EYE *of the* STORM

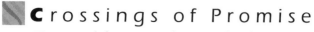

Crossings of Promise

Historical fiction with a touch of romance

Dianne Christner
Keeper of Hearts

Janice L. Dick
Calm Before the Storm
Eye of the Storm

Hugh Alan Smith
When Lightning Strikes

Heather Tekavac
Cost of Passage

EYE *of the* STORM

JANICE L. DICK

Herald
Press

Waterloo, Ontario
Scottdale, Pennsylvania

National Library of Canada Cataloguing-in-Publication Data
Dick, Janice L., 1954-
    Eye of the storm / Janice L. Dick.

(Crossings of promise)
ISBN 0-8361-9253-2
    1. Mennonites—Russia—History—20th century—Fiction.
    I. Title. II. Series.

PS8557.I2543E94 2003   C813'.6   C2003-902895-X
PR9199.4.D52E94 2003

EYE OF THE STORM
Copyright © 2003 by Herald Press, Waterloo, Ont. N2L 6H7. Published simultaneously in USA by Herald Press,
    Scottdale, Pa. 15683. All rights reserved
Canadiana Entry Number: C2003-902895-X
Library of Congress Control Number: 2003106489
International Standard Book Number: 0-8361-9253-2
Printed in the United States of America
Cover art by Barbara Kiwak
Cover design by Sans Serif Design Inc.

10 09 08 07 06 05 04 03 10 9 8 7 6 5 4 3 2 1

To order or request information, please call
1-800-759-4447 (individuals); 1-800-245-7894 (trade).
Website: www.heraldpress.org

This book is dedicated to Wayne,
my best friend, husband, and encourager
whom I thank the Lord for every day

And to our children:
Christiaan and Lorraine Mau
John and Wendy Hiebert and Ashley
Dennis Dick

Acknowledgments

There are many people who have helped with and influenced the writing of this book. Special thanks to my editor, Sarah Kehrberg, for working with me on this book. To my aunt, Sue Enns, for all the precious books from which I gathered much valuable information. To Hope Neufeld for friendship, support, and ideas. To my uncle and aunt, Hugo and Katherine Jantz, for their interest and promotional help. To Dr. Helmut Huebert for his excellent resources on Russian Mennonite people and places. And to the many others who are part of my personal and writing life.

Most grateful acknowledgment and thanks go to my family. To my mother, Margaret Enns, for enduring enthusiasm for this project and for showing me, together with Dad (1918-1994), the meaning of unconditional love. To my parents-in-law, Walter and Edna Dick, for consistent prayers and love. To our children and grandchild, Christiaan and Lorraine; John, Wendy, and Ashley; and Dennis for their constant love and support. To my husband, Wayne, God's gift to bring joy and contentment to my life.

Most important acknowledgment goes to the Lord God who gives gifts and expects us to use them, with his divine help, of course.

Map credit: "Mennonite Colonies in Ukraine and Russia," reprinted from *Mennonite Historical Atlas*, William Schroeder and Helmut T. Huebert, Winnipeg, Man.: Springfield Publishers, 1996, p. 14. Used by permission.

MENNONITE COLONIES IN UKRAINE AND RUSSIA
MODERN NAMES AND BOUNDARIES

■ Mennonite Colony

0   200
Kilometres   WS/HTH/95

Volga

SCOW

River

River

Kazan   *Belaya River*   U

UFA

ALT SAMARA

R   U   S   S   I   A

NEU SAMARA

Samara

ORENBURG

ARKADAK

Orenburg

Don

Saratov   AM TRAKT

River

Ural River

Volga

ATYEVO   *River*   Volgograd

KAZAKHSTAN

Rostov

Don River

River

Kuban

River

Kuma River

C a s p i a n

KUBAN

SUVOROVKA   TEREK

Caucasus Mountains

S e a

GEORGIA

AZERBAIJAN

9

I will take refuge in the shadow of your wings
until the disaster has passed.
Psalm 57:1

Prologue
Succoth Estate, Crimea, May 1879

"'Sixthly: We affirm our most gracious guarantee that no one of the presently settled Mennonites, nor of those who may choose to settle in our empire in the future, nor their children and their descendants, shall be obligated to participate in military or civilian duties at any time unless personal desire for such duty is expressed.'"

David Hildebrandt and his young son, Heinrich, sat behind the massive desk in Succoth library and listened as Elder Jakob Wiebe read aloud from the *Charter of Privileges* set down by Tsar Paul almost eighty years before. "Can you not see, Hildebrandt? We are being persecuted. Our rights have been rescinded. That is why we must leave."

"Our rights—in the name of reason, Jakob, we are simply being called upon as Russian citizens to come to the aid of our nation. Do we turn tail and flee when Mother Russia is in need, after all she has done for us?"

Elder Wiebe pounded his fist on the desk in exasperation. Young Heinrich jumped but kept his ears open and his mouth shut.

"They give no thought to us, to our way of faith and life, our commitment to nonresistance," continued Wiebe. "We do not emigrate in fear for ourselves, but for those for whom we are responsible, our sons and grandsons. We cannot, in good conscience, leave them to be swallowed up by the ways of the world."

"And you hope to keep them from involvement with their neighbors in America? How will you accomplish that?"

"At least there we will have our freedoms. Take to heart

the words of Christ in Matthew's Gospel: 'When you are persecuted in one place, flee to another.' The doors here are closing for us, Hildebrandt. Come with us while there is time. Follow the call of God."

David Hildebrandt frowned at the last statement, and Heinrich's eyes darted back and forth between the two men. His father lifted his chin and looked Elder Wiebe directly in the eye. "With all due respect, Jakob, I do not appreciate your judgment of my calling. I do not agree with your course of action, yours and the many who go with you to a new land. But if you feel you must, I will not attempt to stop you. Nevertheless, do not insinuate that I am disobedient to my Lord, for I am not. I believe he would have us stay in Russia. He has plans for us here, a hope and a future. He did not lead us here to destroy us. I believe we will continue to enjoy great freedom in our adopted homeland, and, in return, all we have been asked to do is lend our young men for a short term to help with reforestation, building of roads, and medical duties. We will not be forced to bear arms, that has been promised."

"And is Tsar Alexander's promise better than Tsar Paul's? For your sake, I hope so." Elder Wiebe spoke quietly and then stood to his feet. "I have done my duty in trying to persuade you, Brother Hildebrandt. I hold no ill feelings toward you—you have always been a fair and honest man. I pray that God would protect you and provide for you here. I take my leave. Farewell."

The two men shook hands, faces grim, but sincere compassion in their eyes. Heinrich watched, and remembered.

PART ONE

1917

The knights are dust, their good swords rust,
Their souls are with the saints, we trust.
Russian Poem

Chapter 1

The blaze from the fireplace warmed Johann's body, but not his soul. Ever since his return from medical duty in the *Forstei*, he had been struggling with the terrifying memories. Even Katarina's promise to marry him had not erased the horror from his mind, and he loved Katya more than life.

She sat next to him now, reading *Pride and Prejudice*, while her father, Heinrich, and Agnetha Wieler played a friendly game of Crokinole at the card table.

January silence settled on the snow-frosted park beyond the windowpanes of Succoth Estate. A reverent hush, a serene stillness, wrapped its arms around the Hildebrandt family, offering needed solace in this time of war and unrest.

But Johann Sudermann did not feel the serenity, the peace. Instead, he remembered the winter past. . . . He and Philipp Wieler, Agnetha's husband, had been forced to crouch in ghostlike silence in a trench of frozen ground, wondering if the stillness would last long enough for them to pull the wounded men out of their premature graves and take them to the questionable safety of the medical tents. With frozen fingers poking out from frayed mittens, he grasped the shoulders of the moaning soldier while Philipp lifted his feet. They gently laid him on the narrow wooden stretcher and hoisted it out of the trench.

Cautiously, Johann raised his head to survey their surroundings. The silent expanse of freshly fallen snow muffled the world in an illusion of peace. With a slight nod to Philipp, he slowly pulled himself onto level ground and lay flat, waiting for gunfire. None came and Philipp climbed up. Swiftly, making each movement count, the two medics of the *Sanitätdienst*, the Forestry Service Medical Corp, ran with the stretcher over the frozen mounds of earth, toward the screen of fir trees.

Three more steps . . . two . . . then a volley of gunfire erupted from behind them, sending them to their knees with the force of the blast. Screams ripped the frigid air. Debris fell from a once placid sky, littering the white snow. Johann looked around wildly for Philipp, but could not locate him in the chaos. Then he heard someone urgently calling his name.

"Johann! Johann!" He struggled to focus.

"Johann? Are you ill?" Katarina's voice was etched with concern. Her father and Agnetha looked up from their game.

"Johann?" Katarina pleaded, her hand on his arm.

Suddenly he shuddered and his eyes cleared as he focused on her. He took in her alarmed expression and was overcome with emotion. "I'm sorry—I was back at the front—Philipp and I. . . ." he stopped, glancing at Agnetha, reminded again that she carried her deceased husband's child. He stood then, nodded to them all and left the room.

Katarina turned anguished eyes to her father, silent tears slipping down her cheeks. "What's happening to him?" she whispered. Agnetha came to sit beside Katya and put comforting arms around her.

"Hush, my dear. He needs time; he must learn to forget."

"But the pain is deep. Will it ever heal?"

Agnetha paused. "Some images will be forever burned into his memory, but with time he will visit them less often.

"We must try to create new and pleasant memories, but most of all, we must allow the Lord God to heal Johann in his time and in his way. Do you believe that God loves

Johann? That he has a plan for him that is better than any we could imagine?"

Katarina wiped her tears and quietly said, "Yes, of course. But sometimes it's difficult to live what one believes."

Heinrich had risen from his easy chair and now stood gazing out into the night. He turned to her. "Katie, come stand here with me."

She hugged Agnetha and went to her father. Without a word he pulled her close to his side with a strong arm about her shoulders, and they lifted their eyes to the night sky. Distant constellations winked coquettishly while a pale orange moon observed in placid benevolence. Moonlight slanted across the snow-dusted lawns and into the windows, washing all with a peace that was palpable.

"This is our Father's world," said Heinrich softly after an extended silence, "and we are his much-loved children. His ways are not our ways, but his ways are best."

Katarina absorbed strength and faith from him. "Yes, Papa," she replied, taking in the moon-washed landscape shimmering with purity and hope.

She reached out a hand to Agnetha and she joined them. The trio stood together, lifting their hearts in silent prayer to the maker of the moon, to the one who pinned the stars each night to the blanket of the velvet sky. Miraculously, the peace of the Father fell upon them like a mantle, and upstairs in his bedroom, Johann drifted finally into a dreamless sleep.

Next morning, Johann was his pleasant, cheerful self. Poking his head into the kitchen, he immediately found Katarina and smiled. "Ah, dear teacher, could you spare some time for a crisp walk? It's a brilliant day."

Katarina sat at the round table in the sunny windowed

corner of the immense kitchen, surrounded by Anna's and Nicholai's schoolwork. Teaching her younger brother and sister sometimes tested her patience, but it also brought its rewards.

It took a moment for Katarina's smile to work its way to her eyes. The memories of the previous evening haunted her, but she decided this was the time to put her faith into action. "Of course, Herr Sudermann. I would be delighted." She smiled as she packed up her books and pencils, calling over her shoulder to Cook and her helpers. "Thank you all for a pleasant morning."

She set the books on the hall table and shrugged into the woolen coat Johann held for her. "Come, Katya," he prompted as he led her out the garden door to the snow-covered walkway. "Leave your deep thoughts for a while and enjoy the sun with me."

She looked into his eyes. "And will you do the same?"

His smile faded and he turned his face forward. She watched his profile as he struggled for composure. Tucking her arm more securely through his, she also concentrated on the path ahead. The snow-robed trees of the orchards and hedges reached out sheltering branches as the couple passed.

"I remember when some of these trees were young," said Katya. "Mama ordered them from nurseries far and wide and planted them with love. Mika and I helped her tramp the soil around them so they could grow tall and strong and beautiful." Johann could picture Katya and Mika, two little girls, one fair and serious, the other dark and spontaneous, helping their mother.

"One winter we had a bad storm. Sleet covered the trees with a layer of ice that bent them to the ground. Mama was concerned. As soon as the ice melted away, she took us outside with her and we staked up the ones that had been damaged.

"The injured saplings struggled, but their branches were flexible enough to adjust. Their roots had taken firm hold in the rich soil, and eventually they straightened and grew strong. Some were tied up longer than others, but they all survived.

"Look at them now, Johann. They are stronger for their suffering, and no less beautiful. It just took time and care."

They had reached the bench in the olive grove and Johann dusted the snow off so they could sit. He looked at her with a tentativeness that tore at her heart.

Taking both his hands she said, "Johann, you have been through a terrible storm, but I am here to help you, and I will never stop praying."

Tears of release slipped down his cheeks and he let them fall, no longer ashamed of his emotions. *Perhaps*, he thought, *this is what my father has missed—someone to allow him to grieve, and then to hold him up as he learned to stand straight and tall again.*

"I am so thankful for you, my Katya." He wrapped her in a strong embrace while the tears dried.

"What do you think of Kerensky?" Paul Gregorovich Tekanin sat holding a cup of hot tea, near enough to the grate for the dancing flames to cast dark shadows on his ruggedly handsome face. Firelight glinted in his black eyes.

Grisha, older and stockier of frame, considered Paul's question as he turned his own cup in his hands. He set it on the arm of the chair as he spoke. "He's an excellent orator, that's an established fact. He knows what he wants and is doing his utmost to get it, within the law."

"Yes, but what is it he wants?"

"He means well, I think," Grisha answered, his head leaning against the worn brocade of his chair, his fingers steepled before him. "As a lawyer, Alexander Kerensky has done much for the revolutionary movement, defending those accused by

Tsar Nicholas. He is a socialist, rather a lonely one in his sphere of operation, but he does strongly advocate change."

"He would not join the Bolsheviks?"

Grisha shook his head and picked up his cup again. "Never. He's a *Menshevik*, a moderate. He believes in political evolution, not revolution. But he definitely sees the writing on the wall for the tsar."

"Yes," agreed Paul. "Everyone sees it but Nicky himself." He stood and stretched, catlike, then moved to refill his cup from the softly hissing samovar. Steam rose from the cup, releasing a pungent aroma. "So where does that leave us?"

"Well, my friend, we must be careful." Grisha stared into the sinking fire. "To pledge our allegiance to either Kerensky's associates or Lenin's Bolsheviks could easily backfire in this volatile atmosphere. Petrograd is a tinderbox of frustration and anger. To stand with the Bolsheviks could be the end of us. We've both seen what uncontrolled passion can lead to." He glanced meaningfully at Paul, whose face paled at the reminder of the violence surrounding Vera's untimely death.

Paul could not keep the memories back. He had convinced himself that what he and Vera had was merely human comfort in the midst of the turmoil of revolution. They had embraced the same convictions: destroy the autocratic regime and allow the people to rule. But suddenly she had been taken, and he himself had clumsily killed any chances of rescue. She was dead and his world crumbled. Only Grisha, mentor and friend, had remained.

"I propose we stand back for a time," Grisha said, jolting Paul back from his reverie. "We may yet be of some use if we are able to keep body and soul together."

Paul sat again in the chair opposite his friend. The glow of the embers now sketched a gauntness into his brooding features, making him look older than his twenty-three years. Finally, he spoke. "We can't go back to *Pravda*, not after all that's happened. If Djugashvili came back, he'd nail us to the wall."

Paul mulled over the enigma of the man, Iosef Djugashvili. Due to the contrary and controversial nature of *Pravda's* pages, Djugashvili found himself on constant alert, but that did not prove sufficient to shield him from his enemies. He spouted a strong revolutionary ideal, a bold and brazen Bolshevik vision which the blue bloods would not swallow. They branded him an enemy of the tsar.

The result was ostracism in the form of exile. They thought, the high brow crowd, to put an end to the man's dangerous obsession by quick-freezing him in a Siberian winter or two, but the experience only served to strengthen his resolve, like the twisting and folding of steel on the blacksmith's anvil. The constant heating and cooling process hammered Djugashvili into the "man of steel" who would later rule Russia with undeniable force—Joseph Stalin.

"Yes, our Stalin is not a man known for compassion," Grisha agreed. "How about the Astoria?"

Paul shrugged, thinking of the stately hotel where he had worked as a waiter and a professional eavesdropper for *Pravda*. "I don't know. I think I've been gone too long."

A sharp knock on the door of their flat surprised Paul and he sloshed hot tea on his leg. With a muttered curse he banged the cup on the table and walked to the door.

"Who is it?" he growled.

A nervous voice filtered through the wood panels. "A friend. I need to speak with Tekanin and Grisha."

Paul opened the door a crack, his foot behind it. He recognized the young man as one of the runners for the still struggling presses of *Pravda*. "What do you want, boy?"

The tall, gangly lad stood awkwardly in the hallway outside the flat, his large eyes darting up and down the length of the corridor. "I have a message for you from the boss," he whispered.

Reluctantly, Paul stepped back and allowed him to enter. "Out with it. What is your message?"

The boy cleared his throat and blinked hard as if to focus on his assignment. His fingers twitched nervously at the hem of his ragged jacket. "The boss wants you both to come back to the presses. He expects to return from Siberia at any time and needs the paper up and running. He says it is urgent and he depends on you to help."

His message relayed, he bowed slightly and turned to leave. "Oh sir," he said, fumbling in his inner coat pocket. Pulling out an envelope, he offered it to Grisha. "He said to give you this if you should doubt me. It's a letter that arrived this morning from Djugashvili himself."

Grisha pulled a sheet from the envelope, glanced at it, and passed it to Paul, who looked it over as well. "Seems valid," he said. "It's in his hand, and the date is stamped on it." He handed the letter back to the boy and opened the door for him to leave.

"Thank you for coming," said Grisha, tossing him a coin. The boy gave a quick nod, glanced at Paul, and hurried out.

Paul shut the door and locked it. Taking a seat, he remembered the first time he had met Iosef Djugashvili, the man many now called Joseph Stalin. His first day in the capital, a nervous Paul Gregorovich Tekanin had sat alone on a bench outside a little Petersburg pub with no plans but survival. He had been studying a discarded newspaper. . . .

"What have we here? A literate peasant?"

The words jolted Paul, and he tossed the paper aside in nervous haste as he stared into the black eyes of the speaker.

"At ease, man. You are a southerner, are you not?"

"Yes," he answered, his bewildered gaze falling to his worn boots.

"Would you perhaps be in search of employ?"

At this question, Paul's head snapped up and his eyes

locked with those of the stranger. He tried to still his pounding heart and hide his desperation. "I might be."

The man chuckled. "Come. I was about to have something to eat. I will treat you and we will talk." Without waiting for an answer, he turned and entered the restaurant beside them. Paul's feet followed even as his brain continued to decide. He ran a hand through his curly black hair and pulled his worn shirt stiff over his baggy brown pants. Hitching his thumbs into his wide leather belt, he followed his free meal ticket into the pub and took a seat across from him at a tiny round table near the back.

As his new acquaintance ordered food and drink, Paul Gregorovich stared around him. So far he had lingered in the small villages near St. Petersburg, anxious but hesitant to enter the city. He had managed to land a few odd jobs to earn a plate of hot food now and then. But today, he had decided, he would advance into the fray, meet the demon of his fear, and slay it. He alone was master of his fate, was he not? Now it seemed fate was on his side.

They sat in the smoky haze of a back street building amid the clamor and clank of pots and plates, the smell of bustling bodies in search of sustenance, and the murmur of voices.

The food arrived, a dead fish only, but sizable enough to quell his hunger. As they ate, the older man spoke again. Extending his right hand across the table he said, "Allow me to introduce myself. Djugashvili, Iosef Vissarionovich."

Paul met his eye as he shook his hand. "Tekanin, Paul Gregorovich."

"Welcome, Tekanin. As I said, I may be able to suggest employment for you. But there are a few qualifications which must first be discussed."

"Sir?"

"First, you must be able to write. Second, you will not question my authority. And third, you must keep your work in strictest confidence." He chuckled slightly. "The last I see as no problem. You don't appear to be much of a talker." A lock of Djugashvili's dark hair slipped onto his forehead, adding a menacing touch to his intense demeanor.

In his heart, Paul thanked his childhood friend, Johann Sudermann, for sharing his education with him. He blinked nervously and cleared his throat. "I both read and write in Russian, as well as French and German. I can certainly apply myself." He stopped to gather his wits. "Are you a newsman then?"

It was Djugashvili's turn to consider his answer. "I gather pertinent information and publish it."

"Pertinent to what, sir?" Paul's eyes now sparkled with interest.

"Pertinent to what the populace needs to know." Running the knuckles of his right hand over his thick black mustache, Djugashvili said, "I see my second condition will need some work." He looked shrewdly at Paul. "However, I think you are teachable. I think you will do."

From then on it was a matter of wits and ingenuity for Paul. He learned to be in the right place at the right time, to extract the facts without arousing curiosity or suspicion, to arrange his material succinctly and in a manner pleasing to his employer.

The opening at the first-class Astoria Hotel had come at a most opportune time for the newly employed Tekanin. His long tunic, belted and worn over loose fitting pants tucked into high boots, was replaced by dark straight pants, white shirt tucked in, sleeves rolled up to mid forearms. After some months working at the hotel, he looked every inch city born. His circle was not of the elite, but Paul carried off a debonair attitude with a flair.

The Astoria management trained him as a waiter, but he worked also as a listener. His fluency in French as well as

Russian proved a bonus. His German he did not flaunt—at present—Germany was the enemy in this worldwide war. But he kept it as a trump card if that particular game came to be played.

Paul put his heart and soul into the work, transforming from a nervous young man bent only on survival, to a sly and cunning reporter who planned, through his and others' efforts, to bring down the Romanov Dynasty by force. His fire was stoked by covert communications from Lenin, self-proclaimed leader of the Bolshevik faction. Although not a large movement in terms of numbers, Bolshevism proved strong in ideals and plans. The Bolsheviks believed they knew what Russia needed, and that was revolution.

Paul's life had picked up a purposeful pace, and his relationship with Vera, co-worker at *Pravda*, had softened the realities of his world.

After Vera's fateful end, Paul had nearly destroyed himself. His vision of revolution had become overwhelmed by black hopelessness. Only now, as he looked over at Grisha, the grief receded and the vision returned.

"We should go back to *Pravda*," he said. "We know the business. We could help."

Grisha, who had been studying Paul as he sat lost in thought, twitched his reddish mustache and pulled absent-mindedly at his beard. "We will go back," he said finally. "We will see what happens."

The new man at the helm of *Pravda* in Joseph Stalin's absence was Mikhail Pavlovich Karakozov. Paul listened intently as the man spoke.

"Lenin is not here at this time, although he would like to be. According to recent communiqués from Switzerland, he works diligently to convince all warring countries to revolution. They do not heed him as yet.

"Kamenev is a strong Bolshevik," continued Karakozov, his gaze lingering on Paul, fully aware of the antagonism between the two men. "Unfortunately, he is also still in exile in Siberia."

"The tsar lacks originality in the punishment of political dissenters," offered Grisha. "Soon Siberia will blossom with Bolsheviks."

Chuckles moved around the room at Grisha's remark. Karakozov quieted them with an upraised hand. "Brothers," he said, "in the absence of these men of vision, and with the incentive of Stalin's return, we who remain must keep the cause alive."

"Here, here!"

"We must continue to propagate radical social democracy. We, brothers, must be the professional revolutionaries of our day."

"We are with you."

"Paul Gregorovich," Karakozov addressed him, "we would ask that you attempt to regain your position at the Astoria. I understand that Henri still commands the kitchens. If you approach him first, he may be able to put in a good word for you with the management. They know times are unstable and may well excuse your sudden unforeseen disappearance last fall."

Paul paled at the reminder. He lowered his eyebrows in an attempt to control his expression and nodded.

"Grisha, you will be in charge of personnel and quality of production here at the presses. All incoming information and final proofing will be passed by you. I will work with you on this. Young Dmitri Soloviev here will be your right hand and the rest of you will do what your hands find to do until we regain control."

Karakozov slapped the table with the flat of his hand and received full attention. "To the work then, men."

As he crossed St. Isaac's Square enroute to the Astoria, Paul was acutely aware of the mood of passersby. An abused and misused citizenry carried their animosity openly, antagonism and resistance apparent on their faces and in their stride. The Cossacks remained on guard, always alert to trouble brewing. *The political and economic pot may not be boiling*, thought Paul as he ran up the back kitchen entrance of the Astoria to find Henri, *but it is certainly simmering.*

Chapter 2

As independent as she envisioned herself to be, Maria Hildebrandt missed her family. She had chosen to stay in Alexanderkrone with the Reimers, but her heart still strayed often to Succoth. She knew her father loved her fiercely, in spite of her headstrong ways, and Katya had become more of a friend than she had ever been. Of course, little Anna was as sweet as ever and Nicholai was growing so fast, she knew she would hardly recognize him when next they met. Letters were not guaranteed deliverable, but she had begun to write home to Succoth regularly, and even made a visit to see her Grandmother Peters in Ruekenau.

The drive to Oma's was short and the old woman was surprised by Maria's call. They talked of many things, including Maria's brother Peter at Bethany Psychiatric Home.

"I hear he is doing well," said Oma.

"As well as can be expected, I suppose," returned Mika. "He has settled into routine and he looks well. Better than he was at home, I must admit. He is still easily agitated, but Susannah manages him admirably." She thought of Susannah, short and jolly, sincere blue eyes lighting her round face, blonde braid circling her head like a halo. Suse and Katya had become instant friends, something that never failed to amaze Mika, who usually claimed the role of socialite. *If Peter has to be in a place like that*, she thought, *at least he has Susannah and Gerhard to care for him.*

"The good Lord has answered our prayers, then, for Peter. If he is content and healthy, we need to be extremely thankful."

"I wasn't at first," admitted Mika. "I was angry that he had to go away and that others were able to do what we could not. But it has turned out for the best." She paused. "Papa and Katya must miss him terribly."

"I believe you have changed, child," observed Oma as the two sat by the fireplace in the visiting room of the Ruekenau Home for the Aged.

Mika felt uneasy with the directness of her grandmother's statement, but after a moment of reflection she realized that this woman could probably read her mind anyway. "Oma," she said tentatively, "do you remember when you were young?"

The old lady laughed heartily. "Do I remember? Do you think memories fade when one grows old? No, my dear, they grow stronger than ever. What I cannot recall is what I ate for breakfast this morning." She looked at her strikingly beautiful granddaughter. "What do you want to know?"

"When did you feel you were grown up, that you could stand on your own and make your own decisions?" She eyed her grandmother and waited for her reply.

Oma Peters smiled. "When did I feel independent? Hmm. Most likely when my Jasch passed on and I moved in here to the home."

Surprise and then consternation crossed Mika's porcelain features, but the old woman continued. "At first I was subject to my parents, and they were loving and kind, but firm. Jasch and I married when I was seventeen years and so I became subject to him, in a way. I don't mean he lorded it over me. My goodness, he was a gentle man with much patience. But because I loved him, I strove always to please him, so I was in a way subject to him.

"When the children came, I looked to their needs. That's

how life goes, Maria. There is never a time when we can do what we want without influencing the lives of others."

Maria rose from her rocker opposite Oma and stood looking out the window at the trees along the streets of Ruekenau, their branches beginning to swell with the promise of buds.

"What is bothering you, Mariechen?"

The girl sighed. "I don't know. I want to be happy and content, but I'm always restless. There doesn't seem to be any purpose to life besides keeping myself amused."

The old woman thought for a moment. "The first step to understanding life is to come to a realization of who the Giver of Life is. What is he like? If we can discover the answer to that, we will be closer to finding our purpose."

Maria turned, hands on her hips, brow furrowed. "Why does everything always come back to God? That's all I hear about at the Reimers'. Be good, go to church, live pleasing to God, don't break the church rules. It never ends."

At the ripe old age of three-score and twelve, not many things surprised Oma Peters. She remained placid and thoughtful as Maria spilled her anger and frustration. Then she asked, "Did you sew that dress yourself, Mariechen? It is very becoming."

Mika looked sharply at her aging grandmother. "Yes, Tante Nela and I made it. What has that to do with anything?"

"Humor me, my dear, I am old." She folded her wrinkled hands on her lap and continued. "When you shopped for fabric, did the bolt of blue floral demand to be chosen?"

Mika stared at her grandmother. Oma continued without taking notice. "When you and Cornelia were fashioning the gown, did the fabric propose that the sleeves be puffed or did you decide that?"

"Oma, perhaps you should rest now. I can return another day."

Mrs. Peters chuckled delightedly. "You think this old

woman has lost more than the color of her hair? Sit down now and answer me this: who do you think created you?"

Maria sat down slowly in the chair and proceeded to rock. "I suppose God did."

"You suppose? I thought your parents taught you better than that."

"All right. God created me."

"That is correct. He chose you, he fashioned you—and made a superb job if I may say so—and that is how you came to be. He did not consult you in the matter." The old woman smoothed her apron. "God simply asks for our allegiance. He wants us to choose sides: for him or against him. Every choice we make is one or the other, and every choice builds upon the ones before it."

"You make life sound so serious."

"So it is. Sometimes we forget how serious."

Mika followed the reasoning. "How do we know if our decisions are right or wrong?"

"Oh, it depends how well we know the one we are following. If you follow the Lord, you spend time in his Word and at church, and he tells you quite plainly what is right and what is wrong. We gather together as a Mennonite people, as do those of other faiths with their own brothers and sisters, to share what God has taught us and to encourage each other in our daily walk. But you must listen and obey, or all the knowledge in the world will not help you. When you decide in your heart to follow Jesus, Maria, he gives you his Spirit to help you discern and then carry through. It is a lifelong process, believe me, but a rewarding one."

"Rewarding? It sounds difficult indeed."

"Not if you consider the alternatives. Some people think they can go their own way and everything will fall into place. They either don't know or won't acknowledge that God is the director of the play and that he writes the script. If you don't follow it, nothing makes sense. You don't know where you are heading. Do you begin to see?"

Mika sighed again. "Oma, why is life so demanding? Why can't it be like Grimms' fairy tales that Mama used to read to us?"

"Because they were stories invented to entertain. Life is real. Life is demanding. I believe when once one accepts the fact that it is so, one becomes much more free to make the best of it." She placed a wrinkled hand on Mika's arm and looked directly into her eyes. "And when we follow the Lord, the paths he leads us on are fragrant with his love and grace. I know this because I have walked his paths.

"Any other path leads to death. There are many walking dead in this world, my dear. Do not choose to be one of them. Choose to walk with God, and he will teach you what you need to do."

In the twilight of a March morning, Dmitri Soloviev trudged along a snowy Petrograd street enroute to *Pravda* headquarters for another day of work with Grisha. His stomach rumbled hungrily and he swayed on his feet. It had been too long since he had eaten, and his mind and body did not want to function anymore.

As he rounded the corner of Apraksin Market, Dmitri passed the same bakery he saw every morning. The ingredients for the baked goods cost five times more now than they had last year, but the baker, a Jew by the name of Ephraim Wiedeman, still managed to scrounge up the necessary items. Ephraim had his sources, much as Dmitri and Paul and Grisha had their sources of political information. These days, one did whatever was needed to get by.

The yeasty aroma of poppy seed rolls fresh from the oven caused Dmitri's stomach to lurch.

He put a hand on the windowsill of Wiedeman's Bakery to steady himself. Several other lean and tattered individuals stopped to see what Dmitri was up to.

"Time for a morning snack, Mitya?" asked one.

"Smells like heaven," said another. "Oh, for just a taste!"

"Well, you won't get one unless you have more money than I do," said Dmitri bitterly. "I wonder how long one can go without food."

The group was quiet for a moment, long enough to notice that their gathering, a thing not encouraged these days on city streets, had drawn a crowd. More and more hunger-pinched faces appeared on the outside of the bakery window to stare in at braided loaves of *challah*, black bread, egg-and-onion buns, and apple strudel.

Amidst the shuffling of boots and the rubbing of hands, which accompanied their muttered grievances, the crowd parted to admit a middle-aged woman and her servant. The tiny bell tinkled over the doorway as the two well-dressed women entered Wiedeman's Bakery and slammed the door shut behind them. The little shop exuded a breath of such rich, buttery smells that the gathered throng heaved a collective sigh. Suddenly one of the young men shouted, "I am starving. I need bread." He elbowed his way to the entrance and pulled open the door.

At first, the crowd stood in shock at the audacity of the young man. But it was the beginning of the end. Hunger overcame all else as they shouted and shoved their way in, grabbing breads and rolls off the cooling racks. When the bakery was too full for any more bodies, they broke windows so those on the outside could also eat. Ephraim Wiedeman whisked the woman and her servant out the back door as the mob descended. There was a time to defend and a time to flee, he knew these things from experience.

The baker and two frightened women ran from the back of

the building, and nearly collided with Paul and Grisha. "Watch where you're going!" snapped Paul irritably as he stepped out of their way. As they neared the bakery, Paul spied Dmitri in the midst of the melée. "What on earth. . . .? Grisha, there's Soloviev. We must get him out before he gets caught. The Cossacks will be here any time to quell this disturbance and I don't know if Dmitri is tough enough to withstand any kind of interrogation."

They moved toward their friend, but were soon caught up in the riot. It was all they could do to keep their feet. Already people were falling and being trampled in the stampede for bread. Paul realized now why Ephraim had been in such a hurry to leave. Soon, several police constables arrived on the scene, but no one paid them any heed.

Wiedeman's Bakery on Apraksin was not the only scene of public disobedience that morning of March 8, 1917. News spread quickly on Petrograd streets, and soon mobs were overrunning many of the bakeries and markets in the city. The tsar's Cossacks came out in full force once the word was out, their bright red coats and black fur caps in vivid contrast to the drab and dirty snow. They trotted up on their sleek horses, sabers unsheathed.

By the time the Guards reached Apraksin, Paul and Grisha had evacuated Dmitri Soloviev, who still clutched a *zemmel* roll well sprinkled with cinnamon and studded with raisins. They moved away from the scene into an alley and ran along it until they came to one of the city's grain storage areas. It seemed this too had become public target for the starving populace. As the trio passed, a bent old woman shuffled up to one of the sacks of grain and reached a gnarled hand to loosen the ties. Her fumbling fingers couldn't open the bag, and Paul stopped, seeing his own mother in this woman.

"Here, Mother, allow me." As he pulled at the strings that tied the sack shut, the sound of horses' hooves interrupted him. Paul and the woman both turned wide-eyed to see a fierce Cossack advancing upon them. He raised his saber, then hesitated momentarily, with narrowed eyes. The blade sliced through the air, but instead of blood, grain poured out at the feet of the old woman. Several other Guards arrived as the deed was done, and at a glance, without a word, proceeded to slice open all the sacks of grain along the row.

With shouts of joy and wild abandon, people descended on the alley, filling their hats and aprons with grain. Tonight they would have bread.

The unheard-of had happened. The people had reached the end of their endurance and now even the tsar's troops agreed with them in their need. From there the rioting increased with a sense of jubilance at an attainable victory. It was not long before university students joined in—they were always prone to revolutionary ideas. Words like "socialism" and "equality" were shouted from soapboxes and balconies. Every wishful orator had his day.

"I wonder how many rioters took part in this today," Paul remarked to Grisha as they set the type late that night at the presses.

Grisha wiped the sweat off his forehead with his sleeve. "Many thousands, I'm sure. We won't know this soon, but I would venture to guess, after talking to our people from various areas, that there could have been close to 100,000. Not just rioters, but strikers too."

"Didn't take long for the mood to spread to the factories and workhouses, did it?" Paul glanced over at Grisha. "Where will this lead?"

"Kerensky will press his advantage, that's certain. Nicholas is obsessed with this European war. We're into the third year of it, we've lost millions of men, and Nicholas won't give in. He has no idea what is happening at home, and public rioting will frighten the empress as she tries to hold the fort alone. She is known to be majestically unreasonable in crises. Perhaps she will insist on public trials and hangings to keep up the Romanov tradition."

Grisha shuddered but shook his head. "I am not a prophet, but I have a feeling that we have reached a new level in our progress."

"Let us hope so."

Come morning, the air of Petrograd smelled of smoke from vandals' fires. With the public disobedience came those inevitable opportunists who stepped out of the shadows when the initial work was done, to collect what they felt was their share of the loot. Many public places suffered the effects of these thieves, sporting shattered windows and broken doors. The only difference between this day and the one before it was the multiplied number of strikers and rioters.

Tekanin dodged from street to street, eyes and ears open for new developments. As he ventured nearer the Winter Palace, he became aware of the sound of marching horses. He saw no sympathy on the riders' stone faces, no mercy in their drawn sabers. *The Duma must have ordered all the tsar's troops out to defend the city center*, he thought.

Before Paul reached the corner of Liteyny, he heard the clash of swords and infuriated howls of pain. Cossacks galloped straight through the crowd, sabers slicing, roaring to intimidate. A student waving a banner lost an arm. An old man too slow to move out of the way lay crushed beneath stamping hooves. But the troops did not achieve their desired effect. Instead of dispersing, the crowd fused together, refusing to retreat. Guns blazed and several more rioters fell, but still the survivors stood their ground.

Paul soon found himself caught up in the mob, shouting for justice and food. As a burly guard rode by him, Tekanin reached up and grabbed his arm. "Are you not Russian too, brother?" he shouted into the coldly chiseled face. "We need bread. Help us in our struggle." The rider wrenched his arm away, but reined in his horse while he stared at Paul.

A moment later, he sheathed his sword and, with a long look at Paul, he too took up the chant: "Give us bread! Down with the German woman!" As the day wore steadily on, the police presence gradually faded and the Cossack Guard, although present, stood mostly on the sidelines, fine horses prancing, riders watching history unfold.

It was almost as if Paul Gregorovich stood in his father's boots. He had strong memories of his father, and the stories told him by his mother had kept those memories alive. . . .

"Your father was angry over the injustice and poverty in our village," his mother would say, "and all the other Russian villages he had heard of. Greshka beggared his way to the capital in 1905. The country was at that time in turmoil over the war with Japan, which had turned from what Tsar Nicholas considered a paltry skirmish, into a full-scale war. In the end, Russia conceded much, barely able to scrape together her dignity.

"Back in St. Petersburg, a revolutionary march led by a priest and revolutionary, Father Gapon, approached the Winter Palace to seek audience with Tsar Nicholas II. Your father marched with them, hoping against hope that the peaceful demonstrations would elicit some response, some acknowledgment from Russia's 'Little Father.'

"The demonstration definitely brought response, but it was not what the marchers had hoped for. Nicholas himself was not at the Winter Palace. In his absence, the Cossack troops were ordered to disperse the crowds by force. Guns blazed and sabers slashed, and more than one thousand of Russia's citizens lay dead and dying, their blood staining the snow in the courtyard of the majestic palace." She always stopped to wipe away bitter tears at this point.

"Among the fallen was your father, Gregory Mikhailovich

Tekanin." The bitterness hardened her already stony countenance. "The world came to know that day as Bloody Sunday,
but it had little impact on our plight, and my Greshka would
never come home again."

Paul would not forget the stories. They fueled the fire that
ignited his passion for revolution.

As the eldest son, he had become the one his mother
depended on to help feed her family. He had paid dearly for
his father's vision. Now he found himself in the midst of his
own opportunity to change the situation of Russia's poor, and
he intended to see it through. He had no wife, no son for
whom to fight, but he claimed the families of others as his
own and fought for them. He would not back down, ever. He
would help the people achieve what his father and those of
his day had failed to achieve. It was almost within their grasp.

"Grisha," called Paul as he arrived breathless at *Pravda*
headquarters. "You will never believe what is happening in
this city. Pandemonium has broken loose."

"How many dead?"

"Some, but not many. The troops are siding with the people, or at least they are not hampering the riots in any way.
It's amazing. This revolt is beginning to amount to something."

"What of the tsar's men?"

"Soldiers and Cossacks are joining the crowds."

Grisha's sturdy form was everywhere in the office, his reddish hair standing up in tufts as he ran his hands through it.
Blotches of dark ink smudged his cheek and forehead. He
scribbled the stories, set the type, and kept the machines oiled
and running. The papers churned out and were offered to a
welcoming public.

Paul grabbed a newspaper off the stack going out the door.
"Insurrection Now! End the War!" The familiar slogans
shouted back at him from the printed paper. Front pages

retold the last days' events with clarity. What amazed Paul the most was that Vladimir Lenin was somewhere in Switzerland, thinking his dream of a revolution would be a long time coming. Joseph Stalin was apparently on his way back from Siberia, and Leon Trotsky remained in New York City, editing a Russian revolutionary newspaper. In spite of the lack of leadership, the Bolshevik movement at home had exploded spontaneously, and the sparks continued to fall.

Chapter 3

 "But why do you wish to go away?" Katya stared wide-eyed at Johann as they sat in the library at Succoth. "You have served your time, and have been honorably discharged. What would make you wish to rejoin the *Forstei* now? What about us?" Her words came in a rush, in a tangle of emotion.

"My dear, I feel it is my duty. I will not go to the front. I will stay at the Schwarzwald Camp and work with the new recruits there. They need medical training, and I can help with that. It is one way I can counter the effects of this dreadful war. If I am able at least to help others learn how to save lives, perhaps my time will be well spent. Here at Succoth I feel like I am hiding from the storm."

Katarina continued to stare at her fiancé in disbelief. "What are we to do here without you? News from the north is frightening, and I don't know if next time you will return."

"I am in God's hands, Katya. Surely I am safer there, in his will, than here, out of it."

She stopped to think that through, but her eyes held the same hurt and sorrow. She stood and walked over to the windows overlooking the park. Johann stood as well, wondering how to communicate the call he felt in his heart. Suddenly Katya's hand went to her throat and she turned to him with stricken eyes.

"What is it, Katya?" he asked, starting at the fresh pain he saw there.

She tried to speak, but at first no words came. Finally she managed to find her tongue. "It's me, isn't it? I always marveled that you could be content with someone plain and tall." She squared her shoulders and lifted her chin, which trembled in spite of her resolve. "If you wish to change your mind about our engagement, I would prefer you tell me plainly. I will not hold you against your will."

Johann's jaw dropped open. He shook his head, but it took him a moment to choose the right words. "Katarina Hildebrandt! Where ever did you get an idea like that? If you were not in such pain, I should laugh uproariously at this notion."

He reached for her hands and led her to a chair, then knelt in front of her. He looked deeply into her devastated green eyes and spoke from his heart. "Some months ago, I came to the realization that I loved you and needed you. It took me far too long to reach that point, but I finally saw the truth. That truth will never change. I love you for as long as I live. My feelings for you will only grow stronger. Do you believe me, my love?"

Katya said nothing, but the stony set of her face began to relax as Johann continued. "I want you to know something about me. Johann Sudermann is a man of his word. He does not make sudden and rash decisions, nor does he renege on promises at a whim. Do you understand me?" Katarina managed to nod her head, now clinging tightly to Johann's hands.

"I have asked you to marry me, and I long for the day. However, the Lord has been working in my heart, calling me back to offer help to those in need. It has nothing to do with us, but everything to do with me. There are so many wounded and dying soldiers, Katie, and perhaps my knowledge and skill can save at least a few. How shall I answer him?"

"How long must you be gone?" Katarina's voice was small and thin. "What if you are sent to the front again? You know better than I that things don't usually work out as planned."

"I propose to go for a month and see if my contribution is needed. It is in obedience that I go. You have no idea how long I have wrestled with God on this point."

"Perhaps he doesn't want you to go at all. Perhaps he only wants to test your willingness—like Abraham and Isaac, you know." They both smiled weakly at the slim possibility.

Within the week, Johann rode off north to help offset the effects of the Great War in the only way he knew. Katarina stood staring down Magnolia Lane long after the dust had settled. "Oh Lord God," she prayed, quoting Job, "I will trust you. Though you slay me, yet I will trust you."

Factories had shut down, due to citywide strikes. Shops and stores had been looted. Revolutionary fervor held the crowds together, and their numbers grew daily.

"The tsar's administration is desperate to maintain control," said Grisha as he and Paul stood amidst the tumult of Apraksin Market, "but most of his troops have mutinied."

"Nicholas has apparently ordered a regiment of loyal soldiers to move in and keep the peace," answered Paul. "They are presently on their way home from the front. The government has gone underground while they await the arrival of the guards."

"When are they expected to arrive?"

"Who knows? Depends on the trains."

A vendor overheard their conversation and called out to them. "They won't make it through. Word is, the railway workers are also on strike and refuse to transport the troops home. No help from the front, I predict."

"Where did you hear this news?" asked Paul.

The man gladly revealed a reliable source, and Paul and Grisha moved with the demonstrators in the direction of the city center. The two brave reporters kept pace with the people, picking up bits of information as they went: Nicholas was doomed, Kerensky would take power, a new government would be formed to rule with justice and peace. Expectations were high. It amused Paul that the utopian dreams he had placed in Bolshevik hands were similar to those the people now expected of Kerensky.

When the mob reached the city center, they gravitated to the arsenal. Guards at the main doors simply stepped back and allowed them in. As Paul and Grisha watched, guns were tossed into the crowd. Paul reached for one, but Grisha stopped him. "We are reporters, not anarchists," he hissed. "Violence always pursues those who use it. We have experienced this." Paul grimaced and turned away.

"Look behind us!" he whispered to Grisha.

As the other man turned, his eyes widened and the muscles in his face tensed. A group of motley looking men entered the compound. "Those are prisoners," Grisha whispered back. "They must be inmates of the St. Peter and Paul Fortress."

The men marched freely, encouraged by those who had evidently emancipated them. "Guns for the prisoners. Guns for the prisoners." The cry was carried along until it became a deafening roar. The two *Pravda* reporters melted out of the vicinity of the convicts, and retreated to a safer vantage point.

"Can you believe what is happening?" exclaimed Grisha. "If they arm those renegades, they will ensure total chaos."

"But many of them have been imprisoned at the whim of the empress, or because of the anger of the tsar. They are not all hardened criminals."

"Look at them, man. How many would you say appear reasonable and of sound mind?"

Paul looked, and had to admit to himself that he did not feel safe in the presence of these convicts. "I still think we should grab a couple of guns. You never know when we will be up against it, and there will be no other way out."

He pushed his way back into the milling crowd, closer to the arsenal. One small-statured, fine-featured prisoner had taken charge of disbursement of firearms. The man took two rifles from those inside the building and turned to hand them out. Paul reached out and found himself looking into a most cruel and calculating face. Both men paused momentarily. The convict narrowed bloodshot eyes and bared his teeth in a bone-chilling smile, then thrust the guns into Paul's hands and turned away to continue his job. "One for me, Machno!" shouted someone in the mob. "One for me."

Grisha noticed the pallid hue of his friend's face. "What is it?"

Paul frowned, a deep crease forming on his forehead. "If the devil is here in bodily form, I have seen him." He shuddered, holding tightly to the firearm. "Let's get away from here."

"Children look!" exclaimed Heinrich as he shook out the current copy of his favorite newspaper, *Friedensstimme*. Katarina and Agnetha moved from their places at the breakfast table to look over his shoulder as he read: *"Tsar Nicholas II Abdicates—New Government for Russia."* He laid the sheet flat on the sleek surface of the cherry wood table so all could see it.

"When? Who is the new tsar?" Katya scanned the print.

"There," pointed Heinrich. "Nicholas abdicated first in favor of his son Alexis, but since the child is ill, he instead chose his brother, Grand Duke Mikhail. But Mikhail doesn't want the throne."

"I don't blame him," commented Agnetha, leaning her growing stomach against the table. "With the fallen economy and the riots and strikes, who could make sense out of anything?"

Katya leaned forward again to continue reading aloud. "*'Yesterday, two representatives of the Duma met Nicholas Romanov in a railway car at Pskov, near the front lines. After a brief discussion, he wrote out his letter of resignation, ending it with the words: 'May the Lord God keep Russia!' Citizen Romanov will return to the capital'*. . . . Citizen Romanov!" Katarina's face paled. "We no longer have a tsar. After three hundred years, the Romanov Dynasty has fallen."

"Sobering thought, indeed," agreed her father. "As ineffective as he was, my heart goes out to him and his family."

"I wonder what they shall do now." Agnetha pondered this, her hands absently rubbing her stomach.

Heinrich read on. "*'The Duma has approved a Provisional Government under the headship of Prince Lvov, effective 14 March. The Soviet, which represents the working class, has decided to support this new middle-class government until such a time as a constituent assembly can be formed. This assembly would then draw up a constitution for Russia.'*

"What tremendous changes have come about in this country! Perhaps, my children, God will yet smile on us through this new administration. A party chosen by the people may recognize our plight as a minority. We must never give up hope."

A gentle knock on the door introduced Fyodor. "A telegram for Miss Katarina," he stated, coming forward with an envelope. He bowed slightly and turned to leave.

"Wait a moment, Fyodor," called Katya. "I'm sure you also are anxious for a word from Johann." She unfolded the paper and read the three short lines, a bittersweet smile on her broad face. Tucking her wayward hair behind her ears, she looked across at Agnetha. "He is fine and greets all of you. I am to continue with wedding plans so that all is ready when he returns." Her smile widened. "It certainly is good to hear from him. I don't imagine it is easy to find a telegraph office."

"Thank you, Ma'am," said the servant, leaving the room as quietly as he had come.

"You are a fortunate woman, Katarina." Agnetha spoke with a faraway expression on her face. "When God gives a gift, we must cherish it." Heinrich's gaze lingered on the young woman who had taken refuge in his home. She was also a gift from God.

"What is happening at the Tauride Palace?" questioned Mikhail Karakozov when Paul and Grisha returned from their foray into the streets. "The March 12 issue of this paper must be set by midnight."

"We managed to pull ourselves away from the crowds at the arsenal," answered Grisha. "More riots, prisoners freed and armed. We would be glad to check out the Tauride."

"Good. Dmitri scrounged up a few poppy seed rolls—they're not fresh, but they are edible—so help yourselves while you write up the arsenal stories. As soon as you can, get on your way again."

"We'll do our best," said Paul, already scribbling away on a notepad. Grisha leaned over his shoulder, adding ideas, juxtaposing information. Soon they were on their way up Nevsky Prospekt, slipping unnoticed down a back street to gain entrance to the palace. All the doors were guarded, of course, but these days the guards were talkative.

"What goes on in there?" questioned Paul. "The people need to know."

"No problem letting the people know," the man said easily. "In this wing," he pointed to his right, "the Duma meets, desperately trying to save the monarchy, if not under Nicholas, at least under one of the Romanovs. That wing," he indicated left with a toss of his head, "is where the Soviet meets. That's the group that claims to represent the workers and soldiers."

As Paul and Grisha pumped the guard for information, a group of workers arrived and demanded entrance to the meeting of the Soviet. "What is your business?" inquired the guard.

"We wish to align ourselves with the new regime. Change is the only way."

"In you go. Left at the top of the stairs. They'll question you there."

As the doors swung open to admit the workers, the two reporters were amazed at the lavish beauty of the palace, the surfeit of gold and tapestries. They were also surprised at the ease with which the workers gained access to the Soviet.

"We wish admittance," Paul said with false authority.

"All you need do is ask. Entire regiments of soldiers have defected from the tsar's side to swear allegiance to the Soviet."

"What of the Duma? What are they hoping to accomplish?"

"Grasping onto the monarchy. But it seems to me like chasing a greased pig. It's impossible to hold on to." The guard laughed loudly at his own joke, and Paul and Grisha stepped inside the palace. While Grisha occupied the guards at the top of the stairs, Paul slipped away to the right, hoping to infiltrate Duma headquarters. He came close enough to hear voices raised in strong argument, led by the unmistakable oratory of Alexander Kerensky.

Paul was intercepted by one of a few tsarist hangers-on, and urged at the point of a rifle to retrace his steps. He returned to find Grisha standing in the doorway of a left wing ballroom, listening intently to members of the Soviet as they debated the most efficient way to force the Duma to disband.

"What do you think will happen now?" whispered Paul.

"This group sounds at least like they have a plan," replied Grisha, "but they have never held the reins before. The

Duma, on the other hand, is used to a form of power, but no one is listening to them anymore."

"I heard Kerensky speaking," Paul informed Grisha. "The Duma is trying to persuade the Soviet to preserve the monarchy, even if not under Nicholas."

"Well, good luck to them, they will need it. Popular opinion does not side with the tsar or with his puppets in the Duma. Kerensky does, however, hold some respect as a socialist."

Johann thought of Katya as he crossed the exercise yard at Schwarzwald Camp. She had been brave at his departure. He felt guilty for causing her such discomfort and self-doubt. But how could she doubt? Had he not shown her that he loved her?

He recalled Heinrich's sage advice on the subject of women: "Understand them never, just love them." Yes, he would have to keep that in mind. As practical and bright as Katya was, she was still sometimes prone to lapses of common sense. Well, he decided as he nodded at the group assembled before him, it would be his pleasure to keep her informed of what she meant to him.

Johann walked with purpose in his step. There were new men arriving on the scene who had come of age and required training. They looked so young, and yet he had been no older at his recruitment. Now he felt older and sadly, wiser to life. As he reached the circle of trees where the young men waited, he assumed control with quiet confidence.

"Where is Eduard Claassen?" he asked, consulting his list.

"In the dormitory, most likely," answered one of the recruits casually. "He didn't want to come out today. Too tired, he said."

"Bergmann," ordered Johann to one of the older men, "you will lead these men in two circuits of the entire field while I speak with Claassen. No walking permitted. Keep up a steady pace."

Johann made his way briskly to the same dormitory he had bunked in on his first assignment. He ducked inside, allowing his eyes to adjust to the dimness before he proceeded. As Bergmann had suggested, Eduard Claassen sat on his bunk, reading a book. He was not in uniform, nor had he made his bed.

"Claassen, why are you not out on the field with the rest of the men?"

Claassen looked up nonchalantly and smiled. "Oh, greetings, Herr Constable. You have found me out. Now I am in trouble." The insolent smile reminded Johann of Isaac Neumann, and only the memory of that man's present situation calmed him enough to repress his anger.

"I am not a constable. You will call me Sudermann, nothing more, nothing less. You will be on the field in five minutes or there will be suitable punishment. Do you understand?"

"And what if I don't?"

Johann stepped near the man's bed and bent over to look directly into his eyes. "Then one day when the enemy comes and destroys those you love, you will watch them die without being able to help. You will faint at the sight of blood and cry for help. Now get up and present yourself appropriately attired."

Although Johann's voice remained quiet and even, his words contained unmistakable iron. Claassen gauged its strength for a moment, then raised one eyebrow and swung his legs off the bunk. "I'm coming, I'm coming."

As they emerged from the dorms and headed out again to the field, the others completed the first round of their run. "Fall into line, Claassen," ordered Johann, "and remember to start counting at one. You will do four rounds, and then report immediately for kitchen duty. I believe there are several bushels of potatoes to be peeled for supper."

At supper that evening, Johann spoke to his men. "Many of you have come here with false expectations. I know because I have watched you, and because I have been in your place. Some of you do not wish to be here. That is perfectly understandable, but we are in a state of war, and we, as Mennonites, will do our utmost to support our country by binding up the wounds of those who have fallen.

"Others of you are here for the glory. You have an image of grandeur in this service, that you will be praised and applauded for your contribution to the cause of justice and mercy. Don't fool yourselves. You will instead be faced with death, disease, and devastation, with hunger, cold, and bone-weariness, with helplessness in the face of need. Medicines and pain suppressants are in short supply, and you will be called upon to be innovative and strong.

"I do not wish to discourage you, but you need to know that this war is real, it is terrible, and there is a limit to what you can do. However, limitations do not preclude that we give up. The Lord gives each a job to do, whether it is to offer a cup of cold water or to bathe a fevered head . . . or to saw off a limb." Johann paused as the weight of his words sank in. "No matter how insignificant or overwhelming our contributions may be, if we are acting in obedience to God and our conscience, we are making a difference.

"Sometimes the minds of the men are in more trauma than their physical bodies. You must learn to deal with that as well. I have also witnessed insolence on the part of new recruits," here he looked pointedly at Eduard Claassen. "It can break even a strong man. Do not waste your energy on selfish concerns. Save it for the real challenges.

"I wish you all the best in your training. We will work together as a team, then you will move out to do your duty for God and for your country. The war has escalated instead of winding down, and it does no good to pretend otherwise.

As an arm of the Mennonite church, we do not go forth with the sword, but with the love of God, to clothe the naked, to comfort the sorrowing, to offer gentleness in the face of hatred, to overcome evil with good. May God help us."

Chapter 4

 Paul Gregorovich Tekanin served the duck à l'orange and parsleyed baby potatoes with the grace and finesse required for a first class snubbing. He did not take the rebuffs personally. He knew that as a waiter he was not considered a valid persona in the eyes of those wealthy enough to dine at the Astoria Hotel. The clientele would surely have responded differently had they known he was a bona fide Bolshevik with strong ties to *Pravda*. But they did not know, and so spoke freely in his presence. The last number of weeks since the Petrograd Revolution had proven interesting in the extreme. The aristocracy had sided with the middle class *against* the monarchy, and *for* the Provisional Government, but they were concerned about their future.

The scrawny woman to whom Paul now served dinner reminded him of one of the chickens that used to run wild in the crooked dirt streets of his little village of Ackerman. Her thin neck did its best to support a tiny head almost hidden beneath the profuse plumage protruding from her crimson hat. Her beady eyes darted here and there. Long skeletal fingers, heavy with rings, clasped each other on her narrow lap, as she relied on her generously appointed beak to accentuate her speech.

Her husband nodded and muttered occasional words in subconscious reply to her constant monologue. His beefy form bespoke more action than words as he handled his eating utensils with practiced dexterity.

"I've heard the tsar is in terrible trouble. His family too." She picked at her food and brushed away Paul's offer of another glass of champagne. "Apparently he has nowhere to go. Lyudmila told me, in confidence mind you, that he requested to take his family to Great Britain, King George V being his cousin and all. But they won't have him. Afraid of the consequences, I suppose." She took a tiny sip of her drink and continued speaking.

"And the empress is Queen Victoria's own granddaughter! Imagine being spurned by your relatives in your hour of need."

"What does it concern us?" countered her husband, much to her surprise. "Nicholas turned out to be a poor leader, and now we have a new government. Can't you allow me to dine in peace?"

The veins stood out on Madame Chicken's neck as she set her mouth in a firm line. The handsome waiter hovered near again, filling their wine glasses, replacing half-eaten rolls. "You will not steal my bread, young man," she scolded Paul. "It is worth its weight in gold these days."

Turning back to her husband, who had subsequently buried himself in his dinner, she said, "This new government now, Lyudmila tells me it has no power at all. Lyudmila says it is only a puppet in the hands of the Soviet. That is not good news, Boris. The Soviet does not have our best interests in mind."

Pravda was not interested in the further welfare of Citizen Romanov and his family, past stating that they had been put under arrest by the Provisional Government for their own protection, but Tekanin found himself in attendance when the family was escorted from their official residence at Tsarskoye Selo.

It had been a familiar place to him two or three long years

ago, when as a fledgling reporter, he had kept tabs on the imperial family. Now, under the auspices of the new regime, the former royal residence had undergone startling alterations. Rich ancient tapestries had been ripped from the walls, carpets pulled up, gold pried off of doors, diamonds removed from chandeliers. The hollow sound of soldiers' boots echoed off the bare oak floors. The place resembled a mausoleum.

As opposed as Paul was to the inequity of the tsarist lifestyle, he still felt a pang of nostalgia for the glory that had been. A way of life had ended and a new epoch had begun. He hoped these times would be better than the sight of the ravaged palace foreshadowed.

As he watched from the lower hall, a door opened on the floor above, and a group of eight people began their final descent of the elaborate staircase. Nicholas came first, resolution written on his face as plain as if it had been scrawled in ink. Huge dark circles underscored his eyes, telling of sleepless nights and deep-seated regrets. He carried himself with dignity, nodding regally to those watching, although most either ignored him or threw back sarcastic remarks. The empress also appeared dignified, although the façade thinly disguised raw fear. She avoided eye contact and clasped her husband's arm with bloodless fingers.

Their four daughters, of varied age and beauty, followed nervously, keeping their eyes averted. Behind them, a large, sturdy sailor carried young Alexis, obviously unable to walk. Pain marred the child's thin face, and a resignation far beyond his thirteen years. The hemophilia had taken its toll.

As the Romanov entourage marched silently by, Paul caught the eye of Nicholas, and the two exchanged the faintest of nods, an allusion to ancient brotherhood. Try as he might, Paul Gregorovich could not but feel pity for this man. Fate had handed him an order too large to fill, and he had failed. Now he would bear the consequences, whatever they might be.

"How is she?" asked Heinrich nervously as Katarina descended the stairs at Succoth.

"Agnetha's fine," answered his daughter with aloof confidence. "She is walking the upstairs hallway."

"Walking the halls! Shouldn't she be in bed?"

Katya shook her head in amusement. "Mama gave birth to five children. Don't you remember how it works? Well, I suppose that was not your responsibility." She bustled by him to the kitchen, then whisked out again, a bottle of tonic in her hand. Heinrich murmured something indistinguishable before settling down again to his record keeping.

April had slipped in on the heels of a rainy March, and now smiled on the estate with a warmth that cheered the soul. The lilacs were in full bloom and sent their offering up on the air currents to the third floor where a serious business was in its last stages. By noon, a tired but victorious Katarina poked her head into the dining room to give Heinrich the news.

"The midwife has delivered Agnetha of a strong, healthy baby boy. Mother and child are both doing well."

He stood to his feet at the announcement. She reached up and kissed his cheek. "Wait an hour or two and you can come up to see Agnetha and the baby. They need some peace now and a nap, and then we will show off the new arrival."

"Where is Mikhail Pavlovich this morning?" asked Paul as he entered the pressrooms. "Come to think of it, I haven't seen him around much these last few days."

Grisha passed him a copy of the paper. "He is busy ingratiating himself with Kerensky, trying to get the inside story about who's actually running the country. I think Kerensky is as puzzled as the rest of us, although he'd be the last to admit it."

"What makes you say that?"

"Well, for one thing, the tsar and his family have been placed under house arrest. They are under the 'protection' of the Provisional Government, but this was done at the suggestion of the Soviet. Who makes the decisions?"

"You won't find that in the paper. No one cares." Paul marched to his desk in a corner of the large room and picked up a sheaf of papers. "We need to concentrate on making the most of the victory of the people. The Bolshevik movement has gained momentum and, according to the men at the helm, we must maintain that momentum."

"Men at the helm? You mean Mikhail Pavlovich?"

Paul shot him a glance. "No. I mean Lenin and Trotsky. Trotsky has come here to Petrograd and Lenin is rumored to arrive any day." Coming near to Grisha, he said under his breath, "If we are going to wear red, we had better be sure of ourselves."

Grisha returned his look and realized the seriousness of his friend's warning. "Of course," he replied, but the conviction never reached his eyes.

As the two finished speaking, Karakozov burst through the door, closing it quickly after him. "I hope we will not have to move," he said with some irritation. "The mobs are at it again, taking over everything they don't like. The government has given them more freedoms these past few weeks than they have had in hundreds of years: political and religious pardons, freedom of speech, of the press, of assembly, even freedom for trade unions to strike. It's too much. They cannot handle it."

He moved over to a window and peered out. Suddenly he hissed, "Disappear!" It was the signal to hide, and Paul, Grisha, and the other workers did so, according to past experience and much practice. They left via a back entrance, and not a moment too soon, for the door through which Karakozov had just entered was broken and flung out of the way. A gang of some twenty angry demonstrators stormed in and began smashing machines, ripping papers and pouring ink over everything.

It did not take them long to completely ransack the place. They left behind a small, smoldering fire, which grew as it consumed the available fuel. As soon as the vandals left, Mikhail returned and put out the blaze. Paul and Grisha found him sitting at one of the desks, surveying the damage. "Stupid fools!" he exclaimed. "We are essentially on their side, if they were bright enough to deduce it. Now they've destroyed our public link between them and the Bolshevik party." He swore as he walked about, checking the machines.

"We will repair the damage and begin again, I assure you," said Grisha. "It's been done before."

"And for now?"

"For now we will have to meet somewhere else and work on maintaining the tide of revolution until we have reestablished ourselves."

Paul sat down carefully on a broken chair. "What did you find out about Kerensky?"

Mikhail sat down as well, hands on his knees in resignation. "Kerensky wants to continue this confounded war. He believes it is expedient to show the world that we are not done for, that there is still life left in us. The Soviet is totally against it, of course, arguing that it is a lost cause and a waste of time and resources, and that we should be concentrating on putting ourselves more securely in power. They are in the process of replacing all local Russian councils with soviets consisting of members of the proletariat."

Paul looked confused. "So why doesn't the Soviet just take over, since they are more powerful than the government anyway? What is the point of waiting?"

"It's all in the timing, I think. First of all, the Soviet didn't expect such an easy victory back in March. This process was supposed to take a much longer, more gradual course than it did. People are unpredictable, that's the bottom line. Second, I think the Soviet decided to let the Provisional Government take the responsibility for trying to straighten out the issues of hunger and land. Much easier to let someone else mop up the mess and then step in like a savior to claim the glory.

"As far as the war goes, from what I've heard, the administration has been quoted at home as saying that Russia desires peace more than anything. Meanwhile, Foreign Minister Milyutin has quietly smoothed things over with the other allied leaders, saying that we have no intention of pulling out of the war."

"That is duplicity at its best," remarked Grisha. "I do believe we are burying ourselves alive here. God help us all if someone doesn't soon take over and set a more realistic course."

"God help us?" Mikhail Pavlovich sneered. "God has no part in this. In fact, he does not exist, my friend. I'd advise you to remember this."

Heinrich entered Agnetha's room with Katya. A serene Agnetha lay tucked neatly into the huge four-poster bed with her little son lying in the crook of her arm. At Agnetha's nod, Katarina gently picked up the baby and showed him to Heinrich.

"Isn't he perfect?"

"His name is Philipp Johann," said Agnetha.

Heinrich could not seem to take in the sight, especially that of the young mother, with her hair loose and brushed to a shine.

"Heinrich," Agnetha interrupted his thoughts, "would you like to hold Philipp?"

"Oh, no. It's been a long time since I held a baby." His

words did not match his expression. Katya offered the child to him.

"Well, Philipp," he cooed as soon as the baby was placed in his arms. "You look like a fine little man. Your papa would be proud of you." He paced around the large room as he spoke to the child who had opened wide blue eyes that seemed to focus on the speaker. Katya and Agnetha exchanged amused glances.

"You are fortunate to have such a wonderful mama, and many others who care for you. Yes, little Philipp, you are a gift to us all from God above. May you grow to love him as we do."

He continued to walk and talk, and soon Philipp dozed off. Reluctantly, Heinrich laid the sleeping infant down beside Agnetha. Holding her eyes for a moment he smiled and said, "My heartfelt congratulations, Agnetha. How good of God to allow us to be a part of this great event. Rest well now." He stepped to the door and turned for one more look at mother and child.

Katya ushered him out, glancing suspiciously at him as he left. Smiling and shaking her head, she silently drew the drapes to darken the room, kissed Agnetha and Philipp, and quietly closed the door behind herself.

"It has been a long time since we heard from your family, hasn't it, Maria?" Cornelia Reimer made the comment as she punched bread dough in the cool morning hours. Marie sat at the kitchen table podding peas. A murmured "Mmm hmm" was her only response.

Cornelia glanced at her over the top of her eyeglasses. "Don't you miss them, dear?"

"Of course, Tante Nellie."

"I'm sure they miss you."

"Are you trying to make me feel guilty again? Because I refuse to do that."

"I'm sorry, dear, I don't mean to make you feel guilty, but I think I would miss my family very much if I were separated from them." She continued to knead the dough until it developed the required elasticity. Then she placed it in a large greased bowl, spanked it soundly, and covered it with a damp cloth. "There. Now, would you like some tea while we finish the peas?"

"That would be nice. Shall I make it?"

"If it's not too much trouble. I must admit my back is tired already, and it isn't even noon yet." She sat down gingerly in the straight-backed chair and winced as she tried to find a comfortable position. She picked up another bowl and commenced shelling peas at an alarming rate.

Maria stared at her. "I will never be able to do that," she said. "Perhaps I shall never have to."

The older woman looked at her questioningly. "What do you mean? How will you eat peas if you don't shell them?"

Mika smiled at her and said, "Perhaps I shall not grow peas, or anything at all. I don't like gardening very much, as you already know."

"But how can you not grow a garden? It is the accepted practice here in the colonies, that each family look after themselves with fruits and vegetables, canning and pickling and making jams and jellies. What would the village council think? And the church? They would say you were lazy!"

Mika chuckled at the response she had achieved. "I don't much care what the council or the church think of me. I would like to live somewhere else, other than in a Mennonite settlement. It is suffocating sometimes."

"Isn't that what you said about life at Succoth?" Cornelia's husband Abram stood in the doorway, until then undetected by the women. "You are prone to claustrophobia, it seems."

Maria set a cup of tea down for each of the Reimers and

brought another to the table for herself. She said nothing until she had sipped the hot liquid. "I tire quickly of the familiar. It is a fact of life for me."

"Perhaps you don't realize that boundaries have been put in place to protect you."

"Abram, you could afford some tact," chided his wife.

Maria grinned. "It's all right, Tante Nela. Say what you mean and mean what you say. I know you both love me."

They nodded and Mika said, "Everything becomes tiresome. If I had to shell peas every summer, I would run screaming from the house and go live in a tree somewhere."

"There are no mirrors in trees, nor easy chairs. You would never survive."

They were all chuckling now, but the truth still lay before them. Maria was restless; trouble was brewing.

"Peter helped me change his bed today," Susannah Warkentin told her husband as she entered his office in search of requisition forms. The early April sun shone warmly into the large window. "He's continued to improve since the Hildebrandts came to visit, but his actions today were most incredible. I don't know what to think."

Gerhard considered his several years as administrator of the Bethany Psychiatric Home. He had seen a miracle or two, but mostly the residents either remained on their particular plateau of consciousness, or gradually degenerated. It was not often he and the staff witnessed significant improvements.

"How does one explain the works of the Lord?" he asked, shaking his head and smiling at his wife. "We petition God with particular requests using all the faith we can muster, and nothing happens. Then we resign ourselves to the way things are, and voilà, miracles happen."

"I know," Susannah responded. "I wonder how much Peter is capable of. Here in these calm and consistent surroundings, he has been able to come to terms with his personal insecurities and even learn and progress. He no longer stiffens so noticeably when someone touches him. He doesn't rock back and forth or try to injure himself. He doesn't actually make eye contact, but he certainly seems to understand more of what is going on around him."

She stood before her husband, her blue eyes alight with joy. "You should have seen him today. His actions perfectly mirrored mine as we worked, which means he had to replace left with right and vice versa."

Gerhard couldn't help but reach out for her. As a man, he was technically the head of their home, the leader, but so often he was inspired by her inner strength, her joy, her beauty. She nourished and sustained him, gave him a reason to do well at whatever he did.

"Gerhard, we are on duty," she reminded him, a smile tugging at her mouth. "There are other nurses on the ward."

"Then we must be quick," he answered with a disarming grin. "I need to hold you close for a moment."

For that moment and several more, Peter was forgotten. Susannah eventually pulled away. "I must return to my patients," she whispered, her heart warm with love for this man God had given her. Reluctantly, Gerhard released her. As the door closed behind her, he noticed the requisition forms on his desk. He picked them up and waited for her to return for them. When she did, his teasing smile caused her face to redden. "That will be enough from you, young man," she scolded softly, "or I shall be forced to report you to the administration."

"I am the administration, my love."

"I will speak to the board of trustees."

"Do what you need to do; I fear I cannot be reformed." Susannah slipped out the door before he captured her again.

Chapter 5

"Abram, have you found her?" asked Cornelia as she rushed to meet her husband at the door. "I am sick with worry."

He looked grim and said nothing as he hung his black jacket on the peg in the entry and set his hat on the shelf. He met his wife's eyes and debated how to break the news to her. "Sit down, my dear," he finally said. "I have heard some disturbing information."

"Go on, then, tell me."

He sighed heavily. "It seems Karl Dirks left on a little journey yesterday morning in his buggy, and he was not alone."

"Maria!"

"Yes. At first everyone who saw them assumed they were out for a drive, but when they did not return, the folks who had seen them drive away were afraid to tell us. What foolishness. How can a problem be handled without knowing?"

"But where did they go? And why just the two of them? What could have happened? Perhaps they were robbed and are lying somewhere. . . ."

"Nela! Calm down, please. A search has been made of the surrounding area and all around Kleefeld and Lichtfelde, turning up nothing."

"But they cannot disappear into thin air. Surely someone would contact us if they had been seen."

"Unless they did not wish to seen."

Cornelia paused as the possibility became clear to her.

"Abram, what are you saying?"

His eyebrows arched and he hitched his thumbs behind his suspenders. "It seems Karl left with the intention of being gone for more than a day. He took clothing and money. Maria must have known as well. Have you checked her room?"

"No, of course not. That is her domain."

"Then I believe it is time we invaded that domain."

Maria had been gone for two agonizing weeks before the Reimers received a telegram from her. She informed them briefly that she and Karl were fine and would return eventually. "I suppose that means when the place they are in begins to suffocate the lady." Abram tried unsuccessfully to keep the sarcasm from his voice. "We must communicate the news to her family. Bring me pen and paper, Cornelia."

"What a scandal," she said as she retrieved the writing materials from a shallow kitchen drawer. "How shall they ever show their faces again? The church must be considering strong punishment for them."

"Maria is not a baptized member. Heinrich always believed baptism should be a matter of choice on the basis of faith, not a requirement for church membership."

"Well, baptized or not, she is a fallen woman. Where will she go? I don't know, I just don't know. I am so ashamed for her."

"Nela, please. I need to think. This is extremely difficult."

The Hildebrandt's response was terse and to-the-point: DEVASTATED STOP SEND M HOME IMMEDIATELY STOP SO SORRY FOR TROUBLE STOP HEINRICH

Heinrich and Katarina met Maria at the station in Karassan. "You look well," offered Katarina in a flat tone. When Maria turned to her sister to respond, she saw the depth of pain lying behind her the familiar greeting. She could not speak but turned forward again and watched the horse's ears pivoting to the sounds around them. She did not notice the beauty of the new crop or the freshly greening leaves and grasses along the roadside, but then she had never noticed these things.

What touched her most was the heartbroken silence of her father. She had honestly never meant to cause him pain. She had never meant anything; she had acted on a whim.

On arrival at Succoth, a subdued Mika greeted Nicholai and Anna with hugs and a quavering smile before retiring to her room. She did not want supper.

That evening the three of them, Heinrich, Katarina, and Maria, sat uncomfortably together before a crackling fire in the library. "It is time to talk," said Heinrich. "I want to hear your story—only the truth, not the justification—and we will remain silent until you are finished."

Maria fidgeted, twisting her carefully manicured hands in her lap. "Well, Karl and I decided," she began to cry and searched in her pocket for a handkerchief. Katarina offered her one wordlessly and she continued. "We decided that we both needed to escape the confines of the village. The traditions and customs were stifling, so we left one day. No one knew, and anyone who saw us thought we were off to a picnic or something."

"Didn't you—"

"Katarina, we promised to remain silent while she tells her story."

"Yes, Papa."

Maria cleared her throat. "We did not consider the feelings of others," here she looked at her sister in answer to her unspoken question, "we just drove off. It was exciting at first, so free to come and go as we pleased. Karl had money. He had recently sold one of his prize stallions, so we had fine accommodations. We drove west to the Molotschnaya River and crossed to the Lutheran side. Stayed in various places and shopped, and pretended we were a fine lady and gentleman out for a holiday.

"After about a week, we began to disagree about things, everything actually, and it became unbearable. We were too proud to return, however, because everyone would say they could have told us as much. Besides, how could we return—we weren't married."

Katarina's head drooped on her chest. She dabbed at her eyes with another handkerchief. Heinrich sat silent and grief-stricken, gray eyes fixed on the beautiful, broken young woman who was his daughter.

"Well," she continued, finding her voice again, "after the second week, we couldn't stand each other's company any longer and I demanded that he return me to Alexanderkrone. He refused, said I could never go back there anyway, after what I'd done . . . what *I'd* done! Like he had nothing to do with. . . ." Here she faltered and paused several minutes while she wept. Taking a deep breath, she managed the rest. "He handed me a small roll of money and lifted me down from the carriage. He told me to go on home, that I was hampering his freedom and . . . and . . . that I was not nearly as interesting as he had thought." Her voice broke again.

"So I did the only thing I could do. I sent two telegrams, one to the Reimers and one to you, and purchased a train ticket back to Crimea. I can never go back to Alexanderkrone." She lifted her eyes to her father's. "That is my story."

His eyes bright with unshed tears, Heinrich considered and

then tossed away many words without speaking them. *What does one say in a situation like this, Lord. You must give me the words. I am dead inside.*

"Maria. You have come home. You are always welcome here, whatever you have done, but you are an adult and have made your own decisions. You have dug a pit for yourself and fallen into it. Now you must carve steps so that you can climb out again. But your actions have injured those who love you. The Reimers have been greatly wounded and no doubt feel somehow responsible for not taking better care of you."

"But it had nothing to do with them. It was my decision."

"Yes, I know. Nevertheless, they will suffer for your deeds. You have obviously torn our hearts as well by flying in the face of all you have been taught. It is as if a knife has pierced our souls, and you yourself have put it there, although, as you said, you did not think of it so at the time.

"All these things have resulted from your decision to live your own way. But the greatest damage you have done is to yourself. You have created an enormous gap between yourself and God. He does not change, but you have removed yourself from him. The pain you have caused him is greater than anything we could ever feel. He created you for good, not for evil, to be a companion to him. He sought to bless you, but you have spit in his face."

Throughout Heinrich's speech, Maria had been crying quietly, but now she raised her tear-stained face and cried out, "No! I would never do that!"

"I'm sorry, my dear, but you have. If you are not on God's side, you are against him. There is no middle ground. God will have all of you or nothing. The choice is yours, but there are only two options."

Mika sank to the floor before her father. "I'm sorry. I'm so sorry." Katarina joined her on the floor, and wrapped her arms around her sister.

Paul Gregorovich Tekanin and Grisha sat in their hot, cramped flat munching on chicken cordon bleu and crème caramel. As long as Paul retained his position at the Astoria, Henri provided him with enough food to live on, delectable delicacies in small amounts.

"I've located another small press," Grisha said, licking his fingers. "I've been passing out leaflets while you were at work."

"Is the rumor true?" asked Paul. "Is Lenin coming back?"

Grisha nodded as he chewed another mouthful of chicken. Swallowing, he wiped his mouth on his sleeve and said, "They say he is enroute as we speak. The Germans put him on a train, sealed it so he wouldn't stop in their country, and sent him through to Russia. He is expected at Finland Station here in Petrograd on April 3."

"That's next week."

"How clever of you," Grisha smiled. "Your intellect is amazing."

Tekanin cuffed him on the arm, almost sending the rest of the meal onto the floor. "Calm down, friend," said Grisha, laughing. "We must not waste this wonderful food."

From the beginning, Paul's friendship with Grisha had given him a sense of family in this city of beauty and evil. They had filled a void in each other's lives.

When he had first begun to work for Stalin, Paul Gregorovich Tekanin had done well. He had become a man of action, capable of split-second decisions, of calm in the face of chaos. Until Vera. It seemed his life was divided into two halves: before Vera and after Vera. She had shared his passion for the cause. She had also uncovered the latent compassion and need which he had tried to entirely exile to his own spiritual wasteland. He had responded to her need with his own, and for a time the meeting had soothed the pain.

But when, by his own foolhardiness, she had died, his soul had died with her. He felt bereft, empty, directionless. All the Lenins and Stalins in the world could not replace or revive the passion in him. He realized now that the utopia he had sought for in the world centered on one specific person, and he had failed her. How then could he have faith in a vague ideal that was to have encompassed the whole of society? Paul's hope had died with Vera Guseyva.

A period of blackness blocked Paul's memory, a time when he could recall nothing but dull pain and darkness. Gradually a spark of light, like the smallest twinkling star, had appeared on the firmament of his mind. The faint light shone in on him through the care of Grisha. No one else paid any attention to him in his depressed alcoholic haze. Grisha had become a Barnabas for his particular Paul.

Little by little the haze thinned and the love of a friend won out. Gradually, as one awakens from a coma, Paul became aware of time and space. He exercised no will of his own, but was borne on the wings of Grisha's will, of his mentor's determination to keep him alive. To Grisha, this was a chance to make up for the brother he had lost, to pour his heart into a cause more attainable perhaps that the political salvation of Mother Russia.

For Paul, it meant life, but as he returned to consciousness, he felt at a loss. What had before been his passion had now become his nemesis. Because of passion he had lost his passion. He had trouble concentrating, believing that Bolshevism would truly bring about the utopia it promised. But he was too far involved to turn tail and run.

And so Paul and Grisha endeavored to adjust. Their main priority had changed from idealism to personal survival, whatever that demanded. St. Petersburg had become Petrograd, the world was at war, and they must find a way to survive in spite of it all.

It had been a difficult journey, but with Grisha's help, Paul had again plotted his direction. The return to *Pravda* and the Astoria had been well timed. His excitement at the return of Lenin surprised Grisha, who rejoiced that the cloud which had hung over his friend's life had lifted. But he shuddered at the direction of his allegiance.

"We are preparing to meet Lenin at the station," said Grisha. "Now that the Provisional Government has granted freedoms, we no longer need to hide our colors. In spite of a faulty ideology, this new leadership has offered some benefits."

"I must assume that you would have told me. I will be there, even if I must desert my wealthy clients at the hotel."

As the train screeched into Finland Station the following week, both Paul and Grisha were present, along with a crowd of the curious and the committed. The doors were opened and there he stood, the man to whom many of those present had dedicated their lives—Vladimir Ilyich Ulyanov—Lenin. A shout went up and soon the entire station was cheering. A young girl walked forward to meet him with a bouquet of flowers while a small band played the *Marseillaise*, the song of the French Revolution. It was not exactly a hero's welcome, but Lenin was not a hero—he was a revolutionary.

He accepted the accolades with a preoccupied nod, then lifted his hands for silence. "Thank you, Comrades," he began. "The time has come. The revolution is in progress. We want peace with Germany, bread for all, and land for the peasants. But we can have no compromise. We cannot collaborate with the *bourgeoisie*. We must bring down the Provisional Government and claim complete power in the name of the Soviets. It is the only way."

One of the foremost in the welcoming group, an old man by the name of Plekhanov, raised his voice. "He's mad!" he shouted. "He's going too far at once, jeopardizing the entire plan!" Some joined him, but most cheered wildly as if the answer to all their ills had been found. Paul disregarded the shouts of Plekhanov and his cronies. Old men with old ideas. Lenin spoke of hope and change, of equality and freedom. If revolution was what it would take to bring in the new, then revolution it would be. Grisha stood beside Paul, quietly battling enormous doubts.

Chapter 6

 "I need you, Mika." Katarina stood halfway up the staircase, trying in vain to secure another garland of greenery to the railing. As her sister appeared at the bottom of the stairs, Katya cast her a pleading look.

"I'm all thumbs when it comes to decorating. If you don't take over, this disaster will be the focal point of the wedding instead of the bride and groom."

Maria took a calculating look at the balustrade and began easily to twist and tuck until it met her approval. "There. That wasn't so difficult, Katie. What else would you like me to do?"

"Everything. I don't know where to begin and the wedding is tomorrow. I'm so nervous, I can't even think."

Mika smiled calmly and walked up to give her sister a hug. "Don't worry about a thing. I checked with the kitchen, and Cook has everything well in hand. The weather looks wonderful for tomorrow, and the grounds keepers have the park all clipped and trimmed. Sorry the lilacs couldn't bloom any longer, but the roses are in their glory. Mama would have liked that."

She was lost in another world for a few moments, then shook herself and turned to Katarina. "You need to spend some time with Johann now. He's only been home from Schwarzwald one week and needs some calming himself, if I don't miss my guess. Go on now and I will get to work. Today I will enjoy myself helping you and tomorrow I will stay out of the limelight."

"Tomorrow you will be with me, Mika," Katya held her sister's eyes. "You are to be my witness . . . Marie?"

"Yes, of course. If you wish it, I will stand by you."

"Good. That's settled. Now, I wonder where I shall find Johann." Her eyes shone as she spoke his name, and Maria knew she was momentarily forgotten. *Ah well, that is as it should be*, she mused.

The next day Johann stood waiting for his bride to join him at the top of the staircase. He adjusted his spectacles constantly, peering over the balustrade from time to time to check on the guests assembled in the main hall. Everyone stood waiting as he did, dressed in their finest, anticipation in their eyes.

The waiting crowd constituted a varied mix. Some families from neighboring estates came in their buggies, dressed fit for a royal gala, while Misha and many of the other Succoth workers appeared in clean peasant clothes. Katarina had insisted they come as equals with the wealthy because they were her friends.

Mika slipped out of Katya's room and came over to stand with Johann. "Almost ready," she said. "Oh look, here she comes."

Johann forgot everything as he gazed at his bride. Katarina wore a snow white satin wedding dress, a simple pattern, long and flowing, made exquisite by the addition of a single strand of pearls about her neck. Anything with ruffles and lace would have looked cheap on her, but this gown brought out the best in Katya. He adjusted his glasses yet again as he moved forward to meet her.

Katya blushed as she tucked her arm through his, then looked up shyly to meet his eyes. There shyness ended and love took over. Nothing else mattered to either of them. Today they would pledge their vows to love each other, for the rest of their lives.

The couple descended the stairs to the music of violins. Mika, head held high, smile in place, walked with her father. Nicholai and Anna came behind them as they walked outside to the gazebo in the park. Rose petals scattered along the pathway added their fragrance to that of the garden and flowering shrubs, and birds' song accompanied the strings.

Heinrich had managed to locate Fritz Hengstein, much to Johann's delight, and that small but powerful man of God stood waiting at the gazebo as the couple and their family approached. The guests took seats on benches placed on the lush lawn. Some raised parasols to shelter them from the sun's rays, while others enjoyed the pleasant warmth.

"Family and friends," began Hengstein, "we are gathered together this fine day to honor God and to witness the vows of Johann Sudermann and Katarina Hildebrandt. . . ." Katarina was so thankful for Johann's hand on her arm. She did not like to be the center of attention. He patted her hand and she knew he understood. She was also thankful that her father had been able to contact Hengstein for the occasion. It was important to Johann. After all, it had been Fritz who had introduced him to the Savior.

"I have chosen my text from a rather unlikely source," the preacher continued. "Many view the book of Ecclesiastes as a writing of discouragement and futility. But there are many lessons to be learned from these words of King Solomon. Chapter four and verse twelve states: 'Though one may be overpowered, two can defend themselves. A cord of three strands is not quickly broken.'

"The braiding of a cord of three strands is what we are witnessing this day. Johann, Katarina, and God are entwining their lives together. This couple before you have pledged 'each for the other and both for the Lord.' Such a cord is strong and dependable for any task."

Mika felt the sermon would never end, so she focused on

her sister. Katarina had never demanded much from life. She had taken what came her way and been contented. What a blessing contentment was. *Will I ever experience it? Or will I wander in restlessness my entire life?* Mika glanced through the trees and sneaked a peek over her shoulder as if expecting something, but all remained quiet and worshipful.

Johann and Katarina vowed their love and lives to each other and exchanged rings. Katarina now wore the brilliant ruby that her mother had received from her beloved on her own wedding day. Papa had retrieved it from the hiding place. It rested as a promise on the ring finger of her left hand. Guests congratulated the couple and began to move toward the tables set up near the house for the celebration supper and the usual program of poems and songs.

Johann and Katarina both heard the sound at once, a faint strum of guitars. Each looked to the other for explanation, but both shrugged their shoulders. They did not need to wonder long. To the utter surprise of all except Maria, a band of brilliantly arrayed gypsies appeared on the lawn. The reds, blues, and yellows of the men's baggy clothes, cinched at the waist with multicolored scarves, were made even more vivid by the women's rainbow-hued dresses, low cut and fitted in the bodice, flowing wide around their ankles. At a nod from Natalya, Katarina's friend of many years, the balalaikas began to strum, slowly at first to accompany the swirling skirts of the women, then increasing in momentum and volume until the scene on the lawn was transformed into a vibrant kaleidoscope of color and sound.

Katya stood transfixed, her lips parted in amazement, watching the solemn occasion give way to festive celebration. Johann took her hand as they watched in wonder.

Some in the audience were not of the same open mind. After all, dancing was not approved of in Mennonite lifestyle, apart from the circle games the young people played at weddings and other social gatherings. It was, to them, a sign of worldliness, an aligning of oneself with the prince of this world and his wicked schemes. Logically speaking, the separation from the world was a means of retaining the purity of their devotion to God, of avoiding the obvious temptations of such contact between the sexes. Besides that, these were gypsies!

The guests turned as one to their host, Heinrich Hildebrandt. Surely he would quell this wild intrusion. Heinrich, after one swift glance at Katarina, knew his answer. Stepping toward the dancers, his eyes on Natalya, he began to clap in time with the music. Some of the guests slipped away to claim their buggies from the shed and ride quickly away from this worldly affair. Others simply observed with unreadable expressions, but many joined in the clapping.

Mika barely kept herself from swirling into the midst of the dancers, but knew she had created enough scandal for the present time.

Little Anna had slipped to the ground, her new royal blue dress covering the grass at her feet, her face a picture of ecstasy. Heinrich glanced at Nicholai who was clapping enthusiastically, a wide smile on his face.

Gypsies mingled with staid Mennonite church members and raw Russian peasant workers. As Katya stood with Johann, she felt as if a piece of heaven had temporarily descended to earth just for her. It was indeed a celebration.

"Come, children, it is time to say good-bye to your father." Agnetha stood at the foot of the stairs and called them, then returned to the front entrance. Anna, seated on the top step, looked over at her brother and waited for his lead.

"Yes, Mrs. Wieler," he answered. "We're coming."

Nicholai stood and held out his hand to Anna. "Come on, don't be a sissy. Papa's only going to be gone ten days or so. He's left us before and we've always been fine."

"I know," she said, her chin trembling. "But we've always had Katya with us."

"She will be back soon, and Mika is here, so we're still a family."

"Mika doesn't make me feel safe like Katya does. I always wonder if she'll go away without warning."

"For shame, Anna," chided Nicholai. "She said she was sorry and we must believe her."

"Do you never feel that way, Kolya?"

He frowned. "We are going to be fine. Besides, Mrs. Wieler is here and little Philipp. It will be fun, you'll see."

"I know. Mrs. Wieler is nice. Papa likes her a lot too, don't you think?"

"Anna, stop that. I don't like to think about it. She is a nice lady and will take good care of us." Together they made their way downstairs to bid farewell to their father.

"Now children," he said in his cheerful booming voice. "I expect you to mind Ag—Mrs. Wieler and Maria. The conference begins tomorrow and I have a long drive ahead of me. I hate to leave you after all the excitement of the wedding, and with Katya and Johann gone, but the All-Mennonite Congress is an important event at this time. We will discuss the economy and our place in it, the political situation and how we will stand as a Mennonite community. In times of turmoil, we must stand together as a people. My hope is that we will be recognized by the Provisional Government as a valuable minority and given appropriate status.

"Now, I need hugs all around and a promise to pray for each other." Anna and Nicholai complied, but Agnetha stood off to the side, silently observing the family tradition.

Mika came forward as well and kissed her father's cheek. "I love you, Papa. Please be safe and come home as soon as you can. And give my regards to Uncle Abram and Tante Nela when you see them."

"And Oma," piped up Kolya. "You must greet Oma for us."

"That I will most definitely do." He seemed slightly distracted as he picked up his luggage and put it down again. He glanced over at Agnetha and nodded. She smiled in return, turning little Philipp around so that he could see Heinrich.

"Philipp wishes you a good trip, Heinrich," she said.

Heinrich walked over and touched the baby's cheek. "You be a good little man, Philipp." Looking again at Agnetha, he held out his hand and they shook hands in farewell.

"Godspeed, Heinrich."

"Thank you." He picked up a suitcase, allowing Fyodor to carry the others. "Good-bye all. God bless. See you at the end of next week."

Katarina relaxed for the first time in days as she leaned back into the worn velvet seat of the train compartment. Johann sat beside her, lulled to sleep by the rhythmic movement of the car and the touch of his wife's hand on his arm. She stared at him in something resembling surprise. Was this beloved man beside her really her husband? It seemed almost too much to take in, this dream come true. Never before had she actually dared to believe that she would be Mrs. Johann Sudermann.

They had been married for several days now, but the sight of him never ceased to set her heart to racing. She laced her fingers through his, to which he smiled sleepily and leaned on her shoulder. Allowing her head to fall back again, she recalled the excitement of the wedding. She had planned, with Maria's help, a simple ceremony with those who meant the most to her, and a few of the others who needed to feel they did. It had ended up being a celebration from start to finish, a solemn, then lively festival of thanks to God for his blessings. She had felt bad about those who had left at the appearance of the gypsies, but Papa had said not to waste worries on that. It was her day, and she had enjoyed it immensely.

A sudden lurch of the train brought her back to the present. Catching hold of the armrest with one hand and Johann with the other, she kept them both from rolling onto the floor. Johann cleared his throat and straightened his glasses. "Well, I suppose I should wake up now before I injure myself."

Katya smiled and lost herself in his eyes. This trip was another dream coming true. They were traveling down to Alushta, to the Russian Riviera.

"If you had remained teaching in Kleefeld, you would probably have traveled down to the coast for a teachers' convention sometime. I've heard the Mennonite Board of Education has built a beautiful retreat center at Alushta."

He reached for her hand. "I'd rather see it with you."

On arriving at Alushta, the two climbed part way up Kastell Mountain to the country *dacha* of one of Heinrich's acquaintances, and with the help of Katya's maid, Dunia, and a young boy to carry their luggage, settled into the airy and comfortable home overlooking the Black Sea. The week spent there was the best time of their lives, alone together, with no responsibilities demanding their attention, other than the joy of getting to know one another.

They sat on the verandah on the last evening, looking out over the sea as dusk fell. From time to time, the lights of ships dotted the dark waters of the Black Sea. "This has been the happiest time of my life," Johann said as he stroked her hand. "Life has been interesting and good, but never have I experienced the joy and contentment I have here with you."

She smiled at him. "I do hope the joy and contentment will continue when we leave, because I am not planning to stay here forever." She rose to stand at the railing. "I know what you mean, though. I have had a wonderful life, but never have I felt quite the same degree of completeness as I do with you."

"We are indeed well matched, my dear. We . . . what was that?"

"Where?"

"Down on the sea. Across the water toward Constantinople."

Narrowing her eyes in the dimness, Katarina noted several flashes of light to the southwest, but nothing more. "Constantinople is too far away to see, Johann. I imagine it's a ship."

He said nothing, squinting across the distance in an effort to see.

"Johann?"

He turned to her, his face a study of restrained emotion. "Something's happening out there, a naval skirmish of some kind. I thought the Ottomans had settled down, now that the Dardanelles were closed to the Allies."

"Oh Johann, let's not speak of the war tonight. This is our last night in Alushta and the beginning of our marriage. Must the war rob us of our joy so soon?"

Johann couldn't keep his eyes from the water. "I'm sorry, Katya. I recognize the signs of war, and I know the results as well, the suffering of the men who must do what their commanding officers demand of them. As far as I know, there are no medical units in this area. The *Forstei* is aware of the possibility of trouble, but no units have been posted here."

It was Katarina's turn for silence. Dread seeped into her being as she stood watching the faint faraway sparks and flashes. Would these battles now steal her husband from her side? Each time he left, there was a chance he would not return. While she admired his courage, compassion, and loyalty, she did not fully understand it. *Perhaps that is the way of a woman*, she thought. *Our first loyalty is always to our men and little ones, while theirs is to the greater good of humankind. A difference in perspective.*

"Perhaps we should turn in," she said. "Tomorrow will be a long day of traveling."

In silent consent, he took her arm and entered the house. The breeze was as sweet, the trees and flowers as fragrant, the air as moist and warm as before, but there was a chill in the hearts of the two young lovers. Reality always follows the dream.

Johann, Katarina, and Dunia stood next morning on the platform of the train station, prepared for the ride back to Succoth. The train was late, as usual. As it pulled in with much screeching and steaming, the crowd grew. Soldiers formed a good part of the throng, most looking weary and wearing clothes that were moth-eaten. A voice rose above the rest, calling Johann's name. He tried to place the direction of the call and was suddenly pounced upon by two neatly clad men.

"Sudermann! Where have you been, man?"

Johann's jaw dropped as he saw Eduard Claassen standing before him along with one of the other trainees he had worked with in Schwarzwald a month ago. "Eduard. Jakob. What are you doing here?"

"Off to Turkey. There's a war going on, if you've forgotten." Claassen's eyes lit on Katarina and he grinned. "Been rather distracted lately, I'm thinking."

Johann smiled. "This is my wife, Katarina Hil—Katarina Sudermann. And Dunia Orlovna. We are returning home from our wedding trip."

"You had better take a detour, Sudermann. We need you. Lots of action right now on the Ottoman shores. Constantinople's still a big prize, you know."

"You sound more like a soldier than a medical officer."

"Sorry sir, but it's the excitement. I know my job. Seriously, we need you. Not enough of us to go around, and the fellow who is supposedly commanding us is not adept as a leader. That's the truth. I don't know how we will survive this assignment with him in charge. Think it over, sir, before your train leaves. I'm sure the ladies will be fine on their own."

Katarina's heart was racing so fast she thought it might leap out of her chest. Her hand held tightly to Johann's arm, as if by clutching on to him she might keep him close to her. Even as her heart rebelled, her head knew better.

Turning aside from the others, she said to him, "Johann, it seems you must go."

"No! I will not marry you and run off to leave you alone far from home and security. I have pledged to take care of you and that I will do."

"Dunia and I will be fine, Johann. Won't we, Dunia?"

"Of course, Ma'am. I know how to handle these degenerate soldier types."

"There, it's settled." Katarina willed herself to stop trembling. It did no good. She shook like a leaf in the wind as she stood before Johann. He returned her gaze with one so confused and torn that she thought her heart would break for him. Reaching out to him, she wrapped her arms around his neck and laid her face on his shoulder. His arms went round her and he held her tightly to him, afraid to let her go.

Murmuring into her hair, he said, "Oh my Katarina, my special girl. Unselfish as always. How can I leave you? And how can I not? Lord, help me."

"Train to Simferopol and Spat leaves in five minutes," came the announcement over the loudspeaker. Still the two stood together, as if trying to make up for the time when they would be apart. Johann escorted Katarina and Dunia into their compartment and checked the luggage. Taking a smaller bag, he threw a few of his clothes into it and hoisted it onto his back.

Johann forced a smile and, with trembling lips, kissed his bride. "I've always come back, haven't I?" She nodded and clung to him for a moment. Then, turning him around, she said, "Now go. Do what you need to do, and I will pray night and day for you, my love."

She stood bravely at the door until he had torn himself away and run off to join his unit. Then she reentered her compartment, shut the door behind her, and collapsed in heartrending sobs beside Dunia. The Russian girl, who claimed to be able to manage the advances of reprobate soldiers, now applied her inner strength to the much more difficult job of calming her mistress and friend.

Heinrich mingled freely with his friends and brothers-in-the-faith at the Ohrloff Congress.

"Heinrich Hildebrandt! Good to see you." The speaker clapped him on the back and Heinrich turned to face Gerhard Warkentin. The latter brought a warm smile of recognition to Heinrich's face.

"Gerhard, my friend. How are you? I didn't expect to see you here."

They shook hands as they greeted one another and Gerhard explained. "As one of the administrators of *Bethania*, I felt it my duty to investigate and participate in this congress. The political situation affects the Home, and we are responsible for our patients. One cannot deny the realities."

"Well said. I am comforted that our Peter is in such capable and caring hands. By the way, how is he? And how is your lovely Susannah?"

"Both very well, Heinrich. Peter has gradually accepted a more active role in the home, following Susannah around, mimicking her actions. It is helpful for her, and she is a woman of great patience, as testified by her tolerance of me."

Heinrich laughed outright at the statement and laid a hand on Gerhard's shoulder. "Save me a place at table later, Warkentin. I would like to share supper with you."

The afternoon meeting began with enthusiasm. Many stood to voice their concerns and views, Heinrich among them. "It is time, Mr. Chairman," he began, "to remind the new government that we are loyal and valuable citizens, and to request equal status with our neighbors."

The statement was met with acclaim all around and the subject was discussed at length. Eventually, a Mr. Ernst Thielman was assigned to communicate with the authorities to bring the matter to their attention.

Another important issue raised at the first meeting was that of redistribution of land. Apparently, the land confiscation edict authorized by Nicholas in 1915 had never been repealed. Although the law had not been enforced, the assembled Mennonite community felt they would be more secure with the law off the books. Plans were made to deal with this matter diplomatically but effectively.

"The officials in Petrograd will be busy keeping up with all the grievances which I am sure will be pouring in." Heinrich said, savoring his snack of plum *perishky* as he visited with Gerhard Warkentin and various delegates. "Just like my Liesbet used to make them," he remarked of the delectable pastries.

"Not so good for the waistline," chided Abraham Kroeker, editor of Raduga Press.

"By the way, Abraham," said Heinrich, "how is the press operating these days? I have missed my copies of *Friedensstimme* for some time."

"Yes, I know. It was unfortunate, but one must sometimes consider self-preservation. With the war and anti-German sentiment it brought with it, we decided to step back for awhile until things simmered down. We are planning to release the paper under another name for the time being. It will be known as *Volksfreund*, and you will receive it automatically."

"*The People's Friend*. I suppose it is a more palatable title to the authorities in this present situation. I like it. Keep up the work, Brother Kroeker. It is imperative that we stay informed."

The Congress proved to be a valuable exchange of information, concerns, and decisions. Heinrich thought it over as he snapped the reins on the horse's rump. He traveled the same road he had taken three years ago when he had first met Johann. *What a miraculous God you are*, he conversed with the Lord. *Life has its difficulties, but in them all, you are there.*

Chapter 7

"May I take my horse for a ride, Mrs. Wieler?" asked Nicholai politely one afternoon about a week into Heinrich's absence. "Anna and Mika are sewing their boring old pillowcases and I need some fresh air."

Agnetha smiled as she looked up from her rocking chair, amazed at how the boy had grown over the last several months. Baby Philipp lay contentedly in her lap, staring up at the voice he heard. "Yes, I think so, Kolya." He liked it that she called him Kolya. It made him like her in spite of himself. "Be careful not to ride too far, and make sure you inform Misha of where you are going."

"Thank you," he called as he ran from the room, hoping that he would remember to tell the old stableman of his intentions. Maybe he could get a few of the boys to drop their work long enough to play Russians and Germans. It was worth a try. He loped out to the barns in anticipation.

Several hours later, Agnetha poked her head into the parlor where Mika and Anna sat embroidering. "Is Nicholai with you? He went out riding with some of the workers' boys some time ago, and should be back by now."

Mika looked up from her work and shook her head. "No, Agnetha, he hasn't returned yet, unless he came in the back way and went directly up the stairs. Anna, will you please go check upstairs if he is there? Perhaps one of the servants has seen him. I will ask Cook if he's been to the kitchen—it's one of his favorite places."

"Thank you. I just put Philipp down for the night and I hate to go too far away until he is entirely asleep."

"Don't worry, Mrs. Wieler," Anna chimed in. "We'll find our Nicholai."

Mika and Anna left immediately on their search, leaving Agnetha standing pondering in the entrance hall. A seed of uneasiness germinated in her mind, from where she did not know. Even as she turned to go to Philipp upstairs, a loud knock sounded at the main doors. Fyodor materialized instantly from the servants' sitting room and opened them. On the verandah stood a delegation of Succoth workers. Agnetha recognized one or two of them.

"We want speak to Heinrich Hildebrandt," demanded the spokesman, a heavyset, bearded man with a loud voice.

Fyodor hesitated. "He is not available tonight. When he returns, I will tell him you wish to speak with him."

The man on the doorstep smirked. "Turncoat," he muttered at the house servant. "I want Hildebrandt. Is important."

"I am sorry, but he is not here."

"Well then, I speak to mistress."

Now Fyodor looked completely at a loss. "Mistress? Mrs. Hildebrandt is no longer . . . there is no. . . ." Clearing his throat he called forth all his minimal authority. "What is it you wish to speak to the master about?"

"The master?! You fool! You work for these wealthy pigs and protect them yet. You are to them nothing. Nothing! They throw you out on cobbles when they finish with you."

Fyodor, making a great attempt to still his quaking knees, tried to shut the doors. "I will have Mr. Hildebrandt contact you as soon as he arrives home, which should be soon. Good night."

The big man stuck his oversized boot in the doorway and pushed it open. He noticed Agnetha standing at the parlor door and pointed at her. "Her," he shouted. "I will speak to her. Move, Servant."

Agnetha came forward quickly. "I will speak with you out on the verandah, sir. Fyodor, go to the kitchen and ask Cook to prepare coffee for these men." The small woman ushered the speechless giant back onto the verandah, where she graciously offered him a seat. Taking one herself, she sat straight-backed and confronted his anger.

"Now, suppose you outline to me the nature of your concern. I am in charge here at the present time. My name is Mrs. Wieler."

She extended her hand to shake his, but he stopped himself and pulled back. "You are Heinrich's new woman?" He laughed raucously and several of his company joined in, making lewd remarks.

Standing to her full height, which amounted to just over one and a half meters, she glared fiercely at the man. "If you wish to speak to me, you shall do so with at least some degree of decency. That is the way a gentleman makes his point."

The giant rose as well, towering over Agnetha, and leaned close to give her the full effect of the alcohol on his breath. She turned her face away, but did not back up. "Maybe I no gentleman, eh? Maybe I real bad man, take you with me, eh?" He sneered at her, but still she would not budge.

"I have asked you several times what it is you want. State your name and your business, man."

Puzzled by her apparent lack of fear, he stepped back and settled into his chair, assuming the air of a benevolent dictator. "I am Ilya Veselovsky. We come for land. We work land, we want land. You Germans," he labeled the race with an indecent epithet, "you come take all our land, get rich, take servants. No more. Land is ours."

"I understand what you are saying, but I am not at liberty to change anything tonight. When Heinrich returns, I'm sure he will discuss this with you and come to some agreement that benefits everyone concerned."

Ilya stared at Agnetha, trying to read her thoughts, her intentions, to deduce the source of her self-control. As he contemplated this, the main doors opened and Fyodor stepped outside carrying a tray of cups filled with steaming coffee, which he placed on a table beside the door. The men helped themselves. Fyodor moved quietly to Agnetha's side and whispered something into her ear. Concern immediately registered on her previously calm features.

The whispered words were a threat to Ilya. He bounded up from his chair and grabbed Fyodor by the collar. "What trouble you make now, Turncoat?"

Fyodor gasped in surprise and fear, unable to speak. Agnetha stepped in like a referee in a wrestling match. "That will be enough. Let him be." She scolded Ilya as if he were a child instead of a hulking menace of a man. In surprise, Ilya released his captive and turned his attention to Agnetha.

"For your information, Ilya Veselovsky, Heinrich Hildebrandt's son Nicholai is missing. He went out riding with some of the boys this evening and has not returned. We are all concerned." Turning to the men with Ilya, she said, "Have any of you seen Kolya tonight?"

Veselovsky narrowed his eyes and tapped his fingers together, then tipped his bushy head down to stare with calculating cruelty at Agnetha. Some of the men whispered to each other and one laughed.

"What is it? What has happened to Kolya?" Agnetha turned her wrath on Ilya. "What have you done, you great bear of a man? Trifling with a child's life to gain a piece of ground. Have you no shame?"

"No, I have no shame. You should fear me."

As Agnetha listened to his words, she became aware of the sound of buggy wheels rolling along Magnolia Lane from the direction of the main road. Heinrich was not due home for at least two days, and Johann and Katarina wouldn't return till the end of the week. Were there perhaps more workers arriving to add to the threat already in progress, or was God answering her unceasing prayer for help?

Veselovsky also heard the sound and turned his ear to listen. "Who comes?"

"I don't know. But I demand that you return Kolya to us at once. Such behavior will not help your cause."

"We decide that, not you," he shouted at her, jerking his head around to the sound of the wheels and hooves.

As the buggy rounded the corner of the house, Agnetha's heart beat in her throat. It was not Heinrich, nor was it Johann and Katarina. The driver pulled his wagon to a stop and climbed nimbly out onto the cobblestones. In the light of the gas lamps, she recognized the owner of the neighboring estate, Wilhelm Enns. He stood for a moment, taking in the scene, his tall, lean figure casting a straight shadow behind him. He removed his cap, revealing short dark hair slightly receding at the temples. His deep-set eyes, shaded by dark brows, sparkled in the dim light as he ran a thumb and forefinger over his well-trimmed mustache.

"Good evening." His nod included all. "Have I come at a bad time?" He caught Agnetha's pleading gaze. "Perhaps you would not mind if I joined you. It is a little trot yet to Tomak and I could use a cup of coffee if you have one."

Agnetha stepped forward and held out a small hand to Wilhelm Enns. "Welcome here, Mr. Enns. We were about to have coffee all around."

As Wilhelm bowed over Agnetha's hand, he gave her a whisper of a wink. "So good to see you again, Mrs. Wieler. I hope you are well. And little Philipp?"

"Very well, Mr. Enns. It is Nicholai who concerns us tonight. He rode off with some of the boys and has not returned. These gentlemen were commenting that they may have seen him." She turned meaningfully to Ilya, who tried his best to see through her eyes into her thoughts, but was thwarted again.

"I only maybe see him." The pitch and intensity of his voice had mellowed considerably since the arrival of Enns, who continued to stand protectively beside Agnetha. There was something of authority and justice about the man that stalled the sinister intent of the group sitting on the verandah. The atmosphere was crisp with tension, broken suddenly by running footsteps approaching the house.

In a moment, the figure of Nicholai burst into the arc of gaslight, chest heaving from his mad dash across the yard. He stopped abruptly, his wide eyes darting from Agnetha to Neighbor Enns to the men on the verandah. He calculated the gauntlet he would have to run in order to enter the house, and decided to stay put until a better opportunity presented itself.

Agnetha stared at him, then at Ilya, who frowned and shrugged. Heaving an audible sigh of relief, the small woman stood regarding the boy. She took several deep breaths before speaking. "Nicholai Hildebrandt, where have you been?"

Kolya swallowed. He much preferred the soft 'Kolya' she usually addressed him with. Dropping his eyes, he said, "I forgot the time, Mrs. Wieler, Ma'am. We, the boys and I, were playing Russians and Germans, and the Russians were losing, so I couldn't. . . ."

"And you commanded the Russian contingent?" Wilhelm kept his smile admirably hidden, one dark eyebrow raised.

"Of course. I am Russian. So I could not leave my unit in a bad place. We managed to hold off the German attack by splitting into two groups with half of us coming up behind them and then. . . ."

Several of the workers began to chuckle, and Ilya looked uncomfortable, as if the meeting he had engineered were also a game to be laughed at in hindsight.

"Kolya," Agnetha's voice resumed its usual soothing quality, "please go inside and tell your sisters you are returned. They have been worried. Then get yourself into bed." As the boy picked his way up the steps, one of the workers slapped him on the shoulder.

"Congratulations, General."

The company laughed and several men stood and stretched, setting their empty coffee cups on the railing. With nods, they trudged away into the darkness, in the direction of their own homes. Ilya Veselovsky snorted and muttered as he followed his troop homeward.

Minutes later, only Agnetha and Wilhelm remained seated on the verandah, now coming alive with moths and other night insects. After explaining briefly what had taken place, she looked over at him, no words enough to communicate her gratitude. Her eyes closed as she leaned back in the rocker and shuddered.

Wilhelm came to her side, his face all concern, and touched her arm. "Mrs. Wieler, you must be most distressed."

She smiled slightly as her eyes opened again. "I am better now, thank you. For a while I wondered."

"You amaze me. You carried it off with such grace and strength. I'm sure the men thought to scare you out of your wits."

"Oh, that they did. But what good would it do to show them my fear? I could not meet their demands even if I wanted to, and besides, they gave me the impression, the scoundrels, that they had taken Kolya." She looked at him in all seriousness. "I thought they had Kolya." Then the trembling began and she wrapped her arms around herself to still the quaking.

Wilhelm Enns felt totally helpless. He longed to hold her until she calmed down, but propriety forbid it. Although he had admired her strength and poise before this night, he now realized the enormous soul hidden in this tiny form. What was a man to do?

He realized then that she was looking at him strangely. "What is it, Mr. Enns? Your eyes carry such a stricken look."

Blinking rapidly, he tried to steady his racing pulse and return to his normal calm. "I was feeling badly for you here all alone, before I came."

"And why did you come?"

"I . . . I don't know." He rose to his full height and turned to put his hands on the railing of the verandah. Looking out into the now peaceful dark, he said, "I suppose I was feeling alone tonight, in spite of the fact that I have three young children to care for. It is one year today that my Liese passed away. I needed something to do and decided to go for a trot in the buggy. I imagine it was the Lord himself who led me here."

He turned toward her, leaning on the railing now, his arms crossed over his chest as if to stop himself from revealing any more of his private pain. He was decidedly handsome in the evening glow, thought Agnetha, in spite of herself.

"I know the feeling, Mr. Enns—"

"Wilhelm."

She glanced up at him. "Wilhelm. It is almost a year since I received the news of my Philipp's death. I am so thankful that I have little Philipp to care for."

"Sometimes one longs for more than a child's comfort." Catching himself again, he exclaimed, "I must go home. The servants will wonder what has happened to me."

Agnetha rose from her rocker and the two stood looking at each other for several moments. Abruptly, Wilhelm reached out his hand and Agnetha responded with the same. "I hope we shall see each other again soon," the man said. "Are you sure you will be all right now? Shall I stay longer?"

"I'm sure we will be fine. I believe Heinrich will be home

day after tomorrow, and Johann and Katarina soon after. Thank you for stopping. God works miracles every day if we but open our eyes and ears to them."

"Yes, he does. Good night, then."

"Good night, Wilhelm." He nodded, pulled his cap down onto his forehead and walked briskly back to the buggy. Climbing in, he leaned forward to wave and turned his horse back toward the main road. Agnetha stood for a long moment, watching the blackness where the buggy had been.

Johann was a landlubber and no doubts about it. His insides rolled with the waves as the vessel nosed toward the Ottoman coast. In a few short hours, he had twice thrown up into the dark waters, and now he stood with teeth clenched, refusing to do so again. Land could not be far away.

Eduard Claassen slapped him on the back. "How are you feeling, Commander? Still feeding the fish?" The younger man chuckled, but not with the sarcasm of his early trainee days. He had come to respect Johann Sudermann and would stand by him in any situation. All he had needed was someone to believe in him, to expect the best of him.

Johann's sunken eyes sought Eduard's in the darkness. "I'll be fine. Thank you for asking." He clamped his mouth shut again, in admirable determination. Unfortunately, his weakness won out and Claassen stood with a hand on his back until it was over.

"You really should stop this, you know. Not good for the system. Well, I'm off to find some bread and cracklings." Johann gagged again at the thought, his eyes striking daggers into Claassen's retreating form.

After meeting with Johann at the train station, the Schwarzwald Unit had jumped into wagons for the short stretch to Sevastopol. From there they secured a couple of world-weary fishing vessels and set out across the dark waters of the Black Sea, running south-southwest on a course to the coast of Turkey. The naval confrontation was being fought in the vicinity of Constantinople, and the Russian-Mennonite medics planned to land somewhere east of the actual fighting to establish a temporary hospital. At this point in time, Johann would have preferred the sight of blood to the incessant rolling of the waves. He wondered how a normal bodily weakness could so upset his mind.

He wondered also how Katya was faring. She should have arrived at Spat and begun the last stretch of the journey in a rented buggy. Thank heavens Dunia was with her, although he knew the girl took most of her courage from her mistress. Why had he deserted her? What a fool he was! Where was the call of God in all this? So often he wished God would communicate with him more clearly. A telegram would be nice. Or a message in the clouds. But he had to put these thoughts behind him and press on if he was to be of any use to his unit. They depended on him, and so far, he had not shown much leadership, clinging to the side of the boat as he was.

He strained his eyes in the darkness in search of the shore. Oh, to have terra firma beneath his feet. "Lord, bring me to the land again," he pleaded silently between clenched teeth.

"Peace! Bread! Land! Peace! Bread! Land!" The chant of the crowds gained intensity as Vladimir Lenin stood on a raised platform in Apraksin Market, his recent speech still ringing in their ears. The average-looking man with balding head and well-trimmed beard stood looking out on the sea of faces from heavy-lidded eyes. The effect of his words was electrifying. Grisha and Paul Gregorovich stood off to the side trying to make sense of it all.

"First we try to align ourselves with the Bolsheviks," Grisha said to Paul in low tones. "And then our noble leader appears and blows us out of the water. Stop the war, toss out the Provisional Government, give the land to the peasants, and hand over industry to the workers. I agree with the basics, but he wants it all done now, immediately. Would it not be better to bide our time and plan carefully?"

"Perhaps he has already planned this all out. He has had a lot of time on his hands lately."

It all made Grisha nervous. "No more clandestine jobs and eavesdropping. He's asking—no, demanding—that we stretch out our necks for him. Are we ready for this?"

"Ready or not, we must take a stand now or never. What have we to lose? We can't go back and we can't stay the same. We may as well climb on board with both feet."

Grisha regarded his closest friend and ally dubiously. Finally, with a heavy sigh, he turned to hear the rest of the speech. If he were to "climb on board with both feet," as Paul put it, he wanted to know the nature of the craft he was riding on and the strength of the political winds blowing against it.

"Kerensky has been appointed Minister of War." Grisha spoke as he and Paul put the finishing touches on the printing press. "He's gone down to the front to encourage the troops to action."

"What more are they supposed to do? They have no equipment and they are suffering from dysentery and typhoid. What does the man expect?"

"Whatever it is, he won't get it." Grisha rechecked the ink and put through a trial run of paper. "There," he said as the copy slipped out onto the drying trays. "I believe we have finally repaired the damage the mob inflicted on our press and we are ready to roll again."

"It's been too long. We have a lot of news to share."

"Ah, but you forget, Paul Gregorovich, that we are not as concerned with what has happened as with the Bolshevik point of view." He spoke low and quiet, glancing occasionally at Mikhail Karakozov, in the far corner, writing furiously at his battered desk.

Karakozov looked up and beckoned both men to approach. "I have some copy ready for editing, Grisha, if you please. Things are happening fast and we must keep up. Kerensky will soon be premier of the Provisional Government if I don't miss my guess, and violence in the cities and in the country is on the rise again."

"I thought Kerensky was at the front encouraging the soldiers as Minister of War." Paul looked puzzled by the discrepancy of the information.

Karakozov answered without looking up. "He was there. Harangued the troops into giving everything they had in defense of Russia against the Germans. They apparently cheered him heartily, and then when he left for home, they threw their empty guns on piles and started for home as well. For all intents and purposes, gentlemen, the war is over for Russia and for us."

"And yet you think Kerensky will be made premier?"

"Affirmative. We need to bring these developments to our readers in a way that will shed a negative light on the present temporary administration."

"Which should not be difficult," added Grisha.

Paul agreed. "They have done themselves more harm than good continuing on with this cursed war. Lenin has been harping on that very issue. Perhaps we can help to convince those who are still undecided."

Karakozov glanced up at Paul then and considered him for a moment. "I am glad to hear you speak thus. I have been worried about your commitment to the cause. It would not be wise to falter now in that commitment.

"It is a good thing we changed locations again before getting the press up and running," Karakozov continued. "The people are up in arms again. They want the promised food and land and an end to the war. They are becoming impatient with Kerensky because he is not coming through on these matters."

"They weren't his promises," reminded Grisha. "Lenin was the one who adopted that slogan and incited this impatience and revolutionary spirit in the people."

"Then perhaps Alexander Kerensky should get out of the way and let our true leader take charge." Paul's fervor was unmistakable. "Lenin would show everyone how this country needs to be run."Grisha grimaced. "It's becoming more and more dangerous out there. No one cares anymore about consequences. They've caught hold of the pendulum of change, and it's on the upswing. Heaven help us when it swings back again."

Karakozov glared at him, then questioned, "Where are they concentrating their efforts today? We should have a man there." He looked at Paul as the likely candidate.

"A large group of peasants and factory workers is descending upon the Tauride Palace. The Provisional Government has, of course, moved underground, and the Soviet is secure because it sides with the people. I think this one will be more vandalism than political negotiation."

"As usual. This entire society is completely out of control." Paul and Mikhail turned to Grisha as he spoke these words.

"That is what happens in revolution." Mikhail Pavlovich pounded the table before him. "Violence is the only way to gain the attention of the upper classes and reduce them to the same level as the rest of the people. Violence is necessary for change."

Although Grisha stood soberly through Karakozov's statement, he cringed inwardly at this inevitable onslaught of violence—again. He wondered why he, a peace-loving man, had been born into such a time as this, and how he would survive it. Perhaps it was time to move on. He cut short his wayward thoughts. Sometimes Mikhail Pavlovich could almost read his mind, and it was much too dangerous to give his doubts away.

"I'll get busy with the latest editing," he said, "while Tekanin runs out to Nevsky Prospekt."

As evening approached, Paul Gregorovich burst into *Pravda* headquarters. Both Grisha and Mikhail Pavlovich stood at his dramatic entrance. "What's happening?"

"A group of armed sailors has joined the demonstrators," answered Paul, leaning over onto a desk to catch his breath. "They are besieging the palace."

"What for?" asked a confused Grisha. "Only the Soviet meets there now."

"Yes, that's the point. The crowds are turning their anger on the Soviet. 'Where are the promises you made?' they say. 'Why are you sitting behind closed doors making deals with the government?'"

"How big are the crowds?" Karakozov was already scribbling details on his notepad.

"I don't know, thousands anyway. But they keep materializing from every alley and street. It's building just like the February riots."

Paul noticed a satisfied look on the face of his boss. Turning back to his work, Karakozov said, "Finally the ball is on the court again. Lenin will be pleased."

Next day the crowds had swelled even more and were becoming increasingly irate. The July heat and humidity added to the volatile atmosphere. As Paul kept to the outskirts of the mob, observing and trying to figure out what their plan was, he came upon a particularly angry group of sailors in St. Isaac's Square. As he edged closer to the action, he noticed a smartly suited gentleman trying desperately to talk his way out of the clutches of the tough seaman.

"I am a socialist, my fellow Russians. I believe as you do and am doing my best to see that this country adopts socialist policies."

He was rudely interrupted by shouts and curses as soldiers joined the sailors, pushing the unfortunate man up against the rough stone façade of Liteyny Mercantile. "We've heard enough of your promises. You are Kerensky all over again, doing nothing but spouting empty promises."

"But I assure you—"

"We are fed up with assurances like clouds that refuse to drop rain. We will have our way. We are the people and we will have the power."

Shouts erupted from the crowd. "Empty promises. We have the power." Soon the chants become more savage and the people's words were: "String him up. Give them a lesson. String him up."

Someone ran for ropes, and a few agile sailors clambered up a drainpipe to lash them around a stone cornice. The victim had resorted to pleading and struggling, but this only incited the onlookers to more anger. All at once, an authoritative voice shouted over the group gathered there. "A moment, gentlemen. What is to be gained by taking this man's life? He is merely a puppet of the government."

The instigators turned on the interrupter with malice in their eyes, but stopped short at the sight of the slim middle-aged man with wire rimmed eyeglasses and pointed black beard. "Mr. Trotsky. We did not know it was you." Hemming and hawing, they eased their hold on the captured socialist and listened as the celebrated orator calmed them down.

"The Bolshevik plan is to take over the government, and we are well along in that process. Please do not set us back by such useless actions. You are men of reason, and to this reason I appeal. Let this poor unfortunate go and attend to his business, and you attend to yours."

By some intervention of fate, or whatever the people believed to be in control of the situation, the prisoner escaped with his neck still normal length, and Leon Trotsky thanked the sailors and soldiers and continued on his way to make sure the riots were effecting what was needed for the Bolshevik cause.

Paul held his breath as he watched the drama unfold and resolve. As much as he wished to become a part of the demonstration, he knew he must keep his wits about him and do his job. By evening there was havoc everywhere. The city was in reality at the mercy of the people, and they were not yet satisfied. The mob at the Tauride Palace was well armed, workers, students, sailors, and more soldiers. As the sun sank out of sight, they decided it was time to take action.

Paul set aside his professionalism and joined the crowd as they battered the doors where the Petrograd Soviet met. Police fired at the crowds to disburse them, and the people returned fire. Already many lay wounded or dead on the wide streets of the city, and still the rioting continued. Again and again, the ramming of posts and poles beat against the finely carved portals of the palace, and finally, with a loud crack, they broke open and the crowd rushed in.

Ringleaders lambasted the assembled committee with their accusations of empty promises and compromises. "Down with the government! Down with the government!" Police attempted to prevent the crowd from hurting the members of the surprised and frightened Soviet and only just succeeded in doing so. It was a situation where no one would win, and reason had again been passed by.

As Paul pushed his way closer to the front of the enormous room where voices were raised in shouts, he wondered what would come of it all. He should take care not to become too involved, but he agreed wholeheartedly now with the angry workers. How long would this war of words continue while every day out on the street people died of malnutrition and disease, and the soldiers still at the front lines offered themselves up as a sacrifice for . . . for what?

Behind him Tekanin noticed a number of government officials trying to make their way through the crowd to be heard. One of them was the lean, hollow-faced Alexander Kerensky. The people grudgingly let him through until he found a place at the front beneath a massive painting depicting the Crimean War. Vestiges of a more elaborate lifestyle still remained in the palace to remind those present of its aristocratic past.

"Workers, soldiers, sailors," began Kerensky. What was he doing speaking up for the Soviet? "You have come out today to demand your rights, and we do not begrudge you that. The Provisional Government believes you are entitled to those rights and are working toward that end."

Boos and catcalls rose from the audience, but the speaker maintained his calm and raised a hand to quell the rising murmurs. "There are, however, some facts you may not be aware of, which will greatly alter your allegiance." He stopped to clear his throat, glancing at his associates. "We who make up the Provisional Government know, and have known for some time, that the forces inciting you to this civil disobedience are not who you think they are. When your Lenin arrived in this noble city, from where did he come?"

He waited for the answer. "Germany." Paul noticed movement out of the corner of his eye and turned in time to see the bespectacled man with a pointed black goatee exit the building with great haste.

"Germany," he repeated. "Now why would he come from Germany? Let me suggest one perfectly good reason: He is a German agent."

The crowd again erupted in catcalls, but Kerensky quieted them. "Think about it. The Kaiser will stop at nothing to infiltrate our nation. Lenin is a prime candidate for this job, and he has hired on with the German government to subdue the populace of Russia. I have documents to prove it. Will you consign your lives to the likes of a man who has sold his soul to Kaiser Wilhelm?"

The effect of this information, whether contrived or truthful, amazed even Paul. The mob swallowed the words as a fish swallows a hook. It caught them and held them in confusing irony. The cause they believed in had once again turned against them. It took the wind out of their political sails and left them confused and helpless.

With much muttering and murmuring, the crowd dissipated, Paul moving with them, and wandered off in various directions. Tekanin took a circuitous route back to the *Pravda* office and reported everything to Karakozov. Grisha, proofing another column, listened with astonishment to Paul's account of the confrontation and the unforeseen conclusion.

"Obviously," he broke in, "the Provisional Government has been scheming a way of putting down the Bolsheviks. We must be on total alert again." He sighed and Mikhail Pavlovich shot a look at him.

"I agree that we must also go underground again, as if we are not already in that position, but we are going to weather this storm. Lenin will be victorious."

As the trio of newsmen pondered this strange new development, Vladimir Lenin packed his bags and beat a hasty retreat across the Gulf of Finland. He had denied the charges of Kerensky, which were indeed false, but public opinion had shifted against the self-proclaimed Bolshevik leader. For the time being he knew of a comfortable villa in Finland.

All the news came out in the papers next morning: "*Lenin, known German agent, flees country. Trotsky and Kamenev arrested.*" In spite of himself, Paul smirked at the mention of Kamenev behind bars. That cold fish deserved a taste of living under someone else's thumb.

Chapter 8

The night was moonless. A stiff breeze blew in bank after bank of steel gray clouds, like a heavy damp quilt over the Schwarzwald entourage. The insulation from above exaggerated the sound of gunfire, and the crack and pop brought time to a standstill for Johann. All his memories of *Forstei* service came together as one long moan. He shook himself alert.

"Keep low, men," he instructed in a quiet but firm voice. "They are not out to get us, but they also can't tell us apart from the Turks." They had come up on the beach of a small bay, as planned. In the shelter of his coat Johann switched on his electric lantern to check again the crudely drawn map supplied for him by Daniel Voth, the man who had originally been assigned command of this forlorn group of newly recruited medical officers. Voth had most gladly relinquished his command when Eduard brought Johann forward and introduced him.

The map showed a small hillock not far from the beach, around which grew a stand of acacia trees, thin protection against the enemy, but somewhat of a shelter. That was where Johann was headed. The men in his command carried canvas, poles, pegs, and mats, as well as their personal medical bags.

Another explosion resounded from the water some distance away, lighting up the skyline for several moments, long enough for Johann to glimpse the hill. "Keep down," he ordered again. "Run for the trees." The group ran for cover, doubled over and stumbling with their varied burdens. Reaching the trees, they dropped their packs and threw their tired bodies onto the short wiry grass to catch their breath. Johann knew enough to let them gather strength before pushing them to set up the tent.

As a blood red sun rose above the Black Sea several hours later, it illuminated a crooked but firmly planted tent in the shelter of dark trees. The men lay sleeping in the quiet of the morning. The warm rays of the autumn sun woke Johann as he turned stiffly on his mat. He sat up with a start, the name of his wife escaping his lips as he stared about him. The roar of a ship's cannon brought reality back into sharp focus. He blinked the sleep from his bloodshot eyes and rubbed life into his face.

Rising to survey their situation by daylight, he silently circled the tent, peering through the trees to the south. The fertile northern plains on which Johann and his men had landed ran the entire length of Turkey's Black Sea coast, according to his map. Farmers raised crops and grazed small herds on its grasses, while the Pontic Mountains rose as a backdrop, separating them from the drier central plains.

The night's work had gone well in spite of lack of light, but it was time to fly the flag of medical mercy and go in search of survivors. Several Russian frigates had approached the coastline in the early morning hours and were now busy unloading the wounded onto small boats to be rowed to shore. Johann roused his tired men and they set out to carry the survivors back to the tent on makeshift litters. It would mean many trips back and forth on the sandy beach, but that was what they were there for.

As Johann, Eduard, and a young *Forstei* recruit named Aron Andres approached the first load of wounded, a large man in decorated military uniform climbed out of the boat and waded to the beach. His naval cap shadowed low brows

over deep-set eyes, a hawk nose the focal point of his broad
face. His thin lips were drawn in a straight, firm line as he
assessed the situation.

"Good day to you, sir," Johann saluted the commanding
figure. "We are medical crew here to retrieve the wounded
and take them back to that enclosure." He pointed over his
shoulder to the stand of acacias and reached into his pocket
for the official certificate of the *Forstei*.

Another naval officer had come alongside the first and it
was he who acknowledged Johann. "This is Admiral Kolchak
of the Black Sea Fleet," he said, gesturing to the rows of
medals on the man's chest. "And you are?"

"Johann Sudermann, sir, of the Schwarzwald Medical Unit.
We arrived last night and erected a tent to shelter the wounded."

The man scrutinized Johann and then turned to his superior.
"Well, Admiral, do we give the survivors over to this lily-
pawed bunch?"

"You may go," Kolchak dismissed his surprised assistant
and focused on Johann. "The battle of last night was not in
our favor, although we came away with our ships. Some cannon
damage to be repaired, so while the Germans are doing the
same, I would invite you to take away these ill-fated men and
do what you can for them. If we are unable to pick them up
later, we trust you will return them to Russian soil."

Johann nodded and backed away to organize his men.
Kolchak stopped him. "Medic, what news from the capital?
We have heard of the sweeping changes and riots. Do you
know anything of the welfare of the imperial family?"

Johann turned back to the admiral and scoured his memory
for information. His wedding and holiday to Alushta had distanced him from some of the realities of the revolution. "It
has been some time, sir, since I was home to follow the
papers, but it seems the people have overthrown the tsar's
government without even a strong leader. Lenin has returned,

and Trotsky has joined him from the States, but they were not in Petrograd when it happened.

"If you will allow me to say so, sir, I have heard that Lenin is also against the Provisional Government which has been set up. He has no patience with this institution, encouraging the people to follow his more revolutionary plan. It seems from the news that has reached us in Crimea, that Lenin's Bolsheviks are gaining power quickly. The people are so enthused and motivated by their amazing victory in the February Revolution that they don't intend to release the pressure until they get what they want, which according to the printed word is 'peace, land and bread.'"

"Yes. That is also what we have heard. We sail around this miniature ocean in a world of our own, trying to hold the German dogs at bay, and sometimes radio contact is poor. But tell me, medic, what of the tsar? Have you heard anything of Nicholas? I joined his naval troops when I was thirteen years of age. Fought the Japanese in '05, and then spent a good number of years charting the polar regions of Nicholas's realm. He is a fine man and will always hold my allegiance."

Johann surveyed the loyal tsarist commander and wished he could tell him what he wanted to hear. "It seems the Soviet became suspicious when Nicholas requested safe passage to Britain, so they arrested the entire family and are holding them in Tobolsk."

"Siberia! When this war is finally over, I will find him there, I promise you." The admiral turned from Johann and marched in the direction of his assembled men. A few strides away, he stopped and looked back at Johann. "Do your duty now as a subject of a proud but broken nation."

Night fell too soon as stretcher after stretcher of injured men was hustled over the beach to the shelter of the temporary hospital. Some carried, others bandaged and stitched. The Mediterranean climate of the Ottoman Empire made the work of the *Forstei* hot and tiring, but the men persevered. Their commander proved to be an able and dedicated example for them to follow. His strength came from God alone, for he had long ago come to the end of his own.

One more run, thought Johann as the brilliant orb of the sun sank below the horizon and a breeze sweetened the air. Surprisingly, the sea had been quiet this day, with ships anchored to reconnoiter and repair. The ships, leaving their last casualties behind for the Schwarzwald company, pulled up anchor before the Turks should force them out of harbor. As twilight fell, the pop of guns and the roar of the cannon resumed. The waters of the Black Sea magnified the sound. It felt as if the enemy was at the doorway of the flimsy hospital tent. Hand torch in his pocket, Johann and eight of his men set out on one more trek of mercy.

"Even with the hospital flag waving in the wind, I will never feel safe in enemy territory." Eduard Claassen summed up the feelings of all of them. "Who would know if we were wiped out or not? So many dead in this crazy war, they wouldn't miss a few more."

Johann needed to keep up their morale. "No more negative talk, fellows. Let's do our job and leave the rest in God's hands."

Eduard glanced over at his commander but did not comment. Arriving at the shore, they picked up the last few unfortunate men and gently lifted them onto the stretchers. "Just get us off this infidel coast, would you?" pleaded one very young navy man whose shoulder was mangled and bloody.

"That's our goal," Johann reassured him. "Best for all of us to get back to the hospital tent as quickly as possible." Then to his men, he said, "Let's go. It's almost dark and we'll be easy targets in the moonlight."

The group carried their patients as fast as comfort would

allow. The young man with the damaged shoulder cried out every so often and his side began to bleed. *Perhaps broken ribs protruding through the flesh* guessed Johann without having examined the wound.

He and Eduard carried the last litter across the grassy beach. Shells were flying on land now, as well as at sea. "Guess the Turks are giving us an enemy's welcome." Eduard threw the words over his shoulder to Johann. About ten meters from the trees the shots increased and a bullet whizzed past Johann's ear. Both men hit the ground on impulse. The young wounded man rolled off the stretcher onto the ground and lost consciousness with an unearthly scream of agony. Eduard abandoned the litter and dragged the man into the temporary compound.

As Johann struggled to pull himself forward, another volley of gunfire ricocheted off the uneven ground upon which he lay. He was temporarily stunned by an intense pain in his foot, but adrenaline kept him moving. Claassen was at his side instantly, his charge having been delivered. "Come on, Captain," he said as he grabbed Johann by the arm. "Almost there." Johann's right foot refused to work for him, and the pain persisted. With a great effort by both men, they rolled behind the cover of the acacias.

As they sat panting out of the range of fire, Claassen's concern surfaced. "You all right, Sudermann? Did they get you?"

"I'm fine. Only a pain in my foot." He grimaced. "Must have stubbed my toe on a rock or a root as I crawled. Probably lose a toenail is all."

"Let's take a look." In spite of Johann's objections, Eduard unlaced his scarred boot and pulled off his blood-soaked sock. Switching on the pocket lamp, he examined the foot. "Plugged you good, sir," he said after a moment's inspection. "Nearly blew your big toe right off."

Johann grabbed the light and looked for himself. "Blasted Turks. Don't they know a hospital flag when they see one?" He winced again as he touched his foot.

"Sit back, Sudermann. I'll get some antiseptic and clean that out before we bandage it."

"No. Leave the antiseptic for those who need it. I'll be fine."

Claassen blew his breath out loudly and knelt down to speak face-to-face with his commander. "I will risk discipline by disregarding your orders," he said. "A small trickle of the stuff will ward off infection. We don't need a disabled captain, or another fevered patient, and your wife would kill me if I didn't take care of you. Now, I promise I won't use any more than absolutely necessary."

The damaged toe was sufficiently doused and bandaged in short order, and with the aid of a stout branch from one of the trees, Johann hobbled from stretcher to stretcher and mat to mat, checking on the work of his trainees. He was surprised how much his big toe had to do with balance and how much pain that minor appendage created.

Johann bent over the fevered form of the young naval recruit. The medics had done all they could, but his wounds were more serious than previously suspected. A rifle shot had blasted his shoulder, flesh and bone were shattered and torn, and loss of blood was substantial. He had also taken shrapnel in his side, causing more blood loss and endangering his heart.

"Will I make it? Mother needs me." His voice was barely a whisper, his breathing shallow.

"We'll do our best, son," assured Johann, his heart breaking as he sent a desperate prayer heavenward. "Where are you from?"

"Tsaritsyn." A sudden convulsion racked the broken body and he coughed up blood as Johann helplessly held him. Even as the young man's eyes pleaded with Johann to help him, the light of life fled from them and he slumped back onto the hard, cold mat.

Johann choked back a sob and signaled two of his crew to take care of the deceased. He wondered, as they carried the lad's body outside, how long it would be before his mother heard the news. He had died too soon, this young son of Russia, one of so many millions of war dead.

Johann rubbed his eyes with the heels of his hands and staggered away leaning heavily on his cane. He decided that if a friendly ship did not arrive within the next few hours, they would load these war victims onto the fishing boats and head back to Russian soil, provided the Turks didn't use them for further target practice. In the meantime, his toe throbbed mercilessly.

"The local *volosts* in the colonies have been given new leadership," said Widower Enns as he and Heinrich sipped coffee in the well-appointed library at Succoth. "The Molotschna administration is now called a Soviet, and peasants from the surrounding areas have been appointed as its officials. I am gravely concerned about their capabilities and their motivation."

"I hear what you are saying, friend," replied Heinrich. "I have read in *Volksfreund* that the concept of the Soviet is being expanded from the cities to the distant corners of the land, but I thought perhaps they would allow the Mennonite colonies to continue to self-govern. We manage quite well."

"To this date it has worked adequately." Enns turned his cup in his hands as he spoke. "Our *zemstvos*, run as they are by Russians, Tatars, Mennonites, and other Germans, accurately reflect the districts which they administer."

Wilhelm drained his cup and placed it back in the saucer.

"However," he continued, meeting Heinrich's eyes, "in the words of Abraham Kroeker, 'The golden age is past for the Mennonite people of Russia.' We will not be able to hide forever from the realities that face our brothers in the colonies."

"I suppose you are correct in that belief. What do you think is ahead for us?"

"You know as well as I do. A guess is only as good as the information we have. We here in the Crimea are more independent, but the colonies are in quite a turmoil. The *Schulzes* and *Oberschulzes* will be looking for other ways of spending their time than in supervising the communities. "

Heinrich grimaced. "You and I are both members of our local *zemstvo*, Wilhelm. How will we deal with the changes that are approaching?"

"I have not yet been asked to resign. I suppose I will continue as long as I am allowed. I believe it was a good political move to call on more of the Tatar *murzaks* to help us maintain control."

"It shows our trust in them. Hetman Skoropadsky was pleased." Heinrich finished his coffee and tapped a rhythm on the arm of his chair.

Wilhelm seemed to have little more to say, and yet he made no move to leave. "What is it, neighbor?" asked Heinrich, concern in his question. "Something is troubling you."

Widower Enns knit his brows and stroked his slim mustache, looking even younger than his thirty-two years. He glanced up at Heinrich and then down again at his shoes. He stood to his feet and cleared his throat. "Has the household recovered from the fright the workers caused last week?"

Heinrich tried to read the man's meaning. With narrowed eyes he answered, "I believe so. Little Anna was not aware of it at the time. Apparently Mika sensed a disturbance and kept her otherwise occupied. They stayed with Philipp while Agnetha dealt with the situation.

"She suffered the greatest fright, but she is a strong woman in spite of her fragile appearance. She handled the situation as well as anyone could. I am proud of her." He smiled. "But she could not say enough about your miraculous appearance to save the day."

"I had no idea what I was walking into. I had merely decided to take a drive in the evening air and found myself on your doorstep." He gazed across the room absentmindedly. "She truly was amazing. Such calm and composure. I admire her fortitude with those angry men."

Heinrich still searched the younger man's face as the blue-gray eyes met his. Enns seemed flustered. "Well," he said at last, "I suppose I should return home to Tomak. Thank you for the visit."

They stepped out into the entry and Wilhelm shot a glance down the long hallway and up the staircase. As they passed the parlor he peeked in as far as possible without seeming nosy.

"Good afternoon, Mr. Enns." The words issued from the parlor where Agnetha sat sewing. Philipp slept in a bassinet near her.

Enns retraced his steps and leaned into the room to acknowledge her greeting. He smiled warmly. "Good afternoon to you, Mrs. Wieler. How are you? I hope the unpleasantness of last week's meeting is forgotten."

"Oh, my meeting with you was far from unpleasant." She smiled primly at his confused look.

"I meant with the workers."

She laughed then. "Of course, Mr. Enns. I'm sorry, sometimes my sense of humor gets away from me. Yes, I have put the unpleasantness behind me and try not to dwell on it. And you?"

Wilhelm advanced further into the room, smiling at his own gullibility. "Madame, that was cruel, but I forgive you." He pulled at his lapel nervously, but could not keep his eyes from her face. "I still think a lot about the encounter and wonder what brought it on. My own workers have not been outwardly angry, but sometimes I sense a quiet rebellion in their attitude. It pays to be aware of these things." He reached out and smoothed Philipp's wisps of fair hair.

Heinrich stood in the doorway observing the exchange with surprise, a dull pain in his chest. *Lord, grant me grace*, he prayed silently as the realization of what was happening became clear to him. *Of course she would prefer a man closer to her own age. I am old enough to be her father.*

Coming forward, he placed a hand on Wilhelm's shoulder. "My friend, excuse my lack of hospitality. Stay for supper with us, if you would be so kind."

Enns regarded him closely, then glanced at Agnetha, who gave nothing away in her expression. "I would be glad to do so, if I am not intruding."

"Not at all. It will give us all a chance to visit with you."

Agnetha stood and gathered baby Philipp into her arms. "I will stop by the kitchen on my way upstairs and ask Cook to set another place at the table." She smiled at both men as she breezed past them into the hallway.

Wilhelm and Heinrich looked awkwardly at one another. Finally Heinrich clapped his neighbor on the back and began to chuckle, although the pain in his chest still threatened to steal his breath. "I do believe she has captured your attention, my friend. The ways of the Lord are truly amazing, are they not?"

Enns grinned and shook his head. "I had no intention of. . . ." He stopped and shook his head again, pulling on his mustache.

"I should not be surprised. She is a lovely woman. And you a man with three motherless children. You should not stay alone; they need a mother's touch."

"But how can I take such a step? Even though my heart leaps at the sight of her, I feel like I am being unfaithful to my

Liese." He paced the room as he spoke, his eyes now gray and piercing. His handsome face appeared gaunt as he spoke of his wife.

"Till death do us part, Wilhelm. Liese is gone, but you and your children remain. Here is a woman who obviously is willing to develop a friendship with you, and who has no family of her own besides Philipp. She too has suffered and endured. She would understand your hesitation as well as your hope." Heinrich stood before his friend. "Pray about it, Wilhelm. Ask God for guidance, and if he does not wish for anything to come of it, it will fade."

Enns nodded. "Thank you, Heinrich, I will do that."

As will I, thought Heinrich as he put a hand to his chest.

Chapter 9

 "Abram, I'm afraid." Cornelia Reimer clung to her husband as he entered the door of their sturdy home in Alexanderkrone. "Two Toews brothers have been murdered in cold blood near Waldheim, and robberies are taking place almost every day in the villages."

Abram looked grim as he listened to his wife recite the facts he had heard minutes before at the church meeting. Wordlessly, he set his hat on the shelf by the door and walked into the large, sunny kitchen. The yeasty aroma of baking bread soothed his senses. He sat down at the table and pulled out a chair for his wife.

Dutifully, she sat, but could not remain seated. "Oh Abram, what you have been warning is coming true and I didn't believe you." She paused to think. "Perhaps I knew what you said was possible, but I chose to deny it."

"Nellie, I wish I were wrong, but the signs have been obvious for a long time already. The unrest that has pervaded Petrograd and Moscow is filtering down to us here in our tidy little settlements. We have already experienced the invasion by way of the local Soviets. *Oberschulze* Friesen has been forced to resign with the rest of his committee, and a group of illiterate peasants now calls the orders in the Molotschna. They do not understand our religion or our way of life. The enemy has stormed our inner circles."

"Thank goodness the church is still allowed to function as we are accustomed."

"Yes, so far." Abram Reimer kept his silence for several long moments before he spoke again. Cornelia checked the bread in the oven and came to stand again at his side.

"I have been trying to decide what to do."

"What to do? What can we do?"

He looked at her with love and pulled her onto the chair near him. Holding her shaking hands, he reasoned it out. "We have several options, as I see it. We could continue to live in denial and pretend that the murders and vandalism are normal and will occur from time to time. Or we can become vocal and demand that the Alexanderkrone Soviet put a stop to these criminal acts and allow us to return to our former way of life."

"By becoming vocal, do you mean protest like they do in the cities?" His wife stared at him wide-eyed.

He smiled slightly. "My dear, I am thinking aloud. I am merely laying out the facts and our choices of response. As I was about to say, another choice would be to retreat, leave here before the situation gets worse."

"Leave? Leave our beautiful home and our village? We have both lived here all our lives. It is like the Garden of Eden and much more organized, Abram. How could we go away and where would we go?"

"I've been thinking." He tapped his temple with his forefinger. "Perhaps we could make a visit to Succoth and stay until the tension has dissipated. What would you say to that?"

She stared at him, trying to digest all that he had said and to consider the implications of such a flight. "For how long . . . of course, you cannot know that. Would the Hildebrandts allow us to stay . . . we know they would welcome us. Abram, we maybe should take Heinrich's mother-in-law with us. What if something happens at Ruekenau?"

"I suppose we could ask her, but I doubt she would come. She is an independent old soul."

"Yes, but we should ask, Abram. We could go tomorrow."

"How soon could you be ready to leave here, Nela?"

"How soon can I pack up my entire life and lift it into a buggy?" She sighed and wiped tears from her cheeks. "I don't know, possibly a week. But I will have to houseclean everything before we go. All the walls and ceilings will need to be wiped down and the rugs beaten and aired. There is much to do. I wish Maria were here to help."

"Nela, don't bother about the cleaning. You never know what may happen in our absence and it will all have been for naught."

"I could never leave a dirty house. It hasn't been washed down in three months." Her husband smiled. "We are coming back, aren't we, Abram? Because I could not bear to leave forever."

"Of course, my dear," he assured her, wishing he believed his own words. "As soon as things quiet down, we will return and you can set to cleaning like never before."

She took the bread from the oven, dumped the steaming golden loaves onto cooling racks, and bustled out of the room to begin her checklist. He watched her go. *Father God*, he prayed silently, *am I doing the right thing? We have been taught to turn the other cheek, to avoid confrontation, but am I a coward if I leave? On the other hand, can I sacrifice my dearest wife for the sake of my pride? Please guide me in my decision, Lord.*

Abram Reimer was awakened early the following morning as the mantle clock began to strike three. The room was dark and would be so for another few hours. As he lay wide awake in the darkness, he distinctly heard voices in the night air. They seemed to come from Theodore and Katie Konrad's yard next door. Rising quickly but carefully so as not to alert Cornelia, he pulled on his pants and tiptoed out to the kitchen to retrieve his shoes and jacket. He thought of Theodore Konrad with his arthritic hip. No doubt his Katie was scared out of her wits by now, unless her deafness prevented her from hearing anything. Their married son and family had relocated to the Terek Settlement on the Caspian Sea, so they were no longer here to come to their aging parents' aid.

Abram noiselessly lifted the latch and let himself out the kitchen door. Pressing his lean form against the house, he inched toward the corner and peeked around it. He could see little on this moonless night, but he could definitely hear a commotion in the Konrads' garden. Keeping low and quiet, he edged closer to the back of the house. Suddenly he thought of Nela waking and finding him gone. He wondered if she would scream loud enough to wake Uncle Schellenberg from his eternal slumber in the neat little cemetery, on the far side of the village, behind the Koop Store.

Throughout his clandestine approach, Abram had been unable to decide what he was going to do about the problem in the garden. He was not a man given to unreasonable fears or violence, but he still wondered what he would do if backed against the wall. Does a man ever know for sure how he will react?

As Abram's eyes grew accustomed to the dark, aided by the faintest hint of approaching dawn, he saw what was happening. Two men bent over the garden, filling sacks with produce, and trampling the plants behind them. Just then he caught movement from the corner of his eye. A stooped figure limped from the shadows of the Konrad dwelling. Before he could so much as warn his elderly neighbor, the man confronted the vandals.

"Go home, Thief!" Theodore Konrad shouted in Russian. "Raise your own food and leave us alone." As quick as a bolt of lightning, one of the intruders slugged the old man on the side of the head and he crumpled to the dirt.

Abram leaped from the shadows of his house and vaulted

across the fence separating his yard from his neighbors. The silhouettes straightened in surprise, and next thing Abram Reimer knew, he lay gasping on the grass, clutching his right arm. Right on cue, a blood-curdling scream from his bedroom window ripped the night.

Theodore Konrad moaned, shook his head and sat bolt upright. "Where did they go?" he demanded. By that time, the thieves had run off through the old man's orchard and into the wood nearer the Juschanlee River. Cornelia screamed again and called out for her husband.

Konrad crawled over to where Abram lay curled up on the grass. "Reimer! Have you been hit?"

"They must have shot me in the arm, but I don't even remember hearing the gun. How is your head?"

"There will be a knot, something to boast about, but I am fine. Let us make our way to your house. I believe your wife is calling." The retired schoolmaster helped Abram to his feet, and pushed opened the garden gate. "Here we go, Abram. Lean on me and I will lean on you. Together we will make progress. Cornelia calls."

Abram grimaced as he stood, fighting off a sudden attack of dizziness. With his good hand on the fence, he and Theodore Konrad stumbled to the kitchen door and entered the house. Theodore set the lantern on the table and eased his neighbor into a chair. "Cornelia Reimer," he called. "It is Neighbor Konrad. Abram is here with me."

A wild-eyed, Medussa-haired Cornelia emerged from the back of the house, her robe wrapped clumsily around her middle-aged frame. Seeing her husband with blood all over his jacket, she screamed again and crumpled to her knees.

"Nela," commanded Theodore in his best teacher's voice, "you must pull yourself together. Abram has received a gunshot to his right arm and needs our help. Give me the belt of your wrapper."

Obediently, Nela slid the cloth belt out of its loops and placed it on the table. "Abram?" Her voice perched on the edge of hysteria.

"Come," said Theodore firmly. "Give your Abram a kiss so he gets some color back and then run along next door and tell my wife I'll be home soon. You may have to shout, she's deaf as a post." The pitch of his voice gave credence to his statement.

Cornelia stepped toward her husband and knelt beside him. She sat thus for a moment, calming herself, then rose and planted a resounding kiss on her husband's brow. Theodore Konrad grinned and Abram smiled weakly.

"Good girl. Now, before you go talk to my Katie, run across the road to Jakob Thielman's house and ask his son Willy to run for Dr. Bittner."

She fished a large safety pin from a kitchen drawer and fastened her robe. Before she could leave, a sharp knock sounded on the Reimers' door and a voice called out, "Is there trouble here?"

"It's Jakob Thielman, himself," declared Theodore, "come in answer to your ear-splitting screams. Let him in."

Mechanically, Cornelia moved to the door and lifted the latch to admit Mr. Thielman. Nodding in greeting, Theodore barked out instructions. "Thielman, rouse Willy and send him for Dr. Bittner at once. Then come back and help me with Abram. He has received a gunshot to the arm."

Jakob Thielman stared at Abram, who sat slouched in a straight-backed kitchen chair, face ashen, the belt of his wife's house robe forming a tourniquet around his right bicep.

"Immediately," he called over his shoulder, already halfway out the door.

"That man will make things happen. I hope his son doesn't think the end of the world has come, being awakened so suddenly at this time of morning." Theodore wrapped Abram in an old blanket that lay folded on the deacon's bench by the door. He kept talking as he worked. "Not that he doesn't deserve a little of his own medicine from time to time. Goodness knows, he has given me a turn or two in my classroom." He continued to support Abram.

"It's all right now, Nela. Dr. Bittner will be here soon and he will take care of your Abram. Relax now and go talk to my Katie."

Abram decided he would recover well enough as long as he could keep his head. Even as he made his decision, shades of gray and black descended upon him like the huge flapping wings of a raven, and he slumped forward in the chair.

"Fine time to swoon, Abram," said Theodore Konrad, holding him up as best he could. "I'm an old man, you know."

"Papa's home! Papa's home!" The two youngest Enns children leaped from their beds as Wilhelm's steps sounded in the upstairs hall.

"I am coming, my dears."

Little Tina met him at the bedroom door and flew into his arms. Sarah was right behind her sister, reaching as far as she was able round her father's waist to wrap him in a hug. Wilhelm knelt and embraced them both at the same time, inquiring how their evening had gone.

"David read stories to us until it was time for bed and then Helen tucked us in."

"Yes, and we had *vereneke* and sausage for supper. You missed it."

Wilhelm smiled. He wanted to give his children all the happiness they deserved and to protect them from all the evils of the world. He knew he could not, but he would do his best trying.

"I had a lovely supper, too, children. I believe it was pork chops, or was it steak? No, it was pork chops and applesauce."

Tina nuzzled her head into his neck. "Why did you wanna eat with the Hilabrans instead of with us, Papa?"

He raised his eyebrows at the question. Why, indeed? "They invited me to stay, and as I knew you were well looked after by your brother and Helen, I decided a visit with the neighbors would be nice."

His explanation satisfied Tina, and Sarah was already yawning. "You two chickens jump back into your beds now. It is late."

Tina giggled. "We'se not chickens, Papa. We'se *Mädchen.*"

"You are little girls, of course. How could I forget? But you still must get to sleep." As he tucked Sarah into her bed, she stared at him for a long moment. Then, in a stage whisper, she said, "Papa, David says you are looking for a new mama for us. I told him he was crazy. You aren't, are you?"

Wilhelm leaned over and planted a kiss on his daughter's forehead. "You are not to worry about that, and you will not call your brother names." He pulled the thick blue comforter up to her button nose. "Good night," he said. "Go to sleep now."

Wilhelm backed out of the room, and continued on down the wide hallway to his son's room. Faint light seeped underneath the door, and Wilhelm knocked softly before he turned the knob and entered. David's eyes widened at the sight of his father, and he hurriedly closed his book and put it aside on the night table. "Hello, Papa. I thought I should stay awake until you came home, in case anything should happen, you know."

Wilhelm smiled and nodded. "Thank you for taking such good care of your sisters, young man. Your sense of responsibility pleases me."

David flushed with pleasure and scooted closer to the wall so his father could sit on the edge of the bed. "Did you enjoy yourself, Papa? Did you talk about the war and the riots?"

"Yes on both counts. The war subject is sad. So many have died. The riots are on and off in the cities, many unhappy and angry people who want everything changed at once."

"What can be done, Father?" David's eyes carried a look too old for his nine years. He had always been a thoughtful and gentle child, but the loss of his mother had made him even more introverted. Sometimes Wilhelm worried. He knew how easily gentle hearts were wounded.

"If I could give you the answer to that, my son, I would be the most sought after man in the country, or in the world, for that matter."

"Jesus would know what to do."

"Yes, he would, and he does, but sometimes he allows people to go their own way until they are ready to call on him. We must pray that folks will sense their need of him." Wilhelm saw the weariness in David's eyes and leaned over to tousle his hair. "Sleep now, my son, and give the worries of the world to the Lord."

Still David gazed at him, as if trying to read his mind.

"What is it?"

"Oh, nothing." The boy slipped back onto his pillow and turned his face to the wall.

Guessing at the questions nagging David's mind and not knowing how to answer them, Wilhelm patted his son's shoulder and left the room.

He opened the door to his own bedroom and walked in. The room hadn't changed in the past year, except that there was only one pillow on the bed. "I only have one head," he had said to Helen, the housekeeper. He made a habit of sleeping in the center of the big, soft mattress. It kept him from rolling over at night and seeing his Liese lying beside him, her hair released from the braid, fanned out on the pillow in the moonlight.

He sat down heavily on the edge of the bed and covered his face with his hands. How could he even think of Agnetha when he still loved Liese? He would always love Liese. But sometimes he ached for companionship. His heart felt as if it might split in two.

Aron Andres was dead, blown to bits by a land mine that had been freshly planted in the night. Apparently, the Turks had decided it was time for the intruders to leave. The hospital flag did not always make a difference.

The wounded from the temporary medical outpost had already been loaded onto the boats and the tent taken down. The dead *Forstei,* what they could piece together of him, would be buried at sea. They could not take him all the way to his home in Halbstadt. Andres had been a good medic. He was only nineteen, but anxious to do his part in saving lives.

Johann recalled talking with the young man just a few hours before his life had been snuffed out.

"It's a beautiful world, wherever you go, isn't it, Captain?" Aron had said as he carried supplies back to the boat. "Even the war can't take away the wonder of God's creation."

"Well, the war just took one of the best, didn't it, Aron?" Johann hadn't realized he spoke aloud until Eduard Claassen approached him with sorrow on his face. "Come on, Cap. Let's leave this heathen place and go back to Russia. Everyone's pretty edgy." He helped Johann up from the stump where he was sitting and retrieved his makeshift cane.

Andres's tarp-shrouded body lay in state in the bow of the first vessel out to sea. As soon as they were well away from land, Johann and one of the medics said a prayer, thanking the Lord for the man Aron had been, and then they released him to the waves, to be reclaimed by God Almighty, on that day when he would gather his jewels from the ends of the earth and the depths of the seas.

The emotion of the moment was quickly pushed aside by Johann's returning seasickness. It even overcame the pounding of his battered toe. Thank goodness the patients lying in the bottom of the boats were sailors and used to the relentless pitching of the craft in the waves. *Get me home again*, prayed Johann, *and I will never set foot on a boat again.*

Abram's arm was healing nicely. Dr. Bittner had removed the bullet and disinfected the area thoroughly before closing the wound. The way Cornelia hovered around him, he had no choice but to heal. Now, as they bounced their way north to Ruekenau, his arm only hurt a little.

Cornelia had been adamant after the confrontation in the Konrad's garden that the time had come for them to head south. "At least until the worst of the trouble is over." She did not sleep nights, and would not go out alone even in the daytime. She worried about Theodore and the lump on the side of his head, but he seemed to be fine. It was his arthritis, he said, that hurt the most.

As the buggy pulled up to the Ruekenau Home for the Aged, Abram jumped out and reached up his good arm to assist Cornelia. She smiled lovingly at him and climbed down to tie the horse to the hitching post. Together they entered the long white building with its neat little suites and stopped at the one that said "Frau Anna Peters." They knocked and stepped inside.

Mrs. Peters looked up from her knitting. It took only a moment for her to recognize these two who had been so faithful in visiting her over the years. "Welcome, children. Sit here on the sofa."

She wrapped her yarn around the knitting needles and tucked them safely into a basket beside her chair. Her warm green eyes twinkled as she looked from one to the other. She raised a finger to Abram's arm. "Cutting wood for the stove again, I see."

Abram smiled and shook his head at her droll sense of humor. "No, Mrs. Peters, I am better with an ax than that."

They chatted for some time, but Cornelia kept throwing meaningful glances at her husband until Anna finally asked her what was on her mind. "Abram will tell you," she said nervously. Abram cleared his throat and forged ahead. "We are leaving the Molotschna and going down to Succoth for a time—"

"—until the troubles are over," finished Cornelia.

"We do not wish you to remain here alone without any family, so we have come to ask you to join us. The Hildebrandts have welcomed our request and you know there is plenty of room."

"It has been years since you saw the estate, Sister Peters. It is even more beautiful than it was."

Anna Peters rocked in her chair, looking from face to face, and said nothing. Finally she smiled. "These old bones are too fragile to go traipsing about the country, running from the enemy."

"But Mrs. Peters," cut in Cornelia, "life is becoming dangerous here." She grimaced and leaned forward in her chair. "Last week, there were thieves in Neighbor Konrad's backyard, vandalizing the garden. When Mr. Konrad confronted them, they smashed him on the head, nearly killed him. And then they turned on my dear Abram and shot him. Shot him, mind you. A little to the left and he could be dead now." The horror of the possibility set the woman to shaking.

"Theodore is fine and I am alive and well. We must not exaggerate."

"It could have happened," his wife cried defensively. "I do not wish to be a widow." She shut her mouth tightly when she turned back to the Widow Peters.

The old lady listened, frowning at the story. "Ja, ja, this world becomes more evil each day. Now you two wonderful friends are doing your best to protect me from it, and I appreciate it. However," she smoothed the folds in her ever-present apron, "I am not going anywhere with anyone."

Cornelia Reimer gasped in surprise and frustration. Abram winked at her. "I told you she wouldn't budge, Nela."

"But she can't. . . ."

"Don't push, my dear. This is Anna Peters's decision and we will not coerce."

"Thank you, Abram. Now Nela, no amount of convincing will change my mind. What if I were to accept your kind offer, and travel all the way down to Succoth, and then the trouble followed us there? Where would we go after that? Can we keep running from it? Besides," she removed her spectacles and shined them with a corner of the apron, "what would the enemy do with a gnarled old woman like me? I am in God's hands and as such, I will remain here."

Cornelia still pleaded with her eyes, but Abram knew the case was closed. "Very well. We will continue to pray for you and we will give your most heartfelt greetings to Heinrich and the family."

"*Ja*. And don't forget to give my love to Maria. That one needs to know."

Abram and Cornelia shared a look and admired the old saint for her compassion. God would take care of her.

Chapter 10

Katarina sat at her father's massive oak desk in the study, poring over copies of *Volksfreund* and *Der Botshafter*. After scanning the first pages again, she began explaining to herself the latest news from the capital, so that she could better relate it to the children tomorrow in the classroom. "Premier Kerensky—Alexander Kerensky—is head of the Provisional Government, and he is a socialist. But he is not a revolutionary and is anti-Bolshevik. That's Kerensky."

She glanced back at the papers. "Now, Kerensky appointed a tough old Cossack as commander of the Russian army. This Cossack's name is General Lavr Kornilov ... Kornilov. It must be imperative that political leaders have names beginning with 'K.' Perhaps the children and I shall make up a song to teach them who's who. . . ."

"Apparently," Katarina said next day in the classroom, as she sat at the long desk with Nicholai on one side and Anna on the other, "this Kornilov was overzealous in his plans."

"What is overzealous?" Anna looked at her sister blankly.

Nicholai leaned forward to look past Katya. "He tried too hard. Went too far."

"Oh." Anna was trying hard to be interested, but all the war games and espionage were beyond her. She glanced at the wall clock but kept her impatience to herself.

"What exactly did he do?" Kolya wanted the details, as always. Tomorrow he would probably organize a game of the situation with his friends from the workers' homes.

"Well, he hates the Bolsheviks, so he called up a crew of Cossacks from the south to protect the Provisional Government in Petrograd. He said he would hang Lenin and his associates, whom he called German spies, and squash the Soviet." Katya knew she may as well tell it as it was, for Nicholai would figure it out anyway.

"So what happened?"

"It seems Kerensky thought that General Kornilov was out to get him, so he dismissed him. Kornilov refused to be dismissed, so Premier Kerensky called on the Soviet for help, and the Soviet in turn asked the Bolsheviks for assistance."

Anna flipped through the newspaper, but Kolya was all ears. "And of course the Bolsheviks refused?"

"*Au contraire*, my brother. Lenin wired from wherever he is staying, that the Bolsheviks would not fight *for* Kerensky, but they would fight *against* Kornilov. A large group of revolutionaries gathered together, and they managed to talk many of Kornilov's Cossacks into defecting to the Government. They also rioted and tore up train tracks and such. Kerensky arrested Kornilov for his supposed coup, but according to the papers, Kornilov escaped last week."

Nicholai's eyes danced at the excitement of it all. His enthusiasm for all the political turmoil concerned Katarina, but Papa said it was normal for a boy. "All boys long to be soldiers," he said. "He needs to know the facts, but we must also teach him to love his enemies, to do good to those who hate him. That will be the real challenge." Katya needed no convincing of that fact. She thought of her Johann, a soldier of mercy, facing the same hazards as the rest of the army. She felt as if she was still waiting to marry him, except for the passionate dreams that filled her nights. She would not think about that now. Dreams could not be avoided, but wandering thoughts could. Straightening, she marked her teaching journal for next day.

"All Power to the Soviets!" Grisha read the lead on *Pravda's* front page. *"Insurrection Now!"* He shook his head as he scanned the sheets. "Lenin is pushing too hard, too fast, Paul Gregorovich. It may yet explode in his face."

Paul considered the words of his associate and friend. "That may be, but the revolution is rolling in Moscow as well as in other major cities. If we do not take charge now, we may lose out."

"We?" Grisha cocked an eyebrow at Tekanin. "We will do as we must, but we are not willing to put our lives on the line in this power struggle. Wait until there's a better indication of who will come out top, and we may align ourselves more concretely."

Paul ignored his words. "The All-Russian Congress of Soviets plans to meet on November 2. I am anxious to see what Lenin will do."

"He will be here." Grisha looked over his shoulder. "If our boss Karakozov were here, you could ask him. He knows much more than he tells, even in the papers. There is something going on, and we do not know because we still own our souls. I believe there will be Bolshevik activity sooner than November 2."

"Then let the games begin," announced Tekanin vehemently. "Enough idle talk."

Grisha frowned but made no comment as he perused the columns of the newspaper. He folded it and tossed it on the desk. "We are nothing but pawns in a complicated game of chess. The kings and queens, and even the bishops, consult one another, even when they are on opposing sides. But the pawns are disposable. We work here for Stalin or Lenin or whoever calls the shots on this publication now; we witness all the major and minor altercations associated with the revolution, but we know nothing. We are at the mercy of the match."

"Cynicism withers the brain, my friend. We must not stoop to that. After all, what is a game of chess without pawns?"

Abram snapped the reins on the horse's rear end as he and Cornelia rolled past the Lichtfelde townsite on their return from Ruekenau. "I smell smoke," he exclaimed, and they both saw the billowing black cloud as they cleared the stand of trees along the Juschanlee River.

"It's coming from our village!" Cornelia craned her neck to try to pinpoint the source of the fire, but as yet it looked like it could come from any of the buildings in the pretty village of Alexanderkrone.

The horse snorted as Abram shook the reins again. He said nothing, but his face was a study of intensity and hard-won control. He guided the buggy down Main Street, his eyes honing in on his favorite corner of the world.

"Oh my!" Cornelia leaned forward, holding to the buggy for support. "It is our house, Abram, I know it is. Oh Abram!"

"Shush, Nela. I don't know if it is . . . no! The smoke is coming from the Konrads.' Heaven help them."

As the buggy pulled up to the Reimer residence, Abram vaulted out, heedless of his damaged arm, and ran to his elderly neighbors' yard. Cornelia quickly climbed out of the wagon and wrapped the reins around the hitching post. The horses could wait, Theodore and Katie would need her.

Already a bucket brigade worked in the backyard, hauling water from a small well used by several neighbors to water their gardens.

"Where are Theodore and Katie?" Abram would not forget the effort the old man had made to help him when he had been shot by the bandits. "Did they get out?" Even as he spoke, he approached the house to check for himself. As he grabbed the door handle, a loud voice stopped him.

"Neighbor Reimer, we are here. Do not roast yourself for nothing." Abram turned to see the old man and his wife huddled together on the lawn, smoke and soot staining their usually spotless attire. Rivulets of tears coursed down Katie's soot-darkened cheeks. She coughed and choked as she cried, "My home, my beautiful home, it is all gone. They have left me nothing." Her sobs were lost in the shouts of the fire fighters as they sought to contain the blaze.

Abram felt ashamed of his relief that the breeze was coaxing the fire away from his house, but he couldn't help himself. Cornelia stood beside old Katie and put a comforting arm around her shoulders. "How did it start, dear friend?"

Abram walked over to where the threesome spoke together. He saw Katie shake her head vehemently, and Theodore's arm went mechanically around her waist. He stood leaning on the fence, without his cane to help hold him up.

"They did this, Abram," the old man said sadly, his usually loud voice subdued.

"Who would do this? Was it an accident of some kind?"

"No!" The voice reached a higher decibel. "Those bandits did it. The garden robbers. I saw them from the shop window."

Abram looked over his shoulder at the small carpentry shop Theodore Konrad worked in most days. The back window had a clear view of the garden and the back of the house. "How do you know it was the same people? It was very dark the other night."

"I know. I recognized their shapes and the clothing they wore. They were retaliating for that night, for the fact that I protected my property. It is mine, I tell you." His property continued to burn before his hurt and angry eyes.

"I saw them too," interjected Jakob Thielman, who lived across the street. "So did my boy, Willy. Bandits. They ran off through the trees again, and Willy after them, but they had horses tied to the trees by the river."

Abram and Cornelia shared a look and watched the back wall of the Konrad home crumple inward. "Back up, everyone!" Abram moved the group toward his home. "The roof is coming down, back away." As the words left his lips, the timber in the trusses burned through and, with a great crash, fell in on the house. The grounds all around had been soaked. The falling roof effectively put out the fire, with help from neighbors who soaked the interior to make sure no smoldering flames remained to ignite later. They would be watching the site all night with water and dirt in readiness.

Old Katie collapsed in a heap upon the grass as her home of fifty years crumbled before her eyes. Theodore held her hand to comfort her, but the man known all over the village for his loud voice and jovial temperament remained silent, assessing the damage, the worst of which was to his own sense of security.

When he knew Cornelia had Katie well in hand, he rose painfully and shuffled across the grass toward his shop. The little building was charred, but the door still opened. He pushed it and entered his sanctuary alone. Abram found him there later, sitting on a stool, head on his arms on the work table. Around him on the floor sat several new cabinets.

"A new project, Theodore?"

The man did not bother to raise his head. "Cabinets for Katie for Christmas. Storage for the spare room." His voice was muffled. "They were almost finished. I guess we don't need them now."

Abram walked over to his neighbor and placed a hand on his shoulder. "I'm sorry, Brother Konrad. Why would anyone wish to burn down an old man's house?"

Theodore Konrad lifted a dirty, weary face to look at his neighbor. "All my life I have worked to earn a living, and I have done well. Now I amuse myself in this little place and make other people happy with what I make. Why do they attack me? What have I ever done to anyone?"

Abram sighed. "I don't believe it was you personally they were after, aside from the garden episode. I think it was meant to be a warning to us all. Our people are strangers in this land, even after so many generations. We will always be strangers."

"Then where do we belong, Abram?"

"Where have you been?" Grisha assaulted Paul with the words as he came in the door of their flat that warm September evening.

Paul gave his friend a crooked smile of disbelief. "You sound like my mother."

Grisha continued to scowl. "Maybe that is what you need, a nursemaid to keep track of you and keep you from falling into danger every step of the way."

"What is the matter with you?"

"Nothing at all, except that you are getting more and more involved with this Bolshevik movement, and it is not safe. After what happened we agreed to maintain our distance from the extremes."

Paul shook his head in confusion. The whole episode was beyond him. "We have always leaned toward the left, and no, it is not safe. Nothing is safe these days. But I do not remember making any promises to you or to anyone else. We each make our own choices."

"Sergei, you must be careful. . . ."

Grisha stopped in shock, realizing his mistake. Paul glared at him. "I am not Sergei. Your brother is dead, and that of his own doing. You cannot hold yourself responsible. I am Paul Gregorovich Tekanin, and I have my own life to live. As much as I appreciate what you have done for me, I must make my own mistakes."

Grisha stared at him, pain filling his gray eyes. Finally he turned and walked to the small grimy window that looked out on another dirty brick tenement building next door. Paul approached uncertainly. "Grisha, I'm sorry, I—"

Grisha cut him off with a wave of his hand. "No, you are right. Go."

Paul tried once again to speak, but his mentor simply shook his head and motioned him away. In confused frustration, Tekanin turned on his heel and marched out the door and down the rickety stairs to the street. He had a meeting to attend.

"Johann is returning home!" Katarina clutched the telegram with shaking hands, unable to keep the smile from her face. "He should arrive tomorrow. Oh, Agnetha, he is safe." Her smile faded as she remembered Agnetha's Philipp, who had not been so fortunate. "I'm sorry, Agnetha. Forgive me for being so insensitive."

"Now, now, my friend. God called Philipp home. I have come to terms with that. How could I not rejoice with you, married only a few weeks, and your husband returning to you unharmed?"

But it was not totally unharmed that Johann returned. As the buggy came to a standstill on the cobbled yard the next afternoon, Johann allowed Fyodor to help him climb to the ground. Before coming to greet his young bride, Johann reached back into the buggy to retrieve a walnut cane with a curved handle.

"Bought it in Spat on the way home," he said as Katya watched him limp toward her. She could not move. "It has a retractable pick at the bottom for better grip out of doors."

"Johann?" Her voice quavered in shock. "What have they done to you?"

He cleared his throat nervously. "Didn't think your husband would be a cripple this early in your marriage, did you?" It was a silly thing to say, and he knew it as soon as the words left his mouth.

The repressed anguish in his words finally shocked life into Katarina. With a cry, she fell against him, almost knocking him over, sobs pouring out of her. Fyodor stood behind Johann with a hand at his back to balance him. Johann let Katya cry until she was spent, then led her up the step, slowly and laboriously, nodding at Agnetha and smiling at a wide-eyed Anna and Nicholai.

Agnetha carried Philipp on one hip and reached out to Anna with her other arm. "Come, child. We will talk about it, and it will be fine. You'll see." Anna looked from Agnetha to Nicholai, and then back to Agnetha. With a loud snuffle, she buried her face in Agnetha's apron and allowed the woman to stroke her hair.

Nicholai was wide-eyed, not from sorrow but from wonder. He could hardly keep his excitement in check as the family gathered in the parlor. Maria sat quietly on a chair in the corner, observing the others. She allowed nothing to touch her too deeply. She had learned to put on a brave face and to harden her heart to accusing looks and judgmental words. With practice, she believed she could close off her heart to the pain.

Johann had lost himself in Katya's green, loving eyes. Coming back to reality he tried to reassure her. "It's only my big toe," he said. "In time I shall be able to walk without a cane."

"What happened, Johann?" Katya had calmed enough to think and wonder.

"Got in the way of a Turkish bullet."

"You got shot by the Turks?" Nicholai was on his knees in front of the couple, all eyes and ears. "Did you get 'em back?"

"No Kolya. The *Forstei* does not fight, it heals." Shaking his head, he continued. "I'm not sure why they fired on a medical outpost, whatever the nationality. The hospital flags were flying all that day."

"Did it hurt?" Nicholai had to know.

Johann grinned. "Of course it hurt. They plugged me good, do you want to see it?"

"Yes!"

"Nicholai!" scolded Katya.

"But he offered, Katie. He said I could see it."

She looked at her husband and shrugged her shoulders. Anna cowered behind Agnetha's skirts, peeking out from time to time, although she did not come near enough to see the actual wound. "Ooh, that's a good one all right," pronounced Nicholai. "Did you see it, Mrs. Wieler?"

"Yes, I saw as much as I wished to." She smiled and bounced little Philipp on her knees. "I would say Johann is a very brave man."

"Will they make you an honorary commander of the *Forstei* now, Mr. Sudermann?"

"Johann. I am your brother now, remember?" He paused before he answered Kolya's question. Looking around at the adults in the room and settling on Katya, he said, "I will no longer be serving in the *Forstei,* nor will anyone else. The entire operation has been shut down due to political instability."

"Shut down!" Katarina and Nicholai spoke the words at the same time. Katya could not keep the joy from her voice as she realized that her Johann would not be called back to the service. Although the reason for shutting down the institution which had operated since 1874 was not an encourag-

ing one, she took comfort that she had her husband back, mostly in one piece.

Kolya's tone of voice bespoke disappointment. "But what will I do when I am eighteen? How will I serve my country? How will I fight against the evil?"

Ah, the naïveté of young men, thought Johann. How many of them had joined the service with such high ideals and left with deep wounds that were not always physical? And how many of Russia's sons had died a soldier's death in the great war, entering the fray with glory-tinted glasses which every day showed a more distorted image of their dream?

Paul Gregorovich Tekanin crossed Isaac's Bridge and turned onto Maly Prospekt, making his secretive way to a flat on Vassily Island, in the growing slum area of Petrograd. His recent argument with Grisha preyed on his mind. Still shaking his head in perplexity, he crept quietly along an alley and across a yard in the shelter of a rickety fence. In spite of Grisha's friendship, Paul was not about to throw away this opportunity to be involved in the upcoming coup. Lenin knew what was best for Russia, and he had a plan.

The small, rundown flat was packed with Bolshevik supporters. Paul squeezed into the room and found a reasonably comfortable spot beside a window near the kitchen area. As he looked around at the gathering, mostly men and a few women, he wondered what their next move would be. The date for the Congress of Soviets was fast approaching. A month ago Premier Kerensky had held a democratic convention to strengthen his moderate socialist stand. The Bolsheviks had been represented by Leon Trotsky who had made his point by marching out of the meeting.

Paul saw Grisha enter quietly and take a place in the back

of the main room. His countenance was troubled. As Paul pondered, the meeting was called to order by none other than his old acquaintance, Lev Kamenev. Apparently, he had been released along with Trotsky, because there he stood, formidable as ever. "We have witnessed Kerensky's attempt to avoid violence," he said coldly, "but as we all know, there is no other way to achieve our goals."

He stepped to a closed door and knocked. The door opened to reveal Vladimir Lenin himself, come out of hiding for this meeting. The intense man frowned in concentration as he spoke to his supporters. "We must act now, while revolutionary fervor is still high. We cannot wait for the Soviet or that pitiable Provisional Government to implement their weak attempts to change society. Ours is the only way. Insurrection now!"

The chant picked up, but Kamenev subdued it. They did not wish police intervention this evening. This time they did not want to create a disturbance. Paul and several others argued for a more evolutionary introduction of Marxist principles, but Lenin insisted on violence. Mikhail Pavlovich Karakozov loudly voiced his support for Lenin's strategy, glaring at Grisha when he offered an alternative. Paul saw Grisha ease his way out of the crowd and into the street.

"It will only take two or maybe three days and we will have control," declared Lenin. He continued his impassioned speech, adamant that the coup must take place before the Congress of Soviets. After the meeting, which ended with a 10 to 2 vote in favor of an armed uprising at the end of October, Lenin slipped away again, and Leon Trotsky and his protégé Kamenev set about preparing for the event.

Chapter 11

Maria found Katya in the library with their father. "I've had the servants prepare a room for Mr. and Mrs. Reimer as well as one for Oma, should she decide to come," she said to them.

"Thank you, Mika, but I would be surprised if Mother came with them." Heinrich had to smile as he thought about his two dear friends trying to persuade the old woman to leave her retirement home. "She may have come if it had been entirely her idea, but she will never be cajoled into anything. When her time comes, I imagine the angels will allow her to wade across the Jordan by herself rather than offering to carry her."

Both girls broke into fits of laughter at the picture their father had painted of their maternal grandmother. Although they loved her dearly and knew beyond a doubt that she loved them, they also knew her to be strongly opinionated and stubborn to the core.

"Mika, relax," suggested Heinrich. "The Reimers love you and will not hold a grudge."

"I didn't know my restlessness showed." She glanced at her father and faltered again at the love in his eyes. How was she to harden her heart to that? Or to a sister who insisted on including her in everything that went on in the household, as if she had never gone off and shamed them all.

"You know what you've done and so do we," Katya had told her once. "You know that we love you and pray daily for you." Mika had left the room before the pain of love worked through the layers of defense she was building up.

As Heinrich had predicted, Oma Peters did not come to Succoth with Abram and Cornelia Reimer, but neither did they come alone. With some apprehension, Abram turned back to the enclosed buggy after helping Cornelia out, and reached his hands up to another woman whose husband followed her out onto the cobbles. It was with difficulty that the old gentleman climbed from the vehicle.

Heinrich stepped forward with a hug for Cornelia and a strong embrace for his friend, Abram. A sincere welcoming smile lit his strongly handsome face as he greeted the newcomers. Abram cleared his throat. "Heinrich," he said, "your mother-in-law refused to join us, but I have brought our neighbors, Theodore and Katie Konrad. Their home was burned to the ground by vandals last week. I took the great liberty of inviting them to Succoth."

"We apologize for the surprise," said Theodore, taking Heinrich's proffered hand and shaking it heartily. "Abram and Cornelia offered us their home if we wished to stay in Alexanderkrone, but we have received two separate attacks of late, and my wife was afraid to stay."

"I heard what you said, Theodore," interjected his wife, loudly enough that she could hear herself. "It was not my decision alone to abandon our village. But as I do not wish to offend your manhood, I will accept the blame." She twitched her nose at her husband of fifty years and took Cornelia's arm to ascend the steps of the verandah. "Men!" she exclaimed, to the chuckles of everyone but her annoyed husband.

Heinrich gestured wide his arms. "You are all welcome, my friends. We have room for everyone."

The halls and rooms of Succoth resounded with life and laughter as two new families joined the group. Katarina caught her father's private look: *We will share what God has given us with those in need.* Each knew what the other was thinking. No words were necessary.

The plans made by Trotsky and Kamenev, in consultation with Lenin, of course, were carried out in a matter of days, but the Congress of Soviets came and went before any violence erupted. The Bolsheviks received a majority vote both in the capital and in Moscow. A meeting of the Petrograd garrison decided, on October 3, to recognize the Soviet as the supreme power in Russia. It was a shock to the Provisional Government, one for which they were not prepared.

Bolshevik meetings were being held everywhere, secrecy no longer a concern. *Pravda* recorded Lenin's dictum, "*Tipyer ili nikagda!*"—"Now or never!" The radical leader emerged from self-imposed exile to take up residence in the Smolny Institute, a former finishing school for daughters of the nobility. From his simple room there Lenin took over the administration of the Second Congress of Soviets. The train of change was on its downhill run, scattering every effort to stop it.

"He's too idealistic," declared a worried Grisha. "He will destroy everything the Bolshevik movement has built up."

Tekanin narrowed his eyes as he listened to his friend expound his opinion. "Why are you so worried? You are not committed to the cause anyway." His voice was low but clear.

Grisha, eyes wide, glanced to the corner where Mikhail Pavlovich worked in his usual frenzy. Karakozov was a dedicated Leninist.

"Don't fret, I won't turn you in," assured Paul. "But you are becoming more obvious by the day, and it may be wise for you to at least pretend you are on our side."

Still Grisha said nothing. He pulled at the collar of his

sweater as if it were choking him and turned back to his editing. Paul leaned close to Grisha, his hands grasping the sides of the battered desk, and met his eyes. "Get on board, my friend, or the train of change will run you over. There's no stopping the revolution now."

"We must transfer the capital to Moscow." The desperation in Kerensky's voice reflected in his eyes. "The Germans and Austrians are gaining ground, even threatening some of the accesses to Petrograd. And we must preserve our government against the revolutionaries at all costs."

"Do we possess the resources to do that?" His personal secretary, Antonin Pugachev, was not being perverse but pragmatic. "You are aware, I presume, of the problems in this country. Burning and looting of wealthy homes is a daily occurrence, as is the slaughter of the inhabitants. Everything remotely resembling order is being destroyed, including forests and livestock. Deserting soldiers are pillaging as they retreat. We cannot ignore these problems and hope to maintain our power."

Kerensky glared at his aide, then sat stiffly in his leather chair behind the massive oak desk at which Tsar Nicholas had also made many decisions.

Pugachev continued. "With the affirmation of the Soviet, Trotsky has put together a military Revolutionary Committee. To protect the capital, he says."

"We must not give in to their demands." Kerensky sat drumming his fingers on the desk. Suddenly, he shot up from his chair and began to pace the floor. "We will present an ultimatum." He spoke almost to himself, pounding one fist into the palm of his other hand. Antonin Pugachev grabbed a pencil from his breast pocket and licked the end of it as he fumbled for a pad of paper, at the same time watching Kerensky over his half-glasses. "We will demand that the

Soviet withdraw their resolution of allegiance to the Revolutionary Committee. Get that out immediately!"

Katarina had suggested that it was time for an outing, and although Johann had at first been reluctant, her enthusiasm was contagious. Now, as their *droshka* bounced over the road to Spat, he was glad for the change. Autumn smiled down on them from a blue sky bronzed by the distancing sun, while the trees cast golden leaves on the roadsides.

"I love autumn," said Katya. "It's so encouraging."

Johann raised an eyebrow at his wife. "Encouraging?"

She smiled. "Yes. Even though the leaves and flowers are dying, they will come again. The heat of summer has receded to a comfortable temperature, and although the winter cold will come, the warmth will always return in the spring. To me it displays a strength of character that is not afraid of the harshness of winter."

"Ah, my dear wife, you are so poetic."

Katya smiled again and squeezed his hand. "I think that Anna and Kolya will enjoy this day, as will Papa. Too bad Mika didn't come."

"Did you really expect her to? She has become more and more reclusive lately."

Katya sighed. "I think she is afraid, of the future and of the past, so she tries to live in denial of it all."

"There you go again, analyzing everyone."

"While I'm at it," she said, a mischievous look flashing in her eyes, "I believe there is a young man in our entourage who is madly in love with his wife, because he knows he cannot live without her. He realizes his dependence on her and so treats her like a queen. This, in my opinion, will never change."

Johann laughed and pulled her close. "As much as I hate to admit the dependence part of your analysis, I must admit that the rest is true. I hope I will be able to satisfy your dreams for our future. I love you, Katya."

"I love you too."

Laughter from the carriage behind them brought Katarina around in her seat. Turning back to Johann, she said, "Apparently Papa and Mr. Konrad are getting along very well."

"Would you expect less from your father? He is a lover of humanity, and especially of those with deep convictions and a sense of humor. He is in his element with Konrad."

They were approaching the bridge crossing the Salgir River into the village of Spat. A great number of people of all description milled about on the streets and in the market area. Instead of crossing the bridge to the windmill and picnic grounds, Johann urged the horse forward. They passed the busy train station and turned west on Center Street, crossing the water past the post office and Langemann's Factory. Johann turned the buggy onto Main Street, which ran by the school and the Mennonite church.

As they neared the windmill, they saw another school and the Mennonite Brethren church.

"What a beautiful setting," declared Katarina. "I have always loved coming here for picnics, especially when we were young and Mama was with us." She paused and pushed a stray curl behind her ear. "Life was so carefree then." She shook off the melancholy mood with effort. "Today we will enjoy what God has given us."

Johann planted a kiss on her forehead as he helped her down from the buggy. "You are an amazing woman, Katarina. A pillar of strength."

Splotches of red crept up Katya's cheeks at the compliment. "It's Papa who holds us all up," she replied.

"You have no idea of your strength or your beauty, my love." He whispered this in her ear and left to unhitch the horse.

The day passed quickly as the group gobbled up the *rollkuchen* and watermelon Cook had packed up for them. Those young or young-at-heart played ball until they were pleasantly exhausted and ready for the *faspa* packed in another huge lunch box.

"Cook has outdone herself again," declared Heinrich, dipping a ladle into the cool fruit soup and helping himself to two thick slices of cold ham. "I am sure she has packed some spicy mustard for this ham too." He slathered this condiment onto his meat and munched happily, even though the mustard threatened to choke him a time or two.

"I offered to help prepare the food this morning," said Cornelia, "but Cook would have none of it. I am becoming lazy."

"We are enjoying it almost too much," added Katie Konrad. After a comfortable silence she continued. "I feel safe here. I miss my home, but it was frightening there of late." She turned to Heinrich. "Thank you again for giving us this time of peace. We don't know how long it will be before we can return home, but this is a time we will never forget."

"Just think, my dear," interrupted her husband. "You almost didn't come today. What you would have missed."

"*Ja, ja,* you were complaining about your arthritis too, but now I had to hold you back or you would have tried to play ball with the young people."

"Who is that coming up the path to the picnic grounds?" The group all followed Agnetha's eyes to the road from the town. "Looks like a band of marching soldiers."

Johann focused on the approaching party, tension building in his expression. Sailors. Attempting nonchalance, he suggested they pack up and head for home while the sun still shone warm on them. Katarina sensed more than saw his tension, and immediately began replacing the dishes and bowls into the food box. The repacking was complete when the troop reached the spot where the family and friends stood, preparing to climb into the wagons for the ride home.

"Hold on there!" One of the sailors approached Heinrich. "Where are you going so quickly? I believe you have some things we would like."

Heinrich frowned as he faced the man. "We are returning home after our picnic. What are you needing, then?"

"Ha, ha. We want food and drink, and maybe women as well. You have some of each I see."

Abram motioned Cornelia and Katie around the other side of the wagons. Katarina stood rooted to the spot beside Johann, while Agnetha pushed Anna behind her and stood straight and still near the second wagon, Baby Philipp held tightly to her chest. Nicholai stood poised for action next to her.

Johann reached into the box and lifted out the leftover food. "There's no alcohol, but you should find a bit of food left over."

One of the sailors approached Katya and looked her over. Johann stepped between them, a fearlessness overtaking his gentle features. Without taking his eyes off the sailor, he quietly told Katarina and the other women to climb into the carriage.

"Hey, I want that one," announced the man. "She will do for me."

"Let it be, sailor," countered Johann. "I will give you whatever material possessions you wish, but you will stay away from the women and the old folks."

"Are you saying I can't have what I want?"

"If you want what you cannot have."

The sailor gave Johann a shove and attempted to move toward the buggy where Katya, Agnetha, and Anna now sat in fearful silence, but Johann restrained him. "I will not fight with you, but neither will I allow you to bother my wife and family. Please be on your way."

Rebuffed, the man's annoyance built into anger, and he motioned for his comrades to join him. "Come. We will take what we want."

As they neared the wagons, one of their company called a halt. A young sailor stood before Johann and studied his face. "You are *Forstei*," he announced. "You removed a bullet from my arm and patched me up so I could rejoin my fleet." Johann recognized the man as one of the Black Sea Fleet to whom he had given medical aid on the Turkish coast. The man turned to his small band of navy men. "We will accept the food they have offered us, but no one will lay a hand on any of them. Is that clear?"

With muttered curses, the troublemakers backed off, grabbing for their share of the goods. "Sorry to bother you," apologized Johann's former patient. "If I had not recognized you, it would not have been a pleasant day for any of you. Get out of here while you can and stay away from the rail lines." With that warning, he moved the men toward the river, where they settled down to eat what they had stolen. Johann, Heinrich, and Abram wasted no time loading everyone onto the wagons and turning them in the direction of home.

"How much worse will it get?" Heinrich asked the unanswerable question of Johann as they checked the harnesses. "Where can we keep our people safe anymore?"

Pugachev again faced Kerensky across the oak desk. His hand shook as he straightened his tie.

"What is it?" Kerensky rose slowly at the look in Pugachev's eye. His chair scraped the hardwood floor.

Antonin Pugachev lifted his chin to summon his courage. "The Soviet does not acknowledge our ultimatum, sir. It's as if we did not exist."

Kerensky pounded the desk with his fist and turned to the window behind him. For several minutes he stood silent, leaving his aide to guess what thoughts ran through his mind. Finally he turned, eyes wide, face strained with tension and anger. "Raise the bridges! Cut off communications! Let the Bolsheviks deal with that. They will not succeed."

To raise the bridges of this city built on the Neva River delta entailed a good deal of cooperation. Pugachev hoped, as he left the spacious office, that he could demand as much authority as his superior expected of him.

Susannah Warkentin sat at the board table at Bethany Psychiatric Home and tried to concentrate on the meeting, but her gaze kept drifting to the windows. Just outside, her favorite oak tree stood straight and tall and white against the still-green grass and winter blue sky. A few brittle brown leaves still clung to their respective branches, shivering in the breeze. Throughout the seasons, Susannah took inspiration from that tree, so stately in the winter, exuberant in spring as it pushed out bright green buds, and ever elegant in summer, adorned by myriad finely shaped leaves.

Now as she stared at the tree through the clean glass of the administration room windows, it seemed suddenly vulnerable. Random vandalism and the burning of the homes of the wealthy was a major concern here as it was in the Molotschna Colony. Several individuals from one of the northern villages of the Chortitza Colony had lost their lives resisting the violence, and the sporadic attacks frightened her beyond words.

"Susannah?"

Jerked back to reality by Gerhard's voice, Susannah felt the color creep into her plump cheeks. She felt the eyes of the administrators and nurses on her as she tried unsuccessfully to recall what was being discussed. Gerhard formed a quick smile and tried to make light of the situation. He knew where his wife's mind had been—they had discussed the situation again last night. But there were important issues to be decided here, and he must see that the discussion kept moving.

"I'm sorry. My mind was wandering. Could you please repeat your question?"

"Of course, Susannah. The resignation of two of our nurses leaves vacancies that will need to be filled. We were discussing the option of rearranging our schedules to cover the openings rather than hiring new personnel. We need your opinion."

"Are the nurses leaving immediately?" asked one of the other health care workers.

Gerhard sighed. "They have already left. Gone south," here he couldn't help glancing at Susannah, "to escape the growing unrest in the area." He dragged his eyes back to the questioner. "Perhaps I should ask if any more of you plan to leave in the near future."

Some of the people at the table looked down at their papers or fiddled with their pencils. After a brief silence, Gerhard returned to his original question. "Susannah, what is your feeling on the course of action. Any rescheduling will directly affect you and the other nurses."

Susannah raised her head bravely and locked eyes with her husband. How dear he was to her, he would never know, although she tried to find ways to tell him every day. What if something should happen to him? How would she exist without his strength and solid faith to encourage her? *You will follow God's leading as you have since you came to know him,* said a voice inside of her. *He will never leave you or forsake you.*

"I think we should reorganize. I would be willing to work longer shifts as needed. The residents here are like family to me, and I will do whatever it takes to make sure they are well cared for."

"Well said," said the head nurse with a kind smile. "I agree, and will cast my lot with yours."

More nurses joined their voices in affirmation of Susannah's sentiments, and Gerhard was encouraged. He accepted the challenge of leadership without flinching, but the threat of danger hovered on the edges of his mind constantly. Whatever happened, he would take the acclaim or the blame for the decisions made in this room. He prayed that God would grant him the wisdom to do the best thing.

Chapter 12

 "They won't do it," insisted Paul Gregorovich. "City officials won't pull up all the bridges. Kerensky had better concede defeat before he backs himself into a real corner."

Grisha and Dmitri Soloviev nodded as they quaffed mugs of foamy beer at one of the tiny tables in a dim corner of Piotr's Pub on Maly Prospekt. The chill of winter had already reached Petrograd and the men were warmly dressed. "So what will it take to complete the coup?" Soloviev sipped, his eyes on Tekanin.

Paul set down his mug and wiped his mouth with the back of his hand. Dark curls danced from under the cap he always wore, softening the hardness in his black eyes. "Not much, I'm thinking, besides the Fortress." He shook his head. "That's one obstacle that could prove a problem. We could lose a lot of men trying to stand against its arsenal."

The three revolutionaries found out the next day how Trotsky decided to face that particular barrier. Instead of taking up arms against the formidable St. Peter and Paul Fortress, the bespectacled Jew simply walked over to the great stone bastion and convinced the defending soldiers to surrender. Not a shot was fired, not a soul harmed. As a bonus, a large number of Fortress guns were given into the hands of the Bolshevik Red Guards. It seemed the capital was changing color before their eyes.

"We've seized telephone headquarters," announced an

excited Tekanin as he rushed into the newspaper office later that day. "Government offices are being taken over as we speak and Kerensky has left the city."

Grisha and Karakozov turned to him. The latter asked, "How in the world did he get past the Bolshevik checkpoints? Everyone knows what he looks like."

"Took an American Embassy car, flag waving in the wind like a democratic banner."

"Ha!" Grisha chuckled in spite of himself. "Sly as a fox," he said. "But he is running scared. He's desperate to find support, and the only place he can hope to do so is at the war front."

"You think he's gone to the front, then?"

"Where else? Switzerland?" Grisha laughed again. "His time's running out. Soon the entire city will be in Bolshevik hands." The knot in his stomach refused to go away, no matter how hard he tried to convince himself that he had come to terms with his revolutionary involvement. It was do or die for him, so there was no decision to make. So he told himself several times each day.

The American embassy car commandeered by Alexander Kerensky jolted to a stop near one of the Russian entrenchments. Waiting a moment or two for the dust to settle, Kerensky and his aide Pugachev stepped out of the vehicle and walked toward a tent in the thinning shade of a few poplar trees. The November sun shone half-strength on the camp and a crisp breeze scattered dry yellow leaves over the dusty ground.

Kerensky pulled back the tent flap and peered inside. The subdued light of a small lantern cast eerie shadows on the flimsy walls of the temporary shelter. A tall, thin man sat on a folding chair behind a collapsible table, pen in hand. He glanced up, annoyed at the intrusion.

"What do you—" Recognizing the face, he jumped to his feet, almost upsetting the writing table. "Mr. Premier, forgive me. I did not expect you. Come in, please."

Pugachev held the tent flap open to allow Kerensky to enter, then stooped to follow him inside. The premier and the general shook hands and stood staring at each other. Kerensky cleared his throat and spoke.

"General Krasnov, my aide and I have come from Petrograd to seek support for the government. As you are probably aware, the Bolshevik faction in the capital as well as in Moscow is trying to take over. I will not waste words. We are nearing the end of our resources. We need your help if we are to resist their advances and stand against them."

Krasnov, beady eyes staring into Kerensky's, stood perfectly still as he mulled over the premier's words. With a grimace, he looked away, then back again. "With all due respect, sir, I have my hands full here resisting the advances of the German army. As you are well aware, we are fast losing ground against them. You are asking me to desert my post at a most difficult time. Have you discussed this with any of the other generals?"

"We have spoken with several, all of whom are of the same mind as yourself." Kerensky raised his chin, his thin cheeks hollow as he attempted to retain his self-control. "I must remind you, however, that without our government, you will be finished here anyway. I am asking you to accompany me back to Petrograd with enough men to make a difference. Your Cossacks are always up to a challenge, are they not?"

"My Cossacks are indeed a mighty force and will do whatever I command them to do." The General lowered his head and pulled at his scraggly white beard. His hands were tough and calloused, his face bore the signs of tension and heavy responsibility. "What you say is correct. I have heard that the Bolsheviks, should they seize power, would call an end to the war." He sighed heavily. "Either way, I am finished here." He looked up and regarded Kerensky for a long moment. "Very well, Mr. Premier," he said. "I will lead my men back to the capital to protect the Provisional Government. May God help us."

Kerensky, visibly relieved, reached out and shook the hand Krasnov offered. Pugachev shook it as well, thankful that this unpleasant begging had achieved its desired end.

"They will save us, you know," Kerensky seemed to be reassuring himself more than Pugachev as they bumped over the rough terrain of western Russia, enroute back to Petrograd. "No one can stand against the Cossacks."

"They are a hard and cruel lot, are they not? I would not wish to be within reach of one of their sabers."

"Then you must not get too near, Antonin Fyodorovich. We will need to remain alert if we wish to keep our heads." Kerensky stared out of the car window at the dry, dying landscape. He could not let his desperation get out of hand. He was the only one who could ward off the Bolsheviks and their insane agenda. "God help us, indeed," he muttered under his breath.

Kerensky worked like a man possessed as he attempted to regain control of power. "Pugachev," he ordered early on the morning of November 7, from his office in the Winter Palace. "Have the military cadets shut down the Bolshevik newspapers. Now! Make certain that *Pravda* is silenced. I have ordered the arrest of the Military Revolutionary Committee and arranged an emergency meeting with the Preparliament immediately."

"But the Winter Palace is effectively surrounded, sir."

"I realize that!" Kerensky shouted. "Do what I have asked you to do."

Antonin Pugachev hurried off to do Kerensky's bidding as the Premier made his way to the front of one of the ballrooms of the palace. Members of the Preparliament sat waiting anxiously as Kerensky took his place at the podium. He wasted no time with preliminaries. In a voice edged with iron he addressed the assembled group.

"Each day we are faced with new and more threatening developments at the hands of the Bolsheviks. We must stand together to stop the insurrection which surges through the streets of our capital. We must not allow Lenin and Trotsky and the other revolutionaries to have their way in our country."

"We agree with you there," said one of the members, "but we must also communicate to the people that we hear their cry for peace and for land. We must acknowledge their plight if we wish to stay in power."

"Yes!" Another member jumped to his feet in agreement. "Cover the city with posters announcing our intention to meet their demands. It's the only way to win back their loyalty."

Kerensky's face became livid with anger. "We will not acquiesce to public outcry. I will not allow such a step to be taken. We will make our own decisions on how to run this country, and giving in is not one of them."

The first man, a moderate socialist who had always seen Alexander Kerensky as a reasonable man, rose again to his feet. "Mr. Premier, I beg of you to consider our suggestions. The will of the people will make or break us this time. They will not stand to be overlooked again. The Bolsheviks are promising to meet their needs, and we should match—"

"We will not be coerced by these radicals." Kerensky repeated the directives he had given Pugachev before the meeting. "By cutting off communications and arresting those in charge we will effectively end this insanity. The cruiser Aurora and her pro-Bolshevik crew has been ordered off on a training cruise, so we need not fear trouble from that direction. And as we speak, a troop of loyal Cossacks under the able leadership of General Krasnov is approaching the city to defend the government."

A wiry little man standing at the doorway spoke up loudly.

"Begging your pardon, Premier Kerensky, you are wrong about the Aurora. She pulled back into harbor an hour ago."

Kerensky stood silent, his face the color of chalk dust. He opened his mouth to speak but no words came. At that moment, a thunderous crash like a cannon resounded throughout the palace. Pugachev, who had been seated at Kerensky's right hand, grabbed the premier by the elbow and ushered him through a door behind the podium. Pandemonium broke loose in the ballroom as the members of the Preparliament fled the room.

The Cossacks had assembled outside of the city and rode in like the yellow horde of Genghis Khan, roaring and flashing their sabers like wild beasts snapping their jaws at their unsuspecting prey. Amid the angry cries and curses of the crowds, the mounted soldiers approached the city center, but their fearlessness was no match for the numbers against them.

Although the deafening crash at the Winter Palace was actually only a blank shot fired from the Aurora, it was enough to disperse any remaining government loyalists in the vicinity. Sailors from the Baltic Fleet swarmed the city center, a determined as the Cossacks. The only army personnel still loyal to the Provisional Government was a women's battalion, which tried to break out of the palace at about ten o'clock. The women were immediately seized.

Members of Trotsky's Red Guard stormed the palace and arrested all remaining Provisional Government officials. Kerensky managed to escape, but the brave General Krasnov surrendered. There was nothing more he could do. He was finished. Besides some scattered rifle and machine gun fire, there was little more resistance to the Bolshevik forces and their growing Red Guard.

Paul Gregorovich had made his decision. With the closing down of *Pravda*—again—he left the ranks of the journalists and joined up with the Red Guard. "It's time for action, Grisha," he said as he informed his friend and mentor of his plan. "Join me if you will, but I will not be kept from this, whatever your decision." His pack lay ready on the chair by the door, easily holding all his possessions.

Grisha passed a weary hand over his eyes and nodded his head. He no longer knew where to turn. Life had become a constant struggle from which there was no escape, and the determination of Tekanin to be in the thick of the fray robbed all his remaining strength. The world at large seemed to swirl around them like a tornado, and they were caught revolving round and round, coming no closer to resolution, only dizzier from hanging on to the wind. He raised his hand and replied, but did not meet Paul's blazing eyes. "Go and do what you must. As for me, I . . . I do not know what. . . ." His voice trailed off and bleakness filled his eyes as he finally lifted them to Paul's.

Paul's heart lurched at the pain in Grisha's face, but he pressed down his feelings and stepped back. "Farewell then," he said in a more subdued tone. "Take care of yourself." Not wanting to risk the rising tide of his emotions, he shouldered his pack, turned and walked out of the door without a backward glance.

Grisha stared at the open door, wanting to follow, but knowing that he did not possess the hardness required to be a soldier of the Red Guard. He wasn't sure Paul did either, but he was determined to go his own way. "Just like Sergei," he mumbled as he quietly closed the door and sank into a chair by the cold fireplace. Sergei had not listened to reason either and now lay cold and dead beneath the soggy soil of one of Petrograd's cemeteries. "Just like Sergei."

"There's been another revolution in Petrograd," said Heinrich to Wilhelm Enns as they sat in the cozy library of Succoth manor. "This one has proven more decisive than the February uprising. The Provisional Government and any immediate hope of a parliament and a constitution have been wiped out.

"The Bolshevik party allowed the November elections and came out with only twenty-five percent of the vote, but the Red Guard forced the Constituent Assembly out of the Tauride Palace anyway. In the morning when they returned, the doors were locked and guarded, and they were forced to disband. We are now under total Bolshevik rule."

Enns, who had become a frequent visitor at the Hildebrandt home, picked up the newspaper which lay on the desk. "I see Moscow has also fallen to the Bolsheviks. A bit more bloody than Petrograd." He looked up at his host. Concern had etched more lines on Heinrich's broad and once lively face. The piercing gray eyes had taken on a troubled tinge, one Hildebrandt could not hide in spite of his efforts to do so. Wilhelm took warning from those eyes. Sometimes he tried to ignore the growing unrest on the mainland, but the disturbances were becoming more frequent and more disastrous.

Abram Reimer, sitting in one of the comfortable chairs, rubbed his fingers on the wood of the armrest. Reimer was never one to speak without thinking, and the others waited as he formulated his thoughts. He raised his eyes to find them staring at him. He grimaced. "Sometimes I wonder if I have done the right thing, leaving my home. I tell myself it is for the mental well-being of my wife, but perhaps the truth is that I am as afraid as she is."

"There is greater danger in not fearing," assured Theodore Konrad, massaging one aching hand with the other.

"Thank you, Theodore. But what do we do if . . . when the

danger approaches us here? Where do we go then? Your mother-in-law was right, Heinrich. Once we start running, where will we stop?"

Wilhelm Enns cleared his throat. "There has been talk of relocating. Of emigrating, actually." He inspected his fingernails as he spoke, then looked up at the other men in the library. "I see no shame in having an alternate plan—I have three children to think of and a. . . ." He stopped himself and hoped the others would not catch his train of thought.

Heinrich stood and began to pace. "How can you speak of leaving? How can we leave all that we have built up over the years? No, I have more faith in human nature than that. The Russian people are going through a maturing process and will come to their senses eventually. This is our home, gentlemen."

"And if we lose our lives and the lives of our loved ones, will that do Russia any good?" Wilhelm stood as well and faced Heinrich. "As much as I respect you, Hildebrandt, I cannot conjure up the faith in humankind that you have. I believe conditions will deteriorate further still." He squared his shoulders and looked at each man in the room. "I am investigating possible ways of leaving the country. I do not intend to lose my life and that of my family for a piece of land."

As the men walked to the dining room for supper, Heinrich spoke quietly to Wilhelm. "Have you discussed with Agnetha your idea of leaving the country?" For some reason, he felt he needed to protect the woman who had come to them last year. Not that she was frail or helpless. He knew the reason even as he commanded his heart to stay calm. He had begun to love the brave young widow, realizing it only when Wilhelm discovered the same. Let the younger man claim the prize, but he would look out for her in the meantime.

Wilhelm regarded him with suspicious eyes, trying to figure out why his neighbor was so concerned for Agnetha's feelings.

"We haven't spoken of it yet. We are not in a position to pursue this course of action together."

"Then perhaps it is time to join forces. What are you waiting for?"

Heinrich's whispered vehemence surprised Wilhelm, but it also gave him food for thought. He had hoped to have some time alone with Agnetha this evening. Perhaps the time had come to broach the subject of marriage. His stomach twisted as he considered the risks. If he didn't ask, she couldn't refuse. Once he gave voice to his feelings, he placed himself in a most vulnerable position. He felt like a schoolboy again, wearing his heart on his sleeve.

After the meal, Fyodor slipped in and quietly handed Heinrich a newspaper. "I thought you would want to know what has happened, sir," he whispered in his employer's ear.

Heinrich caught his eye with a sense of anxiety. "Thank you, Fyodor." Pushing back his chair, he shook out the paper, which still smelled of ink, and perused the front page. His eyes widened at the headlines. "Gentlemen and ladies," he announced, "our war with Germany is over."

A series of exclamations and thanksgiving erupted around the cherry wood table. Eleven expectant faces turned to Heinrich for details. "Vladimir Lenin, new self-proclaimed leader of Russia, has called a halt to the war between Russia and Germany. The armistice begins immediately, with peace settlements to follow." Heinrich looked around at the surprised faces. "The Lord has answered our prayers. The war is over for Russia. Let us give thanks to God!"

Wilhelm was not certain what Heinrich had said to the members of his household, but after a superb supper, garnished with the news of the armistice, everyone dispersed in various directions, leaving Wilhelm and Agnetha alone in the parlor.

"Did you not wish to join the other men in the study?" asked Agnetha with a knowing sparkle in her eyes.

Wilhelm stared at her incredulously. She seemed to read his mind, yet she was not making his mission any easier. He was so nervous, in fact, that he pulled a button off his waistcoat as he sat fiddling with it. Agnetha politely hid her smile behind her handkerchief. She sat poised as a queen and refused to initiate conversation. *What is it about women,* Wilhelm wondered, *that makes them act coy in such situations?*

He cleared his throat for the third time. "Agnetha." He paused, unable to form any words, which was not unusual for him, especially in his present situation. She inclined her head toward him, a serene smile on her face. "I have enjoyed getting to know you," he said.

"Thank you, Wilhelm."

Somehow, the way she said his name, softly and confidently, gave him courage to continue. "Agnetha, I don't want you to think me bold or heartless." Again words failed him. He stood abruptly, unable to stay seated any longer. This time she came to his rescue.

"Say it, Wilhelm. I am prepared to hear your words, in fact, I am anxious to hear them."

With renewed courage, he sat beside her on the settee and took her hands in his. "Then I will tell you my heart." He glanced toward the door.

"Don't worry, Wilhelm," offered Agnetha, "I do believe Heinrich has everyone under oath to avoid this room until we come out."

He smiled in spite of his nervousness and squeezed her hands gently. "I have been alone this last year, very alone. I did not seek female companionship, although it was certainly offered. There are a number of widows and spinsters in the area who would welcome a husband. But when I met you, your face would not leave my mind. And then the night the workers threatened you, and you handled them all with such courage and grace, I . . . I knew then that you were indeed a remarkable woman."

Agnetha listened intently, not interrupting, but encouraging him with a nod now and then.

"If I had been a bachelor, I would have pled your suit immediately, I was so taken with you. But. . . ." he faltered here and looked at their clasped hands.

"But you are still in love with your wife."

Wordlessly, he nodded. "I'll always love Liese. We were childhood sweethearts. Our marriage was blessed with love and three beautiful children. How could I not love her still?"

"My dear Wilhelm, I also had a husband. He was a most wonderful and remarkable man, and our love was a special and holy thing. I will always love him and a part of my heart will always belong to him. But Philipp and Liese are dead, Wilhelm . . . and we are not."

He spoke again. "As much as I vowed I could never love another, since I met you, I find I cannot face the days alone. Agnetha, would you join me in this life God has given us? Would you marry me, you and your little Philipp, and be a mother to my children? They need a mother. I know it is a difficult thing I am proposing, but I . . . we need you."

She smiled at his honesty. "Being a mother is a difficult but rewarding privilege. I realize it may take some time for your children to accept me as mother, but I am willing to try. I too am lonely and in need of companionship. I have come to care deeply for you, and I am quite confident that this is the beginning of a very good love. Yes, Wilhelm, I will join you in this life God has granted us. I will be your wife and mother to your children. And thank you for including Philipp in your proposal. He needs a father just as your children need a mother. When he is old enough to understand, I will tell him how it was."

"Well," Wilhelm sat grinning like a schoolboy, still holding tightly to Agnetha's hands. "We should tell them, since they are all waiting somewhere for the outcome."

Agnetha did not move, but continued to look into his eyes, reading them. He forgot about the others then and everything else around them, everything except this amazing woman beside him. Reaching out to her, he kissed her gently, then again as if to seal their pact. "May the Lord bless us," he whispered in her ear. "I do believe I am the happiest man in the world at this moment."

She smiled serenely as they stood and left the room arm in arm to find the others.

Paul Gregorovich joined the Red Guard with an enthusiasm that surprised even himself. The citizens of Russia had been victorious over the forces of oppression. Utopia was no longer a dream, but an inevitable reality. This giant of a nation, considered prehistoric by the Western world, had something to teach those countries.

Now that the war with Germany was over, Lenin and his followers could begin to repair the damage done by centuries of uncompromising tsars and power-hungry *boyars*. Finally, equality and reason would bring the country to its rightful place among the nations, and Russia could be a leader in spreading Marxist ideology to a waiting world.

Paul shook himself out of his reverie and paid attention to Leon Trotsky, who had risen to address the assembled soldiers. The man carried incredible authority. "There are two main issues which Mr. Lenin is concentrating on at present. One is immediate peace talks with Germany. The other, which is where you come in, is redistribution of landowners' estates to those who farm them."

Trotsky straightened his small round spectacles and gazed

piercingly at the soldiers in the hall of the Winter Palace. "I realize there are not many of you yet, but the size of our army continues to grow daily. I rely on you to oversee the land seizures and assure that the local Soviets are prepared to redistribute fairly among the workers. Your unit leaders have detailed plans for the execution of this new law. They will take over from here."

Tekanin was prepared to follow his unit leader to the outskirts of the capital to begin enforcing the land law, but before they were able to leave the city, some diehard military cadets and loyalist officers staged an anti-Bolshevik demonstration and seized the telephone exchange.

Paul found himself in the thick of the fight, bullets whizzing past his head as he ran for cover behind a stone archway at the gate of the exchange. Not accustomed to carrying or using a rifle, it took some determination for him to squeeze the trigger, with the sights set on another human being. *Come on Tekanin*, he scorned himself, *it's kill or be killed this time.*

The first shot wounded one of the cadets, the next took down an officer. Tekanin tried to pat himself on the back; after all, he was a soldier now, but the churning of his stomach reminded him that he still had a conscience. *You are a murderer*, said a voice in his head, sounding distinctly like Johann Sudermann. Even as the Guard defeated the anti-Bolshevik group and a tentative peace ensued, Paul could not shake the gnawing conviction in his gut. Pictures of childhood days with Johann swept unbidden and unwelcome into his troubled mind.

He remembered working for Johann's father, eating with his family, learning his basic academic skills alongside Johann. Especially after his father's death, Paul had felt a sense of security in the Sudermann home.

Now, however, the memory only caused him intense pain. He thrust his emotions aside and joined the rest of the Guards.

PART TWO

1918

Not everyone ploughs the field,
but everyone wants to eat bread.
Old Russian Proverb

Chapter 13

"What would you say to a sleigh ride this morning, Katya?" Johann leaned over the back of her chair as she sat at the breakfast table. They were early and no one else had yet arrived in the dining room on this sunny January day. He kissed her forehead and fingered the curls at her neck. A smile spread from her lips to her eyes, but faded there.

"What is it, Katya? It's not that cold out today." Johann pulled up a chair and straddled it, facing her.

Katarina said nothing at first, just frowned and looked toward the large sunny windows. Shifting her gaze to his, she grimaced and shook her head. "I don't know what it is. Something doesn't seem right."

"You mean a problem with someone in the family? Is it Mika?"

"No, no, nothing like that." She sighed and tried to put her worries into words. "I didn't sleep well last night. I was plagued with vague dreams, a lot of running and yelling and fear. The uneasiness won't leave me alone today, as if something is about to happen." She raised her hands, palms up. "I don't know, it's probably nothing more than lack of sleep."

Johann took her hands and held them tightly in his own. He was aware of her disturbing dreams, but a little surprised that she related them. Katarina kept many things to herself, even after months of marriage. "I'm sure you were reacting to all the stories of violence in the colonies. This new government seems totally unconcerned with anyone of foreign descent, even hostile toward us. And we thought the end of the war would mean we could resume our former lifestyle."

He grimaced. "Why didn't you wake me if you were afraid. You know I'd listen." He touched the tip of her nose lightly with his finger and smiled into her eyes. "You need some fresh air. How about I ask Misha to hitch up Sunny and we take a drive?"

Still Katarina hesitated. "If you'd like. But let's not ride too far."

"I can honor that wish." Johann marched out to talk to Misha before breakfast, but his light mood had been demoted to a heaviness that slowed his feet and filled his mind. His wife was not given to fears and imagined evils. She felt things deeply, but she was a rational woman. He wondered what had brought on the dreams.

The couple had driven the small sleigh only a few *versts* when Katarina turned to Johann with fear in her eyes and begged him to turn back toward Succoth. "I'm sorry to be such a baby," she said, "but my nerves are on edge. I feel we need to get back home quickly."

Without a word, Johann pulled the driving reins and turned around on the snowy road. The crispness of the wintry air had brought color to Katarina's cheeks, but the tension robbed the freshness from her.

Johann dropped her off at the house and drove the sleigh back to the barn where Misha waited. "Good, you are back. Is not good to go far today."

Johann stopped unbuckling the harness and turned to face the old man. "Why not?"

Misha gave a shrug and kept working. "Something happen today, I feel in here," and he tapped his chest.

The announcement caused Johann's own heart to beat

faster, and he thought of Katya's unusual feelings this morning. "Katya says the same. She is afraid. Please, Misha, if you know something, anything, tell me. There has been too much unrest in this country for your words to be taken lightly."

The old man deliberated for a few moments before he answered. "Peasants want land. Lenin says, 'Take it.' This happens many places. Maybe happen here?" Again the shrug.

"Thank you for the warning, my friend. Please let me know if you hear anything more." Outside, Johann expelled his breath forcefully, sending puffs of white into the clear air. What to do? Should he wait until he had more to go on, or should he speak to Heinrich about it now? Indecision plagued him as he entered the mansion.

Katarina saved Johann the decision by going to her father herself. She realized he did not like to believe evil of anyone unless there was absolute proof, but he had also heard the stories of looting and intimidation that were happening more and more frequently in the area. Bands of soldiers with nowhere to go joined forces, forming groups of undisciplined and desperate bandits who roved the countryside. The problem was much worse in Molotschna and Chortitza and the smaller colonies than here in the Crimea, but it still happened.

"What are you suggesting I do, child?" questioned Heinrich when Katya told him of her anxieties.

"I don't know, Papa," she confessed. "I just had to tell you. I cannot shake this foreboding."

Heinrich drummed his fingers on the desk in his study, mulling over her words. Finally, he looked up, and she could see the ideas in his eyes. "I don't know if your worries are legitimate or not," he said, "but we can take certain precautions in case." He unlocked a drawer and pulled out a sheaf of papers in a manila folder. These he held out to her. "You know where these will be safe. I will put my money and a few keepsakes and valuables into a box and we will make a trip to your mother's tomb. A little pilgrimage, just you and I."

Relief showed instantly in Katya's eyes. She remembered the first time her father had confided his secret hiding place to her. They had walked through the gardens and across the stream, to the little Succoth chapel, or so Katarina had thought. When her father had instead approached her mother's tomb, a brick-enclosed underground room much like a root cellar, Katya could not believe her eyes. Inside, hidden beneath her mother's casket, lay a box of papers, certificates, and ruble notes. And the dried rose petals lying on the casket, a bittersweet expression of love for Elizabeth Peters Hildebrandt. In a way, she stood guard, in death, over her family's most important possessions.

"I'll bring the rose petals and meet you at the garden door," Katya said.

"One year ago we were newly married, riding back to Bethany Home to begin our life together." Susannah smiled up at Gerhard and his arm tightened around her shoulders. The buggy rocked gently as it covered the ground between Einlage and the Molotschna Colony.

"Next to committing my life to the Lord," said Gerhard in a voice laden with emotion, "that was the best decision I ever made."

"Oh Gerhard, I love you so." Their reliable horse kept up a steady pace even as the reins fell slack.

Sitting close together under the heavy blanket, Gerhard and Susannah arrived in Prischib and crossed the bridge into Halbstadt. February continued as cold and crisp as January, but the trip had been inevitable. More help was needed at Bethany Home since several nurses had left in fear of the unrest and banditry, and the Moria Deaconess Home in Neu-

Halbstadt was still training young women as nurses in spite of the war.

Gerhard had hoped to speak with Dr. Erich Tavonius, one of the founders of Moria, but the good doctor had been forced to join the Russian army as the administrator of a reserve field hospital. Instead, Gerhard was ushered into the office of Dr. Franz Wall Jr., son of another *Moria* founder. Wall rose from his desk and met Gerhard with outstretched hand.

"I am Franz Wall."

"Gerhard Warkentin from Bethany Home at Einlage. Pleased to meet you."

"And you. I apologize that you must speak to me instead of to Erich, but one cannot twist the arm of the Russian military."

"So I've heard," returned Gerhard with a wry grin, "but have you any word about Dr. Tavonius? I met him in 1915, and his commitment to easing the suffering of others impressed me greatly."

Wall nodded as they took their seats. "Everyone who meets him is impressed. He is a good man. I pray that the Lord would see fit to allow him to return to us. He was injured in a riding accident a year or two ago, and spent some time at the military hospital at Tsarskoye Selo. Apparently, he met the empress and her elder daughters who helped nurse the patients, but since then we have not heard. But what may I do for you today? You are brave to travel so far in the shadow of the advancing Red Army."

"Brave or foolish, I'm not sure which," answered Gerhard. "We have a need for nurses at *Bethania*, and sincerely hope to return with them to Chortitza before the Reds arrive. At least, that is our plan."

"We?"

"My wife, Susannah, has accompanied me. She needed a rest from the constant busyness of the Home. Several of our girls left after bandits threatened the settlement, so the remaining workers are overloaded. In fact, we must return tomorrow morning. Do you have anyone you could recommend to us?"

Dr. Wall frowned and rubbed his fingers over his forehead. He sighed heavily. "There are two young women, both dedicated to doing whatever God calls them to, and both able to do the job, whom I would recommend without doubt."

Gerhard was perplexed. "Then what is your concern?"

Wall raised his eyes from the papers before him and looked piercingly at Gerhard. "We here at Moria attempt to continue on in an orderly fashion, but our time is short. A great monster stands at the door, ready to tear apart the order and precision we have established." At Gerhard's wide eyes and raised brows, the administrator of Moria stood and walked to the window.

"Warkentin, you need to know the extent of the threat. All our carefully established organizations mean nothing to the Russians. They do not understand or care how much we Mennonites have invested into establishing our society, or how much good it does. They see only wealth where they have none, and injustice because we do well and they are starving.

"The bandits care for no one but themselves and the army; well, Warkentin, we are simply in the way. If you wish to take the two nurses I suggest to Bethany, fine, but I only pray you and your wife will arrive safely, and that the girls will yet be able to do some good before everything is destroyed."

Gerhard stood as well, astonished at the apocalyptic prophecies of Franz Wall Jr. "Is it as bad as that? Is this not another storm we can ride out and then settle back into routine? What makes you so sure that disaster is imminent?"

Franz grimaced. "So many questions, so few answers. All I can say is that you will see, but I hope it will not be firsthand.

We are already under the control of the local Soviet. We have no more say in what happens."

He walked over to his desk and retrieved two papers, which he handed to Gerhard. "Here are the forms for Helga and Tine. I will call them, and you and your wife can interview them after lunch. Then I would invite all four of you to stay at our home tonight and leave as soon as it is light tomorrow. I wish you could be on your way today already, but I would not suggest night travel."

Gerhard left Wall's office in confusion and some mental turmoil. What would he do if the Red Army arrived? How could he protect Susannah? And why had he not considered the dangers more thoroughly before coming? His questions became prayers as he retraced his steps to find Susannah in the Moria Home sitting room. She would read his mind and he must have an answer for her.

True to his expectation, Susannah immediately detected trouble in her husband's eyes. He quieted her with a shake of his head. "We will discuss this at supper," was all he would say.

Gerhard awoke long before dawn on February 6. It took him a moment to remember where he was. Susannah lay peacefully asleep beside him in the guestroom at the Franz Wall Jr., home. As much as he hated to do it, Gerhard woke Susannah gently and encouraged her to dress for their return to Einlage. Sleepy but complying, she prepared herself as quickly as possible and brought their small valise into the kitchen where Johann spoke in hushed tones with Dr. Wall.

She nodded a good morning to him and knocked at the door of another room where the two nurses slept. A muffled acknowledgment sounded from behind the closed door, and within ten minutes, Helga Siemens and Tine Thiessen emerged, ready for a quick bite to eat and then the buggy ride to Chortitza. In spite of the circumstances, the girls, both nineteen years of age, put forward cheerful countenances.

Mrs. Wall had prepared fresh cinnamon buns the evening before and now bustled about her kitchen offering these delicious rolls with cups of hot, creamed coffee to the travelers. "May God grant you safety," she whispered.

"It's all right to speak in a normal voice, my dear," said her husband with a twinkle in his weary eyes. "Everyone in this household is here in the kitchen, and I doubt the sound will carry beyond these stout walls."

Everyone relaxed somewhat with the words and sipped their coffee. As they gathered their bags to leave, a loud knock sounded at the heavy front door. After a moment's hesitation, Franz moved to answer it. He opened it a crack, but could not recognize the visitor in the still-gray dawn.

"Doctor, it is I, Helmut Hiebert. Please allow me to come in."

Wall immediately backed away and opened the door wide. Hiebert burst in, anxiety and fear etched on his young features. He gasped to catch his breath and managed to pass on the message he had come to deliver. "The Reds came in the night. They stayed mostly along the main street and some took the road past Schroeder's Motor Factory to Petershagen. There was such confusion as they broke into homes and demanded accommodation. Several people have been shot, among them a Mr. Herman Suderman and a fourteen-year-old boy. I don't know who he was, but he is dead. I don't even know why these were shot. If the Reds come, don't resist them. Give them whatever they ask." The young man opened the door. "I must continue to spread the warning. God protect you all."

He was gone as quickly as he had come, and the assembled hosts and travelers stared at one another in mute disbelief. Gerhard looked at Susannah, and she knew what he wrestled with—do we go or do we stay? Which is the safest and wisest? She felt sorry for him, but could not offer any additional information to help him make his decision.

Finally, as the light of day began to illuminate the room, the Walls, the Warkentins and the two young nurses stood shoulder to shoulder in a circle, and offered themselves to the protection of their heavenly Father. With a strange peace, Gerhard hitched up their buggy and helped the ladies into it. They waved a thank you to Dr. and Mrs. Wall and rolled down the street past the mill and the School of Commerce.

"I have no idea if conditions will improve in the near future. Perhaps now would be as good a time as any to risk the return to Einlage." Franz Wall's words had clinched the decision for Gerhard as they discussed it a few minutes before in the Wall's kitchen. In a wry attempt at humor, Gerhard had quoted Lenin's dictum: *"Tipyer ili nikagda"*—"Now or never."

In grateful relief, the four travelers reached the outskirts of the town unassaulted, and Gerhard urged the horse into a canter.

The Hildebrandts and company were finishing a lunch of hot rice soup, sausage, fried potatoes, and pickled beets, when they were interrupted by Fyodor. He strode purposefully toward Heinrich at the head of the table.

"There are people at the door, sir, workers, and they insist they are coming in. What do you wish me to do?"

Heinrich, alarmed at Fyodor's apparent fear, threw down his napkin and rose quickly to his feet. "I am on my way. Thank you, Fyodor."

As they left the room Johann and Abram followed, with Theodore Konrad shuffling along not far behind.

"What is the excitement about?" inquired Heinrich when he reached the front doors.

"We come to claim what is ours," answered the

spokesman, none other than Ilya Veselovsky. "The Soviet says we take what we need. The Soviet gives us power to take, now, today."

Heinrich lifted his chin as he considered Veselovsky's statements. He was well aware that the local Soviets had been discussing redistribution of wealth to those who actually worked the land, but he had not believed it would come to this. The tsar had issued such a decree in 1915, and even though he and Johann had journeyed all the way to Petrograd to defend their case and that of others in their position, nothing had eventually come of the decree. It had never been enforced. He had taken for granted that nothing would come of this latest absurdity either. But this time he was wrong.

"We come in, Hildebrandt. Stand out of the way."

"What do you want?" countered Heinrich. "If you are hungry, I will give you more food, although I always make sure you have plenty. Do you need more wood for your fires, warmer coats, what is it?"

"We take our share," repeated Veselovsky stubbornly. "Is ours for we work the land. Move aside."

"Gentlemen," Johann stepped in beside Heinrich. "Listen to reason, if you would. You have no right to demand anything of the Hildebrandts."

Johann's words, meant to calm, had the opposite effect. The dozen or so men and women standing on the verandah began to grumble and demand entrance. If Heinrich and Johann had been alone, the result might have been different, but with Wilhelm, Abram, and Theodore standing in the doorway as well, the workers backed off, although belligerently.

"We come back with paper from Soviet," declared Veselovsky. "Tomorrow we take." Angrily, he turned and stomped down the snow-covered steps, his entourage behind him.

Heinrich closed the door in disbelief. Shaking his head he glanced around at the others gathered there. Together, the group went to join the women waiting in the parlor.

"Wilhelm," asked Heinrich in a pained voice, "can they demand this? Does the new law allow them to enter my house and help themselves?"

Wilhelm tightened his lips and acknowledged Heinrich's questions. With a sigh, he nodded. "I wish I could answer otherwise, but I attended the *zemstvo* meeting yesterday, and the soviet has declared that land and goods redistribution is within the law, and that the workers are within their rights to demand it. I'm sorry."

"And have your workers approached you?"

"Not yet," conceded Enns, "but I have called a meeting of all my employees for tomorrow to negotiate. I don't know if I can avoid trouble and the destruction of my home, but I thought it to be worth any effort I might be able to make. Perhaps you too could call your people together."

Heinrich nodded wearily. "Perhaps. Perhaps without Ilya, but that one seems intent on revenge for his lot in life. He has always been a difficult man to work with, and I have had to put him in line more than a few times. Now he will retaliate."

"They will not take everything, Papa," declared Katarina with determination, knowing he understood her meaning.

The company sat in silence for several minutes while everyone thought his or her private thoughts. Then Heinrich spoke, his strength returning gradually until he stood unafraid before them. "My children and friends," he began, "the Lord has told us not to be surprised when these strange things happen to us, but rather to expect them. We are aliens here in a foreign land. Our home is in heaven, where our true treasure is. Let us not become attached to material things. Nothing can touch us that the Lord Jesus himself has not first sifted for each of us. Should he see fit for us to donate our material goods to our workers, then we shall do so with grace, and wish them well. Let us look at this challenge as a test of our true strength. Can we do this? What is your opinion?"

The shock of the workers' demands had affected each person there in a different way, but each rallied at the words of Heinrich Hildebrandt. They would stand tall, they would show love, they would turn the other cheek, even if the cost was high. After all, everything they considered their own was ultimately from the hand of God.

"The Lord giveth and the Lord taketh away," pronounced Abram, and the assembled group joined in chorus, "Blessed be the name of the Lord."

Katarina shuddered at the words that were usually reserved for funerals.

Chapter 14

 "There is a meeting of the Mennonite estate owners of the area this evening at the home of Friedrich Wientz near Karassan. I think we should go." Nicholai stood before the desk in his father's study and challenged him. Heinrich stared at the boy and wondered when he had grown so tall. He had just passed his thirteenth birthday, but he was as tall as Johann and muscular like Heinrich.

"Papa, why do you stare at me like that?"

Frowning, Heinrich cleared his throat. "What kind of meeting is it, my son, and why do you think we should attend?"

"Because it's important. They will be discussing the problem of bandits and the redistribution of wealth."

"Yes. And the question of defending ourselves, is that not correct, Nicholai?"

"We must protect our family, Papa."

"Well, son, I may go, but you will not. You are not of age to contribute to such decisions."

Nicholai began to argue, but his father stopped him with upraised hand. "Silence. We will not discuss this further."

Kolya stared angrily at his father for several moments, then spun on his heel and marched from the room, slamming the door behind him. *We are to be a people of peace, Lord. Our ancestors died rather than take up arms. Now I hear my own son spouting self-defense. How am I to curb his sidetracked enthusiasm?* Heinrich lowered his head onto his hands and remained still as the marble statues he had seen in St. Petersburg several years ago. He wished sometimes that he were carved of marble, for stones did not feel pain.

However, he, Johann, and Abram rode out to Karassan early that evening, accompanied also by Wilhelm Enns who joined them as they passed his estate, Tomak. None of the men were aware of the shadow who trailed them the entire way, keeping well hidden in the bushes at the side of the road. Nor did they notice the figure find a place behind a lilac bush, under the windows of the spacious study of the Wientz manor.

The room, large as it was, soon became crowded with Mennonite men who had come to discuss their plight. "We cannot depend on the local Soviets to protect our rights," stated one young gentleman from north of Karassan. "Some of us are members of the *zemstvos,* and we know they are not interested in our material well-being."

"I agree with you, Albert Krahn, but what do you intend to do about it? Run for premier?" Chuckles bounced around the room and then receded with the seriousness of the matter.

"No," he retorted, "but I intend to protect my family and my belongings. No one has the right to enter my house and take what is mine. I will stand against them."

"How far would you go in your resistance of evil, son?" Heinrich's voice broke through the murmurs that had begun at Krahn's declaration.

Albert frowned at Heinrich's use of the word "son." "It would depend on what the aggressor did," he answered.

Heinrich pursued the matter. "And if he aimed a gun at you or your family, would you shoot him?"

The murmurs now became agitated as some said, "Of course he would not kill anyone," and others, "He should kill them before they kill him. It's a matter of survival."

A tall, lean man of about sixty years stood from his chair and raised his hands to quiet the crowd. "Johannes Toews," he introduced himself. "Brothers, we need to remember where we come from and what we believe. We, as a Mennonite people, embrace pacifism, not because Menno Simons believed it, but because the Word of God decrees it. Many of our forbears in Holland and Germany gave their lives rather than kill another human being. Others left their homes and traveled to far places to escape military conscription.

"From time to time, the Lord allows testing to see if we still maintain our allegiance to the way of peace. Brothers and sons, let us not betray our martyrs. Let us not now betray our Lord."

Young Albert stomped the floor impatiently with his polished black boot. "That is nonsense. The Lord does not expect us to offer our loved ones to the enemy. He expects us to use our heads and protect ourselves."

The debate ran on for several hours and became so heated that the windows were opened for air and distraction. All the better for the form huddled outside beneath the lilacs. Finally, Heinrich stood and faced the group. "I believe we will not come to agreement here tonight. Both sides of this debate are equally convinced of their rightness. I, for one, take my stand to do what Christ would do. I will not resist violence. I place myself and my family in the hands of God to do with as he sees fit."

There were yeas and nays, but several men, including Johann, Abram, Wilhelm, and Johannes Toews stood with Heinrich in his conviction. Johann's heart raced as he thought of anyone hurting Katarina, but he could not go against Scripture. He prayed that God would not ask it of him. He prayed that he could abide by his decision.

Elder Penner from Karassan stood as well, and offered a word of compromise. "There will be a Mennonite conference in Lichtenau, Molotschna, on June 30. Let us await the decision of the conference."

"A dangerous tolerance," declared Wilhelm as they walked out of the mansion to the barns to saddle their horses and ride back home. So preoccupied were they with their meeting, that they did not pay attention to the hooves of the retreating horse as its young rider urged it homeward ahead of the others.

A bleary-eyed Heinrich pulled on his trousers and shirt and tucked his feet hastily into shabby brown felt slippers, a last Christmas gift from his Liesbet. Fyodor's insistent knocking had roused him from his short sleep, and now he hurried downstairs to see what the emergency could be.

On his way down, Heinrich spotted Misha standing nervously near the entrance doors. He held his old felt hat in his hands, turning it round and round. His white hair stood out from his head in wild disarray, and he looked as if he would rather be anywhere but there.

"Misha," Heinrich addressed this man who had been his friend and stable hand for over thirty years. "What is it, man? It's the middle of the night."

"So sorry I wake you, Heinrich, but you need know. Trouble, she come tomorrow. Trouble. You go. Take family now. Horses ready and wagons too. Bad times come for you, Heinrich. I come back door, one hour."

It took Heinrich several moments to put together the mixture of Russian dialect and German words that the wiry little man spit out in his haste to deliver his warning.

"Who comes, Misha? What trouble are you speaking about? And where are we supposed to go?"

Misha looked ready to burst with frustration, but his face calmed as he glanced up the stairs past Heinrich. Heinrich also turned to look, and saw Katarina descending the stairs, her robe pulled snugly about her. She quickly reached the bottom of the stairs and came to stand before her dear Russian friend and protector.

"What is it, Misha?"

"The workers, they make trouble. They come tomorrow, steal, maybe hurt family. You go away, now."

Katya nodded in understanding. "I have been dreaming again this night. I believe we must flee, at least for the time being. Thank you, Misha, for warning us. I will rouse everyone and prepare them to meet you. Go out the back way now so that no one sees you. Stay behind the yew hedges." She ushered him through the house and out the back without a word, then turned to her father.

"Papa, I have a plan. I have been developing it as I lay awake trying to calm myself from the frightening dreams. We will go to the gypsies. I have not been riding far lately because of a deep uneasiness that has plagued me, but I have reason to believe Natalya and her extended family group are still in the vicinity. Will you help me, Papa?"

Heinrich looked like a man turned to stone. His usually ruddy cheeks were now pale and his face was drawn in the lantern light. "My child, has it come to this?" He let out an exasperated sigh. "What will come next, I ask you?"

"Papa." Katya spoke soothingly to calm her father. She had never seen him quite so agitated. "We won't be gone long, Papa, but we must protect those in our care. Please help me. You will need to wake the Reimers and the Konrads. I'm so glad Agnetha and little Philipp stayed in one of the Enns's guestrooms last night instead of coming home. I hope they will be safe there. I will get Anna and Kolya. Mika will help me. Everyone is to dress and take only one pillowcase of belongings each. Are you able to help me, Papa?"

Heinrich shook off the disbelief and dread and nodded his head. "Of course. We will work together. Precious time is wasting." He reached out and pulled his eldest child into his strong embrace and then ran up the stairs with as much speed as he could muster.

Within an hour's time, and with only soft flickering candlelight, the household assembled near the back door to await Misha. Katya sincerely hoped he would be able to remain undetected. It would be a miracle, bringing two wagons, each drawn by a horse. As it turned out, Misha had instead hitched two horses up to the *backloader*, an enclosed coach with a rear exit door.

Katya and Johann brought blankets for everyone, and Cook, beside herself with worry and sorrow, thrust bags of roasted *zweibach* into their hands, should anyone get hungry during their flight. Johann tried to keep the company quiet, but Mrs. Konrad was not aware of how loud her voice was. "Be quiet, Katie," roared Theodore Konrad, as she commented on all aspects of the adventure. Johann and Katya shared a worried look over their candle, then blew it out and climbed into the coach.

Heinrich crawled in last and Misha closed the doors from the outside. The backloader was crowded by the time they all found a seat, but at least the extra bodies provided heat. The little old Russian then climbed up to the driver's seat with the agility of a much younger man, and clucked to the horses.

The wheels of the backloader crunched through the fresh snow, their sound as loud as thunder to Katarina's ears. Johann tightened his arm around her shoulders. "Remember, my love, we are in God's care."

Katya sought his profile in the darkness. "I know," she whispered, "but I am afraid."

Heinrich sat quiet and still at the rear of the coach. *This is a supremely difficult test for me, Lord,* he prayed silently as he clutched the door handle for balance. *I have never been this lacking in control of my situation. I need to trust you like never before. Oh Lord, please strengthen my faith.*

The trip was not a long one. The steadily falling snow muffled the sound of the coach and horses and soon covered their tracks. Misha knew as well as Katya where the gypsy band had settled, but he did not trust them as she did. To him they were vagabonds and thieves, and sometimes murderers. They were without conscience. He would have argued with Katarina about their destination tonight, but he knew there was nowhere else to go.

As the horses and coach pulled into the gypsy settlement, they were immediately surrounded by men with guns who barked out their questions at Misha. He answered them with a nervously angry voice and came to terms with them only when Misha mentioned Katarina Sudermann. One of the number then took over and barked new orders at the others, opening the back door and shining a lantern inside at the blinking occupants.

Katarina made her way back, trying to avoid stepping on everyone's toes and not entirely succeeding. "Son of Natalya," she greeted the one she had come to know as "the Hawk." "We have come seeking refuge this night. Our home is being plundered. We have blankets. All we ask is permission to park our wagon within your settlement and build our own fire."

The Hawk nodded his dark head at her and shut the door again. Cold air from the outside chilled everyone, and Katya passed out *zweibach* for them to chew on. It was something to do while they waited.

They did not, however, wait very long. The Hawk returned shortly and motioned them out of the backloader. Heinrich helped each member out until they stood shivering in the cold. Katya's faith in these friends had never wavered, but the same could not be said of the others.

Katie Konrad's mouth remained firmly closed, but her eyes widened behind her thick spectacles. Theodore clasped her hand tightly, his fingers throbbing in pain. Cornelia looked as if she were facing a firing squad, but Abram stood straight and unafraid. Mika stood alone, bewildered but unwilling to give in to her fear. Nicholai was his usual self, almost dancing with excitement in the swirling snow, while Anna held fast to her father's hand.

Before any one of them could ponder long on their situation, the Hawk led them to the brightly painted gypsy wagons. Two by two they were billeted out, Heinrich taking Nicholai, and Mika taking Anna. As soon as everyone was settled, Misha turned the horse and wagon toward home, promising to return for them when it was safe.

The gypsy wagons were small and odorous, but wonderfully warm inside, and each refugee was offered a cup of bitterly strong coffee. They, in turn, shared their *zwiebach*. It was a strangely surreal February night, a jumble of fear, faith, and humility that would be scratched into the memories of every one of them for as long as they lived.

Surreal was also the only way to describe what was happening at Succoth. A group of about a dozen workers roamed through the mansion, picking up whatever pleased them and slipping the goods into sacks they had brought. They had not broken down the doors—Heinrich had purposely left them all unlocked. The loyal house servants stood back, watching with horror as fine china and heirloom pieces were dropped carelessly into sacks or onto the floor to smash into irredeemable shards.

Cook threw her large apron over her head and sat moaning in the rocking chair in the corner of her kitchen. She had always thought of it as her kitchen, her helpers, her responsibility to creatively and abundantly feed the Hildebrandt family. The sixty-year-old woman, a widow for more than twenty years, had never been in need since she and her Andreas had come to Succoth in the early years of their marriage. Succoth was home to her, and the desecration that was taking place in the house at the present time was a personal affront. Yes, the Hildebrandts were German Mennonites and she was Russian, but by Saint Peter, they were her family. She cried out as if in physical pain as another piece of china smashed on the hardwood.

The looting continued all day and into the night. A dirty beggar passing by stopped to lend a hand, and fell asleep on the brocade settee, head buried in the cushion that Agnetha had been embroidering the day before. The bedrooms upstairs were ransacked, beds stripped, curtains torn down. In the water closet, the toilet was plugged with garbage and the cord pulled off the wall unit. Men and women exchanged coarse jokes and laughed as they sorted through personal belongings.

"Where his money?" demanded Ilya Veselovsky as he pulled out drawer after drawer from Heinrich's study desk. Throwing the contents of the drawers onto the carpeted floor, he growled and roared as he realized there was no money to be had.

One of the men with him laughed loudly. "You think they leave money for you? You crazy! Hildebrandt not a stupid man, Ilya. You stupid, maybe, not him."

With another roar, Ilya dived at his unsuspecting accomplice and the two landed on the floor, punching and sputtering in their anger. Struggling, they rolled heavily into the desk, sending the burning kerosene lantern onto the carpet. Flames caught immediately and the two fighters stopped their quarrel in a moment. Ilya stood back to watch, but the other man grabbed a sack and began to beat at the flames.

"What you do?" yelled Veselovsky. "Let him burn."

The man continued to fight the dwindling fire. "No, Fool. We cannot take what burns."

His mental wheels clicked slowly, and then Ilya Veselovsky

began to stamp out the remaining sparks, finishing with a pitcher of water from the cupboard near the door. "Out. Fire is out. We take more."

The other vandal looked heavenward and shook his head, wondering why he had followed Veselovsky here this night. His only leadership ability was a big mouth and a cruel hand. The man shouldered his sack bulging with loot and walked to the door. "I go home. Sleep. Tomorrow I come back."

Ilya watched him leave the room and turn in the direction of the back door. A moment later, the man walked past the door again. "I go out front," he smirked to Ilya as he passed. Veselovsky was ready to follow him, but as he looked around at the large comfortable room, albeit charred and vandalized, he decided to stay. Wrapping himself in a soft-hued crocheted blanket, he curled up on the soft leather couch and soon fell to snoring.

The unit in which Paul Gregorovich Tekanin served turned its horses south and east from Petrograd along the road to Moscow. It was a great distance to cover on horseback, but the weather was beginning to turn moderate, and the time passed in a rapid series of events. The unit stopped at every large estate or landholding along the way and demanded money and deeds of possession from the terrified owners.

The first encounter nearly tempted Paul back to Petrograd, had he been free to withdraw his commitment to the Red Guard. The Guard rode up four abreast and sat on their horses looking down at the little old man who answered their shouted summons. He stared, terrified, at the group of sixteen soldiers and cried out, "What is it you want?"

The leader of the troop, Commander Boris Kuryakin, a tall, swarthy soldier, pointed his rifle at the elderly Russian and stated icily, "We want your money so we can give it to your workers. It is their money anyway, is it not? And the deed to your land." At the man's confused hesitation, Kuryakin fired a shot at the man's feet, causing him to leap backward, tumble through the door and land gasping on the floor in the large entry, clutching at his chest.

Kuryakin signaled to one of his men, who dismounted and stalked toward the fallen landowner. "Get up, you filthy capitalist," he growled as he yanked the man up by his shirt front. Coughing and doubling over in pain, the man nodded his head and stumbled to his safe to retrieve his stash. The Guard prodded him all the way with the rifle.

In the end, the commander passed out a wad of bills to the group of gaping workers who had gathered near the big house to find out what was going on. They had, of course, heard the news that they were now free to "accept" their share of the holdings, but they had not considered how to take advantage of this strange opportunity. Commander Kuryakin had given them a lesson. They stuffed the bills into their pockets and aprons and, at the Commander's urging, walked past the paralyzed landowner into the house that had always been closed to them. Kuryakin waved the rest of the money in the faces of his men and put it in his pocket. "You will get yours later," he assured them as he struck a match and lit the deed to the property. It curled into brown ash and fizzled out on the cold ground.

Other raids followed a similar pattern, varying only with the amount of money taken and the reaction of the owners. Some were shot for their insolence by the Guards themselves, or left at the questionable mercy of their workers. As he rode along and added his part to the sinister strength of the Red unit, Paul blocked all questioning from his mind. *The means justifiy the end*, he told himself. *The proletariat deserves to own what they work for, the capitalists must be destroyed to make way for the ideal society*. The ideas were raw and unchewed, but Paul swallowed them whole, starved as he was for something to fill the enormous void in his life.

Natalya and her band of gypsies showed practical support and refuge to the temporarily homeless Hildebrandts. The gypsy wagons, although warm, were crowded with the added bodies, and the money Heinrich offered his hosts for food did not immediately solve the problem of feeding ten extra mouths. But tempers were cooled and claustrophobia abated by the sharing of stories and customs, including carefree dances performed by the gypsies, much to Mika's delight. She had become outwardly quiet since her return from Molotschna, but within her there still smoldered a restlessness.

Natalya took to Anna as she had to Katarina many years before. The two discovered a kinship of spirit that amazed everyone except Katya herself.

Nicholai, however, marched about the camp in restless frustration and insisted upon riding with Johann on his reconnaissance missions to Succoth. His father's statement, "you are too young," only angered him. "What does age have to do with it?" he questioned in thirteen-year-old audacity. "Someone should do something about what's happening to us. If none of you will, then perhaps it's up to me!"

After three days at the camp, much of it spent sitting around campfires in the clearing, the Hildebrandts and company returned to Succoth. When Katarina stepped from the backloader, her eyes filled with tears. Garbage littered the once proud entrance to the house, and the verandah railing had been broken in several places. Johann took her hand and they climbed the steps to the large double doors. A grief-stricken Heinrich followed them, Mika's arm tucked tightly in his. It was the daughter who supported her father.

Johann pushed the doors open and entered with Katarina, surprising Dunia and Cook, who were on their knees, scrubbing the entrance floor. Both servants wiped their hands on their aprons and stood, heads bent in sorrow. Katya forgot the house then and reached for Dunia. "Oh my poor dear," she said. "You had to watch it all. And Cook. I'm so sorry you had to experience this."

Now it was Dunia's turn to cry, which she did on Katarina's shoulder, apologizing profusely for the actions of her people. "It was not your fault, Dunia," Katya assured her. "Look at you, here on your knees scrubbing away the signs of vandalism. You have gone far beyond what is expected of you." She paused before she said the next words. "You have the right to do as you please now, you know. You can take what you wish and leave."

Dunia and Cook were both duly insulted by the suggestion, and said so. Mika and Heinrich had walked farther down the hall, and Katya was shocked by her father's cry. "We didn't get as far as the study yet," explained Dunia. "It has suffered badly."

Katya ran down the hall and stopped short at the sight of the burned carpet and the scattered contents of the desk. Heinrich knelt amidst the mess, trying to sort it all out, while Mika stood helplessly by, shaking with anger and frustration. "Why doesn't someone do something about this chaos?" she cried. "What has the country come to when beggars and thieves can plunder at will, and the rightful owners must run for their lives? This cannot go on." She stormed out of the room and up the stairs, too angry to be afraid of what she might find there.

Chapter 15

"The Germans are coming," announced Heinrich a few days after the family had returned to Succoth. "They reached Kharkov on February 23, so they should be here any day."

Since Lenin had officially pulled Russia out of the war, they would, at least to some extent, be subject to the Germans. The news gave everyone much to consider as they awakened to the task of righting the damage that had been done to their home. The work was exhausting. Theodore and Katie Konrad had suffered the most, physically. The time spent with the gypsies had truly tried their endurance and greatly increased Theodore's arthritic pains.

The old man raised his head at Heinrich's announcement. "Our liberators!" he cried. "The Germans have become our liberators. They understand us. They will save us from the hands of these Bolsheviks."

"The Bolsheviks now label themselves Communists," put in Abram Reimer, who kept a keen eye out for news of political developments. "I don't think it changes their plan, but it's a new title."

Wilhelm Enns frowned. "There have been changes at the local Soviet level as well." Wilhelm had brought Agnetha and Philipp back this afternoon, and stayed to supper. "Many of the landowners suffered as you did and complained to the Soviet. Now that Germany has moved into this country, the peasants and workers have been commanded to return what they have taken. It will be difficult to enforce and will not be good for relationships between the rich and the poor. Local constables have been sent out to see that the command is carried out."

"I'll believe that when I see it," retorted Heinrich.

"And what happened at Tomak?" asked Johann. "Did your workers also vandalize the house?"

Enns shook his head slowly. "We met before they had decided to do anything rash and we discussed a solution to the inequalities." Agnetha smiled and turned admiring eyes on her husband-to-be. "My family and I moved into the manager's house—it has three bedrooms and a large kitchen and sitting room. The workers have organized themselves into the big house. It all worked out quite well."

No one spoke, but all eyes stared widely at Wilhelm and Agnetha. "It is only a house," she said quietly. "One can be as happy in a cabin as in a castle, and I was certainly not used to anything beyond the basic necessities before I came to Succoth. I'm sure we shall manage quite well."

Wilhelm's eyes adored her as she spoke. It had been a long time since someone had shared his heart and voiced his thoughts. He had believed that a man could only have one true love in life, but the Lord had blessed him a second time, and his joy surprised him.

Katarina sat stone-faced throughout the conversation, and Johann put his arm on her shoulder as a silent comfort. He knew what Succoth meant to her, and what it would mean to give it up as Wilhelm had relinquished Tomak. She would not look at him for fear of losing her composure, and everyone was relieved to be dismissed from the table.

The men, except for Johann, met in the damaged but reordered study, while the ladies visited in the parlor. Johann fetched Katya's coat, took her hand and led her out into the orchard. Tiny green buds were forming at the ends of dead looking limbs, and the soil smelled of spring. Several deep breaths of crisp air revitalized Katarina, and she poured out her heart to her husband. "What would we ever do without Succoth? It's home. It's our refuge when everywhere else things are falling apart.

"I helped Mother plant some of these trees. Many of the flower beds are my own design. When we were children, we would play hide-and-seek in the orchards, and it was like a fairy tale. Or we would pretend to be robbers and constables, hiding in the rose garden or behind the old olive tree by the bench. Some of our cousins chased each other on horseback through the orchard, but Mother was angry with them." She smiled at the remembrance. "Kolya fell out of that tree there when he was about five, and we were all so afraid that he would die. Knocked himself out for several minutes." They both chuckled at Kolya's fearlessness.

"There's a world of memories here. How could Mr. Enns leave his home, everything he has worked so hard for?" She looked to Johann for a response, knowing that his thoughts mirrored hers. He too had come to love Succoth in the few years he had lived here and called it home.

"What do you think could make you leave Succoth?" he asked, holding her eyes.

She pondered a while, then shook her head. "Nothing, unless I was driven from it." She paused and tried to swallow the lump in her throat. "Or if God asked me to leave," she whispered. "But I don't want to, I don't want to." They held each other, but Katya could not cry. A fierce determination to remain at Succoth kept the tears at bay. She would stay here always. She could hold the family together at Succoth. God would not ask more of her than that.

"There's a German soldier at the gate, Gerhard." Susannah's voice betrayed her excitement. "He spoke German to me."

"Did you expect him to speak Chinese?" Gerhard kissed the top of her golden head as he opened the door of his office to meet the soldier.

Suse giggled. "But he was kind and friendly. We have had to be so careful with the authorities these last months."

He smiled again and closed the door behind him. Susannah watched through the window as the two greeted each other like brothers. They talked and laughed easily as they approached the office. She slipped out the hall door and busied herself at the supply cupboard nearby.

"Now that the Russian army has ceased its defense," the soldier was saying to Gerhard as they entered the building, "we have advanced unrestrained. The Allies' furious demands that Russia continue the war have gone unheeded by Lenin and his Bolsheviks, and Trotsky's creative position of 'neither peace, nor war' holds about as much water as an inverted cup."

"Neither peace, nor war?" Gerhard shook his head uncomprehendingly. "How does that work, Herr Kesselman?"

"Ha! It doesn't. He wants to pretend everything can go back to the way it was before the war. That, of course, is impossible because we have the upper hand here."

"Well, I must admit, we are glad to see you. We offered our loyalties to Russia in '14, and were kicked aside for our allegiance. Although we did not take part in the actual fighting due to our religious convictions, many of our young men risked their lives and some died in the medical corp of the Forestry Service. And still we are considered foreigners and enemy aliens. If they say we are Germans, then Germans we shall be. The fatherland to which we offered our loyalty no longer exists."

Gerhard enjoyed the beautiful lilt of his mother tongue,

spoken freely and without fear. "How are the peace talks progressing?" he asked, relaxing in this strange friendship. "Will Germany take over the whole country?"

"No, I don't think it will come to that." The soldier, who had introduced himself as Dietrich Kesselman, placed his spiked helmet on the desk between them and crossed his long legs. He drank the coffee that Gerhard poured for him and gratefully devoured the fresh cinnamon *kuchen*, its sugary topping clinging to his clipped mustache. "Lenin is afraid of that very thing, though, and has convinced Russia to agree to our terms. The Bolsheviks are meeting with our people at Brest-Litovsk, on the German side of the war front. Negotiations have been long and difficult, but Lenin will do whatever is needed to remain in power."

"What are the terms?"

"We annex Poland, the Baltic states, and the Ukraine. Finland becomes independent."

Gerhard whistled in amazement. "That must include almost a quarter of our population, including much of the good farm land."

"To say nothing of the coal and iron mines and the factories. Yes, it is a costly peace. But I must continue on. A million thanks for your hospitality and the *kuchen*. Makes me think of home." He stood and bowed to Gerhard, who offered him his helmet and walked with him to the gate.

"Some of my men will remain behind here in Chortitza Colony to keep order. I've been made aware of a good deal of banditry and violence that will be curbed at once. I myself will be moving southward. You may rest easy now that we are here, Herr Warkentin. We Germans believe in law and order. Not unlike yourself, I'm sure." He mounted his chestnut mare and rode away with a salute to Gerhard and to the newfound peace.

As hardened as Paul had become in his new position as a Red soldier, the confrontation at Yaroslavl came close to cracking his self-made armor. A group of counterrevolutionaries had taken over the town, located some three hundred *versts* from Moscow, and Paul's contingent was the first to arrive after the usurpation.

His command, cold as the waters of the North Sea, Kuryakin ordered his men to destroy the rebels. "Take no prisoners, leave no survivors. The anti-Bolsheviks must be completely annihilated." Having given the charge, he led them through the streets, slaughtering every soldier and a number of civilians who happened to be in the wrong place at the wrong time. Paul obeyed orders in a frenzy of commitment, his sword stained with the blood of his countrymen, the bullets from his gun finding their mark again and again. He killed and killed until his own soul lay shriveled and gasping within his breast. So the counterrevolutionaries were effectively suppressed.

By the time Kuryakin's unit had reached Moscow, a major change had occurred. Moscow had been declared the capital of the new Soviet Russia, and Petrograd received its third christening in as many centuries. It would now be known as Leningrad, and no one was surprised in the least.

Grisha slipped silently through the back streets of Leningrad, the fingers of his left hand clutching a crusty roll within the pocket of his worn greatcoat. So far he had avoided meeting up with the *Cheka*, Lenin's new secret police. They were, according to word on the street, every bit as precise and efficient as the tsar's gendarmes had been. Grisha suspected they were more so. Lenin had an agenda to move ahead, and he needed to restore public services and enable government offices to function again. Banks remained frozen, and discipline in the factories was still nonexistent.

But right now, the main thing on Grisha's mind was his stomach. There was little food left in Leningrad, or in any of the other cities. Peasants no longer bothered to bring produce to the major centers because no one had money to buy, and there was nothing for them to purchase with their profits.

Grisha had managed to pilfer a dry roll from Wiedeman's Bakery while Ephraim's back was turned. He suspected that the Jewish baker was far too astute not to notice the theft, nevertheless, the crusty roll was now in his pocket. There were many Jews who played a part in the present political game. Trotsky, for example, was actually Bronstein, and Kamenev, Tekanin's nemesis, was born Rosenfeldt. The Jews had, as from ages past and in many places, been plagued and persecuted in Russia. They had suffered greatly under the nationalistic fervor of Alexander III, although he claimed the persecution should not be permitted. Now they were in place to change the system that had cursed them.

Well, more power to them, thought Grisha as he made his way back to the basement flat he still maintained. As he approached, he noticed a dark figure near the building, pacing back and forth with eyes darting in every direction. Grisha slowed his step and paused to observe. He noted that the uniform of the man was that of the *Cheka,* but it was the face that surprised him. This soviet policeman knew him, knew where he lived, and was waiting for his return. The realization sent a chill through Grisha's bones, for the face of the *Cheka* was that of Mikhail Pavlovich Karakozov.

"It's a happy day, Peter dear." Susannah Warkentin clapped her hands as she entered Peter Hildebrandt's room at Bethany Home.

"Happy day," mimicked Peter, clapping his hands. His face, however, remained as if chiseled in stone. He rose to follow Susannah out of the room for their rounds. It still amazed Suse the way Peter had fallen into this role. His mechanical ministrations to other residents were often accepted better than her own, perhaps because they were offered so unthreateningly.

"You see, Peter, the Germans have arrived to protect us from the bandits and the Bolsheviks, so we need no longer fear." Suse made a habit of chatting about life in general and in specifics as she tended to her charges. She knelt before Frieda Lohrenz, who sat motionless in a rolling chair by the window of her room. Frieda never spoke, never moved, unless someone initiated an action. Her wraithlike appearance alluded to her condition. She had withdrawn from this earthly realm and lived suspended in a void somewhere between here and eternity.

Susannah ignored the obvious as she stroked the skeletal hands. "Did you know, Mrs. Lohrenz, that today is not March 2 as we had thought, but March 15th? Yes, we have a new calendar. Fancy that. My grandmother says it's the same one her mother used in Prussia when she was a little girl." She stood to gently brush the woman's hair and wind it into a small bun at the back of her head. Peter stood waiting, rigid as a tree trunk, until Susannah began to straighten the bedding. He stood opposite her, pulling the sheets and blanket taut, fluffing the pillows, smacking them when done, just like Susannah. He made her smile, and then he did something that caused her to stare. He shuffled over to where Mrs. Lohrenz sat and patted her stiffly on the shoulder.

Smiling, she asked him, "Do you like Mrs. Lohrenz, Peter?"

"Do you like Mrs. Lohrenz, Peter?" he responded, imitating her inflection exactly.

With a shake of her head she left the room with Peter trailing behind. "Let's carry on, dear," she said.

"Carry on, dear."

"Carry on, man," hissed Grisha through clenched teeth as he watched Mikhail Pavlovich from a distance. The sun slithered away behind the outcroppings of tenements and flats, taking with it the thin warmth of early spring, and Grisha felt cold.

"What do you want with me?" he muttered under his breath. "Just because I am not a committed Bolshevik doesn't make me an enemy of the state, does it?" The continuing presence of the *Cheka* answered his question. With an exasperated sigh, he disappeared into the alley and backtracked to Apraksin. Plenty of places to hide amidst the smoke and factories and the confusion of the market. He could vanish for as long as required, and perhaps slip back to pick up a few of his things, that is, as long as the *Cheka* hadn't already confiscated everything he owned.

Dietrich Kesselman sat beside Heinrich at the long cherry wood table in the dining room at Succoth. He had been made as welcome there as at Bethany Home, and in every German settlement between, whether Mennonite, Catholic, or Lutheran. An ethnic revival of sorts was taking place in south Russia, and Succoth welcomed it.

"You people have no sense of self-defense or strategy," declared Kesselman. "You sit here waiting for the aggressor and then offer him everything you have. I cannot comprehend this frame of mind."

"I've said so before, but no one listens to me," responded Nicholai.

"To him you should listen," said Dietrich with a grin. "Here we have a beginning."

Heinrich cleared his throat in irritation. He had spoken at length with his son about his un-Christlike attitudes. "Perhaps you do not fully understand our convictions, Herr Kesselman," he said. "We are committed to nonviolence. It is an integral part of our confession of faith."

"Nonviolence and self-defense are not mutually exclusive," Dietrich pointed out. "You do not necessarily have to take the offensive, although at times there is great merit to that approach, but to sit by while your family is attacked, that is foolishness."

"Yes, Father. I think we should—"

"That will be enough, Nicholai!" Heinrich's voice came louder than he had meant it to. "The men," and here he looked at Kolya to communicate his meaning, "will meet in the study after supper to discuss this topic. I believe you have schoolwork to do."

Kolya was so angry he felt he would explode. *He will never realize that I am no longer a boy,* he said to himself. *When I am thirty he will still tell me what to do.* But he remained silently smoldering, determined to hear the proposed discussion. Dietrich Kesselman winked at the boy covertly, and the small acknowledgment calmed him enough to allow an icy civility. "Excuse me, Father," he said shortly and left the room.

Heinrich shook his head. "He is becoming too headstrong," he said as the men chose comfortable seating in the study. Mika had placed a large potted tree over the place where the carpet had been burned. It mostly covered the damage, although Heinrich complained that it blocked his view of the doorway.

"He is a growing boy with an active mind, Heinrich."
Abram, who had never had a son, offered his opinion. "You
block him out of all discussions and he becomes more and
more convinced of his ideas. Perhaps he would benefit from
being included."

"He's only thirteen!" bellowed Heinrich. "What does he
know of life and convictions?"

Kesselman lit a cigarette and inhaled deeply. "I agree with
Herr Reimer," he said, his words wrapped in wisps of smoke.
"The boy needs to know, or he will likely get himself into
trouble. Better someone fully informed than half aware."

Johann felt caught between the two opinions. He pushed
up his eyeglasses and offered his *kopeck's* worth of information. "There is another meeting planned, dealing with this
self-defense issue. The Lutheran and Catholic villages and
settlements are buzzing with talk, and the consensus is that
we try to come to some agreement as neighbors and friends."

Old Theodore Konrad did not speak, but sat rubbing his
hands and wrists where the joints were swollen. The change
of climate from the Molotschna to the Crimea had not
improved his arthritis. All this talk of fighting back bothered
him almost as much as his physical pain. He tried not to
worry; he had to keep his Katie calm.

"Where is the meeting?" asked Heinrich, resignation in his
voice.

"It's in Karassan again," answered Johann, "but this time,
it's in the secondary school on the east side of town, by the
small vineyard."

"Well, we need to be there to hold up our convictions."
Heinrich glanced over at Abram, then at the German soldier.
"And Kolya will not accompany us." His words ruled out
opposition.

Commander Dietrich Kesselman decided to accept the hospitality of Succoth until after the meeting at Karassan. He enjoyed the company of the men as well as the presence of women. One in particular caught his eye.

"You make a fine mistress of the manor," he commented to Mika as she directed arrangement of the dining table for supper.

"Thank you," she replied demurely, smiling up into his confident blue eyes. "It is a position which comes easily to me and which I enjoy. My mother taught me the art of hospitality."

He smiled in answer, straight white teeth glistening behind his carefully trimmed mustache. "I am indeed a fortunate man to have come to Succoth. Would you do me the honor of giving me a guided tour of the estate? I am quite fascinated by the size and order of your father's holdings."

Maria raised an eyebrow as if making a decision. "I would of course be more than glad to show you the estate, but my father would be much more able to give you background information on the land and animals and his farming practices. Perhaps you should ask him instead."

"Ah yes, perhaps I should." He pondered a moment, watching Maria's eyebrows lower into a frown. "For information he would most likely be the better choice, but," the blue eyes twinkled, "for company he would come in a distant second." He crooked his elbow and she slipped her hand beneath it.

"Where shall we begin?"

Chapter 16

Paul Gregorovich awoke with a low groan in response to a kick in his side. A leaden spring sky greeted his eyes as he opened them and crawled from his bedroll. It would be another day of drizzling rain, the clouds weeping over the creatures beneath them. Paul had begun identifying with nature. It was easier to accept than the men he rode with, who daily seemed to lose their humanity and lived by instinct instead of by logic or honor.

Had they ever lived by honor? Had he? On the other hand, what choice did he have? To stay in Petrograd would have proven fatal. He wondered how Grisha fared, whether he had found a place in Lenin's system or was still attempting to live his own way by his wits. *Grisha*. With a heavy sigh, Paul poured himself a cup of bitter coffee and gnawed on a piece of dried bread. It was all they had until they reached the next village or estate, where they would demand the best of what was available.

Kuryakin's orders had modified of late. Food was in such paucity in the cities due to the peasants' refusal to deliver their goods that the Communist government had begun to take it by force. Kuryakin's unit had been given the added duty of coercing the peasants to give over a good deal of their produce. Tekanin was aware that the governmental robbery left the poor farmers with little or nothing to live on until the next harvest. Lenin's promise of peace, land, and bread was proving to be another empty assurance.

A sparrow sat on a bough of the tree Paul leaned on and sang a lonely song. *Give up, little bird,* Paul said to himself. *There is nothing left to sing about.* Still, the bird chirped as if the heavy skies were something to be thankful for, as if he had not a care in the world. *God sees the birds and tends to their needs,* came a voice that had become almost lost to him. *And he will care for you if you will let him.*

Gulping the remainder of the coffee, Paul Gregorovich grimaced. He pushed away from the tree and his niggling thoughts, and went to check on his horse. *Get on with the day; no sense in stalling the inevitable.*

"If you disagree with the intent of the meeting, Johann, why do you plan to attend?" Katarina tipped her head and lifted her chin as she confronted her husband with her logic. "Best not to become involved in such things." She stooped to plunge her rag into the warm, soapy water, then squeezed it out and stood to wash the signs of Succoth's violation from the upstairs hallway walls.

Johann adjusted his spectacles as he considered his answer. "Perhaps I can make a difference, swing popular opinion the right way."

"Is it popular opinion, this self-defense? Is it not in direct opposition to our Mennonite convictions and traditions?" She scrubbed with an intensity that allowed no dirt to remain, as if by scouring she could wash away this infiltration of unwelcome involvement of her people with the world. "I always thought that nonresistance was one of the main reasons our ancestors left Holland and Germany in the 1500s, why they turned their backs on Prussia when Catherine invited them here. Will we now give it up of our own free will?"

"Perhaps it will not come to that." Johann was hedging

and he knew it, but it was easier than trying to explain why so many of his ethnic brothers were ready and willing to surrender one of the major tenets of their faith. The German presence did not help. They encouraged action, military organization, and drills. Johann had observed Nicholai watching in fascination, and practicing these drills with his friends. He supposed it was in the heart of every boy to fight for what was important to him. Boys seldom paused to analyze their actions and the consequences. Neither did many grown men, Johann admitted. Sometimes God asked much of his people.

"The German soldiers have brought many changes with them, Katya. The illiterate peasants have been kicked out of the Soviet, and the *Schulzes* and *Oberschulzes* reinstated to their positions. They will at least have a say in dealing with the banditry and violence that many of our people have been living in fear of. The villages that had been given Russian names by the Reds have now reverted back to their German names, and we now have the right and the power to reclaim what was stolen from us. The Germans can help us put things back to rights and we can go on as before."

Katya looked at her beloved husband and shook her head in disbelief, dropping the soiled rag into the pail. "Do you believe that, or are you simply attempting to placate your wife because she is a woman and therefore doesn't understand such things?"

"Whoa, easy now." Johann's hands were up to ward off the storm he saw building in Katya's eyes. "I will never underestimate you, my love." He turned and gripped the balustrade as he looked out over the entrance below. "I may be trying to persuade myself of these things as well. I don't know what all the answers are, but I do know I must at least offer my opinion on points where I *am* sure. And I'm sure that it is not God's will that we take up arms to defend ourselves."

Katya moved to Johann's side. "Kolya worries me. He is so angry at everything these days. He used to be such a happy child."

"His personal security and peace have been violated, Katya. He is reacting. I only wish your father would listen to him."

"Surely you don't think he is old enough to involve himself in these meetings too, do you?"

"It's not that, Katie. But a boy of thirteen should be heard, respected. One doesn't have to agree with him, but he is worth listening to. Perhaps if your father stopped to consider that, he would be able to uncover the true source of the boy's anger."

Katya remained silent for several moments, thinking about what Johann had said. When she spoke, it was with hesitation. "I think . . . I don't even like to say it aloud, but I think Papa is afraid. He's afraid to hear what Nicholai has to say."

Johann answered her by wrapping his arms around her. She could lose her worries by burying them in his embrace. His strength seeped into her through his arms, his stable presence. She breathed deeply with her face at his shoulder, then turned her face for his kiss. But even in the bliss of that moment, Katarina Sudermann knew that she could not expect from her husband what only God could give. Johann would care for her to the best of his ability, but ultimately she was in the hands of God.

"You are right, Johann. You must go to the meeting to represent the principle of peace. I must admit that I am disappointed in the stand, or lack of it, that our churches have taken in this matter." She bent to rinse her wash rag. "I believe I will talk with Papa about Nicholai."

"Good. If he will listen to anyone, it will be to you."

"We've sent the Reds away with their tails between their legs," laughed Dietrich Kesselman as he and Abram Reimer entered the barn to help Misha ready the horses for the men's ride to Karassan. The wiry old Russian stableman was beginning to tire quickly. Katya suspected a good deal of his weakness was related to shame for the workers' invasion of the Hildebrandts' home, and fear for the future. He was not alone in his preoccupation. Now Herr Kesselman's flippant manner irked him. It also bothered Abram.

"Good afternoon, Misha," Reimer called. "Put us to work."

Misha nodded, indicated a thick red blanket and saddle, and led the way to one of the stalls. "You will ride Samson tonight. The soldier," he jerked his jaw in the direction of Kesselman, "knows his horse and tack."

Dietrich smirked good-naturedly at the covert condescension aimed at him. He did not care what the little Russian thought of him. He had, however, begun to care what a certain lady at Succoth thought. He sobered and kicked himself mentally for allowing a woman to take hold of his interest. He had always prided himself on his coolness, his ability to remain emotionally detached from others, even if he enjoyed their company. He had always been the one in control of the game, but now he had apparently met his match. Yet, in spite of himself and his duty, he took no steps to withdraw from the relationship.

As the men rode toward Karassan, Heinrich ahead with Johann, Abram riding beside Dietrich, they spoke of the upcoming meeting. "I do not know what has come over your Katya," said Heinrich to Johann, shaking his head. "She came to me and actually suggested I include Kolya in our discussions. Has she been talking so to you as well?"

Johann grimaced and faced the confrontation. "It wasn't her idea to speak about it with you, it was mine. I thought perhaps you would listen to her."

"But . . . Johann Sudermann, what could you be thinking? I sincerely hope you have not been encouraging my son in this direction."

"Father, I would not encourage him against you. My concern is that by not allowing him to speak his mind, his rebellion will erupt in another way that may be more serious. He is becoming an angry young man."

Heinrich lowered his eyebrows until they formed a straight line across his forehead. "I have come to respect your opinions, Hans," he began, and Johann relaxed. "But in this case you do not know whereof you speak. You are not yet a parent. How could you assume to know what is best for my son?" Johann's eyes widened and he turned his face straight ahead, while his mount's ears twitched back and forth, sensing friction. "You need not offer me advice in parenting, and you would do well to inform Katarina of the same."

The two riders following heard snatches of the conversation, and Dietrich set about to change the subject to one that interested him more. "Why do the Mennonites insist on being trodden upon by their enemies? Answer me that if you would."

"We do not wish to be trodden upon." It was Abram Reimer who spoke. "We do our best to discuss and negotiate for the well-being of our people. It is the aggression we back away from."

"Yes, and why?"

"It's very simple," answered Heinrich, throwing the words over his shoulder. "Christ has called us to a life of love and obedience. We are to give to those who ask without expecting anything in return, walk the extra mile, turn the other cheek. We are to live in peace and let him deal with injustice."

"That's absurd."

"You cannot understand because you do not believe."

Dietrich snorted, but rode quietly for some time after that, contemplating what made these men think so differently than he did.

The meeting proved to be much larger than the previous gathering at the Wientz home. Benches had been hauled over to the school from the Mennonite church nearby, and lined up in the larger of the two classrooms, with the students' desks pushed out into the entryway.

The other major difference between the two assemblies was the variety of backgrounds represented. Lutherans, Catholics, and a group of Jews came from the surrounding area, their commonality being their Germanic roots and their distress over the unstable political situation.

"Now that we are here," said Dietrich Kesselman when the meeting had been called to order, "you need not fear for your lives. We are your countrymen and will see to it that you are protected. But you should learn to look out for yourselves."

Affirmative comments scattered over the assembly. To Dietrich's surprise, it was a German comrade of his who qualified the statements. "I would add a note of warning to what my friend Kesselman has said. Some of you have been forced into situations by the Reds and the anarchists which contradict your values and beliefs. Some of you have been threatened, affronted, even evicted. Now that we have come with authority, you are demanding the return of what has been taken from you. I speak here mainly to those of you who are wealthy, who have much to spare." Murmurs could now be heard among the crowd, but the district commander continued.

"As I said, you now have the right, under the decree of Hetman Skoropadsky, to demand the return of at least that which is still available for reclamation. But consider the effect of such action on the relationship between yourselves and the poor who have robbed you. It certainly will not help to bring calm and peace back to this country. Consider whether these actions will bring the results you seek.

"I hope that this warning will suffice, and that tolerance would be more prevalent between you and your neighbors. It is my responsibility to maintain peace and calm, and I will do whatever I must to discipline any who disrupt this peace."

The gathered men were taken aback by the warning of the district commander. They had not expected further sacrifice.

"Thank you for your words of wisdom, Commander," Kesselman said tactfully. "We would all be wise to consider them and their intent. However, there is another matter to discuss, one that I'm sure you are waiting to debate." Dietrich paced back and forth in front of the chalkboard and the large world map that hung beside it.

"Should you again be threatened by the Red Army of the Communists, or roving bandits, you need to organize yourselves for self-defense."

"So tell us how to go about this," called out one of the non-Mennonite men. "We already know the necessity."

Dietrich smiled broadly. This would be easier than he had thought. "We will teach you," he offered. "We will hold drills in various places, giving advance notice of where these will take place. Come out to the meetings and we will teach you how to use your guns properly, how to strategize against the enemy, how to defend your homes and families. All you lack is organization."

As he scanned the audience, he noticed the scowls of some of the Mennonites. The opposition was about to be heard. Heinrich Hildebrandt became the self-appointed spokesman for the naysayers.

"Neighbors and friends," he began, "I realize that what I have to say will not sit well with all of you. Each group is free to form their own decisions on this issue of self-defense, and I thank the good German soldiers for offering their assistance. However, there is a group here that should not be involved in this action." Heinrich continued speaking, in spite of the snarls and negative remarks of many in the crowd, including some of his Mennonite brethren.

"For centuries, the Mennonites have embraced nonviolence, and we need to continue in this persuasion, as it is the command of Christ. I hold no grudge against any of the other ethnic groups gathered here. It is to my own people I appeal."

"We've heard enough from you, old man," shouted someone from the rear of the room. "Go home and hide your head then, but leave us to make our own decisions."

"We have come here tonight to remind those who should know better that they are treading on thin ice," continued Heinrich, in spite of the angry interruption. "Beware of taking up the sword, my brothers. As the Scripture says, 'Those who live by the sword will die by the sword.' We will address this issue again at the Lichtenau Conference next month. And now we will leave you to your further discussions. Only take to heart what I have said."

After his speech, Heinrich, Johann, and Abram filed from the room, followed by Wilhelm Enns and a dozen or so others. "We have been obedient," said Heinrich as they saddled their mounts. "May God grant us the ability to live by our words."

"Where is Nicholai?" demanded Heinrich when the men had returned home late that evening. "He is not in his room."

Katarina put a hand soothingly on her father's arm. "Don't fret, Papa. He often stays out late to play with his friends. They forget the time. Remember when Agnetha was so worried that the workers had kidnapped him, and he was only playing games with the other children?"

Her father was as edgy as a spooked horse. She could feel it through his coat sleeve.

"Send him to me at once when he comes in," said Heinrich, hearing his own irritated tone and attempting to quiet his spirit. "I will be in the library."

He gave his coat to Fyodor and entered the library, where a newly made fire danced in the grate. "I will bring you coffee, sir," offered the servant.

"Thank you, Fyodor. I would appreciate that."

He sat down heavily in the overstuffed burgundy chair by the fire and pushed at the logs with the iron poker, sending sparks erupting from the wood. Fyodor delivered the steaming beverage and backed out of the room, closing the door as he left. For a long time, the man sat unmoving in his chair, eyes unseeing, forgetful of the coffee which now sat tepid in the cup on the corner of the end table. His eyes were closed, but he did not sleep. At times his lips moved, and a tear rolled down his cheek.

With an effort, he raised himself from his chair and stood, stretching out the kinks in his body. Then, grasping the arms of the chair, he lowered himself to his knees, his elbows on the cushioned seat, supporting his head. "Oh Lord, hear your servant. I've been trying to obey your voice. Have I been amiss? The future frightens me. What if, after speaking out, I cannot resist the temptation to take up arms. I am only human, Father God. Have pity on me.

"And Kolya, Lord, what do I do with him? What has happened to my carefree son? Is he growing up so quickly and I have failed to notice? Forgive me for reacting so sternly to Johann and Katarina. They were right, you know—I should at least listen. I pray that I would not be too late."

With a tremendous sigh, Heinrich stood to his feet and turned to find Nicholai staring wide-eyed at him from the doorway. "Katya said to come at once," he said in a small voice. "I am sorry to interrupt your prayers."

"Come, sit," his father invited. "I'd offer you coffee, but it is cold."

Nicholai smirked slightly at the idea of his father offering him coffee. He was never allowed to drink it unless it was "fifty-fifty"—half coffee, half cream. He was told it would stunt his growth. *No chance of that now*, he thought as he lowered his tall, sturdy frame into the wing chair on the opposite side of the fire from his father, fingers playing with the buttons of his jacket.

Kolya searched his father's face. He had not noticed him getting so old. His usual ruddy complexion had gone pale and flaccid, his bright eyes dull and haunted. Nicholai felt a sharp stab of pain, wondering if he was responsible for this change. The pain stilled his hands as they fastened to the hem of his jacket.

Heinrich's eyes connected with those of his son. He blinked, looked away, then returned to the matter at hand. He must care enough for this boy to listen to his heart. "Kolya," he said gently. Nicholai was taken by surprise at the softness of his father's voice. He had been expecting a scolding at the very least.

"Yes, Papa?"

Heinrich sighed. "I must ask your forgiveness, son, and it does not come easily to me. Nevertheless, I will ask it."

"Forgiveness? For what?" The boy was genuinely shocked.

His father knelt on one knee beside Nicholai's chair. "I have not listened to you, have not paid attention to your growing up, your questioning, your natural inclinations to protect. I have been wrong. Will you forgive a foolish father?"

Kolya could not bear to see his father kneeling before him, especially as he recalled his clandestine rides to Karassan for the meetings. He had been willing to risk much to hear the goings-on. But the brokenness of the man before him ripped at his heart. "Papa, please stand up."

As Heinrich struggled to his feet, Nicholai threw himself into his father's arms. They held each other for a long time, and much of the misunderstanding and anger seeped away.

At last Heinrich stepped back and indicated the chairs. Both sat. "Now tell me, son. What is it that goes on in your head? What makes you ride out alone when you have been forbidden to do so?"

"You knew?" The realization shamed Nicholai.

"Of course I knew. I was once a boy also and would likely have done what you did. That is one of the things that spoke the loudest to me—remembering what it was like to be a young man."

Young man. Father is already listening. "I thought you were wrong, to refuse to fight those who wanted to hurt and kill us. I decided that if you wouldn't do something about it, I would."

"And what would you do? Go out single-handedly and begin killing all our Russian workers?"

Nicholai was silent, staring at his feet. "I don't know." He looked up and said, "That was why I had to go to the meetings. I had to know what the choices were."

"What are they, then?"

Kolya considered carefully before he answered. "I think that either we decide we will kill everyone who threatens us— and there would be no end to that—or we just have to wait and see . . . let God take over, I guess. I was hoping there was a middle course, so we could fight and still be friends with God."

"Do you think that's possible?"

Kolya looked into his father's eyes and began slowly to shake his head. "No, Papa, there is no middle course. Either we go with God or we fight against him."

"A strong man is one who is not afraid to admit his fears and to face them. Trusting will be difficult, Nicholai, but it's the only path with promise. We must decide what we are to do, because we may soon be called on to choose. Civil war is upon us, Kolya, and the Reds are desperate to retain their hold on the country. Not much will stop them, I'm afraid. You must remember to be firm in your decision."

"I will try to remember, Papa."

"Good. Now you must go to bed. It is late."

"Yes, sir . . . I love you, Papa."

"And I you. Sleep well."

Chapter 17

Paul dreamed that he was a small lad at home in Ackerman, dozing on his mother's lap. She ran her fingers caressingly through his hair as she sang the songs of their people. Then she tugged at his hair too hard and it hurt his scalp. With a groan of pain, he jolted awake, frightening the horse that had been nuzzling his head.

"You would nibble the hair right off my head, you ungrateful wretch?" he exclaimed. The animal shied away at the tone of his voice, and it was then he noticed Commander Kuryakin watching, laughing at the scene he had just played. Paul felt hot with embarrassment.

"Such pleasant dreams, Tekanin. I thought all dreams had turned to nightmares in this life of ours."

Paul did not know how to respond. He had seen little emotion in the man, and it surprised him. "Relax, Tekanin. I will not shoot your head off for dreaming. Not today anyway." He laughed at his own joke. "At least it was not a rat climbing in your hair."

Paul shuddered as he rose stiffly. He hated rats. They had been regular visitors to his flat back in Petrograd and were common in the old buildings that had housed *Pravda* over the years. But he could not come to terms with them, filthy, brazen creatures that they were.

"Yep. Always something to be thankful for, eh, Tekanin?" The commander sat against a wall of the barn they had slept in last night, and chewed on a supposedly clean piece of straw. This was Moscow and they were still sleeping in barns. "Did you know we have a new set of enemies, Tekanin?" he asked.

Paul's head came up from where he had been tying his bedroll, surprised that this man who usually distanced himself from his unit by sheer unpleasantness and threat, continued to address him. "No sir, I did not."

"No, how could you know unless I told you? Well, it's true and I don't mean the Don Cossacks from the South. We already know their fierceness, but they are not our nearest enemy. No, it's the Czechs we need to beware of."

"The Czechs?!"

"Some defected from the Austrian army to Russia during the war, and others were prisoners of war. We were in the process of shipping them home, about 40,000 of them, but it had to be overland toward the east by rail. Toward Vladivostock. They were strung out all along the Trans Siberian Railroad when trouble began."

Kuryakin spit the straw from his mouth and chose a new piece, twirling it between his grubby fingers for inspection. "Trotsky suspected the Czechs of turning against the Bolsheviks and ordered them disarmed and put into labor battalions, but they didn't like the idea. Fancy that! Apparently the Czechs became suspicious of their Bolshevik chaperones and took over the entire rail, with help from Allied forces."

"Where are the Allies coming from?" questioned Paul.

"Oh, they have crawled in from a few places. In the Northeast, British forces have been landing in Murmansk and Archangel. The Americans and the Japanese occupy Vladivostock on the Pacific, with French and British support. They are afraid the arms they previously shipped to these ports will now fall into German hands, and they do not want to risk that possibility."

"So what has happened?"

Kuryakin leaned his head back against the wall of the barn and stared at Paul through narrowed eyes. "The anti-Bolshevik forces have taken over most all of the communities along the Siberian railway. Now this "White Army," as they call themselves, advances westward, toward us, a force to ally itself with the lunatics from the South."

"What will we do?"

Kuryakin snorted. "Whatever we're told, Tekanin. You should know that by now. Quit wasting time and make some coffee. I'm thirsty."

With the sneer that Paul was used to, the commander stood lazily to his feet, stretched and stomped out of the barn as if the conversation had never taken place. In a way, Paul wished it hadn't. So far he had known what to expect from his commander, harshness and cruelty. Now he was confused. And why had Kuryakin told him all this? The threat of an advancing enemy bothered him like an unexpected movement caught out of the corner of his eye.

Grisha carried a small bundle on his back, all he owned in the world. He had decided against trying to return to his flat, surrounded almost constantly by Karakozov and others of the *Cheka*. What little he had there was not worth the risk. So Grisha set out toward the east. He gleaned snippets of information as he gathered a few necessities for his pilgrimage. Lenin was struggling mightily to survive, to maintain power, while "White" forces grew to the Northeast, the Far East, and the South.

Ephraim Wiedeman told Grisha, as he passed him a tiny sack of roasted rolls and dried beef, that the Whites had taken over Siberia. Where the Jewish baker garnered such facts puzzled Grisha, but it gave him the beginning of a plan.

If he was not a devoted Red, then perhaps he was a White. The two colors swam before his eyes as he passed the Bolshevik flag flapping in the wind, still cool in spite of the approach of the summer equinox.

Avoiding people as much as possible, Grisha attached himself to the Volga River and followed it southeast through Nizhny Novgorod, the birthplace of Alexey Maksimovich Peshkov, known to the Russians as Maxim Gorky. Grisha had read most of Gorky's social novels and plays, and of late, the writer had been aligning himself with the Soviet movement.

Grisha approached the town of Kazan, and from there he took the easterly branch of the Volga, called the Kama, to Molotov. Early summer remained cool here in the heights of the Ural Mountains, but the cleanness of the air and the distance from Leningrad invigorated his soul.

It was while he stayed in Molotov that Grisha heard the news about the former tsar. Nicholas and his family were being kept in Ekaterinburg, a relatively short distance from Molotov. A professor at the local university, where Grisha had been given temporary work as a typesetter, told him of the Romanovs.

"They lived in peace and relative freedom while in Tobolsk, but now they've been moved to Ekaterinburg. The Whites are near, and the Romanovs are being held as virtual prisoners, hardly allowed to see the light of day. That will be difficult for Nicholas. He always touted physical exercise and fresh air as essential to one's health and well-being." Professor Stimsky raked clean, soft fingers through his graying hair and sighed. "So hard to see it end like this."

"Is it ending, then?"

Stimsky peered over half-glasses at Grisha. "The Reds won't let him go, you can be sure of that. Not with the Whites so close. All the antigovernment forces need is a mascot, a champion to give focus to their cause, and that won't be allowed. No, Nicholas is doomed."

"It is unfortunate that he and his family could not leave the country. Surely someone would take them in now." Grisha was surprised at himself, former revolutionary, anti-tsarist, political activist. Now that he had admitted his aversion to what he had been, compassion rose up inside him. He could not quell it, nor did he try. After all, Nicholas Romanov was a man like himself. He had dedicated himself to defending his borders, to sustaining the Romanov Dynasty, but he had failed on both accounts. His misfortune was that he still represented the past, something the Reds sought to destroy utterly.

The professor eyed Grisha. He spoke as he straightened the papers on his desk. "I am going down to Ekaterinburg on university business next week. Would you be interested in accompanying me? I have found it is not wise to travel alone these days, and company is always welcome to me."

"I will consider it," answered Grisha.

So it was he found himself in the town of Ekaterinburg, staring curiously at the walls surrounding the yellow house—the old Ipatiev House—where the Romanovs were imprisoned. Villagers stopped to stare on their way to the town square and back, but the brick walls were high and the guard was tight.

As he passed the Ipatiev place on the second day of his visit to Ekaterinburg, Grisha stared up at the windows on the second floor. A slight movement caught his eye, the whisper of a curtain against the glass. It was portentous, that small movement of white, like a surrender to the inevitable. That day, July 16, 1918, Grisha could not shake the ominous dread that fell on him as he walked in the shadow of the Ipatiev House. He and Professor Stimsky planned to return to Molotov the next morning, so Grisha determined to put the plight of Nicholas and Alexandra out of his mind. He was not successful.

Kolya stood at attention at the back of the meeting hall in Karassan. Beside him stood his father Heinrich, his brother-in-law Johann, and Abram Reimer.

Even though he and his father had discussed the Mennonite pacifist stance and the great price which had been paid in blood to maintain that standard, Kolya could not help the excitement that coursed through his veins at this time. He was no longer a child, but a young man.

Dietrich Kesselman marched to the front of the hall, his knee-high black boots carving a hollow tone from the floor-boards. His smart German uniform fit closely to his well-defined body, his deep blue eyes and trimmed mustache the only warm features on his chiseled face.

"My friends," Kesselman began in his clipped German, "we are gathered here tonight to make a decision." He smiled then. It was obvious that the decision had already been made in his mind. "You Germans of the Crimean Peninsula have been treated shamefully, and there are still many about who seek to harm you and rob you of what is rightfully yours."

"You speak the truth," shouted a German Catholic landowner from Schoental, a settlement north and west across the rail line from Karassan.

Kesselman continued to smile. "Your fellow Germans on the mainland have already banded together to protect them-selves and their interests by forming a Self-Defense Unit. The *Selbstschutz* is armed, and dedicated to protecting the vil-lages. It is time you followed suit. The German army is here to help, but you must decide."

"But why must we take up arms?" asked a Mennonite farmer from Boranger. "Can we not negotiate with the pow-ers that be to regain what is ours? Surely justice will be done. I do not want blood on my hands."

Several voices rose in loud disagreement. "If we don't defend ourselves, there will still be blood on our hands, but it will be our own," said one.

"I agree," said another. "How do you intend to negotiate with anarchists and bandits? Have you not heard of Machno? He has come from the devil himself and knows no negotiation besides bullets and bayonets. You cannot stand against such as Machno without weapons."

Heinrich spoke. "We need to go about this decision making process in an intelligent and organized manner. We need to research the—"

He was sharply interrupted by a short, stout man, whose face had grown red with rage. "We have no time for that," he spat out. "Everything is happening too quickly. You may research all you want, but I aim to protect my family. And I do not wish to be judged for it. We must make the decision."

The hall erupted with opinions and declarations. Kolya stood wide-eyed through it all, staring at the fear and anger tumbling from the words and gestures of those assembled. He glanced at his father and winced at the pain written on that once serene face. There were more and more lines on that face every day, and the booming voice and jovial confidence gradually ebbed away as from a slowly bleeding wound.

And so the Self-Defense Corp spread from the mainland to the Crimea. It was not by unanimous decision or even by majority, but by urgency, or so an aggressive minority claimed.

Back home at Succoth, Nicholai faced Heinrich. "Father, what will happen to us at Succoth if we do not defend ourselves? Is it wrong to stand between evil and your family, those who rely on you for safety? Does God expect us to stand by and let bandits and robbers take everything we have away from us? Perhaps even our lives?"

Heinrich turned eyes filled with pain on his son. "I only know what I must do." He gathered together all the firearms on the estate, at least all he knew of, and delivered them to the local *zemstvo* office. "That I might not be tempted," was all the explanation he gave.

Grisha awoke in a cold sweat from a short and troubled sleep. Rising quietly from his pallet, he let himself outside for a bit of fresh evening air. Distant timber wolves howled to the sliver of moon that peered dimly down through the lush leaves of the poplar trees, while local dogs barked their replies. Here and there a voice called out, a door banged, but most of the town lay in slumber.

He walked in the shadows on the side of the main road, knowing where his feet led him without ever intentionally plotting his course. He did not know why his heart burned so for Nicholas and Alexandra, except that he feared their successors would do no better in ruling vast Mother Russia than they had done.

He felt an entire way of life slipping away in silent screams, leaving nothing but death in its wake. It was the same old story of humankind that had been repeated countless times since creation, a story of dissatisfaction and greed, and the final selling of the soul for power. It had happened before, and it would happen again. He felt, but did not know, that it was happening again this very night.

As he approached the old yellow house behind the high walls, as he knew he would, he heard the rumbling of an engine, and ducked further into the shadows as a truck with a box trailer passed him. To his surprise, it stopped at the gate of the Ipatiev House and waited as a scrawny old man emerged from within and spoke to the driver. After a short consultation and routine check of paperwork, the gates were opened and the vehicle was admitted.

Curiosity overcame Grisha and he slunk through the trees to stand directly at the rear wall of the enclosure. The poplars grew close to the fence, their roots pushing and breaking some of the foundation stones, their branches draping nonchalantly over the top to hang uninvited into the Ipatiev garden. *Ah, to be a tree,* thought Grisha. Perhaps to be up in a tree would also serve the purpose. Like Zaccheus. That little fellow had certainly profited from his climb.

Grisha chuckled softly to himself as he grabbed a firm branch and walked his feet up the side of the trunk. He hadn't done anything like this in years, his muscles attested to it, but he continued his efforts until he was able to reach the top of the wall. He sighed at what he saw. Even in the darkness, he could see a forgotten garden, overrun by weeds and dead produce never harvested. The silhouetted scene matched the strange apprehension that had brought him here.

Searching for a place to descend, he glimpsed light from the corner of his eye. He glanced up and saw the wavering flame of a candle appear in an upstairs room. He strengthened his resolve and dropped his body as quietly as possible to the ground. He was in. *I'm as bad as Paul Gregorovich,* he thought, *diving in without considering an escape route.* But he could no more stop himself from entering the courtyard than could the dogs refrain from barking at their ancestral brothers in the wooded hills beyond Ekaterinburg.

The light of the candle seemed to dim in the upstairs rooms and fade away without completely dying. There was movement within, Grisha was sure, and the waiting truck gave evidence of another post-royal transfer. How would he be able to follow and discover where they were being taken?

As he stopped to plan his next move, he heard a bit of a ruckus from the front of the house, where the truck was parked. He inched forward to peek around the corner and observed several dark figures climb from the truck, rifles in hand, and enter the house. It was obvious that the Bolshevik faction stationed here were determined that this night's transfer remain unknown. To Grisha, ever the reporter, that meant someone needed to spread the word.

Grisha crouched in the shelter of the house pondering his story, when a sudden volley of gunfire jerked him to his feet and set him running back toward the wall at the rear of the garden. He stopped and turned in dismay. The firing came from inside the house, from the basement, and it was still going on, round after round, accompanied by screams of utter terror and agony. "No!" he shouted without thinking. "No!" But even in that moment, he knew that no one heard him, and that the sounds within the house were too muffled to be heard beyond the Ipatiev yard.

He collapsed, sobbing, behind sweet-scented shrubs, and held his large hands over his ears to stop the nightmare, but he could not shut it out. He would never, as long as he lived, be able to erase from his memory the unearthly screams of that night.

It took Grisha several minutes to realize the silence. It lasted only a short time, after which lumbering feet began to ascend the stairs and move out of the door. Watching again from his vantage point beside the house, Grisha observed in horror as a small group of dark silhouettes emerged through the front door, dragging large sacks. These were unceremoniously dumped onto the back of the truck. With growls and cold laughter, the murderers scrambled into the vehicle and roared out of the enclosure and into the darkness.

The skeletal old guard stood watching them, the gleam of a hand torch lighting his face. Grisha scrutinized him as he turned to reenter the house. The small, balding head shook back and forth as he apparently considered the slaughter which had occurred. His beady eyes glittered in the torchlight. His toothless mouth collapsed, bringing his jutting chin close to his hawk nose. "Too bad," he said in the tone of voice of one who had missed a train. "Too bad." And he disappeared inside, rubbing at the dark splotches on his tunic and humming a tuneless song.

Grisha fell back behind the shrubbery and covered his face with his hands. He thought of the Romanov family: of Nicholas, who would in his moment of death take the blame for the murder of his family. Of Alexandra, ever blaming herself for passing on the dreaded hemophilia to her Alexsei. She would wander through eternity wailing for her beloved Nicky and her children. Of the Grand Duchesses Maria, Tatiana, Olga, and Anastasia. And of Grand Duke Alexis, who in other circumstances would have been Tsar of all the Russias.

That time had never come for him, nor would it come for any more like him. That time was gone, as imperfect as it had been, relegated to the pages of history, overtaken ruthlessly by modern thoughts and ways. And Grisha was not convinced that the modern would be better, only different. After a long time, he raised himself up, totally drained of energy, and walked out the front gates and down the street. He would not return to Molotov, he decided. His soul was wounded and bleeding, and he needed to move on somewhere, anywhere.

Lenin had moved his headquarters to Moscow, as the Germans came threateningly close to Leningrad. In spite of the name change from Petrograd to Leningrad, Lenin found it more expedient to continue his plan from the new capital. Wherever he chose to establish himself, he was surrounded by unrest and revolution. The storm had not abated but had increased its fury.

Boris Kuryakin and his platoon of Red Army soldiers continued their equalizing campaign in the surrounding area of

Moscow. After years as a reporter, Paul Gregorovich felt isolated from the center of the action. His unit was told only what Kuryakin deemed necessary. As true soldiers, they were expected to obey without questioning, an expectation which was quickly enforced through the example of punishment of those who did not comply. None of the witnesses ever wished to undergo similar treatment.

It was the end of August when Kuryakin's troops were informed of the news: Lenin had been shot and wounded. The aggressor was a social revolutionary by the name of Dora Kaplan, who was opposed to the separate peace with Germany. The day following the attempt on Lenin's life, the chief of the secret police was also gunned down. The chief died, Lenin lived, and an iron hand descended upon the revolutionaries.

Paul Gregorovich Tekanin and his fellow soldiers were directed into the capital city to witness the execution of hundreds of suspected conspirators. The same happened in Leningrad, with a total of almost one thousand executions in the two major centers. Paul felt physically ill. He heard in his soul the groan of a nation in the throes of death.

It was several days before Grisha heard the official report of the demise of Nicholas Alexandrovich Romanov. With great secrecy, the Bolshevik government decided to feed the curious public the following news: *Ex-tsar shot at Ekaterinburg! Death of Nicholas Romanov!* It went on to state that only Nicholas had been killed, and that the family was safe under Bolshevik protection.

For the time being, as far as the Russian populace was concerned, Nicholas had been removed from the scene, and survival in a violent and poverty-stricken society claimed all their energies.

"It's so sad about the tsar," said Katarina as she and Maria sat in the olive grove at Succoth. "I imagine he did his best, and his family must be terrified without him."

"Obviously his best was not sufficient," responded her sister. "I find it difficult to grieve for someone I did not know."

"Oh but Mika, don't you ever imagine how they would feel, pulled from their life of opulence and prestige to a prison somewhere in a mountain village?"

Maria wrestled with her emotions. As usual, she was unable to express her true feelings. "No, actually. We each must live our lives. My wondering can never solve anyone else's problems."

Katarina remained silent for a time as they sipped their lemonade in the welcome cool of the orchard. She experienced great sadness for others and often put herself in their place, but Mika was not like her. Not at all. She was beautiful and sociable and adept, but her heart was a mystery to Katya. She turned to Mika. "You and Dietrich seem to enjoy each other's company," she said tentatively. Although Marie's temper had cooled in the last months, she was still somewhat unpredictable. Katarina had no wish to anger her.

Maria studied her with narrowed eyes. Then she took another sip of lemonade and stared off into the trees. "We are similar, Dietrich and I. Impulsive, impetuous, restless. He understands me."

Katarina pondered her sister's words without malice. "He is a pleasant person, I will admit, and I'm happy for you. Finding a true friend is a wonderful gift." She paused as she formulated her words. "Have you considered what will happen when he moves on? He is sure to go eventually, being a military man."

Mika frowned. "I know. I try not to think about it. When the time comes, I will know what to do."

Her answer gave Katya chills. Where would her sister's impulsiveness lead her? Would she ever be content and happy in her life? Katarina sighed and converted her fears into prayers. Only God could take care of Mika, she decided. Only he knew her future.

Chapter 18

Maria and Dietrich walked silently along one of the paths that led through the apple orchard. The profusion of leaves sheltered them from the direct heat of the sun, and the sweet smell of fruit lingered in the air around them.

Dietrich took her hand and she did not pull it away. "I have never seen such a place as this." He spoke softly so as not to disturb the serene beauty. "It allows me to imagine that I am part of a story that will never end."

"My, but you are poetic today," laughed Mika.

Stopping abruptly, he turned her to face him. "Don't you feel it? This paradise works magic on a man's soul."

"Perhaps, if it is solitude you are seeking. On the other hand, if you crave adventure, even paradise can be confining."

He studied her, his eyes touching her hair, her arched eyebrows, her unsmiling mouth. "Sometimes adventure does not satisfy any more than solitude," he said, his brows lowering over his warm blue eyes. "You have not seen much of life yet, my dear."

"Not much, but enough," she said, and turned away to continue down the path. He stared after her, trying to see into her thoughts.

"Tell me, then," he said, moving beside her, shortening his steps to match hers. "What is it that keeps you so distant from everyone. I thought we understood each other, but I wonder if we do."

Maria stopped beneath a tree, reached up and pulled off an apple. Inspecting it closely she said, "There's not much to tell. I've never fit in with the Mennonite lifestyle. I cannot force myself to be calm and quiet and content, because I am not. I lived for a time in the Molotschna Colony, and then. . . ." she paused, swallowed, and then looked defiantly up at her companion. "Then I left with a friend, at least I thought he was a friend. He turned out to be a heartless beast and I returned alone, except for my reputation, which has been forever tainted."

If Maria expected Dietrich to be shaken by her revelation, she was surprised. "So you learned a lesson. Choose your friends more wisely from now on."

She glanced quizzically at him. He returned her a small smile and drew her hand through his arm. They continued to walk. "Do not think that I am that easily offended, my dear. I have seen much in my life, and have experienced plenty as well. I do not judge anyone. But I have learned to admire courage and pluck, and these characteristics you have in abundance." He smiled down at her, watching her emotions flit through her eyes.

"Mika," he interrupted her thoughts, "I . . . we need to discuss the future." He felt her tense but did not stop. "The war in Europe is not going as we had planned. Germany is losing ground against the Allies. You must realize that if we should lose the war, the Treaty of Brest-Litovsk will be considered null and void. That is the treaty under which we occupy South Russia."

Maria's fingers around the apple were white. Her mouth was drawn in a firm line, and she remained silent.

Dietrich continued. "If we should lose the war, our army will be recalled and I shall leave with them, go back to Germany. I cannot stay here. And so I. . . ."

Mika interrupted him. "And so you wish to break off our

relationship, because it has no future. Just tell me, Herr Kesselman. I am a grown woman, I can bear it." Bright red spots appeared on her cheeks in spite of her determination to remain calm. "I have been rejected before."

"Mariechen, hush. Let me finish." His use of the affectionate form of her name stopped her, especially spoken in such a stern tone of voice, but she refused to be cowed. Her chin lifted in self-defense.

Sighing, Dietrich rubbed a hand over his face and searched the canopy of leaves as he phrased his thoughts. "Marie, when I leave, I want you to come with me. Do you understand? I do not wish to leave you—ever." He said this last as if it surprised even him. With hope in his face, he turned back to her and searched her eyes which were staring incredulously at him.

Totally unlike herself, Maria stammered. Finally, she shut her mouth, closed her eyes and gathered her senses. He watched in hopeful fear, holding her free hand so tightly she almost winced. She opened her eyes and gazed at his face, which had become so dear to her in spite of her resolve to hold herself aloof. "You said *ever*. Do you mean *ever*, or until you tire of me?"

"Oh, my little beauty, you have been badly hurt. No one understands that, do they? They only consider how they have been betrayed by your actions. Am I correct?"

"How do you know these things?"

"How do I know?" His short laugh held a touch of bitterness. "You and I react to things in similar ways. I recognize in you what I have experienced. Two such as we can surely keep good company. Besides," he said with a bemused smile, "I cannot erase you from my mind. I would go mad if I had to leave you." He shook his head. "Do you realize that you are the only woman who has ever had such an effect on me?"

Mika listened, amazed, and her heart warmed within her.

Could she trust this man? She wanted to, but memories stood always before her, blocking the way.

"If I should agree, to come with you, that is, it would break my family's hearts. I have already hurt them deeply by my past actions. It is against all their beliefs to live together with someone outside of marriage. I am torn between what I want to do and what I should do."

"I don't see the problem. We make a little visit to the priest in Karassan . . . " seeing her eyes widen, he added, ". . . or to one of your ministers, and we say our vows. Surely they could not object if we were married."

She continued to stare at him, eyes wide with wonder, with hope, with light shining from a soul long trapped behind self-built defenses. Turning the apple thoughtfully in her hands, polishing it with her fingers, she began to smile. "*Ever?*"

"Ever."

They moved into a quiet embrace while within them the walls crumbled and trust grew.

Many miles to the east and a good distance north, Grisha sat down at the side of the road to rest. He had walked for several weeks, stopping from time to time to assist some farmer in exchange for a decent meal and a place to sleep. It had been as long since he had a plan. He cared not where he went. *I've lost Sergei,* he mused, his emotions dead within him, *and now Paul is gone as well. I do not even know if he lives. There is no one who needs me, and no cause that is worthy of my dedication.*

The heaviness of his heart robbed him even of a healthy fear which would have frightened most others traveling alone on the dangerous thoroughfares of a country in the midst of chaos. He walked when he wanted, in disregard of those he passed. It was a wonder he continued on at all, but something unknown kept him moving day after day, a quiet tug somewhere in the depths of his subconscious.

One warm day at the end of summer, a day so grand that even Grisha had trouble feeling gloomy, he stumbled upon a cluster of small huts and a rickety Orthodox church near a small unknown hamlet. He was weary and thirsty, so he decided to enter the compound and request a drink. Approaching the largest of the dwellings, which was not very large at all, he reached up a hand to knock at the door. It opened to him as if those inside had expected his coming.

"Good day to you, Pilgrim," smiled a young, gray-cloaked individual from the dark doorway. "Come join us in our repast this glorious day. We are more than glad to share with you." Stepping back, the young man motioned Grisha inside.

Blinking to accustom his eyes to the dimness, Grisha observed a long, low table, around which were seated eight men, mostly young, but two older, all dressed in the same gray, hooded cloaks. One of the two elders appeared well advanced in years, but his eyes still sparkled brightly and his toothless mouth spread in a warm but tired smile. "Welcome!" he lisped in a thin voice. "Make our vithitor welcome, brotherth."

They all rose of one accord—except the old man—and bowed to him. Moving together, they made room for him on the bench on one side of the table. Grisha dropped his small sack in the corner by the door and sank wearily onto the seat.

"Thank you for your graciousness," he said. "I only came for a drink of water, but I will not turn down an offer of food if you have extra."

"We alwayth haf enough," said the elder. "A meal for a thtory."

Grisha stared questioningly at the speaker. "A story?"

"Oh yeth. We require a thtory. Then you may thtay ath long ath you wish."

"A story. Hmm." Grisha wondered no more at the strange gathering. He was well aware that he had come upon one of the many tiny monasteries that dotted the steppes. Each had its own unique slant on wisdom and spirituality, and none were accountable to a higher body, or at least, none were required to report. No doubt these young novitiates, and probably the older monks too, were starved for news and entertainment, secluded here as they were. They would gladly share food for news. And Grisha certainly had many stories. How long did he wish to stay? He would take his stories back to the time of Sergei. They would love Sergei as he had. They would grieve contentedly in the sad tale.

It was a peaceful world that Grisha had discovered, quite by accident, he thought. Quiet company, adequate sustenance, daily chores, and his stories. Yes, he had many of them, and when he ran out, he could as easily create more.

Katarina shared a last embrace with Cornelia Reimer as the older woman prepared to climb into the carriage that would take her and her husband and the Konrads back to Alexanderkrone.

"Heinrich," said Theodore Konrad for the tenth time at least, "I cannot thank you enough for giving us shelter and a sense of belonging these last months. You are a good man, Hildebrandt. God will reward you."

Heinrich patted him gently on the shoulder. "It has been a pleasure, Theodore." He raised his voice, "and you too, Katie." He turned to Abram and engulfed his dear friend in a bear hug. No words were necessary between the two. Their eyes spoke their love, their encouragement.

Mika bade them warm farewells, and Nicholai and Anna did the same, sorrow on their young faces as they considered yet another separation. Johann shook hands all around. "We will miss you all more than you can imagine. We have worked well together as a family. Our prayers go with you."

"*Ja.*" Theodore nodded. "We too will pray for you here. Thank God for the peace he has restored to us through our German brothers. Please give my regards to Kesselman and wish him well for me. And thank God also for friends like Abram and Nela who open their home to us when we return to the colony. I will hope our friendship will stand the test." His eyes smiled, but emotions ranging from grief to hope passed over his lined face.

"Come, friend," said Abram. "You have nothing to fear on that account. But we must go now or we will not meet our train."

The Hildebrandt family stood arm in arm as they watched the carriage clatter away over the cobblestones. Parasols sheltered the two women from the summer sun, but it would be a long, hot ride.

As the group returned to the house, Heinrich, Johann, and Nicholai lagged behind. "The *Selbstschutz* is gearing up," Heinrich was saying. "They have been holding rallies and drills in Spat and Simferopol and Feodosia. Even in Karassan men are being badgered into joining the cause of self-defense. Instead of feeling guilty for going against our beliefs, we are made to feel that way for not taking part." He sighed heavily, his arm around Kolya's shoulders.

The boy was silent, but Johann said, "We cannot simply ignore the issue, but we can take our own stand in a more visible way." He clasped his hands behind his back as he spoke, an unconscious sign of deference to his father-in-law. "There are many travelers hereabouts these days, and I doubt their numbers will be declining any time soon. I propose that we set up an infirmary here at Succoth."

Heinrich gave him a knowing look. "This is Katarina's brainchild, is it not?"

Johann smiled in affirmation. "But I agree with her completely."

Heinrich had certainly come to trust this new son of his, but he was not about to jump into anything without asking the pertinent questions. "And you would not hesitate to contaminate our family with the many diseases that plague these travelers?"

"Please allow me to present my plan," said Johann with more confidence. "We could use one wing of the ground floor and shut it off from the rest of the house. We would take careful precautions to maintain cleanliness. Succoth is a large house, Father. How can we sit by while others are in need? Perhaps someday we will be the ones in need. And I have basic training which I can teach the others."

"Oh, I agree with you, son. I too have been wondering how we could make a difference, now that the *Forstei* has been shut down and unrest continues to plague the country. Let's go to the library and draw up some more detailed plans."

Heinrich and Johann walked off with determination in their step while Nicholai wandered in the direction of the barns, deep in thought.

"Susannah!" Gerhard's voice was quietly urgent as he summoned his wife from her duties in the women's residence at Bethany Home. Peter trailed behind, holding fast to her hand.

"What is it?" She knew Gerhard well enough to realize that his tone of voice meant there was trouble afoot.

"Keep Peter with you and stay here in the women's area. There are bandits at the gate again. I will try to pay them off or bribe them some way so they don't harass the patients, but I don't want to worry about you showing up in the middle of it." He kept her gaze for a moment. "Promise me you will stay here, love."

Susannah nodded. "I promise. And I will be praying. Please be careful, Gerhard. These men are not reasonable. Do not take any unnecessary chances with them." He squeezed her hand and hurried away. "Lord God, protect him," she prayed aloud. "Protect us all."

"Protect us all," mimicked Peter.

With false calm, Susannah and Peter made their rounds, stopping at each bedside or rolling chair to speak briefly with the patients, many of whom seemed completely unaware of their presence. As usual, Peter tarried longer with Frieda Lohrenz, patting her hand and straightening her knee blanket as he had so often seen Susannah do. His strangely withdrawn manner of showing care caused Susannah to forget momentarily the danger at the doors of the Home. *God is good*, she reminded herself. *We are not alone. Everything is under his control and nothing can touch us that does not first pass him.* "Lord, strengthen my faith and my courage," she prayed.

Meanwhile, Gerhard fought to keep his wits about him. He had met the bandits at the gate before they broke in. "What is it you want, men?" he asked. "This is a mental hospital."

"Open up and we not break doors." The self-acclaimed leader bellowed like a hungry bear. He was not a large man, but tough and weathered. As Gerhard pulled back the gate, the man shoved his way in, pushing Gerhard against the wrought-iron railings. "Food." He turned belligerently on Gerhard. "Give us your food." The man's wavy hair was unkempt, although the uniform he wore looked in decent shape. Bushy eyebrows lowered in a menacing line over deep-set eyes. His dirty face showed signs that he was usually clean-shaven except for a moderate handlebar mustache. "Now, Fool."

Gerhard had not much choice but to comply, and moved quickly to the storeroom. He was thankful that the nurses in the main building had been able to move any patients away from the kitchen area. He had guessed the bandits would demand food first. He unlocked the door of the pantry and stepped aside for the men to enter. He had no desire to be taken by surprise and locked into the storage room.

As the bandit leader passed him, he stopped and lifted his chin arrogantly. "You know who I am?" he asked, tugging importantly at the lapels of his coat.

Gerhard paled and felt weak in the knees, but Susannah's prayers held him up and gave him voice. "I can't say that I do, but if you are desperately hungry, I will not deny you food."

"I introduce myself. I am Machno." The man made a greatly exaggerated bow before Gerhard, his eyes mocking, inviting defiance. "Nestor Ivanovich Machno. You are wise to give so generous, because if you refuse, I crush you like bug." He stamped his boot on the concrete floor and mercilessly squashed an imaginary pest, his eyes cold as a Siberian north wind. Then he laughed uproariously at his intimidation and joined his companions in pulling food off the shelves of the neatly organized pantry.

They continued to eat, drop, step on, and destroy everything edible until the room was a shambles. Gerhard tried not to look, tried not to imagine what they would do next. All he could do was send many prayers to the Father.

The vandalism lasted an hour, maybe less, and then the group settled down outside on the grass for a nap. They were obviously unafraid of being bothered by anyone. Gerhard seethed inside, but knew he would sacrifice his life if he antagonized them at all. He had never seen Machno, but he had heard enough stories to send fear through his being at the mention of the name. *Forgive me, Lord, if I have failed to be brave,* he prayed silently, *but I must protect my charges. Please make these men leave soon, and give us strength and wisdom to know what to do next.*

He gave the bandits time to clear out of sight completely before he went for Susannah. She was almost ill with worry, having imagined him dead or hurt, but keeping her promise to wait. She flew at him and wrapped her arms tightly around him when she saw him unharmed. "How ever did you manage to come away unscathed?" she asked incredulously. "I have heard of the exploits of these men, even though you have tried to keep the information from me, and I know that they are without heart or soul. Did they threaten you?"

Gerhard sighed in frustration. "No, my dear, they did not. I gave them no reason to. I simply played the part of a coward and opened the pantry for them. There will be little food for patients or staff until we can replenish it."

"Gerhard Warkentin. You are not nor will you ever be a coward. You are wise enough to know when to stand and when to give over. Thank goodness for that, or you would not be here now to help us set things to rights. I love you, Gerhard, and I think you are the bravest man I have ever met. The cowards are those who must threaten and demand with violence and total selfishness."

"Total selfishness," repeated Peter, who stood as always like a shadow behind her. "Gerhard Warkentin. Gerhard Warkentin." He shuffled over to Mrs. Lohrenz and patted her shoulder, then returned to his Susannah. She and Gerhard broke into relieved chuckles at his unselfconscious antics. "Peter, you are a blessing from God," she said as she ruffled his hair.

"Blessing from God," he said, and crossed his arms across his chest as Gerhard had done moments earlier.

"Come, my dears, and we will see if we can begin to clean things up." Gerhard led the way back to the pantry, but even though his face remained relieved, his spirit boiled up inside him. This could not continue. Bethany Home was no longer safe from the anarchists, even if the Germans still occupied the territory. He had to develop a plan.

Once Katya heard that her father had approved of their plan to set up an infirmary at Succoth, she wasted no time in implementing it. They chose to seal off the wing with laundry facilities and a view of the kitchen gardens. The double wide French doors into that particular wing were locked and covered over with heavy draperies, access available through a side entrance near the garden door. The men were employed in bringing in beds while the women scrubbed walls and floors. It was not long before the wing resembled a hospital, and Katarina wondered why they had not considered this sooner.

"Because it was not necessary," Mika stated. "One does not want an infirmary in one's house unless there is need for it." But in spite of her curt words, Mika rolled up her sleeves and worked with the rest of them. Katarina was thankful for her help, and the lighthearted chatter that they indulged in as they worked was refreshing to Katya's spirit.

Johann did his best to teach his new "recruits" as he had done at Schwarzwald Camp, but they were somewhat more headstrong than his men had been. Maria was forever suggesting more efficient ways of dealing with certain problems, and Katarina kept adding compassion to his treatment schedules. "This is all well and good," he muttered to himself one afternoon after a particularly frustrating training lesson, "but I am supposed to be the teacher. I receive too little respect."

"What are you mumbling about, brother?" asked Mika impertinently. "That you should show your trainees more respect?"

Johann frowned momentarily, then threw his hands in the air and laughed. "Whatever you say, nurse." At her warm smile, the frustration melted away. "I appreciate your help, Marie. When Katya sets her heart on something, she does not give up until it's done."

"I know that. She sets her heart, I set my mind. Together we're invincible."

Johann smiled to see the camaraderie that had grown up between the sisters of late. It warmed his heart and gave him the resolve to put his own heart into the project. Today he would post a sign at the main road inviting travelers in for rest or treatment. Most wandered through anyway, but the sign was one of the women's wishes, and he would comply.

Autumn painted summer bronze and the leaves began to fall. The whisper of change was in the air, and it did not entirely refer to the weather. Rumor was that the Kaiser's armies were on the verge of mutiny. Dietrich, well aware of the implications of Germany's failure, worked almost feverishly to whip the *Selbstschutz* participants into shape. He had hoped to give them adequate training in offensive strategies, of which he observed they had absolutely no inkling, but had to compromise some of his plans as the self-defense units insisted that their role was strictly defensive.

Word came by way of a rider from Karassan on the tenth of November. The tall young man dismounted before his horse had come to a stop and ran up the steps two at a time. Pounding on the front entrance doors, he demanded a hearing. Heinrich reached the door first, flanked by Johann and Dietrich. The reporter wasted no time in the telling: "Kaiser Wilhelm of Germany abdicated the throne yesterday and fled the country. Tomorrow morning, November 11, Germany will sign the armistice to end the Great War." Taking a breath, he glanced disapprovingly at Dietrich in his smart German uniform. "The German army will begin withdrawal immediately." Mika stood behind Dietrich, her hand at her throat, eyes stricken.

The young man tipped his hat, raced down the stairs to his prancing horse and vaulted on without the aid of the stirrups.

The men in the entrance stood silent as the news filtered into their brains. The skirmish in the Balkans has spread around the world, and lasted more than four years. Russia herself had sacrificed nine million men to the ravenous appetite of the Great War, all while she herself gasped in the throes of a great inner struggle.

Chapter 19

 "Gerhard, what are we going to do?" Susannah lay beside her husband in the privacy of their rooms in the cottage behind the Home. An owl hooted in the darkness beyond the compound. "Every day we are in danger of the *Machnovitz* returning. They have depleted our food supply and stolen our medicines. They storm in and brazenly take away whatever they see. Even our linens are in short supply. How are we to survive this?"

Gerhard remained silent, but she knew he was not asleep.

She continued. "I know we cannot stop them from coming, but we must do something with the patients. They are too fragile to be subjected to this uncertainty. And nurses are not willing to work for us anymore. The load is too much for the few of us who remain."

Her husband sighed and turned his head to face her. "My dear, I am sorry that you have to live in such a time. You are an angel who deserves to live freely and contentedly, helping others. Instead, you are forced to think always of the danger and darkness around us."

"Don't be sorry for me. This is where God has placed me. Besides, I am a strong girl, I will survive. It's the patients I am concerned about."

Gerhard smiled at her. "I know you are strong and healthy, but the strain has been wearing on you. You seem much more tired than you used to be. By evening you are totally exhausted."

Now it was Susannah's turn to keep her silence. Her hand went to her belly, a protective gesture, but she did not tell her secret. Gerhard had enough to worry about without another life to consider. She would try to get adequate rest and avoid heavy lifting. The strain of fear would have to be dealt with day by day, hour by hour. When the time was right, she would tell him, but not yet. She prayed God that circumstances would improve.

"I am meeting with the board of directors and a representative from the Mennonite Conference tomorrow morning, God willing," Gerhard said, speaking to the ceiling again. He took Susannah's silence as weariness. "We will discuss the possibility of moving some of the residents back home, as many as possible. They can do no worse there at present, especially if we continue to lose nurses."

"And Peter will stay with us," Susannah said. "He is a great help to me."

Gerhard turned to her again. "I promised you that, my love," he said, "and I do not intend to renege on my word."

Susannah had a sudden idea. "If our residents return home, perhaps we could also leave. We would be welcome at my parents' home, and I believe the Molotschna is safer at present than our colony. What do you think, Gerhard?"

He raised his eyebrows and then frowned. "I suppose it is a possibility, but we have responsibilities here for as long as there are patients."

"I know, but at least it would be a plan."

"We're busier nursing White soldiers than pilgrims or vagrants." Johann stopped to scrub his hands at the basin near the door of the Succoth infirmary. "They are moving northward in droves to ward off the Reds."

Katya finished folding the sheet she held and stacked it with the rest in the linen closet. "I know. And the Germans move ahead of them. I'm glad Dietrich was able to delay his departure. I'm afraid Mika will go with him when he leaves."

"Do you think she will? This is not a vacation or a change of scenery. We may never see her again."

Katya clutched the next sheet tightly to her and fought off the tears. "I don't need reminding, Johann. I fear for her safety. And for her happiness."

"You don't think Dietrich would treat her well?"

"It's not that. I'm convinced he loves her, but his life will lead him away, and she will be left alone in a strange land. She cannot accompany him on his military duties."

Johann reached for a towel and proceeded to fold it. "We are indeed facing strange situations. The events since 1914 have been so surprising and unexpected that I cannot even imagine what will happen next."

"I suppose it's back to perspective then, isn't it?" Katarina determinedly reclaimed her serenity. "We are to do what the Lord asks us to do right now, leaving the rest to him."

"Then we need not worry, only continue to fold sheets and towels." Johann smiled at his wife who so often inspired him with her spiritual strength.

She returned his smile, but it faded quickly. "Well, I would agree, except that Anna has not been feeling well for a couple of days. If she should be taken ill, I would question our decision to set up an infirmary. We are inviting sickness, are we not?"

"Katarina." He spoke her name with authority. "Perspective."

Little Anna awoke the following morning feeling worse instead of better. Katya was immediately concerned, but determined not to alarm her sister. "Stay in bed today and rest. I'll call Dr. Johann and he will make sure you are all right."

Anna smiled at the mention of Johann and settled down while Katya went to fetch her husband. "She's burning up, Johann," she told him when he met her in the infirmary. "I don't know what it is."

"I'll be right with you, Katarina. I want to scrub and change my clothes before I see her. Check her neck and chest for rash."

A few minutes later, Johann climbed the stairs to Anna's room and tapped lightly at the door before entering. "Good morning, Anna." He approached her bed and put a hand to her forehead. Katya moved to the other side of the bed to give him room. "My, you are warm today. How do you feel?"

"Not very well," she said weakly. She sneezed and shaded her eyes. "My eyes hurt." "Mm hmm. Any rash?"

"Katya says there is a rash on my tummy, but it isn't itchy."

"Good. Very good. How would you like a little holiday? We'll pull the blinds and light a candle just for fun, and Cook will mix up some lemon and honey water for you to drink. Does that sound good?"

She smiled and closed her eyes. "Yes, thank you." Katya immediately set about darkening the room. Then Anna's eyes flew open and she cringed in pain. "Please, Katya, stay with me in case the bad people come again. Oh, my head hurts me so."

Katarina was at her side in an instant, smoothing her brow and crooning. "Shh. Be still, sweetheart. Of course I will stay, and no one is coming. Everything is quite peaceful right now."

The child relaxed then and Katya stared up at Johann with concern. He motioned her from the room. "I'll be right back, Anna. I want to discuss your holiday with Johann.

"What is it?" she demanded as she faced Johann in the hallway. "Please, not smallpox. Her eyes are sensitive to light, and the rash. . . ."

"Shh, Katie. I don't know for sure, but we will follow my suggestions and send for the doctor from Karassan. Right now it will do no good to work ourselves into a state. You have always been a calm nurse."

"All I know is my herbal remedies and what you've taught me; I've never dealt with smallpox. If Anna, if she—" Katarina stopped abruptly and closed her eyes to compose herself. He knew she prayed for self-control. Finally, with an expelled breath, she opened her eyes again and looked straight at her husband. "You are correct. I will not panic. Thank you, Johann. Will you send for the doctor then?"

"I will send Misha at once. If he knows who it is that needs him, he will come back as soon as humanly possible with Dr. Klippenstein."

"If the doctor isn't at home, make sure he checks at the hospital. Tell him it's on the east side of town right beside the small vineyard, near the windmill."

"Katie, I believe Misha knows the layout of Karassan. He will find the man we need."

He gave her a calming hug and proceeded down the stairs, looking back with a reassuring smile. Katya returned to Anna's room and lit a candle to cheer the dimness. She sang softly as she moved about the room, then settled down at the bedside and bathed Anna's hot face with a cool, wet cloth. Soon the child drifted into a quiet sleep. The candle flickered, reminding Katarina of the ephemeral quality of life, of the fact that there are no guarantees. *We must burn brightly while we have the opportunity,* she thought. *The only thing that is sure is this moment.*

Moscow was cold. Not the damp, devastating cold of Petrograd, but threatening, all encompassing frigidity. Thoughts of the coldness never left Paul's mind as he pounded and hammered at the rugged barracks he was helping to construct for the growing Red Guard. Trotsky knew exactly what he wanted for his army and was determined to work his plans out practically.

"I did not join the Red Army in order to pound nails," Paul said bravely to his companion Anatoly. "This is not soldier's work."

Anatoly nodded, sucking on the finger which had come between nail and hammer. He rubbed circulation into his bony arms and looked around carefully before he spoke. "I agree with you, Comrade, but what choice do we have?"

"And this cold. It's freezing my brain as well as my body."

"Again I ask you, what choice is there?"

Paul turned to look at his companion. "Perhaps we do have a choice. Not one we would discuss openly, but so far I have no chains on my ankles or wrists. We are not alone in this opinion, my friend."

Alarm registered on Anatoly's pale face, accentuating the dark circles around his eyes. "Be careful, Tekanin. You can trust no one. Perhaps not even me."

"Ha!" Paul laughed and slapped Anatoly on the back. "I can trust you. These days you can't expect anyone else to look out for you, so you'd better learn to trust yourself as well. Now, I will be careful, but I intend to listen around the others and see if there are enough of us who are of the same mind."

The skinny soldier glanced behind him with worried eyes. "You cannot mean revolt or rebel. You know as well as I do that such action would be met with death. Anything but compliance is unacceptable."

"Don't worry, I am hatching a plan. Perhaps we need not freeze to death in this accursed climate this winter."

Misha offered his news gravely. Dr. Klippenstein was over-whelmed with duties in and around Karassan. Soldiers, pil-grims, tramps, and ordinary citizens all seemed to be falling prey to influenza and the war related diseases: typhus, typhoid fever, dysentery, measles, and now lately, the dreaded smallpox. Cases were rare and isolated, but they were there. Even though a vaccine had been available for over a hundred years, the war had destroyed supply and access.

"He comes soon as he can," repeated Misha. "Little Anna, she is bad?"

Katya put her hand comfortingly on Misha's skinny arm. "She is resting comfortably, Misha, but her fever is too high. I cannot get it to break. I wish I knew what we were dealing with so we could treat it accordingly."

Misha shuffled his feet and looked miserably at the floor. "So sorry, Miss Katarina. I try but fail."

"You did not fail, Misha. You summoned the doctor. He will be here soon, I'm sure. Would you like to see Anna?" Katya knew Misha was as fond of the little blond girl as he was of her.

"Oh no." He looked up at her and shook his head vehe-mently. "No, she need sleep. We pray." He crossed himself, nodded to her and left the house.

"I must trust. Only trust." She mumbled the words as she ascended the stairs again to Anna's room. The added nursing time made the days busy for Katarina.

Mika continued working in the infirmary until her pretty hands were rough and cracking. She washed and boiled sheets and towels, scrubbed walls and beds, and mopped floors from morning until night. The maids were busy enough with their regular duties and the extra mouths to feed. "With Dietrich so often away, it gives me something to do," she said to Katya.

"When do you think he will head north again?" Katarina

asked her one afternoon as the two folded linens together.

Maria looked at her sister and then concentrated on her folding. Finally she spoke. "I'm not sure. It would not be practical to try to cross the country in the throes of winter. Perhaps he can postpone it until the spring. He must first make sure all the troops south of here and in the vicinity of the colonies are on their way."

"And he has been training the *Selbstschutz* members as well, has he not?"

Again, Mika stared at her for several moments before she answered. Her dark eyes sought trust, her porcelain features tight. "Yes. He feels responsible for them." She returned to her work. "He says they know nothing of strategy, although they show great courage and daring. So he does his best to explain the ways of war."

"The ways of war. I do not fault him, sister, because he is a good man who is going beyond his call of duty for the sake of others. But do you not find it incredible that our young men are being taught the ways of war? We have always been dedicated to peace. Our ancestors gave their lives for it."

"Perhaps they were wrong."

"No Mika, they were not wrong. They were living their lives according to the Scriptures. 'Thou shalt not kill' was for them a commandment to be obeyed. 'Vengeance is mine, I will repay, saith the Lord' were words they took to heart. They were willing to give up their lives in order to save their souls."

"Have we lost our souls then?"

A chill swept through the laundry room as the two girls stared into each other's eyes. "I hope not," whispered Katarina, stepping close to Maria and wrapping her in hug. "I sincerely hope not."

Mika clung to her sister for long moments before releasing her. "Sometimes I'm so confused, Katya. I love Dietrich, you know I do. He is, as you say, a good man. He treats me with respect as well as love. He also believes strongly in what he is doing, and I know that deep down I am bothered by it. But how else are we to stand against the evil? Can we merely wait while the ruthless enemy steals, violates, and kills? Do you know what the *Machnovitz* do to women? Does God expect us to accept this senseless treatment?"

Katya turned again to the work, shaking her head as she did so. She had no answers but what she knew in her heart was that God does not condone the taking of life. It was a truth that came from the root of her being. "We cannot play God. We cannot assume to know his mind. I am afraid we will be severely punished for this blatant act of disobedience, this straying from the truth we know." She pushed her wayward hair from her face. Bright red spots appeared on her cheeks as she spoke her heart. "I am afraid we have greatly overstepped our bounds."

Mika also shook her head. All the black and white seemed to blend into gray in her mind. "I'll scrub up and go check on Anna."

"Agnetha and Wilhelm have decided to be married immediately." Heinrich shared the news with Katya when he located her in the laundry room. "She cannot remain here with Anna ill and so much disease coming through the infirmary. She must think of little Philipp. And they do not think it is fitting for her to remain at Tomak when she is not married to him. So, that is that."

Katya smiled at her father. "Dear Papa, is your heart still broken, or has it begun to mend?"

Heinrich's head snapped up and he frowned at her. "What do you mean?"

She smiled indulgently and moved to offer a hug. "I am not blind, Papa. You care very much for Agnetha. She is special to all of us and we had her first."

His frown disappeared at her last comment and he chuck-led. "Yes, we had her first, but it was not to be. When I saw how Wilhelm was taken with her, I knew I must quell my feelings. After all, I am old enough to be her father."

"Yes, but the heart sometimes betrays our better judgment."

"Such a wise daughter I have." He patted her shoulder and seated himself at the worktable. "I believe I shall survive. The pain has subsided substantially. I have been praying that the Lord would grant me a broader perspective on my feelings for Agnetha. And I must admit that he is succeeding. I am happy for all of them. Both his children and hers need a second parent." He tried to read his daughter's eyes. "Perhaps you needed a mother too, but I did not find one for you."

"Everyone needs a mother. But as long as you are content to remain as you are, I prefer to remember Mama as your only love. It's comforting somehow." Quickly she covered the loophole she had created. "Of course, should you ever find someone whom you would want to marry, I'm sure we are all mature enough to accept it and to adapt."

Heinrich chuckled again. "Don't worry yourself, Katie. I am not seeking a wife." He quieted and his countenance became sober. "It's too late for that." Standing abruptly, he said, "The wedding will take place on Sunday afternoon at Tomak." He paused. "Katarina, you are doing an excellent work here. So many men have benefited from your care in the few short weeks since you and Johann and Mika set up this hospital. Bless you." He kissed her cheek and left to check on his other children.

Chapter 20

The next time the *Machnovitz* came, there was no chance to move patients to safer places. The bandits stormed the compound of Bethany Home, taking what little was left and threatening the patients. One of the intruders, a huge bear of a man with scraggly black beard and hair, towered over Frieda Lohrenz and shouted at her. She did not respond. Her bony hands picked viciously at her chair, at her clothing, at her hair. He gave her a slap that sent her to the floor, where she lay unmoving.

It was too much for Peter. Disregarding the bandit, Peter approached Mrs. Lohrenz's side and patted her back awkwardly. Still she did not move.

"Leave her, you idiot! She is nothing but a crazy old woman."

"Crazy old woman," mimicked Peter, still patting his friend's back.

"That's right, boy. She is worth nothing."

Susannah appeared on the scene at this last interchange of words. Stunned by what had happened, she ran to the woman.

"Well, here's a nice little girl," the burly man said with interest. "Come to Golitsyn."

Susannah spun toward him, the look on her face enough to frighten an army. "You will leave here at once," she shouted, her arm pointing in the direction of the door. "Get out now. You have done enough for one day."

From somewhere, Gerhard materialized beside her and put restraining hands on her rigid arms. Putting her behind him, he confronted Golitsyn. "Please excuse my wife. She is not herself lately. I have found some lunch for you and the others. It's in my office." He gestured politely for the man to precede him, which he did, casting a dark look behind him at Susannah.

She knelt beside the injured woman and, with Peter's help, lifted her into the rolling chair and moved her to her bed nearby. Susannah was shaking violently by now and the taste of bile choked her. She steeled herself to the fear, and bathed Frieda Lohrenz's pale face, revealing the still red hand imprint on her left cheek and the bruise on her forehead where she had fallen. Still the old woman did not respond. Her breathing was shallow and her pulse rapid but faint.

Susannah felt suddenly light-headed and leaned on the bed for support. Then Peter was at her side, patting her shoulder, holding the rolling chair behind her. She sank heavily into it and let her head fall back against the lean. Blurred spots appeared before her eyes and she concentrated on taking deep breaths and expelling them slowly. Gradually, she recovered enough to notice Peter. He turned to the bed, patted Frieda Lohrenz, then turned back to Susannah and patted her shoulder. Then back to the woman on the bed.

Susannah smiled in spite of the gravity of the situation. "Peter dear, let Mrs. Lohrenz sleep now. Please find Gerhard for me."

"Please find Gerhard," he repeated with vehemence, his hands clasping and unclasping. But he made no move to do so.

At that moment Gerhard entered the room and moved swiftly to Susannah's side. "They've gone. It's all right now." He knelt before her and they locked eyes. "Suse? Did he hurt you? What is it?" She tried to look away, but he brought her face back to his. "Suse?"

She grimaced and sighed. "I . . . I don't know what will happen to Frieda. I don't know if she'll endure this attack. And poor Peter is so distraught with it all."

"Peter is distraught because of you. Did that man hurt you before I came, or is this the breaking point for you?" He frowned and rammed his fist into his open palm. "I should never have kept you here this long, it's far too dangerous. I should have sent you, no, *taken* you home." He stared at her again, and she knew he read something more. "Okay, Susie, tell me all of it."

She blushed and instinctively folded her hands across her stomach. "Um, I didn't want to burden you when you already had so many things on your mind, but perhaps I was wrong." As she spoke, realization dawned gradually on her husband's face, and his look of worry and concern turned to wonder and then to amazement. Rambling now, Susannah continued to speak. "I should have told you sooner, but . . . I haven't been feeling all that bad, but . . . today, I guess the excitement was too much, and if Peter hadn't helped me into this chair, I would have fallen right onto the floor." She smiled apologetically.

"Oh Suse." Those were the only words he could manage in his state of surprise and joy. "Oh Suse." He pulled her to her feet and held her close, hardly breathing. Peter joined the embrace mechanically. "Oh Suse," repeated the boy, which set the two laughing till tears rolled down both of their faces. They laughed away the fear, the anger, the anxiety, and Peter laughed with them.

Susannah put both hands over her mouth and moved back to Frieda's side. "Her pulse is stronger, and she is beginning to show signs of coming to. Praise the Lord."

"Praise the Lord," said Peter.

"We must do something to pull ourselves out of the doldrums," exclaimed Katarina one evening after supper. "It's almost Christmas and we are all moving about in a fog."

Johann looked up from the newspaper. He realized that times were difficult and that this affected everyone, but he had seen worse, much worse. He had known the utter despair of being alone in a whirlwind of hate and destruction. He had experienced the helplessness of trying to provide for others when he himself was empty. Being at Succoth always calmed his spirit, even in the midst of change and uncertainty. Obviously, Katarina was not faring as well under the circumstances.

"What do you suggest, Katya?"

"Oh Johann, if I knew I would jump at it at once. We are all at sixes and sevens. Our hearts are as chilly as the weather. I receive comfort and encouragement from my Bible and from you, but some of the others. . . ." She paused for a moment, then looked at him, eyes alight, head cocked to one side. "Ha! Why did I not think of it sooner?"

Johann cleared his throat and tried to catch up with her train of thought. However, hers was speeding along the rails, while his could only chug. He was too tired to pursue it on his own. "All right, my bright star, what is your plan?"

"Simple, my husband. Bible studies. We haven't held them regularly since the war began." She smiled at him as if this were the most obvious plan in the world.

So began the biweekly studies of God's Word. They worked together at it, Katarina, Johann, and Heinrich, inviting any of the household staff who could be spared from their duties for an hour, as well as all employees of the estate. Patients and temporary residents were required to attend, if they were well enough. It was, Katarina explained, part of their treatment. Mika attended as well, somewhat withdrawn but willing.

Wilhelm and Agnetha attended one of the Bible studies the

week after their marriage. Their ceremony had been a small, practical affair, but neither of them seemed to mind. They were happy beyond words, two young adults with renewed purpose and joy. Both Wilhelm and Agnetha enjoyed the Bible study immensely, and said so. "Only one thing was missing, in my estimation," offered Agnetha. "Music."

"I didn't know you were so fond of music," said Katya with surprise.

"It seemed life was full enough here, and safe enough, and secure enough, that my inner music was sufficient, but I used to play the violin, you know. Unfortunately, I didn't bring my instrument along with me from Grossweide."

"Why not?"

Agnetha pursed her lips in deliberation, then said softly, "I had to sell it to buy food the week before Johann appeared at my door. I decided to hide my music away in my soul where no one could take it. At least I am alive to enjoy the memories."

"Sold it . . . to buy food. Oh, you poor woman." Katya wrapped compassionate arms around her friend, but after a few moments, Agnetha pulled back.

"Don't feel sorry for me. Wilhelm found out my secret as well and bought me another violin. It's not like my old one, all broken in, but I will make it so in time."

Katya answered her with another warm hug and a glad smile. "Would you play for us sometime? I do strum a bit on the guitar and Johann plays it too."

"Misha plays the mandolin," offered Nicholai, who had remained after the study to visit with the men.

"Really? That is fine." Agnetha beamed at the prospect of a string quartet, not caring what the instruments were.

"And Mika has a voice like a song bird when she decides to sing." Katarina held her sister close in her heart these days, wondering how long they would be together.

"Wonderful! Let's set a date." They decided to gather the following Tuesday evening in the parlor at Succoth. Katarina hoped Anna would be well enough to attend. She loved music, but was still confined to a darkened, quiet room. The doctor had still not come from Karassan and the fever had still not abated. Katarina worried for the health of her little sister.

Johann decided to drive out to Karassan to speak with Dr. Klippenstein himself, if he could locate him. He said good-bye to Katarina, hitched Sunny up to the small buggy, and climbed into it, well muffled and wrapped in blankets. The early winter was mild, but Katarina would not chance him catching a chill.

The light buggy whisked smoothly across the snow-dusted road, while the winter sun smiled down on the traveler and his horse. Johann began to whistle, and Sunny's ears twitched back and forth with interest. She was glad for a run this cool, clear day and covered the *versts* quickly. They stopped first at the hospital, but the good doctor was not there. "Gone to a tiny collection of huts between here and Chongrav to check on a possible outbreak of smallpox. We hope to keep that away from our town."

"Did he say when he would be back?"

"Depends what he finds, doesn't it?" The unconcerned nurse shrugged her muscular shoulders and turned away. Johann decided to stable Sunny for a few hours and find a warm place to wait. He chose the general store in the center of town next to the large Mennonite church. When he entered the door, he realized that he had walked in on a meeting. A group of about ten men were present, mostly in their twenties and thirties, their voices raised in anger. They quieted for a moment as Johann nodded a silent greeting.

"Is there a cup of coffee or tea available here?" he asked innocently. "I need a place to wait for the doctor."

"What's up? Your wife having a baby?"

Johann colored and shook his head. "Her little sister is ill and we need a professional opinion. All I have is my *Forstei* training."

"*Forstei* training," noted one of the men. "Which *Selbstschutz* unit are you in?"

"*Selbst*—I am not in any. I do not agree with taking up arms." He walked past them to the counter to inquire again after a cup of something hot to warm himself.

The voice assaulted him from behind. "What do you mean, you do not agree? Are you going to wait until the dirty Reds are upon you or bandits break into your home? Till they molest your wife or your mother? They do not come for tea, you know."

Johann turned slowly to face the speaker. He leaned against the counter to steady himself. Measuring his words carefully, he said, "I saw a lot of killing and suffering in the war, fellows. It did not solve anything. At least there I was trying to save lives. How can I agree with a group of men who are determined to send others to a Christless eternity with the help of a gun?"

One of the younger members growled as he stepped forward. "You make us out to be a bunch of murderers. We are simply going to be prepared to protect our own. As our name suggests, we are a *self-defense corp*." He stepped closer to Johann. "And when some scared sheep calls me a murderer, I am angry." He reached out and gave Johann a shove on the shoulder.

"George." The word was a reprimand from the first speaker. The angry young man whirled around and stuck his finger in the face of the older man. "Do not speak to me like you were my mother. George is no longer a child. George has a wife he is determined to protect and no one has the right to stop me." He stomped out of the store, leaving the remaining group

264

momentarily stunned. Johann guessed that the discussion he had walked in on had dealt with exactly that matter. There was a difference of opinion as to methods of self-defense, and Johann had been the scapegoat for the anger and the blame.

The first speaker eyed him skeptically. "You had better reconsider your decision, brother. There are men around who do not look kindly on those who refuse to join the ranks, or on those who think they are above the rest of us."

"I'm sorry if I gave that impression," Johann thought fast for words to say, "but I have been in on a good number of *Selbstschutz* meetings, and am no closer to agreeing than I was before. I cannot tell you how to respond to the threat of the Reds or the roving bands, but I must be accountable to God for my own decision. I cannot go against my conscience."

"Do not judge us."

"My decision is not judgment, although I believe we will all be held accountable. I can never, on the basis of Scripture, take another man's life for any reason."

"Even if he is going to take yours? Even if he takes your wife and children? It has happened, you know. The colonies are in chaos, especially Chortitza. Machno loots, vandalizes, rapes, and kills every day. Don't tell me you would stand by and allow him or his type to do so in your home."

Johann folded his arms across his chest to control his rapidly beating heart and glanced up at the ceiling to round up his fraying thoughts. Shaking his head, he answered, "I don't know what I would do in a situation like that. I'm sure I would feel like stopping the men at all costs, but the basic commandment is 'Thou shalt not kill.' I must abide by it and leave the rest to God, who is merciful."

"Merciful! I could tell you stories that would curl your hair, brother." The others murmured their agreement, but Johann held up both hands in a truce and spoke once more, just as Dr. Klippenstein entered the store. "I don't need to hear all the stories. I only need to obey." He nodded solemnly at the doctor and walked back out the door with him.

"I know you are tired, sir, but would you consider riding over to Succoth to look at my wife's little sister? She has suffered from a high fever, headache, and sensitive eyes for the past week. She also has a rash that has spread, and we are afraid it might be smallpox. There are also several questions we have about cases we have come across in our infirmary."

"I was on my way. Sorry it took so long, but with the smallpox scare, I've been extra busy. Influenza is bad this year too, all over the world, in fact. Quite an epidemic in some areas. It can be a real killer." He tied his horse to the back of the buggy and climbed up with Johann. "Caught you in the middle of a test of wits, I'd guess," he remarked as they rolled down main street and headed south.

"More a test of commitment," returned Johann. "I understand them, you know: it's human nature to protect yourself and your loved ones. But human nature never stops at that, does it? I've seen war, Doctor, and instinct for survival can be transformed into hateful retaliation in a moment. If we live by our nature, we would surely destroy our entire planet. Some of us must keep our heads, our convictions."

"Calm down, son," the middle-aged doctor said soothingly. "I agree with you. You and I, we are life savers, not life takers. It is in our new nature, am I correct? I'm afraid, though, that this is going to be a bumpy ride down the road of compromise. Be careful what you say to whom. The other side is not easily convinced. You see, our young Mennonite men are aware that their forebears sacrificed their lives for their convictions. They know they are violating one of the foremost principles of their faith, and it eats at them. And you should know that in spite of how it seems, those who follow the *Selbstschutz* are in the minority. There are still many—most—who do not wish to become involved."

"I admit it is somewhat of a comfort to know this. It does seem that all the Mennonite population has grabbed a gun with which to kill the enemy before it kills them. They do not wish to suffer for their faith."

"Yes. Although most of the villages and *volosts* in the colonies have decided to allow if not to encourage self-defense, there are four villages I know of that refuse to take up arms: Petershagen, Fishau, Rudnerweide, and Pastwa. They have decided to take a stand for peace."

Johann and Dr. Klippenstein arrived at Succoth in time for supper, but the doctor went upstairs immediately to see Anna. Katarina stood on the opposite side of the bed as he examined the girl. "Hmm," escaped his lips several times, but he did not comment further until he was done. Then he sat down in the chair beside Anna's bed and motioned for Katarina to be seated as well.

"Different case," he began. Seeing Katya tense, he hurried to calm her fears. "This is not smallpox," he said quickly. "It is a severe case of the measles. Many of the children in the area have come down with it, especially the Russians, because they often do not receive adequate nourishment."

"But Anna gets proper food. She's normally a healthy child." Anna reached out a fevered arm toward her sister. Katarina took it as a sign to remain calm. She smiled at Anna, then at the doctor. "What would cause such a severe case?"

"Well, I hate to admit it, but probably the close proximity to the infirmary. I know you all attempt to scrub before you come in here, but germs have many ways of spreading. It seems Anna is the most vulnerable at the present time."

"What can we do to break the fever? And her rash is a great discomfort."

"You have been doing many of the right things. Johann's training and your instinct have worked well together. I have brought along some salve for the rash, which should be applied several times a day, as long as it lasts. The fever will break soon; I've seen it like this before, and although it does take a toll on its victim, there are no long-lasting effects, outside of weariness."

Katarina relaxed visibly. Anna squeezed her hand and whispered, "See, sister, I will be fine. You're a good nurse." Katya smiled at her and thanked the doctor, who was already at the door. "I will take you to the infirmary," she said to him as she tucked the covers around Anna. "I'll be back shortly," she said, touching the end of the little girl's nose with her finger. "Try to sleep."

"We're shutting the gates to Bethany Home, Susannah." Gerhard entered his office where Susannah was straightening shelves after the last bandit visit. She turned to stare at him in disbelief as he sat behind his desk. "For now we are returning everyone to family. The few who cannot travel that far will be billeted in private homes in the Molotschna. For the time being, our colony is too dangerous."

"What about Mrs. Lohrenz? She's from the Crimea somewhere."

"She'll be staying with the Friesens at Fishau. All arranged. And Peter comes with us."

Susannah absentmindedly adjusted a framed certificate on the wall. "So we are going as well?"

"Of course. Home, just like you wanted."

"Gerhard, what is it? Are you angry with me? You know I'd rather stay here if things weren't so chaotic and dangerous. Please don't blame me for this."

Gerhard slammed his fist down on the desk and Susannah was at his side in an instant. "Gerhard, speak to me."

He looked up at her with angry eyes. "It's not you, love. It's the whole thing. I've failed to keep my end of the contract. I have given up and walked away from the residents."

"What are you talking about? The board didn't tell you that, did they? They better not, unless they themselves are willing to step in here."

"No, no. They didn't say it, I did. I don't like to bail out when times get tough, but you need to go home. I'd never forgive myself if something happened to you."

Susannah walked to the window and looked out at the snow which decorated every bough of the evergreen trees. "So it *is* me. If not for me and . . . and the baby, you could stay and finish your work, take your chances. But now I am the cause of your failure. I'm sorry Gerhard. I will find my own ride back home and you are free to stay here and risk your life to keep the anarchists from taking the rest of the flour and sugar. Then when you feel you have met your contract, if you are still alive and whole, you can join us."

Gerhard rose from the desk and came swiftly across the room to her. "Susannah, stop this. You are being unreasonable. I've never seen you like this." He thought for a moment and added, "I have never seen you pregnant before. Perhaps that's the difference. Now calm down and listen to me, would you?"

He wrapped his strong arms around her and held her to his chest while she cried. He let her, knowing she needed the release, wishing he could vent his feelings as easily. When her weeping had subsided, he spoke again. "Susannah, these last years have been heavenly with you at my side. I wouldn't have traded it for all the contracts in the world. And I am so excited about our child that I can scarcely wait until next summer. I don't wish to be apart from either of you, please believe me, and I do not intend to separate us.

"I am, however, concerned with the future of the Home. It makes me feel defeated to close it now, even though others have told me that many of the schools and industries are closing, both here and in the Molotschna. I can't keep things going without regular supplies and at least a semblance of scheduling. So I am involved in an inner battle. I'm sorry if you felt I implicated you as a cause of my failure. Suse, marrying you was one of the best decisions I ever made."

He held her at arms' length and peered down into her round rosy face, framed by the ever-present golden braid. "Now, tell me you forgive me and show me a smile."

Susannah dried her tears and attempted to comply, but her emotions were not her own, it seemed. Instead of smiling, she began to cry again and tried to speak through the sobs. "Oh Gerhard, I love you so, and . . . I forgive you and . . . I can't stop crying. . . ."

Raising his eyebrows, Gerhard stared helplessly out the window and held his wife while she cried. Someone had warned him it might be this way, but he had not believed his Susannah would succumb to such hysterics. "Come, my dear. You are going to have a little nap. Peter will stay with you." Tired and worn out from crying, she accompanied him meekly to the cottage and took his suggestion. As sleep closed in on her, she dreamed she was shielding her baby from the bandits. The nap gave no peace of mind, even though her body rested.

"The Whites are closing in," said Paul Gregorovich to Anatoly one evening as the two men shared a meager meal near the stove in their Moscow barracks. "I have heard Commander Kuryakin discussing it with another unit commander. This may be our best chance to make a break for it."

Anatoly appeared extremely nervous. "How many of us are there, anyway? How will we know when the time is right?"

"Relax, friend. I will let you know. I'm telling you so you will be alert and prepared. When I see an opportunity, we will move. And it is better for now if you do not know any of the others or how many are willing to join us."

The other man grimaced and tried to shake off the dread he felt. He reasoned to himself that nothing could be much worse than remaining with the unit and working at manual labor for eighteen hours a day, with little protection from the elements. This was not life, but a shadow of death, he decided. Yes, afraid as he was, he would accept the opportunity to escape.

"Where do the Whites get their support?" he asked Paul, glancing around to make sure they were alone.

"Britain, France, Japan, America. It seems they are all afraid of Lenin and his Reds—his Communists. They will back the Whites, but they don't want war. The world is tired of war."

"So am I," remarked Anatoly, "but I cannot find my way out of it. By the way, how do you know so much. I thought Kuryakin guarded his knowledge jealously."

Tekanin shot him a quick grin as he prepared to leave and whispered, "Let's just say I have found a leak."

Chapter 21

Tekanin did not receive the opportunity he had been waiting for. At least, not in the way he had expected. A few long days after his conversation with Anatoly, the men were called to report to Kuryakin's superior. They stood at attention, unit upon unit of Red Guards, wondering what was up.

After what seemed an eternity, a black touring car roared into the compound and a tough, weathered general stepped out. He saluted the men and marched up and down the first two rows of soldiers, examining them carefully. He made several remarks to Kuryakin and the other commanders who accompanied him, and these were scribbled into little black notebooks. Tekanin stood stiffly in the third row, close enough to recognize the general. It had been some time, but Kamenev had not changed, at least not for the better. Without compromising his stand at attention, Paul tilted his head so that his hat shaded his eyes. He had no wish to be singled out, as he was sure Kamenev would do if he noticed him. He did not want to renew their former unpleasant acquaintance.

Paul knew that Kamenev now worked closely with Leon Trotsky, who ordered the Red Army. How long he would last was disputable, but at the present moment the man was in a highly superior position to Paul.

After the limited review, Kamenev shouted, "At ease," and carried on a lengthy discussion with the unit commanders. When he was satisfied with the communications between them, he stepped front and center to address the soldiers.

"Attention, men," he barked. All soldiers saluted again and stood straight and tall, arms at their sides. "The time has come for action," he said. "A disgusting swarm of White renegades continues to challenge us and they must be stopped. These insects irritate and interfere with our plans for Russia and must be exterminated. The units assembled here today will be moving south to meet the factions advancing from Sevastopol.

"Our army is efficient and deadly. We will drive out the Whites and erase all remembrance of them so that we can establish true communism here in our great country. In order to do this, every soldier must be completely and totally dedicated to the goal.

"Further instructions have been given to your unit commanders. Prepare to leave by the end of the week."

Another salute and Kamenev climbed into the vehicle and was driven away. As he passed the soldiers on the way to the gate, Tekanin caught a clear look at the man through the car window and lifted his head to the winter sun. He was sure Kamenev recognized him then, but he looked away abruptly and was gone.

So, thought Paul as he marched back to his barracks. *You have saved me a lot of work, Lev Kamenev. We don't even have to risk execution if we are caught deserting. Stay with the pack and we will come nearer to our destination.*

He whispered as much to Anatoly later that evening before curfew. "Forget the plan for now. We will see what transpires." That night he dreamed of his boyhood home in the South, of the wind soughing over the steppes, of his mother and little sister, Sophia, and of Johann. Not even in his dreams could he conjure up a better friend. He wondered what had become of him.

Attitude is everything, thought Katarina as she lit the lamps and candles in the parlor. *Mary and Joseph had no electric lights the night the Savior was born*. She determined to rejoice that Christmas, even though times were more difficult than they had been.

The electricity no longer worked, and there was no more petroleum for the generator. She was thankful that the winter was mild so far. January could prove otherwise, but as her father often said, "Don't borrow trouble from tomorrow." Katarina rejoiced for many reasons, one of those being that Maria still remained under their roof. So far, Dietrich had not completed his task of evacuating the Crimea. He was gone often and for extended periods of time, but always returned, anxious to see his Mika.

Katya had also noticed that her father seemed more his usual self lately. The war and revolution had taken its toll, but his voice had recaptured a hint of the old resonance, and his smile matched the twinkle in his eyes. For these changes she thanked God.

She thought of her brother Nicholai then, and her smile wavered. He had grown so much in the last two years; she could sometimes scarcely remember the little boy in knee pants and suspenders. She felt a motherliness toward him and worried about his future. He seemed content and yet there was something wistful about him. Johann chuckled and called it the wanderlust. She wasn't so sure.

"Where did the frown come from? It's Christmas." Mika joined her, carrying a box of decorations she and Anna had created for the occasion: tiny angels with silk wings, pine cones sparkling with colors, popcorn strings, circular pictures cut from old cards and trimmed with painted paper rings. She knelt and placed them tastefully on the boughs of the large evergreen tree that graced the corner beside the large stone fireplace.

Katarina smiled in greeting. "I didn't know I was being observed," she said. "Actually, I was thinking of Kolya and how he has grown."

"Ah yes. Sometime in the last months he has grown up. He's a good boy, you know."

"Oh I know, Mika, but I still worry. These are such formative years and there are so many frightening things happening in our country, in our world. He knows what is right, but how will he decide? I wish I could protect him from reality."

Maria stood and took Katarina's hands, looking deeply into her worried eyes. "You can't protect him from everything. Even if you were his mother, which you are not, you could not hold the world at bay." Mika returned to her decorating and continued. "Sometimes there are detours in our lives, but that doesn't mean it's the end of everything. You are a woman of deep faith, Katya. Give Nicholai to God and trust him to work it out. Let Kolya make a few mistakes—they are excellent teachers. God will not let him go."

They both knew she spoke from experience. Katya said, "I've always considered myself to be calm and controlled, but lately I've discovered I am not. The upsets caused by the war overwhelm me, and I'm not at all as strong as I thought I was."

Maria smiled and moved to stand beside her again. "Don't underestimate yourself, Katie. You are strong and courageous." She reached up to give Katarina a quick hug. "I shall miss you greatly when I go." Then she picked up the remaining ornaments and left the room.

The words were a whisper, but they pounded into Katya's mind as if they had been shouted through a megaphone. "I shall miss you greatly when I go. . . ." *Why*, she wondered as she stood in the flickering light, *why is sorrow so closely akin to joy?*

That evening after the others had retired, Katarina and Johann sat in the dimness of the parlor and talked in subdued tones. The shadows encircled them like a protecting cocoon as they remembered past Christmases, some of which they had shared and others when they had been separated.

"We have so many things to be thankful for," began Katya. "Mika's still here, and Anna is getting well again. And Papa seems happier." She rested her head on Johann's shoulder. "It was so good to have Wilhelm and Agnetha here."

"And all four children," added Johann. "They certainly add life to a celebration."

Katya smiled. "Little Philipp is adorable. His brother and sisters dote on him." She was silent then, pensive, and Johann lifted her chin so he could see her eyes.

"Don't worry, my angel," he said softly as he traced her features with his finger. "God will give us children when he sees fit. At present, I am more than happy to devote myself totally to you."

Katarina blushed in the candlelight and buried her head against him once again. Johann was quiet for so long that she broke the silence. "What are you thinking?"

He sighed and stroked her hand. "Something you might not like."

Immediately alert, she sat up and faced him. "What might I not like?"

He faced her. "You are well aware of all the turmoil happening around us. So far we have remained relatively unscathed by it, but unrest and violence are escalating. The Mennonite Conferences have set up an agency, based in Halbstadt, to act as a negotiator between our people and the powers that be."

"*Mennozentrum.* The Menno Center."

"Yes. It was actually instituted by the All-Mennonite Congress at Ohrloff in August of 1917, shortly after we were married."

"That would have been when you so bravely shipped off to Turkey and nearly got yourself killed. I remember it well."

"Yes, well, we won't follow that train of thought right now. You asked what I was thinking." He stood and began to pace the room. "Menno Center has taken the leadership in a number of areas since regular meetings of the brethren are dangerous and difficult to arrange these days. Benjamin H. Unruh is the chairman, and he has been working diligently to organize help for those of our people who are suffering at the hands of the anarchists. He has also been asked to look into the possibility of emigration."

Katya turned her wedding band round and round on her finger as she listened to her husband. "Do you think it will come to that?" she asked. "Will we have to leave all we hold dear?"

Johann knew her words were much calmer than her heart. He knew how much she loved her Succoth, her refuge. "We should be prepared and aware of our options," he answered. "I would like to get involved in this process," he said finally. "I am contemplating a trip to Halbstadt to speak with Unruh."

Katarina looked at her hands as she thought over his suggestion. Contentment and worry warred for control in her heart. Johann expected a confrontation or at least a challenge from her, but her voice was small, almost pleading. "May I come?"

He studied her for a moment in surprise. "It could be dangerous, you know. No place is safe anymore."

"Then I shall not be in any greater danger there than here. And I would be with you."

"Your reasoning is sound, but my gut instinct is to say no."

"Then I shall be forced to stowaway with your luggage, or to disguise myself as your driver." They grinned at each other and he knew he might as well agree. She had made up her mind. With his hands on his hips and a fabricated frown on his brow, he said, "I have decided you may come." They both burst out laughing then, their muffled giggles accompanying them up the stairs to their room.

PART THREE

1919

Our life is determined for us;
it makes the mind very free when we give up wishing,
and only think of bearing what is laid upon us,
and doing what is given us to do.
George Eliot

Chapter 22

Katya did not learn the other reason for Johann's wish to go to the Molotschna until several days later. Johann sat at the teacher's desk in the schoolroom engrossed in his books and papers. Ever since the new Communist government had decreed that all citizens between the ages of eight and fifty be given literacy classes, he had been compiling a format for the classes. He believed both he and Katarina were quite capable of teaching the workers from their estate, and others in the surrounding areas, to read and write.

Without warning, the door of the room burst open, and there stood Katya, hands on her hips, standing tall and angry. Johann slowly set his pen back in its ebony holder.

"Johann Sudermann," she began, putting enormous effort into controlling her words. "Why didn't you tell me about the conscription law? Were you just going to mention it in passing one day that you were joining the Red Army? Did you not think perhaps it is my right to know what is going on with my husband?" She clamped her mouth shut and blinked rapidly as Johann's gentle eyes disarmed her fury. He pushed back from the desk and moved around it.

"What are you talking about? I have not been conscripted. At least, not yet. Who have you been talking to and where did they get their information?"

"That's what I mean. You haven't been conscripted *yet*, but you will be. It's only a matter of time. It doesn't matter who told me, it's true, isn't it? Dietrich said—" She stopped abruptly.

Johann smiled. "Ah. Our favorite German soldier is again waxing prophetic. Did you not think it would be expedient to come to me and discuss the issue and his opinions before descending upon your poor husband like a violent storm?"

"Are you telling me that Dietrich is mistaken? That the Reds are not forcing conscription? I would be happy to know that you have not been hiding information from me."

Johann took Katarina's elbow and led her to a seat, taking one opposite her. "Katarina, I need you to calm yourself. First of all, I did not consider that I was hiding anything from you. We both have access to the news that filters down to us, and we both know that much of it is hearsay. These days it is difficult to obtain the truth about any situation. There are too many players, too much politics.

"Yes, there has been word that young and middle-aged men are being taken into the Red Army." He raised his hand to stop further outburst and continued. "But there is other news as well. According to B. B. Janz from the Molotschna, a group known as the Tolstoyans have been granted military exemption on account of their pacifist stance. Janz believes that the Mennonites too can acquire this exemption if we go about it in the proper way. For all I know, he has already achieved this for our people. Janz is well known in Moscow as an able negotiator. I was hoping to speak with him, as well as Benjamin Unruh when we go to the Molotschna, to see if I can help somehow. Now tell me, have I done anything deserving of this onslaught?"

Katya's eyes had lost their anger, but not their hurt. "I was afraid for you, Johann. It seems we are always on the verge of losing each other." Her voice was a whisper and its pain broke Johann's heart. He reached for her and held her as she fought the demon of her fear. "You could have told me," she said into his chest. "I can bear things better when I know about them."

Frustrated with her logic, Johann struggled for patience. He chose his words carefully. "I am sorry that I overlooked discussing this with you. There didn't seem to be any point at present. Why worry and fret when the answer may be right around the corner? I will know better in the future."

Not entirely assuaged, Katarina murmured a soft "thank you," and gave an excuse to check on Anna. Johann knew that Anna was well looked after, but he accepted Katya's reason. After she had gone, he paced before the windows, looking out at the snow-dusted lawns. Katarina's outburst surprised and confused him. Why did she take everything so personally? He had never meant to deceive her. Had he? He decided she would get over it soon enough if he let her sort it out. She would see that she had overreacted. With a shrug of his shoulders he sat again at the desk and resumed his work, humming in anticipation of the visit to the Molotschna.

Paul Gregorovich Tekanin felt invigorated as he and his fellow soldiers marched down the road heading south from Kharkov. They had been shipped by rail from Moscow—January was bitterly cold in the capital and Trotsky did not wish to reduce his army to frozen corpses before they had accomplished their purpose. Now Paul felt like he was going home. The landscape appeared increasingly familiar as they neared the steppes, and the breeze sang the songs of home. Snow still lay in drifts where it had blown, but the sun shone longer and stronger each day.

As far as Paul knew the White Army was pressing northward through the Crimea and had already infiltrated the south of Russia, which had proclaimed its independence as the Ukraine. As the troops reached the northern edge of the colony known as the Molotschna, they stopped to regroup and strategize. Trotsky ran a tight operation with no intention of anything but victory.

They were gathered near the village of Chernigovka on that January day when riders from the town galloped into the encampment. The visitors, four rough and dirty individuals, gave the impression they were not in the least alarmed by the guns aimed at their heads. They dismounted and the spokesman approached Kamenev.

"Greetings," he said. "We have come to help you."

Kamenev lifted his chin higher and motioned for his guards to hold the man. "Tie them up and keep them for questioning later." He turned on his heel and began to walk back to his tent, but the spokesman was not so easily deflated.

"My name is Machno, and my men have taken Chernigovka and set up our headquarters there."

Kamenev stopped but did not turn.

"I have nearly eight thousand men at my disposal."

Kamenev turned to face him and waved the guards away. Machno swaggered. "Of course I also have headquarters in the Chortitza Colony. A nice home for crazy people that was suddenly abandoned." The man twirled his mustache and smiled as he stood appraising Kamenev. "I am a powerful man and I would offer to help you slaughter the Whites. What do you say to that, eh?"

"I have heard of you. Brutal, they say. What is your reason for terrorizing the populace?"

Machno roared with laughter that chilled the bones. "Why do I kill and steal? Because I enjoy it. It is my turn to be in charge. People fear me for good reason. I like that. Killing suits me. How many men have you killed, General?" He spoke the title with such derision that Kamenev almost winced.

"I will speak with Trotsky. Perhaps we can make use of you and your undisciplined lot. Come back in two days."

"Oh, I will come back," Machno nodded, the evil in his eyes so strong that it was almost overpowering. "I will come back whenever I please." He laughed again and mounted his horse in one jump. He saluted the general and took off again at a gallop, dust rising from the road where the snow had already disappeared.

Kamenev watched for some time as the clouds of dust drifted into the trees beside the road. Giving his head a bit of a shake, he frowned and stalked to his tent.

Maria Wall pulled the curtain back from the window and watched as a buggy stopped before the house. A young couple occupied the front seat, while three other people sat in back. Franz was still at the hospital and Maria was suddenly afraid. No one could be trusted these days. So many horrible things had happened already in Halbstadt and in many of the other villages as well. She had not forgotten the terror of the Red Army's February visit.

Just as she was about to let the curtain fall back into place and escape out the back door into the garden, she thought she recognized the face of the young woman as her husband helped her out of the buggy. Such a sweet, round face with a golden braid wrapped around it like a halo. It had to be Susannah Warkentin, and so the man would be Gerhard. Something was wrong, because she also recognized Helga Siemens, the nurse who had accompanied the Warkentins to Bethany Home in February. Mrs. Wall decided the other two occupants of the buggy must be residents from the Home. They appeared frightened and almost totally helpless as Gerhard and Susannah struggled to help them from the vehicle.

As they approached the door, Maria Wall opened it wide and motioned them in. A tall, thin, young man held tightly to Susannah's hand, and the other patient, an old woman, lay passively in Gerhard's arms. Helga brought up the rear, and soon they were all inside.

"Come, Mr. Warkentin, put the woman on our bed. We will heat some tea for her and tuck her in." That accomplished, the hostess brought tea for everyone else and they sat around the oak kitchen table and stared at each other.

"What has happened, children?" asked Mrs. Wall, seeing the insecurity and fear hovering on the faces of her guests. "Whom have you left in charge of Bethania?"

Gerhard glanced at Susannah, then back at Maria Wall. Holding his teacup in both hands, he stared into its depths. Finally, he met her eyes. "No one is in charge any more, Mrs. Wall. Bethania has been nationalized. That's the official story. The unofficial one is that Machno has established a headquarters there, after vandalizing and terrorizing us for the past several months. Most of the residents have been sent home or are billeted in one of the colonies. Mrs. Lohrenz," he motioned to the bedroom, "will be going to Fishau as soon as I can take her there."

Mrs. Wall glanced at Peter, and Susannah caught her meaning. "Peter Hildebrandt stays with us, don't you, Peter dear?"

"Don't you, Peter dear." Peter shifted in his chair.

Maria Wall smiled and stood to refill the cups. As the steaming liquid poured into the dainty china, she said, "My Franz is still at the hospital, but I am hoping he will be home soon. You will stay here tonight, and tomorrow we will see if the situation looks safe enough for you to travel."

"Safe enough?" Susannah's eyes widened. "I thought we had left the worst behind us. Surely the Molotschna does not hold the terrors we have fled from."

The older woman looked first at Gerhard, then at Susannah. "I'm sorry, my dear," she began, "but Machno is here as well. He moves about as he pleases, with a growing force to back him. We heard he was in Chernigovka, but he could be anywhere by now. And the Reds have returned. They want to try to force the White Army out of the country." She sat again and clasped her hands before her on the table, her lips forming a thin line. "We are all in God's hands, children. Even though evil is having its day, we are not alone in it. But I know how you feel. I myself experience fear almost every day as our situation becomes increasingly unstable." She looked at Gerhard and said, "Would you pray with us please, Mr. Warkentin? I believe we need divine reassurance."

They still sat around the same oak table, as human as ever, but as Gerhard prayed, the divine peace of God descended upon them like a warm blanket, and each one opened eyes wet with emotion. The Lord was with them. He had promised never to leave them, and in this they placed their faith.

Chapter 23

For a time, Succoth infirmary had been quiet. The odd transient still dropped by for a hot meal and a clean bed, but the work eased. Anna was back to her healthy self, although she still tired easily after her illness. Katarina and Johann spent their time teaching the Succoth workers to read and write. Many were anxious to learn but did not want to seem too eager to take any help from these "Germans." Since the program was more or less enforced by local authorities, however, the Russians accepted the challenge.

Old Nadia, who had taken Katya's side at the hog-butchering event a couple of years ago, came gladly on her weary legs to be taught by her young friend. Nadia's enthusiasm influenced others to do the same, making the project much easier and more enjoyable. Katya did like teaching, and Johann, of course, was born for this work.

Time passed quickly and soon February rounded the corner, announcing itself by melting the snow and sending spring breezes. "As soon as the weather moderates," said Johann to Katarina one day, "we will be off to Halbstadt to meet with Unruh and Janz." He winked with excitement and she wrinkled her nose at him. Life had become tolerable as they accepted their situation.

As the new year progressed, traffic to the infirmary picked up again. The reason, said Heinrich, was that the Whites were mobilizing in Crimea and moving northward into the Ukraine. Also, the last of the German troops were headed back to Europe. As the Red Army descended upon the south of Russia, many people fled south across the isthmus to the peninsula. Traffic increased in both directions. Again, the Hildebrandts and the Sudermanns busied themselves with nursing the sick.

Disease and malnutrition swept through the countryside with the many travelers and the war. Typhoid and typhus became the dreaded plagues, and Johann relived many times his memories of his medical duty. The poor had become poorer since the revolution, and the civil war now in progress made things much worse. Many *dessiatine* of arable land now lay fallow because there was no seed with which to sow. Less seeded land translated into less food harvested and more hungry people.

Even Dietrich lent a hand with the work from time to time, but Katarina could tell he was restless. She knew he was thinking of moving on, and she knew Mika was also preoccupied with the inevitability. The German military was gone by now, and the *Selbstschutz,* although strongest in the Molotschna, was also active in the Crimea. There was no more reason for Dietrich Kesselman to remain.

Heinrich spoke to Dietrich about his plans in late February. "When do you leave, Dietrich? What are you planning for my daughter?"

The two sat in Heinrich's study. Kesselman no longer smoked in the house because he knew it was not appreciated, but he sincerely wished he could as his fingers drummed the arms of the chair. "I wish to take her with me, sir. I would marry her first, of course, because I know that it would be wrong to take her otherwise." He stood and began to pace. He ran his hands through his hair and came to a stop before Heinrich. "I love her, Heinrich. She is my match, and although it will nearly break her heart to leave you all, she has agreed to come with me."

Heinrich gave a little smirk and sighed. "You're wrong on one count at least. It would not break her heart. My Maria would die if she were forced to stay. Oh, she will miss us and we her," he assured the young man whose eyes suddenly blazed in defense of his chosen, "but as long as you love her, she will survive quite nicely. As long as you love her." He tipped his head back and fixed his gaze on the German soldier.

Dietrich did something then that he had never done before. He went down on one knee and made an oath to love and protect Maria Hildebrandt as long as he had breath in his body. And as far as Heinrich could read those strong blue eyes, he meant every word of it.

"God grant you grace, my son," he answered.

Maria Hildebrandt and Dietrich Kesselman chose a day in late February to pledge their vows. They arranged to have a private ceremony in the little Orthodox church in Karassan with Father Serge Ivanovich officiating. It was to be a compromise of sorts, between their religions. And then they would leave for Germany directly from Karassan.

There were so many things to think about. So far, Mika had managed to keep their departure in the back of her mind, but as the day drew near, she knew she must face up to the inevitable. "I have to go, you know," she said to Katya out of the blue the next day as the two packed her trunk. "I could never let Dietrich go. But I shall miss. . . ." Her voice petered out into a whisper and she gripped the dress she was packing with such force that Katya thought it would come apart at the seams.

Katya remained silent for several minutes, allowing her sister to gather her dignity. One did not push Maria Hildebrandt. "I shall miss you more than words can say, Marie, but I believe we must finish this packing now. You are about to become *Frau* Kesselman."

Mika turned at the name and smiled through eyes filled with tears she refused to shed. A quavery smile crept onto her face and she tossed the dress aside and took Katarina's hands. "Isn't it amazing, Katya? Both of us married! Of course, I always thought we would be, but it still surprises me that we are both all grown up and independent."

"Yes," smiled Katya. "But the greatest surprise of all is that I married first, and to someone who was once taken by you!" Several tears splashed from Mika's eyes then, but only as she tilted her head back and laughed as she hadn't laughed for a long time. Playfully she reached up, held Katya's face between her beautiful hands and stood on tiptoes to touch her sister's forehead with her own. "There is a love," she whispered softly, "that only sisters can share."

"Where is Dietrich?" Mika paced the parlor while her bags waited at the front door. "He said he would check with the other officers we are traveling with and then return for me."

Katya was concerned. "Did he say how long it would take?"

"No, but he only had to ride to Karassan and back. He should be here by now. Father Serge will be waiting to perform the marriage ceremony."

Silence filled the room as each thought her own thoughts. Eventually, Maria grew too agitated to remain in the house. "I'm going to walk in the garden. Call me as soon as he arrives."

Unfortunately, Dietrich did not arrive soon. In fact, he did not arrive at all. To say Mika was distraught would have been an understatement. Katarina had never seen her so distressed. No one knew what to say, what to do.

Finally, late that evening, Katya convinced her sister to go up to her room and try to sleep. She knew that would be impossible, but the tension was becoming intolerable for everyone. Katya carried her sister's small bag to the room and sat on the edge of Mika's bed.

"What do you suppose could have happened?"

Mika fell into a low-back chair and drooped. "Why don't you go ahead and say it? That he never intended to marry me after all. That he has been false to me. That I have been rejected again."

"I won't say it," she answered, "because I don't believe it. Dietrich had every intention of marrying you and taking you with him. As far as I have come to know him, he is a man of honor and integrity. He may not share our beliefs or all of our values, but he would never abandon you. No, I believe something happened that gave him no choice."

"Oh Katie, that scares me too." Maria sat forward in her chair, wringing her hands. It was not something she was in the habit of doing. "Thank you for believing in us, in our commitment to each other, but what would happen to force him to leave without me? It must be something dreadful."

"Mika, let's not think that way. As Mama used to say in tough situations: we need to expect the best and prepare for the worst. I—*we*—will stand by you. Let's pray."

Without waiting for a response, Katarina raised her heart to the Lord, carrying her sister's pain and uncertainty to the Father. And she knew—they both knew—that the Father heard.

There had been no word from Dietrich, and it was time for Johann and Katarina to travel north to the Molotschna to see B. B. Janz and Benjamin H. Unruh.

"I'm coming with you," announced Mika the evening before their departure. "Perhaps I can learn what happened."

Concern carved more lines in Heinrich's face. "What then, Maria? What if you find nothing? Or if you do find a trail, will you follow it? How will we know what becomes of you?"

Mika blew out a heavy sigh as she faced her father. She reached out her hands and placed them gently on his shoulders. "I must go, Father. We are committed to each other, Dietrich and I, and I must follow him, find him. We promised that. . . ." she paused to gather strength and courage. "We promised each other that if we should ever be separated enroute, we would meet at Dietrich's home in Germany. I have directions. I could find it."

"But consider the situation, my child," Heinrich pleaded. "There is civil war in our country. Bandits and madmen rage across the countryside. Life is cheap to them. How could you get through?"

"I don't know, Father. I only know I must go. To give up would be to lose myself. I'd rather die trying."

"Then I will come with you. You will need protection."

"No, Papa. This is not your path. Please," she began to weep softly, "set me free with your blessing and your prayers. I will trust God to protect me. I know in my heart that I must walk this road alone."

Heinrich held her to his chest, his tears dripping onto her dark, silken hair, hers staining the front of his vest. His lips moved silently as he gave her up to God, whom he trusted, even with his own child. He held her in his arms and released her in his heart. The cost was great, but such is love.

The next morning, Johann, Katarina, and Mika piled into the buggy and set off north. Heinrich strode out to the barns to check on the animals and to discuss seeding with the field supervisors. He ended the day kneeling at his wife's tomb in the little Succoth cemetery, explaining to his Elizabeth what he had allowed to happen. He did not understand it himself but hoped things would be clearer when he talked them out.

Johann, Katarina, and Maria stopped at the Orthodox Church in Karassan on their way. The priest greeted them warmly. When they were secure in his office, Father Serge immediately faced Maria.

"Dietrich came here before he left," he said. "Offered his fellows the excuse that he needed to confess, to leave his Russian sins on Russian soil." The priest gave a humorless smirk. "He said I was to tell you when you came—and he was sure you would come—that he was being forced to evacuate at once. The others would not even give him leave to send a telegram. This was the only excuse he could think of."

"So what did he say? Where did he go and what am I to do?" Mika gripped her shawl in her fists, trying to maintain some semblance of calm.

The priest put up a hand to quiet her. "He and his companions were dressed as Soviet officials. They all know enough Russian to get them through. They will travel by train to Kiev and then west. He said he would leave word where he could, and that you are to come when you can. He will wait in his hometown for you. He said not to take unnecessary chances, but he also confided in me that he knew you would come no matter what."

"I'm going. I will continue on with Johann and Katarina to the Molotschna, and then I will set out on my own."

"I will leave that for you and your family to discuss," he said, one hand holding the large cross that hung from his neck. "But I will pray for you and your beloved, that you will be safely reunited."

"Thank you, Father Serge," murmured Maria, clearly touched by the gentle words of this man. She bowed slightly as they left. Katarina did the same and Johann shook his hand. Then they were off to the colony.

"Come," said Johann as he guided Katarina and Maria toward the Great Southern train preparing to chug its way north along the border of the Molotschna Colony, paralleling the Molotschnaya River. They jolted and bumped through Lindenau and Fishau and several other Mennonite villages, arriving finally at Halbstadt about noon.

The air in Halbstadt was electric with fear and uncertainty. People moved about cautiously with watchful eyes. Red soldiers patrolled the streets searching for Whites. Johann grabbed their bags while Katarina held onto Mika's elbow. They hurried to the station and hailed a cab, then waited nervously for its arrival, speaking in hushed tones, standing well in the shadows of the sprawling building.

"What is happening, Johann?" Katya asked, her eyes wide.

"I didn't know it would be this bad or I never would have brought you here."

"I never would have let you come if I'd known either. It feels as if everyone is waiting for a bomb to blow up, but no one knows its exact location."

Mika remained still, fighting to retain the courage she had pulled together for this trip.

Johann peered down the street, looking for the cab. "We will go to see Unruh as planned. Perhaps he can give us information and advice." He looked at Katya with guilty eyes. "I'm sorry, Katie. Pray. Pray harder than you ever have before." He glanced at Mika and she nodded. Yes, she knew how to pray too.

The cab pulled up to the curb and the three scrambled inside. The car took off immediately as Johann gave the driver Benjamin Unruh's address. Johann tried to get some information on the situation from the driver, but he was tight-lipped. "I only drive car," he said. "Not on nobody's side, no."

With a frustrated sigh, Johann leaned back and put his arm around Katarina's shoulders. She was shaking, her eyes darting from one window to the next, as if anticipating attackers from both sides. "Calm down, my dear," Johann whispered. "We should be almost there."

As they came to a stop outside a large home on the north side of the village, a stocky, broad-shouldered man about forty years of age opened the house door and came to meet them. Johann paid the driver, and he, Katya, and Mika climbed out and stood facing the man. Unruh was handsome, his thick, dark hair curling boyishly around his ears, with a friendly demeanor that in this instance remained serious as he led them quickly into his house.

"Not a good time to stand in the street, my friends," he said as he took their bags and invited them into the parlor. "Bring tea please, Frieda," he called toward the kitchen.

"What is happening here?" Johann sat stiffly in an armchair while Katarina and Mika shivered on the settee. "We have just arrived from Crimea, and although we knew the *Selbstschutz* was fighting against the *Machnovitz,* we had no idea that the Reds were back this far."

Unruh toyed with his mustache, but before he could begin his explanation, his wife brought tea. She moved slowly, obviously nearing the end of her pregnancy.

"How many children do you have?" asked Katya, eager for a distraction from the heaviness she had sensed since their arrival in Halbstadt.

"We have seven," she answered with a smile, "and this will be eight." She placed her hand on her extensive tummy and patted it softly. "Once you have four," she said, "they begin to look after each other. Soon I shall have nothing at all to do." The women laughed together and it felt like a balm to Katarina's soul. Mrs. Unruh settled back as comfortably as was possible in her condition and looked to her husband to speak. He winked and sent her a crooked little smile before he began.

"The Reds returned a short while ago. Machno has joined up with them."

"Machno joined them!" Johann's voice reflected his horror.

"Yes. He has devastated the Chortitza and now comes here. He has many, many followers, each as wicked as he."

"Why do they come here?" Katya wanted to know.

"He lives to terrorize the German populace. I believe he has an enormous chip on his shoulder from his childhood days and is determined to take it out on us. Anyway, Bethany Home was forced to close its doors when the bandits vandalized it continually, and now Machno uses it as one of his bases of operation."

Katya's head jerked and her hands went up to her face when Unruh mentioned Bethany Home. "My brother is there. And Gerhard and Susannah. What . . . what happened to the residents? Were they all killed?" Her voice rose in pitch and volume as she imagined the evils that could have befallen her family and friends.

Mika put her arm around Katya's shoulder, but it was plain she was as distraught as her sister.

"I don't believe any of the residents were physically harmed, Mrs. Sudermann," said Unruh in a calming voice. "The director and his wife were here in Halbstadt. They continued on to his wife's home in Lichtfelde."

"Were they alone, or did they have a boy with them?" Johann took up the interrogation. "They have taken Katya's brother in, and we need to find him if he is no longer at Bethania."

Shaking his head, Unruh blinked his eyes slowly and said, "I don't know, my friends, I don't know. There have been so many comings and goings here lately, that I do not remember everyone I have seen or who was with them. We must trust that the Lord is looking after your brother."

"Yes, of course." Johann reached a hand to Katarina and she grasped it like a lifeline.

"Why don't you ladies and Mrs. Unruh relax in the kitchen, Katie, and we will discuss this emigration business,"

Johann suggested. "You look overwhelmed." She hesitated, but he could see the exhaustion in her eyes. "I promise to tell you everything," he smiled at her.

With an answering smile, she nodded and turned to Frieda. Katya stood and helped her hostess to her feet, then followed her out of the room.

Maria stood as well, but waited until the kitchen door closed behind Frieda and Katya. "I will join them in a moment," she said, "but first I need to speak with you." She straightened her shoulders and lifted her chin. "I am seeking a German commander who was scheduled to return to his homeland this week. He will have come through here on his way. Are you aware of any German contingent still remaining in the vicinity or have they all gone?"

Unruh stared at her in shock. "The Germans have all left, months ago—it would be suicide for them to remain here now that the Reds have returned. Why are you looking for this man?"

"He is my fiancé. We were to be married and then head back to Germany together, but something happened to him before we could do so. I need to find him." She remained still and straight, but her eyes pleaded.

Unruh shook his head. "I don't know, Miss. I cannot help you. As I said, all the Germans have long since retreated, and if there are any left, they will be in hiding, or at least in disguise to save their lives. Perhaps your young man waited too long and was forced to flee."

Johann could see Maria's heart breaking. The light of hope went out of her eyes and her head drooped forward. She gripped the back of a chair and looked back at the men. "Then I will set out for Germany in the morning."

She turned and walked toward the kitchen, but Benjamin Unruh stopped her with his words: "Miss Hildebrandt, I am traveling to Germany, Lord willing, as soon as our baby is born. Perhaps you could accompany me."

She stopped in mid stride and whirled around to stare at him. "Do you mean it?"

Unruh hesitated only a moment before answering. "Yes, I mean it, but you must know that my journey will not be direct. I will be traveling to Moscow to speak with authorities there about emigration, then west to Riga, and around by ship to northern Germany where there will be more meetings."

"But that would take months. And what would I do until you leave?"

"You could stay here until then and help Frieda. Her time will come any day now. But I would never advise you to go alone, no matter how direct the route. What do you say?"

Mika paused, deep in thought. *Months! How will I endure it? But it seems the only course open to me.* Finally she said, "I will come." She moved a few steps closer. "I will try to be patient, and not hinder you."

"Then consider it done. I will arrange it in the morning."

Mika gave a slight smile and a bow and turned to the kitchen.

After she was gone, the men looked at each other grimly. "Are you sure about this?" asked Johann.

"I cannot guarantee her safety," Unruh answered, "but it would be better than letting her go alone, and I think she is determined and would do it."

"You are correct in that assumption," said Johann with raised eyebrows. "Her mind is made up." He looked into Unruh's eyes and said, "She has experienced some difficult times in her life, some of her own doing, but I believe she would go to the ends of the earth to find Dietrich."

"Nothing these days is simple or safe, but with my travel papers, I do not usually have trouble. She will travel as my sister—not a lie, as she is my sister in the faith—and so we will attempt to reunite her with Dietrich."

Johann did not know how he felt about that particular deception, but he dismissed it for the present.

"This German must be a good man to warrant such sacrifice and bravery," said Unruh.

Johann nodded. "I have come to know Dietrich Kesselman over the past months, and he is a man of his word, a person of integrity, and he loves Maria. I just hope he has not been killed somewhere. Then everything would be for naught."

"So is the way of our world," said Unruh. "Every day is filled with uncertainty and fear. Oh for a faith that would not waver.

"But I must carry on this mission of finding a way to rescue our people. This alliance between the Reds and Machno's men spells ill for us and death for the *Selbstschutz*. I don't know what will happen to them."

"Then it is high time we make plans for emigration," remarked Johann, pushing up his glasses with his forefinger and focusing on Benjamin H. Unruh.

Chapter 24

Tekanin's unit was stationed between Halbstadt and Neu-Halbstadt near the commercial district and the road to Muntau. So far, action had been scarce, but Paul knew all chaos could erupt at any time. He had not seen any of Machno's men, but he knew of their presence. His chance meeting with Machno a year or so ago at the armory still caused him to shudder. How did he now find himself aligned with the likes of that devil?

As he pondered his situation, he and Anatoly patrolled Ekaterinoslav Street, walking northwest toward Halbstadt's residential area. He noticed the Orthodox church standing proud and lonely and the livery barn with its beehive of activity. Everyone had somewhere to go, something important to do. He walked on, as usual, wondering when his life would again make sense.

Tekanin and Anatoly continued up the adjoining street past the hardware store, peering inside as they marched by. Paul's heart lurched at the sight of a man who looked so like Johann Sudermann he could have been his twin. In the years since leaving South Russia, Paul had often seen Johann on the periphery of his field of vision, only to turn and find it was not, could not have been him. With a tremendous sigh that caught the attention of his companion, he blinked away the apparition and carried on up the street. He looked again on their return, but the man was gone.

"We need to talk to the men who gather at Jacob Epp's Hardware Store," said Benjamin Unruh. "It is the meeting place about town, and there are those who can give us the mood of the people on this topic of emigration. I already have told you the opinions that prevail at the learning institutions." As they got up to leave, Johann cast a worried glance toward the kitchen. Unruh waved aside his concern and said, "We will be back within the hour. The women will be fine here."

As the two men entered the store, the group gathered there welcomed them and moved together to make more room. Standing in the doorway waiting for a chair, Johann turned to see two Red Army soldiers saunter past, hats pulled down low on their foreheads. One of them, the tall one, turned at that same moment to look into the store, but Johann could not see the man's face because he himself looked into the sinking sun. Frowning, he felt the old familiar tug at his heart as he thought of Paul Gregorovich. He shook his head and sat, willing himself to pay attention to the discussion at hand. He would delegate thoughts of Paul to those lingering early morning moments between sleep and wakefulness, when his mind wandered in the realm of memory and imagination. For now he must reconcile himself to realities.

Susannah awoke and sat up in bewilderment as she found herself in her old bedroom in her parents' home. Seeing Gerhard asleep beside her, his features lulled into sleep's peace, she remembered their return. Was it only yesterday that they had arrived? Her parents were ecstatic to see them. It had been impossible to send word, as she and Gerhard did not know exactly when they would arrive. They had managed to move Mrs. Lohrenz in with a caring family in Fishau, and then Gerhard had turned the horse onto the road that would take them from Lindenau to Lichtfelde.

"Peter!" Susannah threw back the covers and pulled a robe from her bag.

Gerhard sat up, blinking sleep from his eyes, shaking sense into his brain. "Susannah, what are you doing?"

"I have to find Peter. He must be beside himself in this strange environment. I have to make sure he's all right." Her waist-length blonde hair billowed about her like a cape as she ran out of the room in search of her charge.

Gerhard fell back heavily onto the bed in sheer exhaustion. He could not get his mind into gear. Suddenly his shoulders began to shake with laughter. "Susannah will be right back, Peter," he said to the figure that lay stiff and straight in the alcove by the window.

"Be right back, Peter," the figure replied, accompanied by mechanical gasps of laughter.

The two still laughed as a sheepish Susannah returned to the room moments later and closed the door behind her. "Well," she said, trying hard to maintain her dignity. "Anyone can forget." In spite of her resolve, she too began to giggle. A knock on the door silenced them all.

"Are you all right, Suse?" Her mother's voice filtered through the door and her silence awaited an answer.

"Yes, Mother," she managed. "I lost something but I found it again. We'll be out shortly."

"Fine, dear. Breakfast is about ready." They heard her retreating footsteps and Gerhard and Susannah giggled again as their worn emotions began to fray. For several moments they again forgot Peter, but a voice from the alcove captured their distracted attentions. "Breakfast is about ready."

Susannah could not remember her mother looking so old. Of course, she had been gone from home for several years, but the aging had taken place lately. Susannah decided it was from the worry that daily faced these people. Bethany Home was not the only place that had suffered at the hands of bandits.

"Several of our townspeople have been killed in raids," Mrs. Loewen informed them over bacon and eggs and fresh biscuits. "Young men too, just boys, really." Her tone was bitter and afraid.

"Boys," commented Suse's father. "*Scheuztler* is what they were. They signed up for it, Hannah. Those who live by the sword die by the sword." Even though his opinion differed from hers, the emotions were the same. A depression had settled over the home, over the village, and over the many villages that made up the colony. A dismal cloak of fear enveloped the Molotschnaya Mennonites as their way of life disintegrated around them: fields used as battlegrounds, woods burned, gardens vandalized, businesses disrupted, families divided physically and philosophically. Their whole world was being turned upside down.

Johann and Katarina had spent several eventful days with the Unruhs, but were now packed to leave them. Mika would remain until Benjamin was ready to leave for Germany.

"You need to talk to B. B. Janz," Unruh advised. "He is the one who is in touch with the authorities. That man has an uncanny ability to negotiate. I have plans to visit Holland, Switzerland, and Germany, perhaps even the United States and Canada. There is much to be done to pave the way for a mass migration. Yes, Janz will be the ticket for you."

"It's been a blessing to be in your home and get to know your family," said Johann. Katarina voiced her agreement and they all exchanged handshakes and hugs. The farewell between the Sudermanns and Maria was much more difficult. The sisters held each other for long moments, then looked deeply into each other's eyes to capture their souls, to last for as long as they would be separated.

"I love you and will pray for you every day," whispered Katarina into Mika's ear.

"I will depend on it," she responded.

Johann also embraced Mika. "Good-bye, little sister. Take care and send news in any way possible."

"Of course. I will find a way." She turned again to Katarina. "I have given you Dietrich's address. Memorize it. If worst comes to worst, we will use that as a rendezvous point." With a last hug, she stepped away and watched Johann and Katarina board the train.

"Godspeed to you," said Unruh as they stepped onto the train and headed south. Johann had suggested renting a horse and buggy and taking the direct route through Tiegerweide, but the Unruhs had challenged that decision. "Far too dangerous," they had said. "Stay nearer civilization in case you come upon bandits." Johann and Katarina both had trouble getting used to the idea of bandits around every corner, but they decided to take the advice and travel as far as possible by train.

Mika waved bravely as the train chugged away.

Once back in the south of the colony, Johann and Katarina stayed at the Reimers' in Alexanderkrone, with frequent visits to Johann's home in Kleefeld. But it wasn't like the old days. Gone were the efficiency, the aura of success, the order that had always characterized the villages. In their place cowered uncertainty, fear, and restlessness; and Johann and Katarina were struck by the contrast.

The Reimers too had changed. Theodore and Katie Konrad now lived with them, and although all four appreciated the comfort of company, they also lived beneath the pall of civil war and anarchy. There was, it seemed, no escape from the oppression.

B. H. Unruh's prophetic words came back to Johann several days later as news of the *Selbstschutz* reached Alexanderkrone. "This alliance between the Reds and Machno's men spells ill for us and death for the *Selbstschutz*," he had said. The self-defense corp, now under the command of German officer Heinz von Homeyer, had been forced to surrender. Every household was aware of the last battle, every home affected by its outcome.

Johann and Katarina learned the dreadful details from Johann's younger brother, Ernst, who had managed to escape with his life. "We were up against the Reds and Machno's men," he said breathlessly. "Homeyer situated us in such a way that we would not be surrounded, or we would all have been corpses by now. It was supposed to be so noble, facing the enemy in defense of our families, driving them back and returning in victory. We had a paltry 2,700 infantry and 300 cavalry. Ha! What a joke. We were playing at war, but the enemy doesn't play. They are real and war is not a game. Not a game at all."

Ernst Sudermann, twenty years old with the eyes of a man three times that age, paced the parlor as he told his story. His hair was blonde like Johann's, but there the resemblance ended. He was not as tall, nor did he wear spectacles, nor were his eyes the gentle blue of a placid woodland lake. Rather, bitterness glinted in his gray eyes. He spoke quickly because he could not stay. It was not safe, and so he would flee to Crimea with those of his comrades who had survived their last stand.

"Most everyone turned tail and ran," Ernst continued. His father sat in pitiful silence, a tired husk of a man who had never nourished dreams even in good times. "Some have joined up with the Whites in another effort to withstand the Bolshevik advance, but they don't have a chance. And so many . . . " he stopped to clear the lump from his throat as he thought of his boyhood friends who had joined with him to take up the sword against the enemies of his people, "so many died. Albert and Willy, Johann Wiens, Peter Friesen, George Neufeld, all of them. All for nothing.

"The *Machnovitz* are brutal." His eyes hardened as he remembered. "They don't just kill, they hack and chop and dismember. They …" Ernst's face began to tremble and crack, and he collapsed on the floor in sobs wrenched from the depths of his wounded soul. His mother tried to console him, his father sat watching the spectacle from agonized eyes, constantly wringing his hands. Johann and Katarina knelt beside the overwrought young man and prayed, even harder than they had prayed in Halbstadt.

Slowly the sobs eased, but Ernst was totally drained of energy. He dozed for perhaps an hour on the sofa, but awoke with a start, gathered his things and ran out the door to the barn. Saddling one of his father's workhorses, and they were lucky the army had left them that, he shoved his gun into his belt and bid his family farewell with the hope that someday they would meet again. Somehow he would be in touch, he said. Then he was gone. His sister, Mariechen, wept openly for her brother and clung to Katarina. His mother cried aloud, but Heinz Sudermann sat silent, shoulders stooped, hands splayed on his knees, eyes vacant, as if he had turned to stone.

The troop of Red soldiers, of which Paul Gregorovich Tekanin was a part, pushed south through the Molotschna Colony, through the town of Waldheim and on to the next sizable village, Gnadenfeld. The commanding Red officer was General Dobenko, an imposing figure, if not for his size, then for his powerful presence. His frustration over the Mennonites' formation of self-defense units drove him to fury. As if he did not have his hands full with the Whites, now he had also to deal with these misfit soldiers pretending at war.

Galloping up to the headquarters of the Gnadenfeld *volost,* Dobenko pulled his horse to a sliding stop, leapt off and burst through the door. Several of his men followed, Tekanin and Anatoly Kovshov included.

Two men rose, startled, from their places within and came to stand before the general in quiet strength. One of them, a Kornelius Martens, held up both hands, palms forward and cried, "Mr. Dobenko, forgive us!"

Dobenko was not in the mood to forgive anyone anything, particularly the sin of taking up arms against the Red forces. "You damned renegades from the faith of your fathers!" he bellowed. "For four hundred years you could not take arms, but now for your damned Kaiser Wilhelm. . . ." The general continued to rant and rave, and Martens and his associate expected that these would be their last moments alive. With pale countenances and prayers on their lips they listened as Dobenko railed at them.

Paul watched in horrified fascination, his thoughts on his dearest friend, Johann Sudermann. Where was he now? Paul knew that the outcome of this plea for mercy would affect the people Johann loved, perhaps even his family. *How could he have known,* he wondered, *where his decision to join the Red Army would take him and what confrontations it would lead to? How would he feel if it were Johann standing before them now, pleading for the lives of his people?*

Once more Kornelius pled, "Please, Comrade Dobenko, forgive us!"

With a huff, Dobenko cursed again and then shouted, "I will not kill all, but my soldiers may plunder for three days, and where they find *Selbstschuetzler,* they may execute them."

Martens and his companion shook violently after the general and his men stormed back out of the building, knowing that although revenge of the Reds would be terrifying, total annihilation had been averted. Together they thanked the Lord and ran to spread the news. Paul saw them as they flew out a back exit in two directions. Privately, he wished them luck. They were going to need it.

Chapter 25

The Mennonites of the Molotschna cowered behind closed doors those early March days of 1919. Machno and the Reds had declared extermination of the *Selbstschutz,* and wreaked havoc on villages and farms as they rode a hunt of horror, rounding up and executing any members who remained in the colony. More than a few innocents also came beneath the deathblows of guns and bayonets, as bandits and Bolsheviks sought revenge on their enemies.

For three days the destruction continued, three days of terror that no law could stop. This fiery baptism burned across the colony, leaving fear, pain, and desperation in its wake. It left smoldering wounds on the land and the people, wounds that would not heal.

Benjamin H. Unruh, accompanied by a special delegation from Menno Center, presented the case before the Communist authorities that the *Selbstschutz* had been established as a peacekeeping force to protect their villages. Through his patient and humble negotiation, the Mennonites of the Molotschna Colony were granted impunity from the Reds on the condition that they surrender all their weapons within three days. As a result, eleven students from Halbstadt were released. It was a small victory, but a victory nonetheless. Following that, Unruh boarded a train headed for Moscow, and Maria Hildebrandt traveled with him.

Abram and Cornelia Reimer's home, where the Konrads and Johann and Katarina were staying, was spared violation during the onslaught. They remained at the ready to hide in the orchard or the pumphouse, or even a neighbor's chicken coop, but the worst of the devastation passed them by.

Not so for Gerhard and Susannah. The Loewen family spent many hours quaking in their underground refuge beneath the trapdoor in the kitchen. Twice the sound of boots on the floor above brought them to their knees in fervent prayer. No one was hurt, but the Loewen's neatly kept house was left in shambles. Canned goods and fresh food was taken from the pantry, and several windows were broken.

Through it all, Susannah feared mostly for Peter. This present life had no resemblance to the carefree existence at Bethany Home, and she expected Peter to react strongly in one way or another. He did not. Rather, he sat quietly, picking at his fingernails, twisting his hair around his fingers, humming an almost audible tune continually. *Perhaps*, thought Susannah as she sat on a sack in the cool damp of the cellar, *perhaps this is what his mind sees all the time: the darkness, the loneliness, the mental prison beyond the realm of reality. Perhaps this cellar is not so unfamiliar to Peter.*

The Loewen household emerged from their earthen sanctuary and quietly began setting their home to rights. Susannah's mother fingered the torn draperies as silent tears slipped down her chubby cheeks. "We can fix them, Mother," assured Susannah, putting a hand of comfort on her mother's shoulder. "It's only fabric, not a life. No blood has been shed here." Peter stood rigidly by, also placing a thin hand on the woman.

Hannah Loewen nodded her head numbly and whispered, "You are right, child, I know. But what about next time? Does it pay to fix things so they can return and do it all again? And will we come away without bloodshed next time?" She gazed into her daughter's eyes with great anxiety, waiting for answers she could not give. "The Boldts hid their two sons in the strawstack, but the bandits found them and murdered them. Kornelsen's home is a pile of rubble, all because they did not willingly offer their husband and father for execution. Willms is dead now anyway, and so is his wife. His oldest daughter wishes she was dead. What will the children do? There's no end, Susie, no end. This cloud of oppression has not yet passed by. May God help us, if he even is listening. Perhaps he has turned his back on us for our sins, our involvement in this war. Perhaps he no longer hears."

Susannah sat heavily on a chair with her hand on her abdomen. Peter sat on a chair beside her, mimicking her actions. She had no words to say. If she were completely honest with herself, she would admit these same thoughts had been churning in her mind as well. But she knew she must trust that the Lord knew. Otherwise, what good was her faith?

"Mama, come sit down," she said. "We will pray."

"We will pray," echoed Peter.

"God does hear, you know, and he cares. But it seems the time is ripe for judgment, and whether it is a punishment upon us or not, we are in the midst of a terrible storm. If all else is taken from us, we must preserve our faith." Reaching for her mother's trembling hands, she prayed. "Dear Father, we here in this corner of the world are suffering greatly, as you know. We request your strength and courage for what you have for us. And Lord, if you would show yourself to my mother so that she could know you as I do, I would be forever grateful. Please fill us with the peace that surpasses knowledge and understanding, the peace that comes from a heart reconciled to you. In your holy name we pray, Amen."

Mrs. Loewen remained with bowed head, shaking almost uncontrollably. Susannah moved to her knees beside her mother's chair and held her. "Mama?"

Her mother's voice was raw. "What must I do?" she rasped. "I cannot bear it alone."

"Oh Mama, tell him so. He waits so near to you."

"Help me, my child."

Susannah held her mother's hands tightly and bowed with her, her head in her mother's lap. Her ever-present shadow knelt in a forlorn heap beside her. "Dear Father, forgive my sin and rejection of you," she paused as her mother repeated the prayer, and longer as Peter also repeated each word with similar inflection, "I acknowledge Christ's sacrifice on the cross for me personally . . . and I thank you for it . . . . Cleanse me and fill me with your loving Spirit . . . and grant me the peace that only you can give. . . . Amen."

"If the way is so simple," Hannah said through her tears, "why has it taken me so long to find it?"

"The Bible says we must come to him as little children. Their minds are less complicated by the worries of this world and their faith is simple and strong. So must ours be."

"Even when we cannot see the light at the end of the dark tunnel?"

"Even then, Mama. You are his child now, and he will never leave you nor forsake you, no matter what comes your way."

They talked for some time, torn drapes and stained floorboards forgotten. A bond stronger than any earthly one formed between them, but temporal joys also surfaced. "Susannah," said Hannah, looking knowingly into her daughter's eyes, "is there something you have been wanting to tell me?"

Susannah blushed and smiled, new tears rimming her beautiful eyes. "Yes, Mother."

"Then it's true, what I see in your eyes? You and Gerhard are to have a child?"

Susannah nodded. Peter nodded also, and the two women laughed and cried together as their spirits shared the joy. In time, Hannah's face clouded again. "Such a terrible time for a child to enter the world, Susie. You will need much of God's strength and courage. Perhaps this is the great tribulation of which the Scripture speaks, and we will be taken up, away from this chaos."

"Perhaps, but we need to keep trusting until that day. The Lord will see us through."

Nodding, Hannah rose and lifted Susannah to her feet. "Let us get to work, daughter, but take care not to stretch too much. Bad for the baby."

"Bad for the baby," repeated Peter.

"Oh my, but life is strange," said Hannah, patting Peter on the arm. "I feel that my spirit is about to burst."

Later that afternoon, a subdued couple approached the Loewen residence, walking from the direction of Alexanderkrone. They were greeted at the door by Hannah whose swollen face attested to her struggles.

"Mrs. Loewen." Johann felt slightly embarrassed addressing the woman who had once claimed him as her future son-in-law, but she quickly put him at ease.

"Ah, Johann, come in, come in. And this must be your wife."

"Katarina."

"Welcome here, my dear. Susannah has told us how dear you both are to her and Gerhard. Suse is cleaning up the parlor. They . . . they left an awful mess, but at least none of us was hurt or killed. Unlike some of our families here in Lichtfelde."

"I'm glad you are safe," said Katya. "There have indeed been several casualties here, but some other villages have fared even worse. Many of the young men have been executed. This is a sad time for all of us." As she spoke, Katya's eyes roamed beyond her hostess, looking in vain for Peter. Ever since the beginning of the plunder, she had been beside herself with fear for him.

"Susie," called her mother. "You have visitors." Then to them she said, "I will make you some tea. We still can pretend to be civilized, even if the world is not." She bustled away to her kitchen with a song on her lips. Johann and Katarina stared after her in wonder. They turned as one to see two figures emerge from the parlor.

"Susannah," cried Katarina as they fell into each other's arms. "And Peter, dear Peter." Mechanically, he patted shoulders as those around him were doing, then stood stiffly, looking at nothing.

Susannah reached out and shook Johann's hand warmly. "Hello, friend," she said. "Welcome to our messy home. Come to the parlor. I believe we will be able to find enough room to sit in spite of the shambles."

They took places in the front room. Peter followed closely and took a seat on the far side of Susannah. Then he stood and moved between the two women. "Is he. . . .?"

"He is fine," replied Susannah to the unfinished question. "By God's grace."

At that moment, Hannah joined them with steaming tea and a few biscuits she had saved from breakfast. "I'm sorry it's not more fancy, but we haven't recovered from the last storm." Pouring the tea and handing it around, she said, "I heard you speak of God's grace as I came into the room." She paused nervously but pressed on. "I have this day experienced God's grace for myself." Her face shone. "I am a child of the King." Her smile touched each one.

"I am a child of the King," mimicked Peter, also grinning at the others.

Surprised, Katarina focused on Peter. "Have you asked Jesus to live in your heart?" she asked.

"I am a child of the King," he said.

Katarina visited often with Susannah after that first meeting, and Mrs. Loewen found renewed and deeper friendship with Cornelia Reimer. Meanwhile, Johann traveled several times to the village of Tiege, which lay near the western border of the Molotschna, not far from the river and the rail line, to meet with Benjamin Janz. B. B. Janz, as he was known by most, had returned to teaching at Tiege after the dismantling of the Forestry Service, with which he had served during the world war. That is where Johann found him that sunny April afternoon.

The woman who answered the door at the Janz home on Johann's first visit invited him to step inside. "Let me tell Benjamin you are here," she said. She returned in a few moments. "Benjamin asks that you join him in his study." She waved a hand in the direction of the room from which she had come and Johann stepped to the door and knocked tentatively. The door was ajar, and he could see the man diligently pouring over books and papers. A large black leather Bible lay open at the side of the desk.

Janz looked up at the knock. He was a lean man, in his early forties, Johann guessed, with deep-set blue eyes, long thin nose, and ears good for listening. A slight smile lifted the corners of his mouth, and he stood and reached out a hand to Johann. "Good day to you, my friend."

"Good day. I am Johann Sudermann. I hope I am not disturbing you."

Janz waved him into a chair and resumed his seat with a chuckle. "I am always occupied with one thing or another," he said. His eyes drew Johann, for in them he saw a wealth of knowledge, a zest for life, and a clarity of purpose. This man knew who he was and what God wanted of him. The observation encouraged Johann and made him glad he had come.

"You have come about emigration, have you not?" He straightened the papers on which he had been working and set them aside, then reached beside him to retrieve a thick folder. "I am keeping a list of those who have personally spoken to me about the issue. We are compiling names so that we may be prepared to offer statistics to the authorities. One must always know at least as much as those one asks favors of." The slight smile returned, then vanished as he licked his finger and paged through the papers inside the folder. "Johann Sudermann, you said? Have you spoken to me of this before?"

Johann cleared his throat. "Actually, I would like to add the names of my wife and myself to your list, sir, but the real reason I have come is—"

Janz's pen stopped in midair as he met Johann's eyes.

Johann plunged ahead. "I am interested in helping with the project. I would like to offer my services in whatever capacity you need them. I served in the *Forstei*, Schwarzwald Unit, for a couple of years, sometime in the area of training new recruits. I am also a teacher by profession. I recently traveled to Halbstadt to discuss the issue with Benjamin Unruh, and he suggested I talk with you, as he is leaving on an extensive tour to scout out the possibilities of mass emigration. There is much to be done and many who would benefit by our work." He paused to catch his breath. "What would you say to my offer, Mr. Janz?"

The older man had been studying Johann as he spoke and had noted the passion in his voice, in his eyes, as he spoke of his countrymen. "How old are you, Sudermann? Wife? Family?"

"I am twenty-five this year. I am married to Katarina Hildebrandt of Crimea, but we have no children as yet. I have been living in Crimea for the last while, when I was not on *Forstei* duty, but I was raised in Kleefeld, so my heart goes out to those of my people who live within direct range of the civil war. I feel a need—no, *a call*—to become involved in this most important project."

Janz said nothing, but sat and nodded his head, his eyes on Johann's. Finally, he nodded again and pointed his pen in Johann's direction. "You might do. I've been thinking. . . ." He opened a drawer and pulled out two thick manuals, which he handed to Johann. "Read these and summarize them for me. I have, of course, read them over, but they need to be analyzed more closely. They are directives from the Bolshevik government. They may not be in control here yet, but in Moscow they are. Now, I have discovered that a group known as the Tolstoyans have requested and been granted exemption from military service as conscientious objectors. Perhaps we can do the same. There is much information on government policies in these manuals."

Johann accepted the books with a puzzled look on his face. "Excuse me, sir, but what does our military status have to do with emigration?"

"Hmm?" Janz lifted his head and raised his left eyebrow. "It is where we must begin, my friend. We must convince the present regime that emigration would not rob them of fighting men. Do you see my point? We must portray ourselves as dispensable in order to procure permission to leave en masse. But it is a fine line to walk, Sudermann, and the *Selbstschutz* has made that job most difficult. How does one persuade the government that those who marched against them with rifles and grenades cannot take part in further military maneuvers for conscience sake? We have shot ourselves in the foot, so to speak, on this matter. But," he tapped his pen on the manila folder, "we are not defeated. There is more than one way to skin a cat, my friend, and I—*we* shall find it."

"I'm in, then?"

"As you wish. Keep in touch often and let me know what you find out. I will give you further work next time we speak. And, Sudermann, thank you for your sincere interest. Our people desperately need men like you. God bless you for your offer."

He stood and shook hands again with Johann, signaling the end of the meeting. Johann at once felt lighter and yet more responsible, but the prevailing feeling was one of satisfaction at making a contribution for the good of his people. He would do his best.

Johann was not prepared for what he found when he returned to the Reimer home. Katarina was in tears, and the older women were trying their best to console her. It took some time for her to tell Johann the reason she was so upset.

"It's Gerhard," she sobbed. "They've taken him away to the army and Susannah is expecting their first child. They've taken her father too. Peter clings to her, and she is totally overcome. . . ." The storm was not yet over, and Johann held her while she cried.

When the sobs had eased he began questioning her. "What happened? I thought the Reds were still being kept in the north of the colony."

"The Whites, Johann. The White Army, the 'volunteer army,' has forced him to join up to fight against the Reds. What are we to do for Susannah?"

"The White Army!" He sat down beside his wife and stroked her hand as he held it in his own. "I don't believe there is anything we can do about the conscription, volunteer or not. All we can do is look after Susannah and Peter."

"And the baby. I hope it doesn't come too soon with all this upset."

"When is the baby due, Katya?"

"Sometime end of July or beginning of August, I believe. And conditions here are so frightening for such an event."

"Yes. Katarina, I think the only thing to do is to take Susannah and Peter to Succoth with us when we return, which should be as soon as possible."

Katya turned to him and threw her arms around his neck. "Oh, I was hoping you would suggest that. I know her mother would prefer her close, but it's too dangerous, and if one has an option, one should take it."

"I suppose the decision would be up to Susannah. How is she handling it?"

Katarina lifted her eyebrows and tilted her head to the side. "About the same as I would if you were swept away from me without an hour's warning. Devastated, overwrought, not knowing how she can go on. Oh, Johann, what if they come for you too? I am so afraid of that."

"We've talked about this before, Katie. We must trust God for each day. Whatever he has in store for us, he will also provide the resources to endure and even to bring good out of it. I will need to travel here to see B. B. Janz from time to time, but I am in God's hands. And I want you at Succoth."

Katarina sighed heavily and laid her head on his chest. "Life is not a picnic in the sun, is it? Perhaps if we didn't expect it to be, we could cope better when hard times come."

Johann sighed and held her more tightly. Both were lost for sometime in their own private prayers.

"I must go to Susannah," whispered Katarina. She gave her husband a kiss and straightened her unruly hair as she moved swiftly from the room.

The flight of Johann and Katarina from the Molotschna was a frightening one, with threat of being overtaken by one or the other of the warring factions in the area. The political regime in the colony changed almost monthly as of late, and it was difficult to keep abreast of the changes. Johann guided the horse and buggy over the ruts in the pounded-out roads and Katarina prayed for her friend Susannah. She had not been willing to travel to the Crimea. "What if Gerhard should be released, and he searches for me and I am not there.

Besides, my mother needs me now with Father gone." The pain in her voice had been almost more than Katya could bear, but she understood and respected her wishes. Besides, Susannah's mother needed her presence, both to help and to be helped by her.

Peter would not seek solace in Katarina, his own sister. He had been too long gone and had replaced her with Susannah. They all knew the truth of this, but it did not help the present problem. Susannah needed peace, and he would not let her go. So Peter too had remained in Lichtfelde at the Loewen home.

Katarina touched the telegram in her pocket, thankful that Maria had sent it to the Reimers. *Safely through Kharkov*, it said. *Love to all.*

Oh Lord, Your ears must be tired of my pleas, thought Katya as they bounced along the Old Coach Road to Dzhankoi, but she continued to pray. On occasion, Johann reached for her hand or winked at her in a manner that meant for her to keep trusting and praying. She simply could not understand why her husband remained beside her while Susannah's Gerhard was somewhere, who knew where, forced to do who knew what. *Faith, Lord*, she begged. *Please give me faith.*

Johann and Katarina were well aware that many *Selbstschutz* men also fled south, or had already done so. Somewhere in the Crimea, or perhaps across the Black Sea in Constantinople, Ernst Sudermann sought refuge and anonymity.

Unbeknownst to any of them, another group of refugees gathered on the southern coast of the peninsula. The surviving Romanovs, Nicholas's extended family, waited nervously at Livadia for the *H. M. S. Marlborough* to carry them away to safety. European relatives had reconsidered, sufficiently shocked by the regicide. There would yet be asylum for the last of the Russian royals.

Their Russian hearts wrenched within them as they pulled away from the shores of their homeland, possibly never to return. Nicholas's mother, the Dowager Empress Maria Fedorovna, would retain the belief to her last breath that somewhere her son still lived. After all, there was no absolute proof to the contrary. It was hope alone that kept one alive in times like these.

The sun woke Grisha as it shone through the cracked window of the tiny hovel he shared with three of the monks at the monastery. The warmth of the morning called him from his pallet outside into the new day. For some weeks now he had been experiencing the old restlessness that had plagued him in that life that had come before. It had eased somewhat as he rested and worked and shared the simple life with the monks, but now that summer approached, he felt a strong urge to move on.

He would have simply begun walking, but the brothers had become friends. He cared for them and owed them at least a farewell.

"But why must you go?" asked Vanya, the youngest who hung on his every word. "What will we do for stories?" The young man seemed next to tears.

The others chimed in with similar pleas. "Don't leave us, friend. Surely the Lord brought you to us and he would not have you leave."

"And why do you think he would not have me leave?"

"Oh, because you have brought us joy. The Scripture says we are to rejoice, and you have helped us to do so."

Grisha continued with the debate, a form of entertainment that he knew they all loved. "Perhaps you focus on the wrong person to give you joy. Should not your joy be in the Lord?"

"He uses us for his purposes," they rallied. "You are a vessel for his use."

The old wise man lifted his shaking hand then to quiet the contest. "Enough brotherth," he lisped, his mouth puckered into itself, his cheeks hollow with age and self-denial. "If it ith time for our brother to leave, we mutht allow him to do tho." The elder motioned Grisha closer and placed his hand of blessing on Grisha's head. The others gathered round and wept and prayed for this friend who had arrived from nowhere and was now leaving again. Grisha shouldered his pack and, with a final wave and smile, walked up to the road and trudged off toward the southwest.

Chapter 26

 Mika ground her teeth in frustration. The train she rode with Benjamin Unruh had been detained for several days in Kharkov while inept Soviet officials searched and questioned passengers and scrutinized their travel documents. Only by humble diplomacy and flattery had Unruh succeeded in recovering their papers.

Now they were finally in Moscow, and Maria sat in a small coffee shop while her companion met with more officials. At least she had been able to send a telegram from Kharkov so her family would know she was safe. She had sent it to the Reimers, knowing that Johann and Katarina would stop there on the way back to Succoth. Papa would be sick with worry for her, and she did not want to give him further grief on her behalf.

Now she sat at a small round table sipping sweet tea and drumming her fingers on the tabletop. The June sun warmed her as she stared out the window, waiting for Mr. Unruh, waiting to leave Moscow, to leave Russia altogether. Dietrich's home village was in Bavaria, in the south of Germany, a world away.

Mika sighed. Unruh's work was important, and she realized that. "But I knew this before I agreed to come," she declared under her breath. "I should have gone straight to Germany. How can I sit here drinking tea while Dietrich might be waiting for me in Schwandorf?"

"Pardon me, miss?" The waiter appeared to be a young student from the university.

Mika swiftly returned to the present. "I'm sorry, I must have been thinking out loud."

"Of course." He leaned over the table and spoke softly, "If I were you, I would not speak of Germany. It is best to keep such things to yourself, yes?"

Her face paled, and she nodded. "Yes, thank you." Perhaps she would stay with Unruh until he was able to accompany her to Germany. *What an incompetent fool I am,* she berated herself mentally.

"I hope you find him," whispered the waiter as Maria stood to leave the coffee shop. She stopped and stared at him.

"Thank you." It was all she could manage. He smiled, winked, and returned to his work. As she left the shop, the student watched her go.

She hurried along the street to the private home in which she and Mr. Unruh were staying; and she thanked God they were leaving the next morning. It made her skin crawl to think people were always listening, always trying to find out things about others. According to what she'd heard, the secret police knew everything about everyone. *Well,* she thought, *they must never know about Dietrich. They would arrest me for much lesser "crimes" than knowing a German officer.* She quickened her step and deliberately hummed a Russian folksong as she turned in at the gate of her hosts.

Word of refuge spread like prairie fire as the Red Army, under its supreme commander, Leon Trotsky, extended its tentacles of control over the Molotschna Colony. As April gave in to May, and that usually merry month melted into June, refugees from the mainland poured into Crimea in droves. Ebenfeld, Annenfeld, Schoental, Karassan, Spat, were some of the destinations of the fleeing Mennonites and other

German colonists. Many knew of Succoth Estate, knew Heinrich Hildebrandt personally, and were now enroute to the estate for safe haven. It was a time to put the Golden Rule to the test. The Hildebrandt household rallied to the needs of the refugees, every hand required to meet daily demands.

On the morning of June 8, those Succoth residents who were so inclined walked down Magnolia Lane and across the bridge to the little chapel for a Pentecost service. The three-day commemoration of the coming of the Holy Spirit, as recorded in the book of the Acts of the Apostles, was held in high esteem among the Mennonites as well as many of the Russians.

"When times were better," said Katarina to Anna on their walk to the chapel, "we decorated the house and even the barn for Pentecost. The Russian people always used tree branches to beautify the outbuildings. The house was filled with boughs and flowers, almost like a green Christmas."

"Why can't we do that now? I think it would be beautiful and God would like it if we celebrated."

Katarina's hand rested lovingly on her little sister's curly blonde hair. "Ah yes, I believe he would. But he would also understand that this year is different. There are so many people in our care that we simply cannot find the time to do all the special extra things we used to do. Lord willing, we can still have service today and tomorrow."

"What about the third holy day? Don't we have service then too?"

"No. That's picnic day." She smiled as Anna's eyes lit up. "Yes, my dear, we will have a picnic. We'll sit on blankets on the lawns and eat outside too." Satisfied, Anna held to Katya's hand and skipped over the bridge.

"I think the old ways and traditions are empty and meaningless," her brother Nicholai commented as they neared the church. "Why would I accept all those traditions without first examining them for myself?"

"Nothing stops you from doing so. I do not defend the empty traditions or our religion or even our way of life," clarified Katya, "but the truth of God's Word. That is the foundation upon which we build our faith and our hope." She placed her hand through his arm as they mounted the chapel steps, and his head lifted higher, independence seeking to assert itself.

The chapel was filled to the last pew as Heinrich rose to read the Scripture. There was a strong sense that by congregating here, these people were holding firmly to their traditions, to their beliefs. It was a strength that would stand them in good stead as the world changed around them.

Apparently, the Lord was not willing that the Pentecost celebration that year would last three days. On the evening of the 8th, a loud knock sounded at the front entrance doors to Succoth manor. "We demand to see Heinrich Hildebrandt," ordered the local *zemstvo* leader.

Heinrich came as quickly as he could, wondering what the commotion was about. "Good evening, Pavel," he said and graciously extended a hand of welcome to the men. The man called Pavel straightened his shoulders and ignored the proffered hand.

"Heinrich Hildebrandt," he said, not meeting Heinrich's eyes, "you are under arrest. You will come with us at once."

Heinrich and Johann, who had joined him at the door, were dumbstruck.

"I said—" Pavel ventured to repeat his order.

"We heard what you said," Johann assured him, "but we were not sure you meant it. On what grounds are you arresting him?"

The second-in-command, a wiry fellow with a crooked nose and a shock of red hair, pushed his way forward and glared at Johann. "We do not need to explain ourselves to the likes of you. Get out of the way." He grabbed Heinrich by the arm and yanked him forward.

"Be civil, Ivan." Pavel was obviously embarrassed at having to do what he was doing to a man he had worked with on the *zemstvo* committee. His accomplice glared at him but released Heinrich's arm.

"Father?" Katarina approached the doorway as her father was being ushered out. "Father, where are you going?"

Heinrich turned a perplexed face to his daughter. "Don't worry, child. I have been requested to report to *zemstvo* headquarters. I'm sure I will return soon." He glanced at Pavel as he spoke these words.

Katarina was not satisfied. "What is this about, Papa?"

"He's under arrest," said Johann in a flat tone. "We do not know why."

"Under arrest? What has he done?"

"Apparently, they do not have to tell us."

"What. . . .?" Katya felt her blood boil as she attempted to reach out to her father, but Pavel intercepted her.

"I am sorry, Miss," he said, "but these are our orders." He and the one called Ivan flanked Heinrich as the head of Succoth manor walked with stooped shoulders out the door of his home and down the wide verandah steps to a waiting buggy. He stumbled slightly as he climbed up into the conveyance, and Katya moved to follow him, but Johann held her back.

"Not now, my love," he whispered. "We must pray now." Both stood stricken as the buggy jolted onto Magnolia Lane in the direction of the main road.

Paul risked discipline to slip away from his regiment that day in early June. They had been camped south of Ohrloff, directly north of his home village of Ackerman. It was too much to resist the call to return to the place of his birth. It had been five years since he had been home, and he needed to find out how his family was faring. Anatoly was not willing to risk leaving, so Paul went alone. Borrowing a horse from the small herd, he quietly led it away from the encampment, mounted, and took off at a fast pace for Ackerman.

At first glance, the village remained the same—dirty, run-down, poverty-stricken. Then he heard it. Silence. *There should be dogs barking, calves bawling, chickens squawking,* he thought, *but there is nothing, no sound.* Cautiously, he approached the *izba* that had belonged to the Tekanin family. The rickety door stood slightly ajar, as if someone had merely run out for a bucket of water from the river and would be back shortly. But whoever was the last to leave had not returned. In fact, there was evidence that no one had entered or dwelt there for some time.

"Mother? Sonya?" Paul pushed the door open until it stuck in the dirt floor and refused to move any further. His heart began to beat heavily against his ribs as he absorbed the emptiness within. It did not take long to assess the condition of the hut, as it consisted of only one room. He whirled at a scuffling sound in the dark corner nearest him. A large rat ran between his feet and out the door. With a yelp, Paul danced from the house and up onto his horse, heart in his throat. He swore at the rat, at the poor abandoned hut, at the bad luck that seemed to haunt him whatever path he took.

As his horse pranced nervously in place, a grizzled old head peered out at him from a nearby hut. Pulling himself together, Paul again dismounted and approached the woman. He did not recognize her. "What has become of the Tekanins?" he asked. "Mother Tekanin and Sonya?"

The weathered, withered face grinned toothlessly at him from beneath a filthy shawl and cackled, "Gone. The Tekanins are gone. Everyone is gone."

Paul was overcome by shock and disbelief. He lowered his head until he stared straight into the cloudy eyes of the old woman and spoke slowly, trying to remain calm. "What . . . happened . . . to them? Think . . . and remember."

An impish grin on her simple face almost reduced Paul to screaming, but he knew within himself that he could not force anything from her confused brain. Grabbing a large stump of wood, he seated himself in the doorway and waited. "What happened to Mother Tekanin, old woman?"

She mused and smiled, looking in the direction of his voice. "Mother Tekanin. Mother Tekanin." A look of victory spread across her rumpled face. "Died of a fever. Her little girl nursed her, but she died anyway. Horrible." She shook her head in grief, but the emotion fled as quickly as the memory. "Too dry for the crops this year. Watch out for fires, young man."

Attempting to swallow the huge lump in his throat, Paul tried again. "What about little Sonya?" he questioned, a catch in his voice. "Where did she go after her mother died? Is she still here in the village?"

"Here?" The wizened woman cackled again. "No one is here. There's no food. I ate the cats, and now they are gone. Everything is gone."

A bad taste filled Paul's mouth, but he willed himself to continue. "Where is Sonya Gregorovna?"

"Sonya Gregorovna? She's not here, young man. Her mother died of a terrible fever. The girl left with that soldier." She shook her head, her face filled with concern. "I do hope he was good to her. Those soldiers are a bad lot, you know. You watch out for soldiers, young man."

Paul sat on the stump for long minutes, his head in his hands. Could he believe anything the crazy old woman had said? On the other hand, did he have a choice? She offered the only clue to the mystery. It didn't matter anyway; they were both gone. His childhood home now empty and dark. In profound grief, he raised his head to the woman, but she no longer stood in the door of her shanty. She shuffled down the crooked path leading to the river, stick in hand, herding imaginary chickens before her.

A heart-rending moan tore Paul's soul as he pulled himself onto the horse and rode slowly back the way he had come. If he had ceased to breathe at that moment, he would not have lamented it at all.

Heinrich staggered beneath the load he carried to the wagon. Since early morning, he had been forced to cut and carry firewood from the stand of trees near the branch of the Salgir River that flowed west of Succoth and south of Karassan. Pavel and his associate had refused to give any information as to the reason for his arrest, or of its duration. "I'm sorry, Hildebrandt," Pavel had ventured in a brief moment when the two were far enough away from eavesdropping ears. "I must do what I am told."

"But who tells you this?" Heinrich's question was spoken in the tone of voice of a perplexed child. It was obvious his plight bothered Pavel, so he pressed on. "Have I not opened my house to the sick and needy? Do we not follow all the new rules, teaching our fellow comrades to read and write?"

"Don't ask me anything more!" Pavel interrupted as he stormed away from the wagon.

So Heinrich cut, carried, and sweated beneath the June sun. He had always been a hard worker, but steady physical labor was not his constant fare, and his muscles complained even when his lips remained pressed firmly together. A tight pain in his chest caught his attention several times as he exerted himself beyond what he was accustomed to doing. "Lord, give me grace," he prayed. "And let me forgive them as you forgave your captors, as you have forgiven me."

Whenever Pavel's second-in-command, Ivan, caught Heinrich alone, he railed at him and forced him to increase his pace. "Work, you filthy *kulak*," he roared. "It is *your* turn now to work for *us*." Heinrich's passive acceptance of this treatment seemed to infuriate the man even more. Threateningly he said, "I'll get you, rich man. The time will come."

Heinrich continued to pray as he worked. Perhaps that was what the Lord wanted of him right now. There was nothing else he could do about his situation. He was in no condition to flee on foot, besides, his cruel taskmaster watched him like a jealous wife did her straying husband.

Later that night, Heinrich lay curled up beside the wagon which he would fill as soon as first light touched the morning sky. His body was exhausted, but his spirit rested in a supernatural peace that had gradually overtaken his perplexity and near despair. As he lay beneath the navy canopy of night, all the stars of the firmament winked at him as if to say, "We are watching over you."

The sudden crack of a twig alerted him and he tensed, ready to spring up. An animal? He did not think so, although he would have preferred it to a person. A movement in the shadows showed him the indistinct form of a man and he knew which man it would be. Something glinted in the tree-filtered moonlight, and Heinrich knew death awaited him at the hands of this man. Thinking fast but moving ever so slowly, Heinrich adjusted his position so that he could roll beneath the wagon. He watched in incredulous fascination as a glinting blade was raised upward to strike.

Katarina awoke from her restless sleep with a start, sweat clinging to her upper lip. Her whole body felt drenched. "Johann!" She shook him awake and whispered, "We must pray. I feel a great dread for Papa. Please help me pray."

Throwing off the covers, the two knelt beside their four-poster bed and interceded for their father, friend, and mentor. They pleaded for mercy, begged for grace, and did their best to give him over into God's hands. "Thy will be done," Katya rasped brokenly. "Oh Lord, you know best." They climbed back into bed and Johann held his wife closely for a long time. Finally, her even breathing assured him that she had fallen asleep. He lay awake, considering all the terrible things that could be happening to Heinrich. He struggled to release his father-in-law to the able arms of God, but the struggle continued all night.

A rustle of squawking and flapping in the trees almost stopped Heinrich's heart. He saw the knife fly into the air, the body of the attacker fall back onto the forest floor. Apparently, he had disturbed the nest of a couple of partridges. Heinrich used the disturbance to roll to the other side of the wagon.

"What is going on here?" Pavel's voice cut through the night as he stumbled sleepily toward Heinrich. The official had stayed at the site that night, against the advice of his companions and his own comfort. Now he knew why. "What are you doing?" he demanded of the would-be attacker.

"The prisoner was trying to escape."

Pavel snorted and settled himself beside the wagon near where Heinrich had slept. "Get out of here," he said disgustedly to the redhead.

The night slipped by peacefully after that, but on the evening of the second day, Pavel personally escorted Heinrich back to Succoth, dropping him off at the main road. "War makes men into animals," he said in attempted explanation for the disgraceful actions he had taken against a man he had worked with on the *zemstvo* committee for many years. "It forces men to do things they would never have thought themselves capable of in saner times."

Heinrich looked up at the man in the buggy, a man just like himself. "You have a family, Pavel. Think of them when you do these things. God grant you mercy as you have shown me mercy by returning me to my family." Then he turned and trudged down Magnolia Lane toward the manor house, and Pavel whipped his horse into a gallop on his way back to Karassan.

After Heinrich had walked for several minutes, a tremulous smile curved his mouth and lit a tiny fire in his weary eyes. "I'm alive, Lord be praised." Then a frown pulled at the muscles of his lined face. "They will be worried." And he quickened his pace, a hand over the pain in his chest.

Johann urged his horse to a canter as he rode from his meeting with B. B. Janz in Ohrloff back to Kleefeld. Last Sunday, June 18th, the church in Lichtfelde had held a baptism service for ten young men and women, and he had attended. Sometimes he missed the grandeur and majesty of the large churches in the villages near his home. News of the civil war was that the front approached Steinbach, which was only a short distance east of his home village. He knew he should get back to Succoth, but he had a few matters to take care of while he was in the colony.

One of these matters was a visit with Oma Peters. It was a favor to Katarina and Heinrich, although he had come to love the old woman dearly himself. The other matter was to check on the Reimers and Konrads in Alexanderkrone. He knew they lived in fear of the violence that was consuming the colonies, but they refused to flee again.

"This is our home, and here we will stay," pronounced Theodore Konrad as the men sat in the Reimer's parlor the next day. "I am too old to run from this enemy anymore." Although the words were spoken sincerely, Johann still detected an uneasiness in the man. Konrad eyed him and finished with the words, "When once one loses trust in his fellow man, there is no safe haven anywhere for him."

He brushed an arthritic hand over his eyes and tried to still the quiver of his chin. "Our paradise is gone," he whispered as he stared out the window on a world still green and lush, denying the terror that lay upon a similar village a dozen or so *versts* down the road. Johann thought Abram did not look quite as convinced that there was nowhere else to go, but then, he was some twenty years younger than Konrad.

After a visit and supper with the two couples, Johann left the house with a heavy heart. As he stepped into the street toward his horse, he heard cannon fire and noticed the smoky redness of the darkening sky. He had delayed his leaving, counting on returning to Kleefeld in a matter of fifteen minutes or so. Now as he looked toward the east, he decided he had better hurry. As he mounted his horse and turned it in a westerly direction, he became aware of dust and fire from that direction also. He was caught in a crossfire here in Alexanderkrone.

Dismounting quickly, he hastened his horse into the barn and returned to the house. "There is trouble coming. Do you have a cellar to hide in?" He said the words as he closed and locked the door behind himself. The Reimers and Konrads still sat at the supper table finishing their coffee. Cornelia jumped up in alarm, clutching at Abram's arm.

"Abram, they've come. We are doomed."

"Don't be melodramatic, my good woman," retorted Theodore Konrad in a tone reminiscent of the man he used to be. Then to Johann, "What did you see?"

"The sky is alight with cannon and gunfire to the east, no doubt the Red Army, and there is an opposing force approaching from the west. If my guess is close, the Reds and the Whites will meet in this village. We must make quick preparations to hide." He looked to Abram.

Abram Reimer tried to hide the dread that struck at his heart, but everyone recognized it, as it mirrored their own. "Cornelia, food and water. Katie, blankets. Theodore, a lantern and some kerosene. Johann, open the trap door here under the kitchen table and help the others down." Abram himself ran to the bedroom to collect a few valuables he knew Cornelia would want. Within ten minutes they were closing the trap door, pulling the rug and table over the top to conceal their hiding place.

Their concealment came none too soon. The rumble of cannon and the crack of gunfire filled the air in the street beyond their home. The Reimer house stood on the front line, with the no man's land of the deserted Konrad property next to it. For two hours the battle raged while the five sat in the cellar awaiting their fate.

"I wonder what happened to those who did not have time to hide?" Katie tried to keep her sharp voice quiet, and almost succeeded. "We could not have done this without Johann's help." She looked over at him and patted his hand. "Bless you, son," she said. "May you return safely to your family when this is over."

When the noise of battle moved on, the five still sat in their refuge and waited, afraid to come out. What would greet their eyes when they emerged? What further terror awaited their exit from their underground hideaway?

"It must be midnight," guessed Johann. "I am going to see what I can see." He climbed the ladder and raised the trap door slightly. Everything lay in unmolested darkness. Cautiously, he raised the door fully and crawled out into the kitchen. The quavering flames of several fires outside cast eerie shadows on the walls, but all else was quiet.

Abram emerged behind Johann and the two ventured outside to assess the damage. "It seems the fighting was heaviest right here in the Konrad's empty yard," said Abram. They could see silhouettes darting here and there, then clipped voices directing fire-fighting efforts. For the time being, the battle had moved on. Again, the Reimer's home had been spared, but for assorted bullet holes in the kitchen wall. Abram did not know why, but he hesitated to rejoice too soon. The war was far from over.

Johann had insisted, upon his return to Succoth, that the family prepare for the possibility of trouble. His seriousness in the matter bothered Katya, though she tried not to think about it. Memories of their past flight to the gypsies and the arrest of her father remained clear in her mind. She liked to think that what was happening in the Molotschna could not happen here, not at Succoth, but she knew there were no guarantees.

"If anyone should threaten us," instructed Johann, "Katya, Anna, and Nicholai are to run out through the garden door, or the backstairs door, whichever is safest, and hide in the garden. Heinrich and I will deal with the problem."

"I'm not running off with the women and children," announced Nicholai angrily. "I am not a child."

Johann blew out his breath forcefully. "I realize you are not a child, Nicholai, but the women and children need protecting. Can you understand that?"

Nicholai lifted his chin in resistance. "I will see them to safety, but I will not hide with them. I will face any intruders with you and Father."

Johann looked at him for some time, then tightened his lips together. "Fine. I cannot force you."

Johann had also brought a telegram from Maria, again sent to Abram and Cornelia Reimer.

It read: LEFT M STOP LONG ROAD TO R STOP DREAM ABOUT SUCCOTH STOP LOVE TO ALL M

Commander Kuryakin's unit retreated from Alexander-krone as the White Army forced them back east. Paul had been in desperate straights during the fight, his mind constantly on Johann. He knew this was his friend's home territory, these three villages sprawled comfortably along the banks of the Juschanlee River.

He dreaded the thought of killing a relative or friend of Sudermann's. He did not know when this dread had taken hold of him, but Paul was fast coming to the limit of his endurance as far as violence was concerned. He had been greatly convicted as his unit ravaged its way from Leningrad to Moscow a year ago, but he had not known any of the landholders personally. Nor had the perpetual slaughter reached its present level. No, Paul decided, he had reached the saturation level of cruelty, filled to the measure with shed blood. He could not go on this way.

"Anatoly," he said as they marched toward their encampment at Steinbach, "I'm done with this. I'm leaving. Are you with me or not?"

Kovshov turned wide eyes on his fellow soldier. "Tekanin, you cannot leave whenever you want. This is the Red Army. Do you know who is in charge here? Trotsky's own train is parked on the tracks of the Great Northern Railway not far from here. He sits in his office in his iron-plated rail cars, protected by sand bags and concrete, as well as at least twenty leather-clad guards."

Tekanin nodded and continued for his friend. "I know, I know. He has a printing press, a telegraph, a radio station, a restaurant, an electric power station—"

"—a bath, a library, garages for several cars, a fuel tank, and two engines to pull the outfit. You do not want to get on the wrong side of this man. He would squash you like nothing."

Tekanin let out an angry laugh. "If Kuryakin catches me, there won't be anything left to squash. So you're in?"

Anatoly Kovshov gave an exasperated sigh and slammed his right fist into his left hand. "Why did I ever associate with you, I ask myself."

"Because there was no one else sane enough to consider."

"Sane? You call yourself sane?" Kovshov shook his head and continued marching. In a subdued voice he asked, "What is your plan?"

Paul remained silent for so long that Anatoly stared at him through the darkness. Finally he said, "I don't have a plan. I'm just leaving. If you're in, follow me. That's all."

The opportunity Paul Gregorovich had been waiting for came sooner than he had expected. During the night after the temporary retreat, the Red unit under Kuryakin's command settled near Steinbach again. The several units gathered there were in disarray due to the unexpected defeat, and commanders huddled together to strategize. There was no moon, and clouds hid the stars. As Paul sat beneath a tree at the outskirts of the village, he decided that the time had come. What did he have to lose? His life? He felt as if he had already lost that months ago, so it didn't matter anymore.

He elbowed Anatoly Kovshov and the two edged their way deeper into the woods that lay beyond the settlement. Moving soundlessly to avoid detection by one of the many guards, the men melted into the forest and paralleled the road that led south from the village. They walked for hours in fear, then relaxed somewhat as they passed by Apanlee, the estate belonging to David Dick. All was quiet here in this southeast corner of the Ukraine. They would head toward the Sea of Azov, thought Paul, and then follow the coast west again until they could cross to Crimea. He had heard that the political situation was somewhat quieter there.

Chapter 27

Grisha strode along the coast road from the southern Ukrainian city of Berdyansk, the July sun browning his already darkened face, a gentle cooling breeze from the Azov caressing his skin. He had spent a day in Berdyansk, but something tugged at him to keep moving westward.

He prayed as he walked, a strange habit that had implanted itself in him during his time at the monastery. The monks practiced unceasing prayer, and it became the norm for Grisha as well. He was not well acquainted with the one to whom he prayed, but he was convinced that God heard the prayers that wafted up to heaven. But what he pondered now was did this God care enough to converse with his creation? He sniffed and pulled his hat down over his forehead to better shield himself from the sun.

A steady stream of tramps, beggars, and fugitives trickled southward from the Ukraine, and Grisha fell into step with them. Some were eager to talk, others kept their silence for fear of their lives. Grisha also preferred silence. When his mouth was silent, his mind could sort through all the questions of life, even though conclusions were rare.

At the moment he was lost in thought, back at the monastery, listening to the debate and theological discussion of the brothers.

"Grisha?"

He remembered how young Vidya had idolized him, asking

often for his opinion on matters spiritual and otherwise.

"Grisha!"

It took several moments for Grisha to realize that his name was being spoken in the present, not in his memory. Startled, he glanced up and into a pair of dark eyes wide with incredulity. He could not speak, thoughts whirled in his head and flew out again, leaving him absolutely vulnerable. *How could this be . . . who could have thought . . . impossible!*

"Are you not going to greet me, my friend?" Paul's voice shook with emotion.

Grisha's arms opened then, and he wrapped Paul Gregorovich in an embrace that robbed them both of breath. Tears streaming down their faces as the two beheld each other.

"How did you come here? How did you find me?"

"I didn't. God must have found you for me."

"But we could so easily have missed each other."

"But we didn't. Ah, Brother, it is so good to see you."

Anatoly was introduced and the three sat down beneath a shrub at the side of the road to catch their emotional breath. There was much to tell, but it could be told on the walk. They would travel on together now and see what the future held.

The tug at his heart back at the monastary had indeed meant something, thought Grisha to himself. Something so amazing he could hardly comprehend it. Not just something, but Someone amazing who knew him and cared. A strange warmth coursed through the man's blood, an assurance, a promise of more to come. A confused but accepting Grisha knew only one way to handle the discovery—he would continue to pray.

The trio gradually made their wandering way to the Crimean Peninsula and crossed over the bridge which led them to Dzhankoi. Grisha strongly urged the others to turn east at the junction, to put more distance between themselves and the rail lines. "Too many people," he said. Eventually, they left the main road and wandered in a southerly direction, using paths through woods and across streams. The way was becoming more beautiful by the day, and they were all ready to camp in one of the valleys in the shade of acacias and rest. Spend the summer. For food and company, Paul, Grisha, and Anatoly joined a work team overseen by a man known as Pavel. He seemed a likable fellow, even if some of his men were not.

As Pavel and his recruits carried out their work of maintaining control of their portion of the Crimea, the newcomers observed a barely concealed rebellion in the second-in-command, a redhead named Ivan. "The revolution was supposed to bring freedom from the tyrants," he said sourly. "But what has it gained us? More servitude. *Batko* Machno has the right idea: Liberty or death!"

Ivan's anger and lack of cooperation irritated Pavel, but he put up with him. Better that than let him go off on his own. No telling what trouble he would get himself into.

"I'm going to a meeting in Biyuk-Onlar tomorrow," said Pavel to Ivan one day in early July. I will be gone one week. See to it that the men continue to fill the wagons and deliver the wood to the *zemstvo* office." He paused as he looked at Ivan through narrowed eyes. "I am forced, against my better judgment, to trust you. Do not disappoint me."

Ivan bowed and scraped before his boss, partly in sarcasm, partly to speed his leaving. He had plans and he could scarcely wait to instigate them. Pavel put his left foot in the stirrup of his saddle, lifted himself up and threw his other leg over the horse's back. Again he glared at Ivan, sensing something amiss but not able to pinpoint it. With a snarl, he wheeled his mount and set off at a gallop for the Old Coach Road.

Bowing to the ground in mock obeisance, Ivan elicited the laughter of his troop. Paul laughed along with them, feeling a freedom he had not experienced for many years. Anatoly kept his distance, but smiled so as not to attract undue attention. Grisha, on the other hand, neither laughed nor affirmed Ivan's attitude. He purposefully rose to his feet and walked away from the group, showing his disgust.

"What is the matter with your friend?" Ivan addressed Paul and Anatoly.

"Don't mind him, he'll be all right," assured Paul. "He's had a hard time of it."

"So have we all," muttered the redhead. A sadistic smile slithered onto his face. "But our hard times are over, at least until Comrade Pavel returns." Conspiratorially he motioned his men toward him, and they gathered around the fire. "We are going on a little raid tomorrow evening. There are many wealthy landowners here who continue to feast and enjoy their wealth while we live out in the open without enough food. It is time for a reckoning."

"The army calls it 'requisitioning,'" interrupted one of the group.

"Call it whatever you wish," Ivan snarled. He looked over at Paul. "You should be good at this kind of thing, shouldn't you? You have had much experience."

Paul glanced at Anatoly, wondering how Ivan knew of his past involvement with the Red Army. His companion shrugged his shoulders and shook his head slightly at Paul's unspoken question.

"We need weapons," remarked one of the group.

Ivan laughed. "Do you think me so dull? There are—were—many such weapons at the *zemstvo* office. Until last night. I have them in one of the wagons. Enough for everyone."

Another of the men spoke up. "Why are we waiting for tomorrow? Why not go right now?"

Ivan was silent a moment, thinking. Would Pavel return to

check on them before he set out, or was he already well on his way. "Why indeed? Now is a good time." He handed out firearms to everyone, including Paul and Anatoly. Grisha had still not reappeared, and Paul thought it better that they leave before he did. He did not want a confrontation at this time. They would return later and work it out.

The group rode out as soon as dusk muted the light of the day. They traveled a distance south so as to be farther from Karassan and discovery if things did not go as planned. As they rode, the men worked each other into an angry mob. Complaining of their poor treatment, they were soon laying blame generously on anyone and everyone beyond their little band of renegades.

Ivan led the way, of course, and he seemed to know exactly where he was going. "There is a stop we need to make first of all," he said, his voice smooth as oil. "A little debt to pay."

The collection of soldiers and peasants reached a wide private roadway. Ivan turned his horse in at the road and led the men down a long, tree-lined lane sweet with the smell of flowers and fruit. Moonlight drifted on and off as soft clouds scudded across the sky. Paul rode along with the others, a strong feeling of déjà vu almost strangling him. *Didn't you leave the Red Army to escape such actions?* The voice inside him refused to be silenced.

Katarina hummed her way through her duties. The infirmary had emptied, the refugees moving on to more permanent dwellings. For the time being, Succoth Manor was family again, and Katya enjoyed the peace. It had been a beautiful day, and she and Anna had helped Cook prepare a summer picnic for the family at the gazebo on the lawn. Johann had returned home safely from the Molotschna, and Papa had recovered from his unexplained arrest. Nicholai concerned her. He was sullen lately, especially as news of the chaos in the Ukraine came to Crimea with the refugees and the sick. She needed to pray for him.

She thought she heard voices as she prepared for bed, but assumed it to be Heinrich and Nicholai. Perhaps her father could talk some sense into the boy's head. She supposed it was the in-between years he found himself in, no longer a child but not quite a man. She smiled at the thought of her Kolya all grown up. Mama would be proud of him, so tall and handsome. And usually cheerful, until lately. Oh well, she thought, he would come through it.

A sudden explosion of gunfire shocked her back to the present and she cried Johann's name in alarm. She could hear his running footsteps approaching the room and ran to meet him at the door.

"Take Anna and Nicholai and run. Bandits at the door."

"Johann! Johann, please be safe. You do not need to be a hero for me—I need you."

Johann gave her hand a quick squeeze and pulled her out into the hallway. "Go quickly." He pushed her in the direction of Anna's room and ran down the stairs toward the front of the house.

Obediently, almost stiff with fear, Katya pulled Anna from her bed and threw a sweater about her shoulders. "Come quickly, my Ännchen," she said, already drawing her out of the room. Nicholai met them at the back stairs and ushered them ahead of him. His face was pale and his eyes wide at the unexpected terror. Cook met them at the door, her ruddy face lined with worry and fear.

"This way," Nicholai instructed as they left by the back door. Several more shots were fired at the front of the house and Katarina stopped short, stifling a scream behind raised hands. Nicholai grabbed her arm and hurried her away from the house, from the sound of guns, from the man she had given her life to and the other who had given her life. The four of them ran a crooked course through the orchard, until Kolya stopped in a thick olive grove and ordered them to wait there.

"Not here," declared Katya, recovering her courage. Leading the way, she darted across Magnolia Lane and over the bridge to the church. Cook followed and Kolya helped Anna.

The girl was crying. "Where are we going? What's happening to Papa? I want to go to Papa."

"Shh, Anna," said Katya in a voice choked with emotion. "God will look after Papa. He needs us to be safe."

"Why are we here?" the girl shrieked. "I don't want to go to the graveyard at night. I'm afraid."

"Nothing to be afraid of, my love. I come here all the time. It's a safe place." When Nicholai realized what his older sister planned, he helped her open the heavy door of their mother's tomb and lit the candle on the shelf within. He helped Cook into the small enclosure and handed Anna in to her.

"Please, brother, don't go back there," Katya whispered. but she saw that he was determined. She reached around his neck and kissed him on the cheek, then stepped back into the tomb with her two companions, while the eerie light of the candle danced around their heads and distant shouts assailed their ears.

With a scraping sound, Kolya pushed the door shut on them. Katarina focused on Anna then, for the girl was nearly hysterical with fear. For long minutes she simply held her and smoothed her long blonde hair. Then they talked and Katya sang to her and told her stories of the mother she could scarcely remember. "She is not here, dear child," she said. "She's with Jesus. Don't cry anymore. We are safe." And then as Anna dozed fitfully in her arms, Katya's prayers poured out for Johann and Heinrich, and for young and impulsive Kolya. Cook sat on the dirt floor and wept, while outside the tomb, a storm roared. Katya knew that only a mighty force could protect her beloved family this night.

Even as she prayed, Katarina imagined how the sight of his creatures wantonly destroying each other must cause her heavenly Father's heart to break. She saw in her mind's eye the jagged fire that tore his heart as it streaked across the night sky. She heard his thundering roar of pain, and she wondered how much he would allow. "Thy will be done," she whispered hoarsely to herself, the words choked in the musty grave.

The band of men forced entry into the mansion, seeking shelter from the impending storm, pushing aside Heinrich and Johann. They began helping themselves to whatever met their fancy and destroyed the rest. Ivan pinned Heinrich to the wall with his rifle, hoping to see him squirm and plead, but the pale face of the head of the house did not plead. Heinrich spoke quietly, offering forgiveness to those who now plundered his house and his family. His presence of mind infuriated Ivan, and he smashed the barrel of the gun against Heinrich's head, causing a trickle of blood to course down his cheek. Even then, the older man did not show fear.

Johann was similarly held at gunpoint by one of the bandits. It was at this instant that Paul and Anatoly entered the house. When he recognized Johann and Heinrich, Paul fell back against the door in utter disbelief. Johann stared at him with matched shock. Stammering, Paul called out, "Ivan, we have other places to visit tonight. Let's move on now. I'm sure there will be more than enough at the next place."

"What's the matter with you?" demanded the redhead. "We've only begun. Besides, I have a score to settle with the old man." He turned to Heinrich again and backhanded him across the face. Johann struggled to come to Heinrich's defense, but his captors held him back.

Paul grabbed Ivan's arm. "Come, man, let him be and take what you've come here for."

Ivan turned on Paul with a growl and threw him back. "Do not touch me. I will do what I came to do." Turning to the man who held Johann, he ordered, "Bring him." They and two others led Heinrich and Johann outside into the building storm.

Paul tried to follow, but was detained by strong arms. "What's the matter with you?" hissed Anatoly into his ear. "Are you trying to get us killed here? What does it matter if they get the rich ones. There are too many of them anyway."

His face taut with shock, eyes black with dread, Paul watched the men push their captives ahead of them out of the door. Johann. "Anatoly, please! I must save them!" He struggled again, but his accomplice merely laughed at him, having no idea of the intensity of Tekanin's pain. After the others had teased him for his weak stomach for plundering, he finally managed to escape and fled outdoors in search of Ivan and his prisoners. It was not long before he found them, and then time stood still.

Ivan and the other bandits led their prisoners in the direction of the barns. A cold sweat broke out on Heinrich's face and ran down his collar. The wind had picked up and howled through the trees. Another deadly slice of lightning cracked into a large oak tree ahead of them, and it fell across their path. The superstitious peasant-bandits shrieked and fled, leaving Ivan alone with the two prisoners.

"Run, Johann," shouted Heinrich through the whipping wind. "Save yourself."

But Johann could not desert his friend, his father-in-law. He leaped at Ivan, but was met with a blow to the head that sent him reeling. Pushing himself up onto hands and knees, he shook his head and rose to try again. His glasses were gone, but had cut his face at the impact of Ivan's fist. Dizziness assailed him, but he lurched toward Ivan. This time the butt of Ivan's gun met him on the side of the head and he lost consciousness even as he fell. Blackness enveloped him and he could not fight it any more than he could still the storm.

It was still night when he awoke, a hellish night of fire and storm. Remembering, he looked around for Ivan and Heinrich, but they were nowhere to be seen in the flickering darkness.

He glanced toward the house to see flames shooting out of the study window. Someone had ignited the kerosene. Fire gobbled the drapes and the books, spreading quickly to the other rooms. Soon the bandits were forced from the mansion with whatever they could carry. Several of them carried lanterns, and proceeded to set fire to the trees in the orchard.

As Johann watched helplessly, the entire estate became an inferno. It began to rain, and Johann felt as if the God of creation wept huge tears that fell in slashing sheets on the fiery scene, reducing it to smoldering embers. Johann also knew that although God saw and cried, and kept the boundaries intact, he would not force his hand on these his creatures who had chosen to reject him. He withheld his hand to allow evil its time.

Suddenly Katarina stood before Johann, her hair dripping with rain, her clothing drenched from the deluge.

"Katya!" Johann gripped her shoulders, facing her toward himself and away from the flames. "What are you doing here? Don't you know what they do to women?" His eyes, large with fear and determination, held her terrified eyes, dark in the night.

"I don't know where Kolya is," she sobbed, her tears mixing with the raindrops.

"I will find Kolya. And I will come back for you." He was glad she could not see his battered face. "You must trust me."

She willed herself to nod. Biting her lip to keep the sobs back, she hung her head in resignation. Johann pulled her into his strong embrace and whispered into her ear. "Katarina, the others need you. You must be strong for them."

Again the silent nod.

"Go back to the tomb and stay with them." He led her back to the little earthen mound in the cemetery. She turned one last time to ask the unspoken question.

"I will come back for you, my love. Do not come out until I come for you."

She stooped and climbed down into the flickering dimness as he closed the door once more. Taking a deep breath, Johann sprinted to the back of the church where for one long moment he rested his head and prayed, "Father God, please help me to keep my promise." As he emerged from the shadow of the chapel, a thunder of hooves could be heard from Magnolia Lane, accompanied by hoots and shrieks of hideous laughter.

His heart trembling within him, Johann stumbled across the wet cobblestones in the direction of the barns. Smoke billowed from the house, and the smell of burned wood permeated the air. Where would he find Kolya? Why had Paul Gregorovich appeared this night, in this place? What had they done to Heinrich?

All three questions were answered for him as he opened the door to the main barn. He staggered back against the wall as his mind refused to take in what his eyes beheld. Before him on the straw-covered floor lay Paul, reduced to a heap of convulsing agony. His sobs were almost inhuman, filled with remorse and pain.

Beside Paul stood Kolya, chest heaving, face twitching, his entire body quaking with the effort of holding the rifle to Tekanin's head. His finger shook on the trigger, savoring revenge.

But the worst part of the scene that assaulted Johann on that dawning day was the body which hung from the rafters above Paul's head. *Oh Lord, no!* his mind screamed. *Not Heinrich!* He heard Kolya change positions, growling at the prostrate form on the barn floor. Choking back his pain, Johann advanced toward his young brother-in-law and spoke softly.

"Nicholai, do not do this thing. It will only bring you down to their level."

Kolya's chin came up and his lips quivered as huge tears rolled down his pale cheeks. Johann tried again. "This is not the man who did it, Nicholai. You know that. Besides, to kill him will not bring your father back."

Kolya did not ease his grip on the rifle, but he seemed to be listening. "Remember what your father always told you, Nicholai. He said, 'Forgive your enemies. Do not take up arms against them.' Do you remember that?"

Kolya let the gun down slowly, considering Johann's words. Johann eased forward and took the gun from the boy, who backed up against one of the stalls. His eyes traveled up to the gently swaying form of his father, and suddenly he let out a cry of anguish that stilled even Paul's wails. "NOOOooo. . . ." He collapsed on the floor and Johann ran to him and gathered him in his arms. He half carried him out of the barn and moved to close the door on the grisly scene inside. As he left with Kolya, he turned to the man on the floor.

"Cut him down, Tekanin. Now."

Chapter 28

Katarina's mind wandered as she sat in the tomb waiting for Johann. She wondered that she hadn't felt the tension that day. Why hadn't she sensed it as she folded tablecloths in the dining room and checked the pantry for supplies, that this day would be the end of life as she'd known it. The end of Succoth. The destruction of her security.

It wasn't as though the violence was a surprise, the entire country had been rife with it these last years, especially since Russia had been fighting in the Great War. The cause and effect syndrome that resulted in the ostracism of anything and anyone remotely Germanic, had spread like prairie fire down the Dneiper and even leapt indiscriminately across the isthmus to Crimea.

Those desperate renegades in the *Selbstschutz* had practiced their protective offensives with courage if not sense, and the backlash of their maneuvers fueled the fire until the heat was suffocating and all consuming.

Why on such a day had destruction come? The sky had been clear and blue, the wind whipping shreds of cloud along distant air currents. Birds busily hunted provision for their young who waited still ugly and eager in haphazard nests. Why had Katarina's personal peace not been overcome by the more ancient premonition of doom?

She started violently at the scraping of the door as it was opened from without. Johann's face peered in at her. A cry of joy and relief escaped her lips. Beyond him the sky had lightened, but all was silent. No birds' song this morning. She saw Kolya there too and scrambled out of the dimness to embrace him. He did not respond although his entire body shook.

"Where's Papa?" she asked as she reached for Johann. He took her in his arms but did not answer. She wrenched herself free. "Johann, where's Papa?" At his silence, the pleading in his eyes not to make him tell, she screamed at him, beating at his chest with her fists. Her response broke into Nicholai's brain and he took one of her arms while Johann took the other. "Leave me alone. Tell me where he is!" But they would not release her.

"Katya, you must listen to me," commanded her husband. "Heinrich is . . . he is. . . ."

"Papa's dead," stated Nicholai flatly. "They killed him." Then sobs silently shook his body as he slid to his knees on the grass by the graves, his head on the ground. Katya turned to stare at him and she had no choice but to believe his words. Nothing could shake them all so thoroughly as this.

Behind them, Cook was holding a terrified Anna, who had awakened at their screams. Johann reached for the girl who ran to Katya, and then he helped Cook climb outside. The woman staggered to the church steps where she sat down heavily, threw her large white apron over her head and wailed.

The others stood within the circle of each others' arms and cried out their hearts' grief. Finally, worn out by grief and tension, they joined Cook on the chapel steps, helpless to know what to do, each lost in his or her own personal pain.

Katya wondered in what dark corner the notion was conceived to extirpate a family home, to remove forever from those who lived there the habitual serenity and trust, and with it, to take the life of one so noble, so compassionate, so trusting. Why Papa? And why like this? Papa had never knowingly hurt anyone. He was, to her, the epitome of justice and fairness, of loving the Lord his God with all his heart, and all his soul, and all his mind, and his neighbor as himself. Yes, the war and revolution had taxed his strength and tested his faith in humanity, but it had also stretched his soul, and this ever-growing strength had filled them all with a sense of purpose. "God has a plan," he had always said.

Now that conviction was gone, snuffed out of Katarina's heart like a candle flame in a draft of wind. She wanted, even longed to believe that God had a plan, and that it was a plan for good and not for evil, but how was a mortal to process the events of that day and all the days previous and arrive at such a conclusion?

Perhaps that was the secret key: Though she could not comprehend it this night, Katarina's God was not flesh and blood, but God of the universe, Spirit of Light and Truth, Supreme Judge, and Father of the Fatherless. *I must believe!* she hissed to herself through parched lips as she stared at the devastation through red rimmed eyes, watching the smoke rise contemptuously from the rubble in an obscene offering to the gods of darkness. *I will believe! I will carry on. I will do this for you, Jesus, and for Papa.*

As she rose and walked slowly across the bridge, tears coursed down her soot blackened face, dripping in dirty stains onto her once white blouse. She walked resolutely toward the ruins of Succoth estate. Her eyes saw burned skeletons of once beautiful magnolia and cherry trees, and the blackened trunk of a gnarled olive, but her mind painted rows of fruit laden trees, branches bending invitingly over the river of life which flowed through the center of the city in heaven. That's where Papa walked now with Jesus.

A slow, sad smile transformed her filthy face. As she meandered around and through the smoldering rubble, she envisioned heavenly mansions supported by enormous glittering jewels and the softest of lawns, and the vision encouraged and strengthened her.

Then Johann stood before her, studying her, trying to decipher her thoughts and her heart. Returning to the present, she reached out her hands to him and said, "We will endure." Then she cried out, "Oh Johann, please help me to endure," and fell weeping into his arms. His lips moved in silent prayer as he opened his heart and soul to the Lord and pleaded for solace for his beloved, for her family, for himself.

The contractions that tightened around Susannah's middle robbed her of breath. "Concentrate, my dear," exhorted the midwife as she guided her patient through the overwhelming waves of pain. But even then, the pain was not as devastating as the inner grief she felt for her husband. She cared not for herself. Her only motivation lay in how everything related to him: as Gerhard's wife she must be strong, Gerhard's baby needed her, she wanted Gerhard to be proud of her. She clung desperately to the belief that somewhere her man was alive, and that God would bring them together again. If she did not hope, she would die now.

Even as she looked into the pink and wrinkled face of her baby, the joy, relief and sorrow braided themselves together into a lifeline of hope. *Gerhard, you have a daughter. I don't know who she looks like right now—she's very new, but I hope she resembles her papa. Gerhard, you are a papa now, imagine that. I wish you could see her. . . . Oh Gerhard, how can I do this without you?*

Cradling her baby close to her breast, she wept for what she—what they—had lost. Her mother Hannah rubbed her shoulders and brushed out her waist-length blond hair. The actions soothed her, and after the women had helped her into clean nightclothes, she lay back against the pillows, still clutching her child to her heart, and both slept in utter exhaustion.

"Grisha, you missed a party," raved one of the bandits upon their return to the camp. He pulled a handful of jewelry from his pocket and held it out for him to see. Grisha grunted his disinterest.

Ivan, the redhead, the ringleader, slid smugly from his mount. "I got what I went for," he boasted, but all the men were caught up with their own prizes.

Grisha noticed that Anatoly remained reticent, and looked about for Paul. "Where is Tekanin?" he asked the man.

"He'll be coming along any time," returned Kovshov, but his eyes told another story.

"Let's get a fire going," Grisha suggested to him, jerking his head in the direction of the forest. "I am in need of some good, strong coffee." Anatoly caught his meaning and followed him deeper into the trees to look for dry wood and kindling. As soon as they were a distance away from the others, Grisha turned to his companion and demanded, "What happened? Why is Tekanin not with you?"

Anatoly paled at the sternness of Grisha's countenance. "He reacted strongly to our raid. Apparently, he knew the estate owner and tried to protect him. I held him back, but later he escaped and I haven't seen him since. When Ivan returned without the *kulak* and ordered us to leave, we did not linger. Something about Ivan . . . I wouldn't trust the man to saddle my horse."

"You don't have a horse. You are a poor deserter with nothing at all. And now you have deserted my friend, your friend. Have you no sense of responsibility? But for him, you would still be feuding with the Whites, or maybe dead along some rutted road between villages. They would care as much for you as you have for Paul Gregorovich. Now, where is he?"

"I do not know. I swear, I left with the others. Didn't see hide nor hair of him."

"Well, saddle up that imaginary horse of yours. We are going to find him."

"We're going . . . back there? No, I don't want to go back. We've done enough there."

Grisha shoved Anatoly ahead of him, weaving his way through the trees away from the camp and in the direction from which the band had come. "Keep moving. I will need you to guide me. I haven't found Paul just to lose him again."

"But I haven't eaten. What about our coffee?"

With a snarl, Grisha pushed him again, and they made their way toward the main road.

Hoofbeats approached on the dirt trail, and Katarina fearfully peeked out the window of the chapel, eyes wide. Johann came to her side immediately and pulled her back. "It's a lone horse," he said. "Not bandits. Relax, Katya. You're like a deer, ready to run."

She didn't answer him, put out by what she believed was a condescending tone of voice. She turned away and went to sit beside Anna on one of the pews.

Sighing in frustration, Johann let himself out of the little building. "Wilhelm," he called in greeting, relieved beyond measure to take a breath of pure air away from their shelter of sorrow. "I have never been so glad to see you."

Wilhelm Enns was speechless, his grey eyes roving over the creek, taking in the black skeletons of trees, the still smoldering remains of the manor. Leaping from his horse, he marched straight to Johann, took him by the arms and embraced him. Standing back, he said, "My dear friend, I am so sorry. We heard word via one of our workers that there had been trouble here last night, and I came over immediately." He looked again at the scene across the stream and winced, shaking his head. "What happened?"

"Bandits," said Johann, tensing as he prepared again to tell of the nightmare that had overtaken them only a few hours before. He tried several times to speak, but the words would not come. He too shook his head and rubbed his face with his hands.

Wilhelm, alarmed by Johann's state, led him to a bench on the cemetery side of the chapel.

They sat and he gave Johann time to collect himself. Even then, the telling was like dragging a mule across a river. Words came hard and harsh. When it was all told, it was Wilhelm who held his head in his hands and wept, great heaving sobs for his dear friend and mentor, Heinrich Hildebrandt. Eventually, he rubbed his reddened eyes again and asked, "Where . . . is he?"

Johann answered so softly he could scarcely be heard. "We have a few faithful workers yet. They have prepared the body and it is in the icehouse. The funeral will be tomorrow in Karassan. Many will wish to attend, and we can host no one here anymore. Never again." His eyes turned in the direction of the house, and there was nothing there to make him smile. No wide verandah overflowing with flowers, no windows topped by brick eyebrows, no large welcoming front entrance, no schoolroom. "A haunt for wild animals," he whispered, "and demons."

"You must come to Tomak. I will return and send a carriage for you at once. We will give you everything you need."

"I appreciate that, Wilhelm. We have no other course but to accept."

"You would do the same for us," he answered, and Johann knew it was true.

"Something else bothers you," stated Wilhelm intuitively. "You should tell me, it would ease the burden."

Johann stood and paced before the bench, hands deep in his pockets. He stopped in front of Wilhelm and met his eyes. "Do you remember me telling you of my childhood friend, Paul Gregorovich Tekanin, the one from Ackerman who had gone up to St. Petersburg before the war?"

The other nodded, clearly puzzled.

"Well, he was one of the band who plundered Succoth last night."

"What?" Wilhelm was on his feet, anger and perplexity drawing his face tight.

"He didn't know Succoth was our home." Johann motioned Wilhelm back to his bench, surprised to find himself defending the scoundrel. "We were each as astounded as the other when he marched into the house." Johann began to pace again, head down, plowing through the memories. "When he saw us, he tried to stop the carnage, especially the mistreatment of Heinrich, but the others held him back. He caught up with Heinrich, but he came too late. The deed was already done. I found them together, with Kolya holding a rifle to his head. Paul was completely broken up about it."

"Did he speak to you at all, explain anything?"

Johann huffed into his mustache. "I did not engage in a conversation with him, Wilhelm. I ordered him to cut Heinrich down and left. I had to get Kolya out of there."

"Where is the boy?"

Johann ducked his head in the direction of the chapel. "In there with the rest. Hasn't spoken since we came back from he barn. Sits alone in the corner totally mute."

Wilhelm grimaced again and nodded in sad understanding. "And what have you done with Tekanin?"

"I haven't done anything. I believe he is still around because I heard him calling my name early this morning outside the chapel. That is surprising enough, for a Russian to set foot in a cemetery at night." He shrugged. "I don't think I have anything to say to him. He was always impulsive, but this time there is no way back."

Wilhelm Enns was silent for a long time. Then it was his turn to pace. Choosing his words with utmost care, he faced Johann. "When you say there is no way back for Paul, are you saying there is no forgiveness for him?"

"That would sum it up in my mind, yes."

"Johann, I realize you are suffering greatly, but I beg you to consider what you say. Forgiveness is not for the easy times. It comes at great sacrifice."

"How can I forgive him for associating with the men who killed Heinrich, who was more like a father to me than my own father? What do you expect from me?"

Wilhelm persisted. "Hans, you cannot let bitterness take root in you." He tried another tack. "You are the one on whom the rest of the family will depend from now on. You cannot lead with a heart of bitterness. How then can you expect your family to heal?" With a gentle smile, he took Johann's arm and waited for him to meet his eyes. "I will not browbeat you any longer. I will look in on the others and then ride back for a carriage. Tonight you will be cared for with all that we have to offer."

Johann embraced the man again. "Thank you, my friend. I know you speak the truth, but it may take some time to obey it."

Enns nodded in understanding. "Don't let it be too long."

Susannah sat in her mother's rocking chair on the verandah of their Lichtfelde home, holding her baby close. She had named her Marianna. The sun was as warm as any July day, the sky as blue, but the landscape had changed. Weeds had sprung up in yards and gardens as people tended to the more urgent needs of finding food and nursing the sick. In places, trees had been cut down for firewood or had fallen victim to fire. The tidy village was no longer as perfect it had been.

Politically, the air had cleared somewhat, and for that Susannah thanked God. Denikin and his White Army had routed the Reds, also keeping Machno away. That devil in human flesh had dedicated himself to decimating several villages in the Chortitza Colony and Zagradovka. From what she had heard, several hundred people had been murdered, shot, hung, or hacked to death by the bloodthirsty *Machnovitz*. Their campaign of death had left the people in desperate straits, having been robbed of all food, clothing, seed, horses, and dignity. Many of the women suffered from diseases left behind by the bandits' lust. Such disgraces proved more devastating than hunger.

Although the opposing armies had also drained the Molotschna of much of its bounty, they were still better off than their brethren in Chortitza, so packages of food and clothing were being gathered to send to the needy. Susannah's mother had scoured her house to send aid to the suffering souls in the Old Colony.

For now, Suse made the best of the relative calm. The White Army was a visible presence, and requisitioning still took place, but at least they did not fear for their lives as with the *Machnovitz*. The requisitioning was, in Susannah's mind, nothing more than legalized theft. Soldiers could come around anytime, demanding anything they wished, and the people had no choice but to acquiesce. Life had become strange indeed.

One of the miracles that God had worked in the midst of the chaos was the adoption of Hannah by Peter. He had taken to her without question, and although he still often trailed after Susannah and held onto her sleeve or her apron, he also attached himself to Hannah. It was as if she was the mother figure he had so long missed. The woman seemed content with the new development, adapting easily to the constant company. "During these trying times," she said, "we must do what the Lord requires of us and look ever to the needs of others." And this she did with devotion and compassion.

As Susannah sat rocking Marianna, she prayed for Gerhard. She remembered how he had often called her his angel, adoring the thick golden braid that encircled her head. She still braided her hair daily and put it up, but her face had changed. Deep hollows robbed her cheeks of their roundness, and their ruddiness had been replaced by a pallor that even the summer sun could not remedy. She would never be the same Susannah as she had been, she decided. Some wounds never healed; some scars went too deep. But through the pain, she must keep her eyes on the Lord, because he had promised that he would walk with her through the valley, and that on the other side, there would be life and beauty and freedom and love. Forevermore. She must always hope.

Chapter 29

The funeral of Heinrich Hildebrandt took place in the Mennonite church in the center of Karassan, as it was the largest Mennonite church in the vicinity of Succoth. The spacious brick and stone structure easily held five hundred people, and it was filled to capacity. Friends and acquaintances had traveled from as far away as Spat and Simferopol, with a delegation from the Ebenfeld congregation in northern Crimea.

A sweet summer breeze blew through the twenty-foot, arched windows, rustling the leaves of open Bibles. It was a welcome cool to those experiencing the staleness of shared air, the claustrophobic grief for the man to whom they bade farewell. Differences of opinion were laid aside as those who had supported the *Selbstschutz* greeted those opposed, and they took seats next to each other. In the final end, Heinrich's passing brought about a unity that his life had not accomplished.

Following several hymns of comfort, the first minister, an Isaac Dyck from Karassan, opened the Word of God to one of Heinrich's favorite passages, Micah 6:8. "Our brother Hildebrandt modeled his life after God's Word," he said. "He set out to act justly, to love mercy, and to walk humbly with his God. He lived this out in his home as well as in the broader community. He held to his beliefs even in the face of severe opposition. . . ." A nervous shuffling could be heard at this comment. Brother Dyck continued, ". . . and beneath the pall of persecution, he clung to mercy, even forgiving his murderers."

After Brother Dyck had offered a lengthy sermon that encouraged the mourners to focus not on Heinrich, but on his God, a second minister from Spat shared from the book of Matthew, the Sermon on the Mount, where Jesus exhorted the people to forgive their enemies and to love those who hated them. The words sank into Johann's soul as he sat beside Katarina in the front pew of the church. He glanced over at Wilhelm Enns, and the other nodded faintly as if to confirm the words he had spoken to Johann earlier that week.

The way was clear, Johann knew. He was to forgive. No qualifications, no exemptions. Now that the truth hit him again, he needed to pray that he would be willing to do this. After all, as the second speaker was saying, did not Jesus die for all, for sinners, offering salvation freely in spite of one's past failings, no matter how gross? Reaching for Katarina's hand, he prayed for grace to forgive.

Katarina sat stoically on the pew beside her husband. She wore a small hat with a low brim that shaded her eyes. They were red and swollen from unending tears that she had willed to cease in the presence of these others. But her eyes were empty. She sat in self-enforced calmness, waiting for the interminable sermons to be done, hearing nothing, absorbing nothing. She was as numb as her brother Nicholai beside her. Only his numbness was beginning to give way to a deep anger.

The two sermons were followed by several choir songs, and then four more brothers offered short tributes to Heinrich and his faith. A graveside benediction was given at the end of the service, as Heinrich's body would not be buried there, but in the cemetery at Succoth, in the same tomb as his dear wife.

Katarina keenly felt the absence of Mika. She needed her sister more than ever now, but she was farther away than she had ever been.

"Do not think that God watches dry-eyed from heaven,"

said Preacher Willms during the benediction. "No, brothers and sisters, his heart breaks for his children, for those he created to live in harmony with each other. He collects our tears in a bottle, he knows the extent of our pain. We do not know why he allows us to walk this path of sorrow, but we know that he walks with us, and that he knows the beginning from the end. We know also that this life is not the end. It is but a brief proving ground before we enter paradise, the beauty and peace of which cannot be described in human language. Remember that our brother, father, and friend, Heinrich Hildebrandt, is now a resident of that place. Pay heed that you are also on the path that leads to heaven. Amen."

According to tradition, a lunch of *zweibach* and cheese was served in the eating area of the church. Everyone felt obliged to file by the family of the deceased to offer condolences and encouragement. For Katarina, this was the worst part of the entire day. Exhausted by her grief and the effort of putting forward a controlled face, she felt like a puddle on the floor.

The event floated by as a fog, and in spite of her resolve to accept and adapt to the trials the Lord had allowed them to endure, she could not bring herself to do so. She shut her mind to everything and everyone. Johann knew and took the burden from her as much as he could. Agnetha did her best to answer the people who waited for some comment from Katarina when none was forthcoming. Anna clung brokenheartedly to her sister, not understanding any of the grief, but the huge, gaping hole in the midst of her being.

Father Serge Ivanovich did not enter the church, but stood outside after the service to speak with the family. He took Katarina's hands in his own and simply bowed his head, slow tears making their way down his face. His presence touched them deeply. He made the sign of the cross and handed them a piece of paper before turning back down the street in the direction of his own church. It was a telegram from Mika:

SHIP PLEASANT STOP PAPA SHOULD SEE THIS STOP MISS YOU ALL LOVE M

The ride back to Succoth chapel was rough and quiet, no one wishing to break the silence, because no words were worth speaking. The body of Heinrich Hildebrandt was interred beside his wife. Before they carried the coffin into the vault, Katarina claimed the papers and money from beneath her mother's casket. For those who did not know, they assumed she was paying her last respects to her mother before Heinrich's coffin filled the remaining space in the small tomb.

They rode off then to Tomak, to accept shelter there and to try to come to terms with their loss and their future. Johann especially struggled with the future. What would God have them do? Where should they go?

For two rubles, fifty kopecks, Abram purchased the latest copy of *Friedensstimme*. Editor Abraham Kroeker had devoted three pages to the death and funeral of Heinrich Hildebrandt and the razing of Succoth. They sat in stunned silence that evening, the Reimers and the Konrads, as they read and reread about the horrifying events from the Crimea.

In the Loewen household also, the words were read and processed, accompanied by many heartbroken tears. "Oh Peter," cried Susannah as he sat beside her on the sofa. "You are an orphan now. Your dear papa has gone to be with Jesus."

"Gone to be with Jesus."

A small house near Wilhelm and Agnetha's had been readied for the Hildebrandt-Sudermann family. The Ennses had

given over the manor house to the workers earlier on, and had taken up residence in the foreman's previous abode. The unpretentious arrangement suited them well. The recently bereaved family settled into a house with five small rooms. Johann and Katarina occupied one of the bedrooms, Nicholai another, and Anna the third, accompanied by Cook whom they refused to leave behind. A kitchen and tiny parlor made up the other side of the house. They often shared meals with the Enns family, whose house offered a large enough eating area to seat them all.

Anna, being young and more adaptable than the rest, soon became fast friends with Sarah and Tina Enns. They had known each other all their lives, but now they shared the unenviable bond of the loss of a parent. They spent most of their days together and some of the nights as well. It was a relief to Katya, who could not seem to pull herself together at all.

Nicholai passed his days out of doors, disappearing for lengthy periods of time without having much to report of his activities when he returned. "He has lost the most," said Johann to Katarina. "He is young and has no one to confide in."

"He has us," she cried stubbornly.

Johann raised his eyebrows and she looked away, knowing it was far from being that simple. "We must pray that he does not lose his way through all this."

"You must pray for both of us, Johann," his wife returned. "I feel as if the skies were made of impenetrable steel, and my proffered prayers bounce off and strike me."

"Katarina, when are you going to let it go?"

"Let it go? Are you referring to the murder of my father and the desecration of my home? I should let it go? Pray, tell me how this can be accomplished and I would be glad to do it. Believe me, the burden is excruciatingly heavy."

Johann sighed and bent to kiss her head as she sat stiffly at the kitchen table. "I will be at Wilhelm's if you need me," he said.

"Typical man," she fumed when he had closed the door. "Doesn't care about my pain, only that he can distract himself in someone else's company. He'd rather be anywhere but with me. He used to love to be near me." Dropping her head on her arms on the table, she wept bitterly, but the tears were not healing. Her sobs drowned out the polite knock at the door, and suddenly Agnetha appeared at her side.

Agnetha did not ask what was wrong, because she knew. She did not try to pull Katya from her sorrow or tell her tomorrow would be better. She did not say that all things would work out for the best. She simply sat and cried with her. Her empathy worked like a salve on Katya's soul, and as she took a huge cleansing breath and dried her eyes, she felt more relieved than she had since that terrible night at Succoth. Partly from intuition and partly from the leading of God, Agnetha continued her compassionate presence with Katarina, and ever so gradually, the walls of emptiness and anger began to crumble. After all, Katya still knew the kind of God to whom she belonged.

One day into the second week at Tomak estate, Katya had gone over to Agnetha's for tea, leaving Nicholai in his room alone, as usual. When she returned, he was gone. *Another one of his solitary rambles*, she thought. He did not return for supper, and everyone became concerned when night fell with still no Kolya.

As they prepared for bed, Katya asked Johann, "Dear, have you been sorting through the Succoth papers I took from the tomb?"

Johann glanced over at the small chest of drawers and the folder Katarina held in her hands. "No I haven't. Do you wish me to do so?"

"No, no. It's just that . . . I don't know. It seems as if some-one has gone through them." She shrugged her shoulders and replaced the file in the drawer beside the toiletries Agnetha had given her. "I wish Kolya would come home. I don't like the idea of him staying out so late, with all that's happened."

She looked to Johann for his support, but he also shrugged. "There's not much we can do about it, I'm afraid."

"Don't you care?"

"Of course I care. But he is a young man who must find his own way."

Katarina huffed, her hands on her hips. "A young man! Kolya is only thirteen, even if he looks seventeen. He is a lost little boy."

Johann was silent, and although he knew it infuriated Katya, he could not think of a way to solve her problem for her, and Katya took his silence as lack of concern for both Kolya and herself.

"Please come to bed, Katie. I'm sorry I cannot put your world back together, but I do love you."

Frowning, she climbed into the bed but stayed neatly on her side. When he tried to touch her, she tensed, so he turned over and went to sleep. Katarina turned her face into the pil-low and cried herself to sleep.

"Johann, come quickly," cried Katarina next morning. She was in Nicholai's room. "Johann, Kolya has not returned, and I found this." She held up a bill, a piece of money. "It's a *kerensky,*" she said. "Papa thought they might be of some worth yet." Her face registered alarm. "The only place he could have gotten it was from my drawer, from Papa's file. He has taken money and. . . ."

Gasping and covering her mouth with her hand, she pushed past Johann and ran to their bedroom. Pulling open the top drawer, she took out the file and leafed through it.

"It's gone. Oh Kolya, why?"

"What are you looking for?" asked Johann, peering over her shoulder.

She hesitated a moment, then turned to face her husband. "He has taken Peter's certificate of birth."

"Why would he . . . oh. That would confirm his age at almost eighteen years, would it not?"

Katarina merely nodded her head, her hands again covering her mouth. Recognizing her fear, Johann reached out and brushed a few curling tendrils of hair from her face and pulled her into an embrace. "There is no end of trouble for us, is there?" They sat down on the end of the bed in silence.

"What now?"

"I don't know."

Grisha and Anatoly walked Magnolia Lane, the latter with great anxiety. "Go back to the camp if you wish," said Grisha, not breaking his stride. "Your fear will not help me here."

"But they will kill me if they see me and realize I was here the other night. You were not a part of the raid."

"No, I was not," said Grisha pointedly.

Anatoly Kovshov paused. "Very well," he said. "I will leave you. I hope you find him."

Grisha did not answer, but kept walking beneath the shade of the magnolia trees, along the well-trimmed hedges. As the lane curved, he saw the destruction, the burned trees and shrubs, the ruined orchards and gardens. And he saw what was left of the house, a pile of rubble behind a charred limestone fence, as if the lowly border had been insufficient to protect the manor. His eyes narrowed as he noted the dimensions of the former estate home. Impressive.

He stood and scanned the buildings across the cobbled

yard and headed toward the barns. Perhaps someone there would be able to offer him some clue as to Paul's whereabouts. He reached the main barn and pulled open the wide door. Squinting in the dimness, he called out, "Anyone about?"

Silence greeted him, yet he did not feel alone. He stepped inside and walked along the rows of stalls. He imagined the fine animals that had once graced these stalls and supposed the requisitioning of the soldiers had claimed most of them. Still he felt as if invisible eyes watched him. Instinctively he looked up and saw a movement in the loft. Catching hold of the ladder nailed to the corner wall, he hoisted himself up.

"Whoever is here," he said, "I mean no harm. I only need information."

Silence. He sat down on an overturned apple box to wait out whoever hid here. After several minutes, he heard a sound in the far corner behind a pile of straw. An old man emerged painfully from his hiding place, a wiry little Russian with wizened, sun-darkened face, his thatch of grey hair stuffed under a moth-eaten cap. The small man stood silent and stared at Grisha as if reading his mind.

When Grisha moved to meet him, he came hurrying over, as if he did not wish the stranger to inspect his refuge. Grisha noted the fact, but settled back onto his crate. "I am Grisha. I have come in search of Tekanin, Paul Gregorovich. Can you tell me where I might find him."

"Misha," he said, nodding in Grisha's direction, but remaining between him and the hiding place.

"Misha, do you know of Tekanin? I have come because we have always been friends—he is like a brother to me." He spoke slowly and clearly. "I know of the raid that took place here some nights ago, and I have seen the tragic devastation of the estate. I also know that Paul was here that night, although he did not know to whom the estate belonged." He directed his words past Misha, toward the corner where the old man had been concealed. "I have come that I might be reunited with him."

He waited silently as the day faded into evening. Finally, he said, "I will not leave here without you, Tekanin," and he made himself a bed from the loose straw and lay down to sleep. Misha had long since sat down against the back wall and nodded off.

Grisha awoke suddenly, lost in the darkness of a strange place. "Where. . . .?" He sat up and felt the straw beneath him. "Paul?" He felt more than heard the presence beside him. As his eyes accustomed to the dark, he could see the silhouette of a man sitting a meter or so away from him on the apple box, staring at him. Shifting slowly, he spoke. "Paul Gregorovich, I have come for you. I do not know where we will go, but we will go there together. I will not leave you."

"You sound like Johann's God," commented the deep voice from the darkness.

"Not God, but perhaps an angel." He chuckled at the irony. Paul's guardian angel again. He heard a faint chuckle from the apple box. In the corner, Misha awoke and lit a lantern, careful not to ignite the straw. As the circle of light grew, Paul and Grisha beheld one another, and Paul's chuckles turned into sobs. Head in his hands, he allowed his wounded soul to bleed and cleanse itself. Grisha sat nearby, head bowed, waiting for the emotions to run their course.

When Tekanin had exhausted himself, he rested, and once daylight filtered into the loft from the floor below, they talked. For hours they shared experiences, fears, hopes. "I cannot leave here without speaking with Sudermann," said Tekanin brokenly, "but he will have no part of me. I watched them. They have taken up residence, at least temporarily, at a neighboring estate, Tomak."

"Then we will go there."

"But if he will not accept my words?"

"We will have tried. I have learned from the brothers at the monastery that forgiveness is the only way to peace. I would not have you fall into the pit of depression which almost claimed your life after Vera died."

Paul Gregorovich shook his head. "Seems like an eternity ago since all that happened." He studied Grisha. "You would accompany me to Tomak? To try to speak to Johann?"

Grisha gave a nod of his head and Paul took it as a solemn oath. "And after that," said the older man, "we will live day by day."

Misha, having been privy to most of the conversation, was now at ease with Grisha, recognizing him as Paul's saving angel. He gave them directions to the Enns estate and kissed them both in parting. "One thing," he added as they opened the barn door to leave. "Please give deep regards to Katarina Sudermann. She has been like daughter to me. Tell her I light candle for her before the priest."

Nodding his promise, Grisha put a hand on Paul's shoulder and the two of them crossed the cobblestones and the creek, passing the little cemetery where Heinrich lay buried. Paul paused and made the sign of the cross, then turned resolutely to the road ahead, to make amends with the living.

Chapter 30

 "Where do you think he's gone, Johann?" Katya paced Nicholai's small bedroom, hands clasped at her waist. "Did he go alone or are there others who feel as he does?" She looked to her husband for some miracle answer, and he, of course, had none.

With a sigh he added his thoughts to her questions. "I'm afraid with all that's been going on both here in the Crimea and in the Ukraine, I have not been watching Kolya closely. I assumed he and your father had made peace about the self-defense issue and that he would settle down. I should have known better."

"Why would you have known better? What do you know about my brother that I do not?"

A small sad smile tilted his mouth. "I, too, was a boy not long ago. I know the earnestness and passion of believing in a cause, as well as the natural restlessness that accompanies growing up. There's something in it of protecting the ones you love."

"But how can running away protect the ones you love? It makes no sense." Katarina stood with her hands on her hips, a frown pulling her face taut. In the July sun, her freckles had again made their profuse appearance, much to her dismay.

"It obviously makes sense to him, Katya. He can't do anything here, so he has gone to find somewhere he can make a difference."

"The colonies?"

Johann shrugged.

"What would you have done?"

He smiled more broadly now. "I would have packed up and left my family, no matter their consternation, and traveled by train several hundred miles to a previously unknown place to teach the children of a man I had met only once."

Katarina relaxed slightly and took a chair beside the bed. She sat with her hands unmoving on her lap and stared at the floor. Looking up at him, she said, "So you think he had a plan?"

He held out his hand to her and she took it. "Of course he had a plan. Why else would he take Peter's certificate and the money? Now we must discover what that plan was and where it led him."

"And pray that God would watch over him until we find him again."

"Katie, do you not think he already does?"

She nodded mutely, then looked up at him again. "We must find a way to send a message to Mika in Berlin. She will be there soon."

Johann thought for a moment. "Perhaps if we sent a telegram to Mrs. Unruh, she would know where to get in touch with her husband. I will go to Karassan to inquire about Nicholai and also contact Mrs. Unruh."

A knock at the door startled them both. They had received no visitors since taking up residence at Tomak except Wilhelm and Agnetha, and they would have made themselves known. Glancing at Katarina, Johann stood and walked into the kitchen. Katya followed him, hoping that there would be news of Nicholai. When Johann opened the door, a man he had never seen stood before him, a rather husky man, at least he had been before the obvious ravages of war had thinned his frame. His thatch of red hair and thick red-grey beard made him one not to be missed in a crowd. The man's eyes as they met Johann's held a certain confidence, an air of self-knowledge that commanded attention.

"My name is Grisha," he said simply. "I come to you, Johann Sudermann, on a personal matter." He glanced past Johann into the room. "May I come inside?"

Johann hesitated only a moment, then inclined his head in assent. He opened the door wide and stepped back to admit the strange man. "Have a chair. This is my wife, Katarina."

Grisha studied her face, then bowed slightly. Katarina was slightly taken aback by the dignified behavior of the man who looked more the peasant than the aristocrat.

"What may we do for you, Grisha?" Johann sat and stretched his legs out before him, crossing his feet and folding his arms at his waist.

"Actually, Sudermann," rejoined Grisha skillfully, "you have said it precisely. You may indeed do something for me, and in doing so, for someone else."

Suddenly suspicious, Johann glanced at the door, but there was no one there. "What do you mean? Who do you speak for . . . ahhh." He sat forward, his elbows on his knees. With an enormous sigh, he said, "Where is he?"

Grisha smiled disarmingly. He liked Sudermann. He could see already why he and Paul had always been friends. There was an honesty there, a transparency. "He is sitting in nervous dejection in the shade of the tree at the side of this house. Shall I fetch him in?"

At Johann's slight hesitation, Katarina rose and walked to the door. "Fetch him immediately, Grisha. We have much to say to him."

Johann sensed her anger rising. His voice was a gentle command. "Katya." She turned and stared at him for a long moment. Her lips tightened, her freckles standing out against her pale face. "Very well, Johann. I will be at Agnetha's." She turned on her heel and left the house, leaving the door open.

The two men looked at one another in understanding. Grisha spoke. "She has lost much." Johann nodded grimly and followed him outside to meet his estranged friend.

Paul Gregorovich sat beneath the oak tree, knees bent, head and arms resting on them. He heard the cadence of voices coming from the house, rising and falling, then a female voice raised in anger. He rubbed his face with his hands. What had he done? In rebellious thoughtlessness, he had destroyed people, again. Paul would never have hurt Johann or his family in any way, but his alliances had made him equal to the one who had done the deed. And that old man had not deserved to die. Why not himself? Why had Paul Gregorovich Tekanin not died in the line of duty before now? Why had God allowed him to continue to draw breath when he would destroy lives, again? His whole life fell before him as a series of wrong choices and catastrophes.

The door of the cottage opened and Paul heard the shuffling of feet approaching. He pushed himself to his feet and raked his fingers through his hair. He felt like a confirmed traitor before a firing squad. He closed his eyes for a moment, then opened them wide to meet his fate. He would face Johann squarely and honestly, if it was the only proper thing he ever did.

Grisha rounded the corner of the house, followed closely by Johann. They stood and stared at each other, Johann's eyes filled with disappointment and the beginning of disdain, Paul's with vulnerability. No words were spoken, but many thoughts traveled the distance between them. Some were instinctively understood, some blocked by pain and a need for justice.

Oh, Lord God, prayed Johann in his heart. *How am I to forgive this man?*

How are you not? The words were as plain as if they had

been spoken aloud. Other words came back to Johann: "In the measure with which you measure, it shall be measured to you." And he prayed for grace, and for Katarina, whose heart had been sorely wounded.

Grisha stepped back and leaned against the house, allowing the men to confront each other. Johann stood with his arms akimbo, legs astride. Tilting his head to one side in an effort at self-control, he stared Paul down. "What do you wish to say to me?"

Nervous still, Paul's hands shook as he tried to find a more comfortable stance. Finally, he shoved both hands into the pockets of his army pants and took a deep breath. Pain wrote its signature in his eyes and across his face. Johann saw, and felt somewhat justified.

The words were difficult for Paul to assimilate. Words were useless to describe the wretchedness that tore his soul, the worst of which was the damage, irreparable, done to the relationship the two of them once had. But it must be faced squarely. "I . . . I have been . . . a fool." The words came fast then, tumbling over one another in the relief of acknowledgment. "I have aligned myself with the wrong side every step of the way. First it was Djugashvili—Stalin. His sadistic character is becoming ever more apparent. Then the radicals, the extremists, trying to fight for justice for the masses, at any cost, not realizing the cost would be so great. Then the Reds." He shook his head in utter dismay, his hand at his brow. Meeting Johann's eyes, he said, "You have no idea the atrocities I have been involved in. I . . . I have killed my own soul."

The heart wrenching confessions moved Johann, in spite of his deep wounds, but he fought for composure and allowed Tekanin to finish his disclosures. "Finally I could not stomach the violence any longer and walked away. Somehow, I dreamed, I would leave it all behind, as if it had never been." He laughed coarsely. "But it followed me, Johann. It would not let me go. I met up with Ivan the Red, and in some bizarre twist of fate, found myself at Succoth."

He stepped closer to Johann, who eyed him with caution. "Sudermann, you must believe me, I did not know that was your home. I had no idea. You must have realized my surprise when I saw you there." He began to cry, endless silent tears welling up from a spring of sorrow and regret. He wiped his face with the heels of his hands, his voice shaking with emotion. "I would die in his place if I could have the chance. He was a good man and I . . . I am a useless mistake of nature." His sobs became audible. "I . . . am . . . so . . . deeply sorry."

He covered his face with both hands and his entire body shook. Grisha stood leaning against the house, eyes wet with tears, face quivering with the effort of control. Johann's chest heaved with a similar effort, but he could not win it. "I know it," he said in a rasped whisper. "I know it, and by the grace of God, by his grace alone, I stand here and extend forgiveness to you."

Paul's head came up in surprise, but his hope faded as Johann continued. His words, at first compassionate, became wooden. "Our hearts have been broken, especially Katarina's. I have lost, for the rest of this life, a superb friend and mentor, a man of such high moral and spiritual ideals that he stands in a class of his own. But Katya," he took a deep breath and tried to keep the anger from his voice, "she has lost everything. Her father, her friend, her spiritual advisor, her security, her home. And I am quite certain her faith is facing a great trial as well. That, as you know, would be the ultimate loss. I pray she will be able to recover it."

Paul stood throughout Johann's speech with bowed head, wringing his hands pathetically. "I . . . I will speak to her as well, although she will most likely strike me. But I have withstood worse." He raised his head. "Shall I go to her, or will you bring her?"

Johann raised his chin and regarded Paul. As he looked, he

saw the man he had been, and the boy before that, the fatherless waif trying to take care of a family in abject poverty. Johann remembered the pinched face, the skinny body, and how these had changed with proper food and companionship, as well as help for his family.

He still saw the joy spread over Paul's face as he discovered the treasure of reading the written word. A certain freedom had been offered to him then, but that freedom was farcical in the light of reality. When a poor man learned to read, it only educated him as to the extent of his condition. In Russia, few literate poor had been able to pull themselves out of the bog of perpetual poverty. Paul had tried, but his choices had lacked wisdom. His alliances also. He had fought the fight on the wrong side, not realizing his mistake until it was too late to change.

"In the measure with which you measure. . . ." The words repeated themselves in Johann's head and he knew what his response needed to be. Slowly, deliberately, he lifted his right hand and held it out to his childhood friend. At first, Paul did not see it, for the tears in his eyes. But when he saw the hand of mercy and grace offered to him, he first jerked his head up to meet Johann's eyes. Like a man in a dream, he too raised up his hand, which weighed like iron, and reached for the one extended. Both were shaking, but as they met, their grip was firm and enduring, forgiving and accepting. Raw emotion poured forth as the two held each other in a strong embrace, brothers once again, stronger for their deliberation. Joy and peace welled up in the soul of Johann Sudermann, for so it was measured to him.

Grisha and Paul walked along the dirt road in silent contemplation. The meeting with Katarina Sudermann had not gone well. She had refused to listen to Paul's words, laying all the blame of her loss at his feet. Johann had looked profoundly sorry, but did not assume to contradict her. *She has her right to hate me forever,* thought Paul.

"You have done your part," offered Grisha. "The rest you must leave in God's hands."

"You speak like a saint," Paul retorted. "When did the transformation take place?"

Grisha accepted the sarcasm with good humor. "You forget, my friend, that I spent many months in a monastery. A lot of theological discussion goes on at a place like that. Can't avoid it." He tilted his head up to the sun. "I suppose some of it is bound to rub off on a person."

Paul did not argue, his sarcasm draining away. Instead he spoke softly, almost to himself. "Who am I to judge any man?"

They camped under the stars that night. It would have been more uncommon to sleep in beds. Life had become a fragile thing that one balanced as one moved through the days, taking what came, not lamenting what one did not have. They both, Grisha and Paul Gregorovich, had come to prefer this kind of life because it gave a certain amount of freedom, if not security.

The following day they were caught up by a rider, flying along the dirt road at breakneck speed on a heavy-boned horse which was not made to run, but to work. On seeing the two pilgrims, the rider pulled up in a cloud of dust and slid from his mount. It was Kovshov.

"Anatoly Andreievich!" exclaimed Tekanin. "What are you doing? If that is a stolen horse, you will hang."

"Not stolen, just borrowed." He gasped for breath. "They do not know I am gone." He grasped Paul by the arm and said, "You must hide. Ivan is out to get you, and he will not rest until he does. He says he will find the rest of the Hildebrandts also, for all the fuss they've made—"

"All the fuss? The man is not only a murderer, but insane. He was the perpetrator at Succoth, not the Hildebrandts." Tekanin shook his head in amazement. "When does he plan this attack, and does he know where Johann and the family are?"

"He does. He comes tonight. I had to warn you because you have been good to me." He glanced at Grisha, knowing he must think him a coward for deserting the other day. It did not matter. He had little to do with Grisha.

Tekanin thanked him heartily and encouraged him to remain with them, but the informer refused, so they sent him on his way. "You must return that horse before they realize it is gone." Kovshov nodded and climbed aboard the panting, sweating animal and reined it around, kicking it viciously to encourage it to move faster.

As they watched him ride away, Grisha said, "He's dead."

"Yes. They will know he has gone. Anatoly Andreievich is not smart enough to delude them. But he would not have stayed."

"No."

With a frown and a grimace, Tekanin turned back in the direction of Tomak. "We must warn Johann and Katarina."

"And then make ourselves disappear," added Grisha. "Any ideas?"

"We cannot stay here forever, living off Wilhelm and Agnetha," said Johann to Katarina after the ordeal with Tekanin was over. "I need to find a way to earn a living, to put food on the table for you and Anna, and for Nicholai when he returns."

"If he returns."

"Katarina," Johann knelt in front of the chair in which she

sat and held her by the shoulders. "You are developing a pessimistic and bitter attitude. It does not become you."

She rose, pushing him away. "What would you have me do? Welcome with open arms the one who killed my father and chased away my brother, not to mention destroying my home?"

"Katarina, we've been through this many times. It was not Paul Gregorovich who did these things. He was in the wrong place at the wrong time, a bad mistake, but a mistake nonetheless. Your bitterness will only eat away at your own soul. He has asked for your forgiveness for his involvement, and that is as far as he can go without your cooperation." He paused as he chose his next words. "Do you think your father would approve of your handling of this situation? Is this what the Lord teaches us to do in his Word?"

She swung around, an angry retort on her tongue, but her eyes reflected pure misery. Stammering, she beat her fists against the window ledge and cried. "No! No, Papa would be ashamed of me. But I cannot help myself. I am so torn inside that I cannot take the step I need to take. If I cannot blame your friend, then who will carry it? I will be giving in to the terrible deeds they have done to us. These things must be suffered for."

He had come to stand by her again, at the window. "Listen to yourself, my love," he said softly. "This sounds not like the Katarina I know and love, but like a *Selbstschutz* leader, and I have heard you say what you thought of them. Release your hatred and anger and let the real Katarina out again. I—we—need her."

Sobbing, she could hardly get the words out. "But how?"

"With God's help. Only with his help. He gave me courage to do so, and he will give it to you also. And be assured that God will deal with those who need to be dealt with. It is not ours to take vengeance." He held her supportively around the shoulders and prayed quietly for victory in her struggle.

Finally he felt her nod, and they both went down on their knees and cried out to the one who forgives and comforts, and he answered their prayers. Katarina managed a smile through her tears. "The pain is still excruciating, but the dark burden is lifted."

"Thank the Lord," said her husband.

A sharp knock sounded and brought them to their feet. Opening the door, Johann beheld Grisha and Paul again, in much more of an excited state than they had been before. They entered the house and Paul glanced at Katarina. She felt the pain again, but breathed a prayer for strength.

She moved toward him, her hand outstretched. "Paul Gregorovich, I . . . ." her voice faded, but she cleared her throat and began again. "Paul Gregorovich, I forgive you. I will not bear a grudge that will destroy me. As I have been forgiven, so I forgive."

In utter astonishment, Tekanin stared at her hand, then at her face again. He glanced at Grisha, whose eyes twinkled with an unfathomable light, and he knew something miraculous was happening. Turning back to Katarina, he took her hand, knelt before her, and placed his forehead on her outstretched hand. Tears of compassion and joy pooled in Katya's eyes, and she cast Johann a look of thankfulness. Reaching out with her other hand, she pulled the repentant man to his feet and smiled at him. "It is good you gave me another chance to forgive you," she said. "I did not expect you to return."

"I, we. . . ." he turned to Grisha for help, still lost in the wonder of being forgiven.

"A friend caught up to us in the road and warned us that Ivan, the redhead," Grisha absentmindedly ran a hand over his own mop, "is out to get Tekanin." He met Johann's eyes. "And the rest of your family."

"Us? Why us? Have they not done enough?"

"Apparently not." Grisha ducked his head in shame at the

conduct of the anarchists. "Once they pass a certain point, they lose all conscience. You've heard of Machno? Well, Ivan applies to the same lack of standards."

Paul spoke up. "Whatever the case, we need to warn you to leave here. Find a place to hide."

"What about you?" asked Johann. "You are in as much danger as we are."

Grisha shrugged. "We will disappear."

"For how long?" It was Katarina who spoke. "You cannot hide forever, moving from place to place."

"Do you have a better idea, my dear?" asked Johann with a small smile.

She returned his doubtful smirk with one of her own, only with more confidence. "Yes, as a matter of fact, I do. But we must hurry."

The men were surprised at her proposal, but saw the wisdom in it. The four settled down to plan and gather what they needed, then shared a sad and final meal with the Enns family. Anna was especially sad to leave Tina and Sarah, but adjusted to the idea as she had to all the other interruptions and difficulties of her young life. Katya worried at her calmness in the face of these things, but had no time to delve into it. Perhaps soon a day would come when they could relax enough to share what was deep within their hearts.

Berlin. A bustling industrial city of nearly four million people who spoke her first language. Maria Hildebrandt knew she should be content to be so near her destination, yet she knew she would not sleep this night. Tomorrow she would catch the train to Bavaria, to Schwandorf, to Dietrich. If it would help, she would start walking now.

Although the people of Berlin were plagued by strikes, food

riots, and inflation, the political air in Germany was calmer than in Russia. The German Empire under Kaiser Wilhelm II had collapsed at the end of the war, and the Allies were making huge demands on its citizens, but a new democratic federal republic had been established—the Weimar Republic—and so there was a ray of hope. Mr. Unruh remarked on the sense of purpose, if not contentment, so different from the chaos in Russia.

Unruh was now in meetings with several people he knew from his university days. He had studied in Basel, Switzerland, and had many friends and acquaintances in Germany as well. They were interested in helping with the emigration process, and all help was welcome.

Midafternoon Maria left the house of the Schroeders where she and Unruh were staying and walked along a branch of the Spree River on her way to the telegraph office. She needed to send word to Succoth. She debated sending the message to Karassan, thinking her family might check with Father Serge as well. That might be the best way. She began to compose the letter in her mind, anxious excitement coloring her thoughts.

Greeting the operator with a smile, she wrote out her message on the pad of paper lying on the counter. He then transcribed it: DEAR FAMILY STOP ARRIVED B STOP TOMORROW SOUTH STOP ECSTATIC STOP LOVE M

As she signed her name to the receipt, the telegrapher looked over his round glasses at her. "Maria Hildebrandt," he said, narrowing his eyes. "I believe a message was dispatched for your lodgings a few minutes ago."

Mika raised her eyebrows and smiled again. "Wonderful," she said. "I'm sure it's news from home."

He did not comment. She paid and thanked the man, and was about to leave when the door opened to admit another customer. A tall, heavy-set German in military uniform walked through the door, removed his helmet and nodded politely in her direction.

Mika hesitated, hoping for information.

The soldier stalked to the counter and began to dictate a telegram: CHANGE OF PLAN STOP CONTINGENT SENT WEST STOP RETURN DATE UNKNOWN G He passed his money to the telegrapher and turned to leave.

Maria squared her shoulders. "Excuse me, sir," she said. "Would you perhaps know of a Dietrich Kesselman, recently returned from South Russia?"

He frowned and narrowed his eyes. "Why do you ask?"

"I need to find him. We . . . he is a friend of the family."

The soldier continued to stare at her, making her feel distinctly uncomfortable. Finally he said, "I do not know of him or his whereabouts, but if he is with the troops heading west, he will be on the train as we speak. If you will excuse me, I must hurry or I will miss that train." He nodded and walked swiftly away in the direction of the railway station.

Mika hailed a cab and instructed the driver to take the shortest route to the station. "I must intercept someone," she explained. Why hadn't Dietrich contacted her as the other soldier had just done? Why had she received no word from him?

The station bustled with travelers, soldiers, and former soldiers—the Allies insisted upon disarming Germany and diminishing the size of its armies. Maria scanned the crowds, desperate to catch sight of Dietrich, if he was even there. She pushed her way through the press of people as they hurried to board the train. Several times her heart jolted as she picked out a tall soldier, but each time she was deeply disappointed that the face was not the one she sought.

"All aboard!" The shouted words of the conductor sent Maria into a panic. What if he were here and she missed him?

The cars began to move with a *shush, shush, shush*, faster

and faster as they picked up speed. She scanned the windows, searching for the face she longed to see, but it was not there.

She moved to the end of the platform, leaning over the railing as far as possible. It seemed the train was pulling her heart along with it. Tears coursed down her cheeks. No one paid much attention; tears were not uncommon in the aftermath of war.

Eventually Maria took a taxi back to the Schroeders, arriving there in time for tea. Benjamin Unruh had already returned from his afternoon meeting and greeted her warmly.

"Well, well, Miss Hildebrandt, I feared we had lost you."

Seeing her troubled face, he asked, "Maria, what is it?"

She shook her head and a tear escaped each eye. Mrs. Schroeder, a warm and comforting woman, took over. "Come, my dear," she said, leading Maria to a chair. "Now tell us the problem."

"I went to the train station—there are many soldiers and ex-soldiers coming and going there—hoping to catch sight of Dietrich, but of course I did not. He is probably at home in Schwandorf as he said he would be." She dried her tears and lifted her chin.

"I'm sure you're correct." Her hostess smiled reassuringly. "We have received a telegram for you, Maria. Perhaps it is good news to cheer you up."

Mika reached hopefully for the envelope and pulled out the single sheet of paper. Her eyes scanned, then stopped, backed up and opened wide. A wail tore from her throat and she slid to the floor. Alarmed, Unruh lifted her gently to the chair, then read the message for himself. There were no details in the telegram, just the words: DEAREST SISTER STOP OUR PAPA DEAD STOP SUCCOTH BURNED STOP SEEKING SAFETY STOP WILL SEND NEXT MESSAGE SOUTH STOP PRAYERS J & K.

Mika wept for the father who had been taken. She wept for the pain she had caused him but mostly she mourned for the love between them, such love as she had seldom seen between a parent and child. She mourned also for Succoth, that beautiful idyllic fairy tale of a place that had at last been invaded by reality. Even though that place had at times represented tradition and control, it still symbolized solace. There was no more solace on this earth, she thought, no more place the mind could go for peace, for tranquility. Even the memory disappeared like a puff of smoke.

They talked of it later, Benjamin Unruh and the Schroeders. She heard them from the bedroom where she lay tucked snugly into a comfortable four-poster bed. Her emotions raged through her, tearing at her heart, making a mockery of any sense of poise or composure she had ever maintained. She threw off the quilts in an agony of despair and paced the room, never-ending tears streaming down her cheeks, dripping off her chin.

Tomorrow she would take the train to Schwandorf. She had suffered many disappointments in her life, and she did not now have the faith to believe that Dietrich would be there. If he was, they would find a way to build a place of solace in their lives. If he was not, well, she would deal with that. As much as she wanted, at this moment, to shrivel up and die, she knew she would not. She would continue on.

Her heart was convinced that the love between her and Dietrich was real. She also knew that her papa was now safely with Jesus, never again to be threatened, never again to suffer. But the rest of her family was in danger. Whatever God thought of her, she loved her family enough to send pleading prayers heavenward for them.

She slumped into an overstuffed chair, weeping softly, then finally falling asleep, completely exhausted, with a prayer on her lips.

A dilapidated wagon, pulled by a thin and weary horse, rattled steadily down the dirt road in the direction of Karassan. Night approached, but the days were long, and the moon almost full. The wagon, with its passengers, had already traveled many *versts*, and the horse needed a rest. After only a short stop by the side of the road, the driver again encouraged the beast to draw on all its hidden resources and continue. A little oats was the encouragement the old nag needed, and she plodded on again.

The driver squinted his eyes at the way ahead, as if to see farther than the natural light allowed. Every so often, he pushed at the bridge of his nose with a forefinger. Beside him sat a child—a girl—and beside her, a tall peasant woman, dirty kerchief tied around her head, hair escaping from beneath it. When the wagon came upon other travelers, the woman brought a rag up to her face and coughed horribly. Once the travelers were gone, she dropped the rag and stole a glance into the back of the wagon, a look of great concern on her face for the pile of straw filling the box. With a glance at the driver, she turned again to the front and sat quietly.

Although Pavel's return was imminent, Ivan the Red ventured out with his gang of anarchists looking for Tekanin. After a cursory search of Succoth and a nasty questioning of Misha, they rode off madly for Tomak. Wilhelm was ready for them. His loyal workers had gathered at the main house, where most of them lived, and waited for the attack. Their number and their loyalty to Wilhelm threatened the bandits enough that they left, after more threat than action. Turning their horses roughly, they galloped off in the opposite direction from Karassan, creating more than a little havoc on their way.

As the first pink shades of dawn streaked the slate blue sky, the wagon pulled to a weary stop under the trees behind the Orthodox Church in Karassan. The driver jumped down from his seat and helped the woman and child from theirs. They stretched their weary bones, spoke a few quiet words to the load of straw in the wagon box, and patted the old horse, which was ready to collapse. Together, the couple and child entered the church by the vestry door and sat in a pew to wait for the priest.

He was not long in coming. Approaching the altar, black vestments flowing around him, the priest did not at first notice the visitors. He stopped in mid stride and turned to stare at them, then walked purposefully toward them. "Welcome," he said.

The couple glanced at each other in the semi-darkness, then the woman pulled back her kerchief. "Father Serge," she said in a panicked voice. "Please, we need help."

He leaned forward, an incredulous look on his face, eyebrows raised. "Miss Katarina!" he exclaimed. "What brings you here?"

The priest nodded a greeting to Johann, patted Anna on her golden head and returned his still startled gaze to Katya, his eyes taking in her peasant clothing. "Please, come with me." He stood straight and led the way along the side of the sanctuary to the room where Katarina had first met him. He closed the door and turned to them in alarm. "What has happened now? "

"We are being hunted by a group of bandits, that is why we could not stay at the neighboring estate of friends." She glanced at the window and the brightening day. "We have not come alone, our cargo waits in the wagon." Here she met and held Father Serge's eyes. Anna clung tightly to Katya, her face pale, lips trembling.

"We thought the double-headed eagle was devouring us,"

the priest said, referring to the emblem of tsarist Russia, "but the beast that has taken its place is more hideous by far. God help us. Who else is with you?"

"Two who may well be more comfortable here than we. Two men who have been involved politically and are in need of asylum."

The priest answered in some alarm. "Bring them inside, children, quickly before the sun is fully up. We cannot risk them being seen."

Johann hurried outside and returned with Grisha and Paul. "This is Grisha," he introduced him to the priest, "and this is Paul Gregorovich Tekanin. Father Serge Ivanovich." His gaze lingered on Paul. "If you will excuse me, I must take care of the horse. She is near dead with what we have expected of her." Johann left the church again and the others sat down to discuss what was to be done.

"Katarina," said Father Serge. "Have you heard from Maria or Dietrich?"

"Yes," she replied. "Last telegram she was in Berlin, planning to go south to find Dietrich." The next words became a whisper. "We sent word about Papa and Succoth. I'm not sure if she'll get it or not. Maybe it's better if she doesn't."

"She won't know where we are," cried Anna. "How will we let her know?"

"Don't worry, Ännchen," said Katarina, sitting down beside her. "We will try to keep in touch with Father Serge, and we will also send another telegram to Germany as soon as we find a place in Molotschna."

The child accepted the reassurances and leaned her head wearily against her sister's shoulder.

Johann returned from stabling the horse in the rundown barn at the back of the church. With heavy hearts they began to lay their own plans. They spoke much that day, and the priest shared his supper with them.

"What will you do, Sudermann?" asked Paul as they sipped tea.

"Teach. It is what I am trained to do, what I enjoy." He turned the cup in his hand. "With all that has happened in the colonies, I am sure there is a shortage of teachers."

"But are you not afraid to return to the civil war front? The Whites are recruiting again."

"I think things have simmered down," said Johann. "The Whites have driven the Reds back and are also managing to hold that beast, Machno, at bay. We will be fine there."

Tekanin did not look convinced, but he had no other suggestions. There was nothing back at Succoth. He had helped make sure of that. He wondered if he would ever walk free of the horror of that heinous night. Perhaps Father Serge could advise him. Yes, he would ask Father Serge Ivanovich.

That night they all slept soundly on straw ticks in various corners of the magnificent but weathered old church. None of the few worshipers who came and went were aware that anyone else but the priest was there.

Next morning before the sun rose, Katarina, Johann, and Anna bade their farewells. Still dressed in tattered peasant garb, they bowed before the priest and thanked him from their hearts for his assistance. They did the same to two black-robed priests, both tall, one dark-haired with eyes black as coal, the other with a thick thatch of red hair and unkempt beard. Johann looked long at Paul, then embraced him. "God keep you," he said, tears in his voice. He turned to Father Serge.

"Take care of him, Father. He is my brother."

They turned to leave, and Katarina looked back at the priest. "Thank you for everything, in the name of my father and of our Lord. God bless you." The heavy wooden doors closed, separating them, each destined for a new situation that would require of them much courage. But they did not go alone. An unseen hand guided them as they forged ahead into the unknown.

Glossary

batko—Russian, "little father"

bolshevik—literally "majority"; original Communist party believing in socialism by revolution

boyars—wealthy aristocratic landowners in the days of Imperial Russia

bourgeoisie—middle class

Cheka—Lenin's secret police

Cossacks—historically nomadic horsemen; troops loyal to the tsar

dessiatine—measurement of land area; 2.7 acres

Duma—Russian parliament, "elected" but virtually powerless because of lack of cooperation by the tsar

faspa—light meal served in the late afternoon instead of a heavy supper; usually cold cuts and buns

Foretei (For-shtie)—Forestry Service; a Mennonite-instituted alternative to military service. Duties included roads building, reforestation, and medial service

Hetman—a Tatar clan leader, chieftan figure (Crimea)

kulak—someone who owns land

murzak—old families of the Tatar nobility

proletariat—working class

rollkuchen—strips of rich dough deep-fried in oil

Sanitätdienst—German; Forestry Service

Scheuztler—members of the Selbstschutz

Schbstschutz—self-defense corp

Tatars—aboriginal people of the Crimea

vereneke—cottage cheese dumplings boiled or fried and served with cream gravy

verst—unit of distance; 2/3 mile or 1 kilometer
volost—administrative district in Russia after 1871
zemstvo—self-governing indigenous administration
zweibach—German; a two-tiered bun

LYSE C. CANTIN PHOTO

The Author

Janice L. Dick lives with her husband Wayne on a grain farm in central Saskatchewan. She is a member of Philadelphia Mennonite Brethren Church. Russian history has intrigued Janice since her high school days. Her parents were born in Russia, and her husband's family has roots there. Her novels are based on years of interest and research.